"[A] wonderful surprise . . . Wolitzer's strongest, most accomplished and most affecting novel yet . . . In *Silver*, all of Hilma Wolitzer's considerable talents, comic invention, surprising twists of plot, trenchant and witty dialogue, power of close observation have come together brilliantly. Read the book."

Newsday

"Wolitzer has the impeccable timing of a fine, stand-up comic. Her zingy one-liners and flip, funny scenes make *Silver* lively reading."

Los Angeles Daily News

"A deeply affecting story of choices made, avoided and regretted."

West Coast Review of Books

"Hilma Wolitzer shows an understanding of how awareness of mortality can change people's lives. Love and death can be daunting themes, yet she tackles them successfully, and gives us a good story to boot."

Worcester Telegram

"Delightful, warmhearted Wolitzer is back in full, sweet, sad, comic force. . . . Richly imagined, warm, and winning meditations on the funny and sad ways in which life's puzzles never end."

The Kirkus Reviews

"In this suspenseful, wildly funny and deeply moving novel, we are avid to find out what happens to all the indisputably human friends of Paulie and Howie, and mostly of course, what happens to them."

Publishers Weekly

SILVER

Hilma Wolitzer

IVY BOOKS • NEW YORK

Ivy Books
Published by Ballantine Books
Copyright © 1988 by Hilma Wolitzer

Library of Congress Catalog Card Number: 87-073490

ISBN 0-8041-0485-9

This edition published by arrangement with Michael di Capva Books, an imprint of Farrar, Straus and Giroux, Inc.

Manufactured in the United States of America

First Ballantine Books Edition: August 1989

ACKNOWLEDGMENTS

The author thanks the National Endowment for the Arts
and the Corporation of Yaddo for their generous support
With gratitude also to Linda Pastan for allowing me
to borrow six lines from her poem
"A Winter Prothalamion,"
and for her friendship

I've had a very happy life,
and I wouldn't do it otherwise.
I even got married once and survived.
HELEN HUMES

1

ONE NIGHT IN AUGUST, UNDERSTANDING ALL AT ONCE why I'd been so sad, I decided to leave Howard. This was the real thing, not just the fireworks of battle or some transient post-battle blues. We hadn't even had a decent argument for months. And I wasn't giving Howard up the way he kept giving up cigarettes. I mean that I meant it. But do we ever know what we mean? Light-years before, when I still believed we had mated for life, like wolves, Howard left and went to live with another woman. After a while he came back, and the children and I made room for him in the kitchen and the bedroom, ready to forgive, if not forget.

I wish I could say that *I* had fallen in love this time, that I was rushing from the house with my skin on fire, and that Mr. Wonderful was going to roll me across the lawn and put out the flames. It wasn't like that, though. Howard and I were getting ready for bed, as we'd done for most of more than twenty-four years, moving through our old ballet of dropped shoes and emptied underwear. I realized that we didn't look frankly at one another's nakedness anymore. Waning interest made us glance away, and shyness of how we were changing. I guess Howard saw me the way I saw him, in hasty flashes of softened flesh before the lights went out.

"Good night, Paulie," he said, yawning hotly on my shoulder, making me shiver. "Whatever you do, don't wake me up tomorrow."

It was Saturday night, about ten o'clock. We used to laugh our heads off when our parents went to sleep that early, all worn out from the effort of their indifference. "Saturday night is the loneliest night of the week," I sang, but Howard was already gone, snoring lightly, his hand a ballast on my hip.

He'd always hated waking up to Sunday, especially if he'd played a late gig the night before. Sometimes he would fall into bed as the room was getting light, still wearing his tuxedo trousers, his starched shirt front bruising my breasts. A few hours later I'd have to rescue him from the gloom of Sunday's Hopper stillness. It was my job, my very mission. I would clear the static from a radio sermon or an opera and turn the volume up high enough to startle the dead. I would dump him out of bed like a rowdy nurse, lure him back to life with waffles and coffee, and with a restorative drive into the countryside.

Lately I just let him sleep. For one thing, we *lived* in the country now, or at least in that purgatory, the Long Island suburbs. If he wanted to look at flowers and trees, he could go to the window and open his eyes. For another thing, I'd learned to be moody on Sundays myself, and I didn't have the heart to cheer him on anymore. In the old days, when the children were young and still in captivity, it was a family project to make Daddy happy and whole again. I tended to get carried away at times, and Howard would become headachy from the commotion of my zeal. "Calm down, for God's sake," he'd say. "You're not waking Lazarus." But when he said it, he was upright, and almost resurrected from his depression.

For several months before that August night, I'd suspected he'd been seeing someone else. But until then I was only going on intuition. I wasn't the ardent girl detective I'd once been, sniffing out sexual scent, tuned to his metabolic rises and falls. He wasn't even acting nicer to me than usual, which my friend and colleague, La Rae Peters, says is always the first sign. That night I simply knew that what I'd suspected was true, and that I'd known it for a long time. But like Scarlett O'Hara, I had put off thinking about it until tomorrow or the next day. As I lay there, random repressed clues fell into place with fatal clicks. Those phone calls with nobody there when I said, "Hello? Hello?," not even a breather. The crazy diets Howard started—the Protein Purge, the Wheat Grass Fast—and broke with bouts of gluttony. (That very evening, right after supper, he'd stood in the light of the open refrigerator eating a whole pound of sliced ham, as if he were feeding coins into a slot machine.) The scratches he'd had all over his neck once, that he said was a rash, an allergy to the laundry detergent. Those long showers he took after working late, the water pounding and pounding against my denial. And when had we last made love with rapture and invention?

The terrible thing was, I didn't care very much. There were pangs of something like jealousy, an itch in my throat I couldn't scratch, and that was all. I missed my lost, crazed self, the indulgence of genuine rage and grief. When Howard went away that time, I went after him armed with murderous love, and he came back. Now he lay beside me in our bed, where he belonged, and I made up my mind to go. Why not? I wouldn't miss this house, in which I'd always been a sort of visitor. And my friends and I would never lose one another, no matter where any of us lived. Katherine, La Rae, and I would travel by dogsled, if we had to, to sit in somebody's kitchen and talk and eat.

I could be a part-time clerk in some other library, and I could write my column anywhere at all. I mailed it into the paper, anyway, since they'd moved their offices to Westchester, just as I used to mail my poems to famous and obscure magazines. Was "Paulie's Kitchen Korner" the culmination of all that literary ambition? I hadn't written a poem in ages, but sometimes I broke up a few lines of copy before I sent it in: To remove those white / Rings from your favorite / Table, try applying / Toothpaste, the abrasive / Kind, with a damp cloth, and / Later, polish clean. And I still kept the big box of rejection slips. It had once held a pair of Jason's fuzzy sleepers, and blue lint clung to all of the slips, like mold.

A few years ago, I'd seen a picture in the newspaper of a seventy-year-old woman graduating from college in the same class as her twenty-year-old granddaughter. *Never too late*, the caption read, and under it the article said that they both planned on entering law school in the fall. Reading that, and looking at their smiling faces, made me want to try and finish the education I'd interrupted to marry and raise a family. That afternoon, without telling anyone, I drove to one of those schools that give you credits for life experience and let you work quickly and independently toward a degree. I sat next to a plumber's helper who wanted to be an aeronautical engineer, and filled out the forms, listing housework and child-bearing, all the jobs I'd ever held, and the two years of college I'd completed. Suddenly, it seemed pointless—I'd wanted to be a *poet*, not a lawyer or an engineer. I knew that learning enriched poetry, but there was no law against being self-taught, and I had thousands of books at my disposal at the library. I even managed to read between the stacks as I was shelving them. And if ordinary life experience— preparing hamburger a hundred different ways and nursing sick children—was good enough for college credit, its ultimate worth to a writer was infinite. I would join a poetry

workshop, instead of matriculating, and I'd carry my notebook everywhere again, in case of inspiration.

I never got around to any of that, though. La Rae and I
took the Great Books course at the library, and that was about
it. If you didn't become what you'd expected to be, it had to
be someone else's fault. Howard never said that he blamed
me for the breakup of his combo, the loss of his free and
jazzy night life, but I knew that he did. And I blamed him
for one thing and another. How coldly I reasoned everything
out, while he slept on in guilty innocence. Our twenty-fifth
anniversary loomed ahead, next June. Although we both dis-
dained all those greeting-card occasions, we observed them,
anyway. Children trap you with their pure faith in sentiment,
with the valentines made secretly in school for their first
loves. I can still feel the heft of the construction paper, the
hidden clumps of damp paste. Howard would hand me the
requisite roses in exchange for the requisite tie, the transac-
tion taking place over the children's heads. "Now kiss
Mommy," Ann would command Howard, and he would.
She'd never let any anniversary go by uncelebrated. She and
Spence traded gifts a few times a month, to mark the day
they'd met, became engaged, got married. The possibilities
of this milestone year would drive her to extremes. I had to
get out before Hallmark unfurled the tinfoil in a roll of thunder, before the mockery of a party with everyone jumping
out of closets yelling "Surprise! Surprise!," bearing gifts of
silver we'd have to return before they'd had a chance to tar-
nish. Who could be more surprised than Howard and me that
love, along with lust and eternal friendship, could ever escape our vigilance? Hi-yo Silver, away, away.

Never mind, we had set the right examples for our children
already, had shown them the value of anger and of concilia-
tion. Now they were on their own. Jason was living in the

Bronx with Flame, his rock group's lead singer. That wasn't her real name, of course—it was Sara Lynn Bartlett. I'd caught myself thinking of Sara/Flame as my actual child, she reminded me so much of myself at her age. She was half beast, half tamed creature, with both halves dying to please Jason. Her pulse was probably synchronized to the beat of his drums. I understood her obsession—hadn't I followed the golden notes of Howard's golden saxophone all the way into this life? When Flame sang with Blood Pudding, in her affecting, croupy style, she clutched the phallic mike as if her hand were joined to it by an electrical charge, and her pink, spiky hair stood on end.

Despite their talent, she and Jason didn't earn very much, and they seemed to take turns getting mugged in their neighborhood. I sent them a few dollars whenever I could—for taxis, I said, for the treat of dinner out. Young love needs to be spared the false romance of poverty. Mimi dies of it, in *La Bohème*, and Rodolfo has to throw his manuscript on the fire just to keep warm. In real life, nobody would have been singing. And nowadays his manuscript would have been backed up on a soft disk. From what I could tell, Jason and Sara only bought pot with the money I gave them, but she would send little thank-you notes, decorated with those inane, noseless smile faces. "Dear Mr. and Mrs. Flax, Jason and I want to thank you very much for your thoughtful and generous gift. We will enjoy spending it on something special, and think of you when we dò. Fondly, Sara."

Jason looked a lot like Howard. They both had the swarthy, redeeming beauty of gangsters, and what my mother once disparagingly called "bedroom eyes," Jason had experimented with various guises, including the current modified Mohawk that didn't quite work with his ringlets. He wore a tiny gold hoop through one earlobe, which Sara had pierced for him with a sterilized sewing needle. At fifty-two, Howard had developed a Kennedy jowl and Onassis pouches under his bedroom eyes, and he sucked in his gut whenever he surprised himself in a mirror.

We could work out the finances of separation—Howard was doing well at the studio, and a few months before, my column had been picked up for syndication. We'd made some good investments in the past, and Ann's wedding was almost paid off, our only debt beside the dwindling mortgage. She and Spence were married a little more than a year. They lived in Larchmont, along with their Swiss housekeeper, in a house about twice the size of ours—only a few miles and several worlds away from Jason and Sara. Spence was a junior partner in his father's brokerage firm, and Ann was in the M.B.A. program at Columbia. She had insisted on having one of those horribly lavish weddings, like the coronation of the Shah. God, the fittings we'd suffered, the agony over the color scheme, the menu, the type style on the invitations! How had we raised such a shallow little materialist? But I wept on cue when she appeared in the doorway of the chapel on Howard's arm—our blond darling, our confection of light. As she glided in slow, triumphant motion toward her blood-drained groom, I wiped my eyes and wondered if she'd ever get there. I'd never taught her to move like that. Howard and I had hurried breathlessly to the altar, with Jason our invisible witness. Howard had to force the ring over my swollen knuckle, but I practically shouted, "I do! I do!" I wouldn't think about any of that now, I wouldn't be sidetracked by nostalgia. There was nothing to hold me back.

I certainly didn't have to stay married for my mother's sake. Divorce was no longer a stigma in her crowd. Most of her friends' children had been through it at least once. And she didn't live with us, the way La Rae's father lived with her and

Frank, so there'd be no awkwardness of eviction or custody. My mother was still in Brooklyn—that borough of widows and yuppies—dead-bolted inside her apartment, wearing her Med-Alert beeper. My news would only confirm what she had known from the moment I'd burst in with that other news, twenty-four years ago—that it wouldn't last. It just took longer to end than she had expected. She would have loved to tell my father she'd been right all along, but it hadn't happened in his lifetime. Over the years, though, she'd grown grudgingly fond of Howard, or used to him. He changed her burnt-out light bulbs, moved her furniture back and forth across the room, and praised her heavy-handed cooking.

We would have to let the dog choose between us.

It was a hot and humid night, and the crickets must have been carrying on out there, but we were sealed in, with the air-conditioner going full blast. I began having one of those aural hallucinations I'd often get in that maddening hum. It was an old Harry James number that Howard's combo used to scramble into riffs and flourishes. I heard the melody straight this time, and started to silently mouth the words. You made me love you, I didn't want to do it, I didn't want to do it, you made me—

Next to me, Howard stirred and groaned. His hand slid upward from my hip to my breast. He muttered something. Oh, no, I thought, not now. It wasn't like him to become horny in the middle of the night. Not recently, anyway. I turned carefully away until his fingers were merely grazing my spine, and thought that maybe we *should* make love this last time, as a ceremony of conclusion. La Rae had something about that in her lonelyhearts column a few weeks ago. What was the heading? *Regrets Sex With Ex.* No, this was different—I was still married to Howard, even as I planned not to be.

"Paulie," Howard said, and I whispered "No!" into my pillow as fervently as I'd once cried "Yes, yes!" into his hot and hectic mouth. Then he said, "This pain. Boy."

"What pain?" I asked, and he took so long to answer I thought he'd spoken in a dream or had gone right back to sleep. I turned to look at him. My eyes had adjusted to the darkness and I could see that he was on his side, facing me, he errant hand on the fur of his own chest. "Here," he said. "Wow."

"Howard, wake up," I told him. "You're having a bad dream." And then I saw that his eyes were open. I put my lamp on and looked at him more closely. He hadn't moved at all, not even the hand, and he was frowning. He seemed about to make a heartfelt speech. "What's wrong?" I said. "Are you okay?" But it was clear that he wasn't okay. He was moon-pale and there was a sheen of sweat on his face and torso. The room was freezing; the music in my head had stopped.

"Oh, shit," he said, and belched deeply. "I shouldn't have eaten that lousy ham."

I got out of bed and brought him some Gelusil, thinking that Howard's father and grandfather had both died of heart attacks, and that profuse sweating was a sure symptom. Wasn't nausea, also? Men Howard's age, even those who ate sensibly and didn't smoke, dropped dead every day, playing tennis or just sitting at their desks. I didn't know how to suggest any of this to him; mortality is Howard's obsession, but it's not his favorite subject.

"Listen, Howard," I began cautiously, "maybe you should see somebody . . . maybe it isn't indigestion."

He looked at me in terror.

"Just to be on the safe side," I said.

"It might pass soon," he said, without conviction. His

voice had altered, grown thinner and hoarse, as if he were parched.

I wiped his face with the edge of the top sheet. I took his clammy hand between mine. "Let me call Stuart," I said. Stuart was an internist Howard saw from time to time, mostly on the softball field.

"California," Howard said. "Convention." It was becoming difficult for him to speak, to unclench his jaw and let the words out.

"Well, then," I said, "I'll just call an ambulance." I said it causally, as if I were about to call a cab.

But Howard wasn't fooled. "No!" he gasped. His face was shiny again.

"You have to check this out, Howard," I said sternly. *"Please."*

"Car," Howard said.

"You want me to drive you to the hospital?"

He squeezed my hand in affirmation.

It was a long walk from the bedroom to the garage. All the way there, I silently instructed him not to die. Nothing was settled between us. Don't you dare, I ordered. We have unfinished business, you bastard. Suddenly I wanted to know who she was, and how it had happened, and why. Had there been others? I was afflicted with jealousy; I'd forgotten its stunning pain, the way it rides the lining of the body, frantic for release. Howard leaned heavily against me as we started out, slowing our pace. We went past the collage of photographs on the dresser, our own smiling faces blessing our journey. I watched us go by in the big mirror. I'd pulled clothing for us both from the floor and the closets without taking my eyes off Howard. Now he wore an open tropical shirt over gray sweatpants, and I had a wrinkled pink sundress on, inside out.

We paused in the kitchen, so he could rest. Our old black Labrador, Shadow, half rose from his mat near the door. He wagged his tail with mild, sleeping curiosity. Was it morning already, time for his walk? When it came down to it, he would choose Howard, with whom he set out every day to rediscover the neighborhood.

There were our places at the table, the sturdy appliances letting us pass. In the garage, Howard's garden tools hung on the pegboard, next to his red satin softball jacket. It was a setup to get me, stage props of touching personal effects. The smells of grease and gasoline, the decaying spears of grass in the teeth of the rake. I helped Howard into the car and went around to the driver's side. When the automatic garage door lifted, like a theater curtain, I saw a portion of blue-black summer sky through the rearview mirror, and a handful of stars.

On the way to the hospital I tried not to talk, but I couldn't help it. I said anxious, stupid things. "Look," I said, "the Castellis are having a party. We weren't invited." I did seventy-five and eighty on the Expressway. Howard usually hated being my passenger, but this time he didn't complain or start pumping his imaginary brake. He didn't stir or say a single word, not even to let me know he was alive. So I had to keep glancing at him, veering out of lane, with the horns blaring all around us.

At Nassau General, I pulled into a just-vacated space near the emergency-room entrance. "Well, *that* was lucky, anyway," I told Howard as we got out. The reception area was brightly lit and busy, and most of the rows of orange plastic chairs were filled. There were parents with crying or sleeping children in their laps; a young couple in evening dress, holding hands; a hugely pregnant woman, who was reading; and an elderly man in a bathrobe, watching a baseball game on the ceiling-mounted television set. I led Howard to a seat and went to the inner doorway, where a security guard stood watch under a sign that said: *Have Your Insurance Cards Ready.* I hadn't even brought my purse with me. I peeked inside the doorway and saw two clerks typing. The triage nurse was sitting at her desk, taking a man's blood pressure. He had a blood-soaked towel wrapped around his other arm, and he was chatting gaily with her about the Mets. "Excuse me," I said. "My husband is having chest pains."

I expected her to leap up in concern, and maybe the bleeding patient, too. They continued sitting there. She wrote something on a chart; the man winked at me. If we had come by ambulance as I'd wanted to, Howard would be inside now, attended by doctors. I'd given in and driven him, honoring the old contract of compromise we'd made after he came back to me. I had to back off—to give him *air*, he'd say, as if we were talking about an accident victim—and he would be faithful. When the nurse finally looked up to acknowledge me, I was practically dancing with anxiety. *"My husband,"* I repeated carefully, the way you do with a foreigner, or a lip reader. *"He has chest pains."*

She signaled to the guard and he ducked into the room behind her and came back with a wheelchair. "Which one?" he asked, and I indicated Howard, who was paler than ever and watching the ball game, it seemed. He looked absurd and pathetic in his improvised outfit—a dying Hawaiian jogger. The guard wheeled him away, holding me back with a raised hand when I tried to follow. "We'll call you," he said, with the insincerity of a casting director.

I remembered going to the hospital in Queens to give birth to Jason. They wouldn't let Howard go up with me at first, even though I told them he was a Participating Father. We had practiced our breathing for months, but no one had taught us how to say good-bye. "We're in this together!" Howard called after me, and we waved and blew volleys of kisses until the elevator door closed between us. Hours later, when he showed up in the labor room, haggard with waiting and worry, I snarled that he was a filthy, stinking liar, that I was in this alone. Now I waved at Howard and he didn't wave back.

One of the clerks beckoned me inside the office. I sat at the side of her desk and filled out the medical and insurance forms. Why did they need all that information? Why did they want to know Howard's religion and his mother's maiden name? I wondered if I should call her. There was no way to break anything to her gently; she had an uncanny instinct for disaster. I'd say, "Hi, Henrietta," and she'd start screaming, burning up the wires all the way from here to Miami Beach. I had nothing to tell her yet, anyway. Any minute, Howard could come walking out, his lips white with Gelusil, swearing he was going to watch his diet from now on.

It was so quiet back there. A city hospital would have been jumping on Saturday night, with victims of gunshots and stab wounds staggering in, and people OD'ing on everything from crack to vanilla extract. Oh, why did we ever move? We wouldn't have grown bored there, or so isolated from one another. We'd have been forced into intimacy because there wouldn't have been enough room to have such secret, separate lives. In Port Washington, Howard had the whole backyard jungle to escape into, and I had my choice of two and a half bathrooms in which to sulk. I knew this was not rational thinking. After all, Howard had first betrayed me when we'd lived in that tiny apartment, and you could die of loneliness lying right next to someone in the same bed. Our move out here twenty years ago had symbolized our growing maturity—irresponsible kids don't take on mortgages and school-budget referendums. We told ourselves and the children that we had done it mostly for their sake, that we wanted them to live in nature, to know about trees and grass. One day, when Jason was about fourteen and still being chauffeured everywhere, he growled from the backseat of the car that it was the wrong *kind* of grass. Ann had adjusted quickly, showing signs of suburban matronhood before she was three.

I handed over the completed forms and the clerk stamped and stapled them and told me to wait outside until I was called. I took a seat next to a sleeping man, after grabbing a handful of magazines from the rack on the wall. The baseball game was still in progress, and the couple in evening dress were still there, the camellias browning fast on her wrist. The young woman smiled at me and rolled her eyes, and I rolled mine and smiled back in exasperated sympathy. What a way to spend Saturday night!

I thought of calling our children, not to scare them, of course, but to let them know what was happening, and for their company. But Jason and Flame were playing a dance on the Lower East Side, and Ann and Spence were at a fancy dinner party in Katonah. And they *would* be scared, especially Jason. When he was little and didn't want to hear whatever we were telling him, he'd race around with his fingers stuck in his ears, chanting "Liar, liar! Pants on fire!"

I opened one of the magazines on my lap. It was a copy of *Sports Illustrated* from June 1984. The lead article was about surf-casting off the coast of Ibiza. The magazines were all soiled and tattered, like the ones in the laundromat. This *place* was like the laundromat—the orange chairs and the trapped cigarette smoke and that oppressive sense of humanity. I shuffled through the pages, unable to read anything. They should have let me stay with Howard—we were in this together.

One of the clerks came out then and called a name. A

whole family rose like flapping birds and rushed after her. Why hadn't she called me? I was here first. A woman went to the pay telephone near the magazine rack. She said, "Henry? I'm still here. He doesn't look so good. You know, yellowish. We're waiting for the doctor."

As soon as she hung up, I called La Rae's number, collect. It rang and rang, but no one answered. I sat down again and began working my fingers together nervously. Howard hadn't looked so good, either. Bluish. Jewish. Mother's maiden name: Henrietta Gold. She was a bride once, and then—bang!—a widow. Well, not that fast, really, but maybe it seemed that way to her. What was going on in there, anyway? I tried to think of something else. That man with the bloodied towel around his arm, a chef, probably, or a butcher who'd missed with his cleaver. To remove bloodstains from fabric, soak in cold water and coarse salt for several hours . . .

The sleeping man next to me came awake and said, "Well, *hello* there." I moved two rows over and looked up at the ball game in time to see an instant replay of a home run. The pitcher wound up with excruciating slowness. The ball moved from his hand in a languid course to the plate, where the batter swatted drowsily at it. It arced across the diamond to the rim of the left-field wall and the outfielder leaped, as if for joy, and watched as it passed his glove and disappeared into the stands.

The clerk stood in the doorway and called another name. I couldn't make it out for a moment, and then, when no one else responded, I realized it was mine. I followed her past the offices into the inner sanctum, an enormous room partitioned by curtains into cubicles. Someone was moaning loud and fast in one of them. Not all of the curtains were drawn, and I saw bare feet, sheeted bodies, and bleeping heart monitors. Everyone looked like Howard. The clerk motioned me to a middle cubicle and there he was, behind the curtain. Or somebody pretending to be him. His hair was thinned a little; he'd lost some weight. He had clear tubes up his nostrils for oxygen and something clear dripping in through his taped hand. A jagged line went up and down across the screen of his monitor, like the profit-and-loss chart of a company in trouble.

"Howard," I said. "It's me, Paulie," as if I, too, had changed while we'd been apart and he might not recognize me.

He lifted his free hand; the wrist was banded with a plastic I.D. strip. "Paulie, I'm having a heart attack," he whispered. "This is it."

The moaning patient began to scream, and a baby cried somewhere with ascending rage or panic. "No, no," I said. "We don't know that." I looked around behind me for a nurse or a doctor, someone to refute what he'd said, but they were all busy elsewhere.

"Myocardial infarction," Howard said, and I knew he hadn't made that up; it had the terrible ring of truth. Why hadn't someone told me first? Then a doctor appeared. He looked very young, about seventeen or so, with recent acne scars and big, goofy-looking ears. "I'm Dr. Forman," he said, and he shook my unwilling hand. "We seem to be having a little problem here." He unhooked the chart from the foot of Howard's bed and glanced at it. "From what we can tell, your husband has suffered a small myocardial infarction." Howard's eyes blazed with victory before they dimmed with despair.

"Oh, *small*," I said, insisting on the bright side of things— my worst fault, according to Howard, after my inability to be serene.

"We're admitting him, of course." the boy-doctor continued, "to our cardiac care unit."

How could he know anything about it? I imagined him carrying a toy doctor's kit, like the one Jason once had, with a little play stethoscope and a jar of pastel candy pills inside. But a real stethoscope hung from his neck, ruthless rubber and stainless steel, and he leaned over Howard to listen to his heaving chest with solemn, grown-up interest.

I watched the erratic line of Howard's monitored heartbeat. It flattened out completely once, and an alarm buzzed for a few seconds before the line moved into peaks and falls again. "That thing's not working," I said to the doctor, and he smiled at me and patted my shoulder before he left.

An aide came and told me I could take Howard's personal belongings home. After I'd signed a release, she handed me a plastic bag. I opened it and took out Howard's shirt and sweatpants. They were sopping wet; he might have gone swimming in them. At the bottom of the bag, I found a smaller bag with his watch in it. He always wore it, even to bed and in the shower, as if he might be cheated of precious time if he didn't keep careful track of it. "Here, you'll want your watch," I told him, and I fastened it above the plastic wristband. My hands were trembling and I could hardly see through my brimming eyes. "Do you know what time it is?" I said. "We haven't stayed up this late in years." Shut up, I told myself. Stop twinkling, you dummy. It was cruel to be so cheerful at the bedside of someone who was sick and frightened. Was I still that angry with Howard, even now? I took his hand and brought it to my cheek. I wasn't really cheerful. Even as I blathered I felt like weeping, and my own heart had squeezed into a fist that wouldn't open. "Sweetheart," I said. "I'll stay here with you." And I did, until two orderlies showed up to take him to the cardiac unit. Again, I tried to follow, wishing I were smaller and less conspicuous. They told me to go home and come back the next morning. "Go home, Paulie," Howard echoed bravely. When I began to protest, the tears spilling onto his hand at last, he said, "The dog."

Of course. I'd have to walk him in a few more hours so he could water the world. I'd have to feed him, too. Life goes on, I thought. That's the way it goes. As if my mother had taken control of my brain and was stuffing it with clichés. I kissed Howard and went back through the reception area and out into the parking lot, shocked by the heat and darkness after that brilliant, air-conditioned chill.

I drove home with Howard's limp clothing on the seat beside me. He might have been removed from them by a wicked spell, and could be restored by the incantation of the right words. I stayed in lane and didn't exceed the speed limit, as a replay of the night's events began to unreel behind my eyes. I saw us getting into bed again, Howard's hand moving to my hip. Everything that had happened—my thoughts about leaving him, his pain, the whole hospital drama—seemed as inevitable as that home run I'd watched on television. I couldn't have stopped any of it, any more than the outfielder could have stopped the home-run ball. And I would have left Howard—I really would have—but he couldn't leave me. Not this way, not yet.

At home, Shadow barked twice, a complaint more than a warning. *You* again, his glance seemed to say, but where's Howard? I petted him for our mutual consolation, and endured his breath while he lapped my face. In the bedroom I turned on the air-conditioner, knowing I'd hallucinate Harry James again in that hum, and hear the phone ringing all night with bad news, and my own voice practicing to say good-bye.

2

PAULIE LEFT AND THEY TOOK ME UPSTAIRS. I COULDN'T
get over what was happening; it kept throbbing in my head
like a news bulletin: *This is it. This is it.* I had the Flax family
heart, that treasure my father and his father had smuggled
past the Czar into America.

I was in another big room, the same striped curtains. How
could you tell what time of day it was in here? I didn't see
any windows, and they probably always kept the lights on,
the way they do in prisons. At least I had my watch. 1:15. A
nurse came through the curtains, a pretty blond kid like our
Annie. She played around with the tubes and she gave me a
shot—to relax me, she said, to help me sleep. I told her I
couldn't take a chance on ever sleeping again. "Think positive thoughts now," she said, whatever that meant. Her perfume made me sad.

Poor Paulie—I'd scared the hell out of her. She'd talked
nonstop there for a while, and I figured she'd kill us on the
way here, driving like Andretti on uppers, but I didn't give
a damn. It had to be better than dying from this—the pain
getting bigger and bigger until the time bomb inside you goes
off—kaboom!

The quiet was spooky; I could hear all the respirators

breathing around the room. Small coronary, that prodigy said, and Paulie was thrilled, as if we'd just won the lottery. Ah, she was only trying to cheer herself up, poor kid. I should have let her call for an ambulance, though. I'd never felt so rotten in my life, with pain all the way up in my jaw and down through my arm. I threw my guts up the minute they took me in, and I thought: Food poisoning, after all— that lousy ham! Then a whole team of them went to work on me, and when they wired me into their system, I knew it was the real thing.

What I wanted more than anything now was a cigarette, just a couple of deep drags to relax me. That shot wasn't working, and how long was I supposed to lie here like this? I'd go nuts before morning. Jesus, it was only 1:22. That had to be wrong. I shook the watch, making the heart monitor go berserk. The pain in my chest was still there, but dulled, as if I was only remembering pain. I felt wrung out, dead tired, but not sleepy.

If I died, Paulie couldn't stay in the house forever. The mortgage was almost paid off, but the place was too big for her to handle alone—shoveling snow, hauling out the trash, putting up the storms. She'd get married again, maybe. I saw some faceless guy, some joker like Frank Peters, working my garden, smiling over at Paulie lying spread-eagled in the hammock, the way she does. It was the wrong thing to think; the pain came closer and louder. What? What did I mean by louder? That shot was making me punchy.

I vowed to give up smoking, midnight snacks, all my bad habits. Stu had a fit whenever I lit up after a game. "And with your family history, Howie," he'd say, shaking his head. Well, thanks a lot, Dad and Granddad. Jason, that dumb little stud, was going to lose it when he figured this whole thing out. For no reason, I thought of how he'd looked right after he was born, like something squeezed through a cookie press, but kind of beautiful, anyway. I loved him as soon as I saw him, and I felt sorry for him. I still loved him, of course, but I also hated him a little, for being so laid back, so easy to lead around by his cock, the way I used to be. That girl he lived with was kind of cute, under the fright wig and the makeup. She reminded me of Paulie, I don't know why. Sara is small and skinny, and Paulie has such a full, curvy body . . .

The nurse came in with the doctor and said, "You were sleeping, that's good." She said it really loud, as if I was deaf. Did I look that old to her, like somebody's deaf old grandfather? The doctor poked around and asked how I was feeling. I told him okay, except that a truck had run over my chest, and he wrote it down and left. The nurse peeked under the covers—I had a tube down in there, too. "So," I croaked, "do you come here often?" At least I got a smile out of her and a pat in the vicinity of my feet before she went out again.

Maybe Paulie wouldn't get married again. She'd probably just get more involved in her causes: mothers against war, against drunk driving, against the nuclear-arms buildup. Years ago, during the migrant farmworkers' strike, she'd stood outside the supermarket and yelled at people going in not to buy scab grapes. I remember that teenaged boys yelled back and threw grapes at her. And she and La Rae handed out flyers near the railroad station for at least three losing Presidential candidates. Paulie used to look then the way she looked in bed—I mean passionate, and *there*. I couldn't help feeling jealous whenever she talked about Chavez or McGovern. I never told her that, of course, and I did my share, picking up and delivering the flyers, nailing picket signs to broom handles. But my heart wasn't in it. Jesus, my heart.

The phone was ringing. I reached for it and was jerked back by the IV. Shit, it was still true. I must have dozed off for a couple of minutes; there wasn't any pain now. I looked at my watch. 4:25! Tomorrow, *today*, I'd be neighborhood news. People would feel bad when they heard about it, and a little glad it wasn't them. Like reading the obits and realizing how nice the weather is, how good the dinner smells.

Paulie would call Mike—he'd have to run the studio alone for a while, or hire somebody. I had a ten-thirty appointment to cut a demo for a C&W group from Merrick. Mike could handle that. But I forgot to tell Paulie not to call my mother. She'd come up here like a bullet and drive us all nuts. When my father died, I went down to Florida for the funeral, and to stay with her for a couple days. Every night she played out another episode in the hit series that was their life together. She had anecdotes, photographs, letters, souvenirs.

I used to wake up to their fights when I was a kid. They were mostly in Yiddish, but somehow I always got the drift. He was a gambler, my weak-hearted father. After a morning's work at the funeral home, he'd head for the track. I guess he looked at a few of those boxed bodies and decided he had nothing to lose. He lost plenty, though, and she wasn't going to let him forget it. She cursed him in two languages, calling him a thief and a *gonif*. He'd stolen not only her money but her youth and good looks as well. He didn't say much, he just banged his fist on the walls and the tables. As they got older, they both mellowed; I suppose even she saw how all quarrels eventually end. They moved down to Miami, to a smaller apartment, like a couple of newlyweds. They bought everything in pairs: Barcaloungers, place mats, heating pads. When their ailments started piling up, they grew really considerate of each other, keeping careful track of who took what pill, and when, from that drug arsenal on their kitchen table.

My sister, Beverly, had come from L.A. for the services

and then gone right back again. She claimed that her own husband wasn't well, but she and my mother had never been close. After Beverly left, my mother and I lay on the twin Barcaloungers and talked about my father. She told me that he hadn't chosen the mortuary business—it chose him. His cousins, who had come over earlier, had started it, and they took him in. It was a living, she added, and shrugged at her unintended irony. The pictures she showed me were from the good times, when my sister and I were little and our parents were in charge of the world. She didn't bring up the Depression or the war, or any of their own knock-down, drag-out fights. She was canonizing him and rewriting history. I felt sleepy and relaxed while she told me all that crap. She was like Scheherazade, keeping herself alive with her stories and keeping me from going home to Paulie. "It's winter up there," she reminded me. "Get in a little sun while you can." It wasn't just that she was lonely. Neighbors came and went all day. They had each other's keys, in case of emergencies: strokes, broken hips, sudden death. They were all old women like her, curved into commas and baked to a crisp under that Florida sun.

Paulie called up all the time, even during the day rates. "What's going on?" she asked. I could practically hear the snow falling in the background. She put the kids on to babble and scream "Daddy! Daddy!" in my ear. The heat was off in the building, Paulie told me, the super out on a bender. Some creep in the laundry room had a fix on her, and the whole family had coughs. She made Jason cough into the phone.

I came to my senses after two weeks and prepared to go home. My mother cried and said not to worry, she would be fine. Although she knew that I wasn't a believer, she begged me to pray for my dead father's soul, and for hers, too, when her turn came. Soon, she assured me. She gave me a box of my father's things to take home, the kind of stuff you end up shoving into a drawer and never look at again: shoe trees, street maps, his green golf cap.

The earth that Paulie's second husband turned over in my garden, in my mind, might be for me. Would she be as forgiving as my mother, and sign me up for sainthood? When I went crazy that time, and ran away with Marie, Paulie said that I'd broken her heart. It healed, though, didn't it? I thought of her eyes last night, bright with tears, and the way she'd kissed my hand. I saw a box of my own belongings being divided between my children. Annie would take my bathrobe and wear it, like she did when she was little. Jason would choose my saxophone. It was what he knew me best by, and he could always hock it if he had to. When had I played it last? It was shining away right now in its dark case in the dark hall closet. I would be like that, without music, without light. Oh, boy, these sure weren't positive thoughts. I ransacked my head for something better and came up with the old days, with our combo, the Fantasy Five, playing a club date. How good it always felt under the pink heat of the spots, the crowd buzzing in the shadows while we warmed up. Carl and Alex noodled around the melody on the piano and guitar, JoJo did paradiddles and rim shots, and Roy thumped out the beat on his bass. When I blew my sax, the sound went right through me like a hit of something pure and expensive. One night, we played a dance downtown at NYU, and there was this big, lovely, flushed-looking girl leaning against the wall, listening and watching. A few days later we were in my car and I was moving down her body as she was climbing mine. I thought we'd go right past each other in our excitement, but we didn't; we made Jason, and later we made Annie.

My mother was right, I'm not a believer, except in some nameless force that probably gets you for not believing. But as I started drifting off again, I prayed a little—just in case— not for my father's immortal soul, but for the rest of my own unused life. I swore I'd stop smoking for good this time. I'd start working out and eat right if I could have another chance at everything. I'd even march with Paulie, against grapes and lettuce and pestilence and war. And I would give up Janine.

3

"SO, IS HE GOING TO DIE, OR WHAT?" JASON ASKED, as soon as we were back in the CCU waiting room.

"I don't believe you just said that," Ann said, jabbing him with her elbow. "What's *wrong* with you?"

There was nothing wrong with Jason; he was only being himself, suffering this news in his own way. His eyes had the furious, tearful look they'd get when he was little and couldn't learn to read. His first-grade teacher had explained on conference day that he was a bright, but disabled, little boy, that he saw things backward on the page. Mirror-reading, she called it. Later they'd call it dyslexia, but they still didn't have a cure. The teacher told us he was frustrated, as if Howard and I hadn't noticed, as if we hadn't mended the ripped reader over and over again in the aftermath of Jason's little storms.

Ann had taught herself to read before she started kindergarten. She read road signs aloud as we whizzed past them in the car, and was always in an advanced reading group in school. Still, she wasn't very sympathetic or charitable to Jason. She claimed he got away with plenty, even if he was dumb. I explained over and over again, for her benefit and his, that he wasn't dumb at all, that he only had a little problem he'd outgrow. And he did learn to read finally, although without exceptional skill or joy. But his real redemption was his gift for music. We'd bought the drums for him as a therapeutic toy, and were surprised by his concentrated interest and his talent. He started improvising right away, like a little Mozart of rock and roll. Music was the thing that bound him to Howard more than to me, despite the competition, the enmity between them. It was a secret language they shared, that made Ann and me feel like outsiders sometimes, even though she was Howard's known favorite. If his father died, Jason would lose the comfort of that connection, and be left with the argument they'd never resolved.

"No," I said. "I really think Dad's going to be okay." Just as I used to hold the taped-up reader and say, "See, Jasie, this is Farmer Brown's cow."

We had all just visited Howard for the allotted five minutes. At first the CCU nurse had said only two of us at a time, but Ann stared her down and said she'd come all the way from Saudi Arabia to see her father, that our family hadn't been together for five years. She might have come from anywhere, with that stunning tan and crisp safari dress, the armload of gold bangles colliding with a crash at her elegant wrist. Jason and I gaped at her, amazed by her nerve and invention, and the nurse, who appeared mesmerized, if not convinced, said, "Well . . . all right, but just this time."

Ann had achieved other goals in her life with the persuasion of charm and self-confidence. At her admissions interview at U. Penn, the school of her choice, she'd claimed she was going to become a corporate executive before her twenty-fifth birthday, and she'd rattled off the names of female role models in the Fortune 500. Howard used to say that she was the brains *and* beauty in the family, driving another wedge between himself and Jason. Ann's ambition held up—before she'd completed her undergraduate degree, she was accepted by the M.B.A. programs at Wharton, Harvard, and Columbia. She'd chosen Columbia so that she could be near Spence. They had met right after her junior year at Penn, when she was a summer intern with his father's Wall Street firm and he was its rising star. Now she managed to merge her schooling nicely with marriage, bolstered, no doubt, by their hefty income. Looking at her and then at Jason, in his impoverished disarray, I understood why they didn't get along better, and why there were revolutions in small, underdeveloped nations.

"Dad looks lousy to me," Jason offered, earning another elbow jab from Ann.

"He looks better than he did last night," I said, which was actually true. Last night he'd looked ready for Madame Tussaud's.

"Do we have the best doctor?" Ann asked.

"Yes," I said, and by then we did. That morning, after I'd called the children and my mother, I called Katherine, who was the source of various useful references for all her friends. Someone she knew put us in touch with an anesthesiologist at Nassau General, and by the time Howard woke up, his tests were being reviewed by the chief of cardiology. He was going to confer with the other doctors and speak to us later. Spence and Sara were expected soon, and I felt as if we were forming an army against the medical opinion. I had the irrational idea that if there were more of us, Howard would get a better prognosis.

He'd tried to control his emotions when the kids and I approached his bed. "Look who's here," he said in a wobbly, strangled voice. "Did you come to spring me?" His overnight stubble made him look more like a derelict than a patient.

"Nah, to borrow money," Jason said.

"Oh, Daddy," Ann said, truthfully, almost undoing all of us.

We hadn't said much of anything else before our time was up and we were ushered out of there. I saw Jason's furtive glances at the sick and dying in the other beds and I knew we were both having the same nervous, speculative thoughts.

The two-hour stretches between visits with Howard were unbearably long. We were like strangers trying to make conversation at an airport during a flight delay. The cardiologist, Dr. Croyden, didn't show up until late afternoon. Spence and Sara were there by then, too, but we were an untrained, makeshift army against the power of his opinion. He told us that Howard had indeed had a heart attack. He didn't use the young resident's medical jargon, and he said that the damage was moderate, not small. So, is he going to die, or what, I wondered, but I couldn't bring myself to say it.

"What's the prognosis?" Spence asked.

"Good, I'd say," Dr. Croyden said. "Of course, the first forty-eight hours are crucial. Then we'll keep him here a couple of weeks, to watch him and let him rest. I expect he'll have to make some changes in his lifestyle once he gets home."

He meant diet and exercise and giving up cigarettes, but my first thought was of the plans I'd been making just before Howard got sick. Last night I'd left the hospital heavy with fear, with the weight of love and love's history. If Howard had died, I would have howled and keened like any bereaved widow. I probably would have wanted to die, too. Yet I'd kept my secret intentions on hold, in some chilly, dark corner of my heart. This changed everything, of course, for now; but in the long run it didn't change anything. I felt justified and guilty and miserable all at once. I wanted to confess, to unburden myself, but Croyden was a clinician and a stranger, and the kids had their own troubles. Ann had developed dark circles under her eyes in just a few hours. And she loved Howard unconditionally; she would think I was some kind of monster. Jason was more likely to understand my ambivalence, because of his own, but this was no time to test him. Maybe there would never be a right time. They were both adults, but they still belonged on the other side of our bedroom door.

My friends had volunteered to sit with me at the hospital, and I'd told them to wait a few days, until Howard had improved a little. Even my mother had asked if I wanted her to come, without complaining for once about how sick *she* was. "Oh, no!" she cried when I told her the news, as if she wanted to deny it. Did tragedy bring out the best in everybody?

Sara sat quietly in the waiting room all afternoon, nibbling on her ragged fingernails. I asked her if she'd like to see Howard and she blushed and said she wasn't family, that only family was supposed to go in. "When he's feeling better," she added. She was there for Jason to lean against during the two-hour intervals, to absorb his unhappiness. I watched the way she waited for cues from him, assessing his mood before she touched him or spoke. She had a store of things in her pockets she could offer him at the right moment: chewing gum, crumpled pink Kleenex that she ironed with the flat of her palm before she handed them over, quarters for when he needed to make phone calls. Once, she plopped down next to me on one of those wheezing vinyl sofas, squeezed my arm, and gave me a cracked and linty Chiclet. I thought of Ruth, in the Bible, cleaving to her mother-in-law, and I was moved. It was sentimental, I knew, but everything seemed to affect me that way: the other families waiting for the five-minute visits with their patients; Howard rallying to talk to us one time, and lying there fast asleep the next; Spence bringing sandwiches and coffee for everyone; Ann coming from the ladies' room with her lipstick freshened and her eyes red and swollen. Whenever it was time to see Howard again, two of us would rise, queasy with suspense, and go in. Nothing dramatic happened, for which we were all grateful, and ultimately a little bored. Mostly we flanked Howard, careful not to jar the bedside paraphernalia, and watched his heart monitor, the way other families watch television reruns together.

When I got home that night and La Rae came over, I was exhausted, and ready to tell her everything. Bless friendship, I thought, as we sat together in the kitchen, sipping iced tea. Sometimes I think we bully men with the mystique of closeness between women, another phenomenon besides childbearing we can torment them with. But the affinity is real, whether the women are teenagers in perpetual crisis, or forty-five-year-olds like us, surprised to still be in the thick of things. La Rae listened without comment, like a nondirective analyst, pushing my own Kleenex dispenser toward me when the waterworks began. "It's weird," I said, after I blew my nose. "I feel as if I've wronged *him*, somehow. And maybe I have, but I don't think so. You just *know* when you know these things, don't you?" I wasn't fishing—La Rae had told me a long time ago that Frank had had numerous casual affairs, from the very beginning of their marriage. Her complacency about it stunned me. I remembered my rampant craziness when Howard was with that woman, Marie, how I'd wanted to kill them both.

La Rae had tried to explain her position. "Look," she'd said. "It's something you get used to, as part of the package, that you accept—like gambling, or snoring, or sloppiness.

It's only one more accommodation you make, like all the others," she said.

"No, it isn't," I said.

"You're right," La Rae quickly agreed. "It isn't. So let's just say that I'm sick—lovesick. It qualifies me to do my column. When people write to tell me they're heartbroken, I can honestly answer that I understand. It's that visceral, personal response that makes me so popular with my readers."

Now she said, "Here's some free, unsolicited advice for you, Paulie—you'd better talk to Howard about all this."

"I know that," I said, "but not right now, not when he's so sick."

"Yeah, not now. There'd be no point in killing him when he's in bed alone."

I sighed, feeling some of the tension leaving me. What a relief confession was, even without absolution. But I couldn't help thinking that if I'd spoken to Howard—if I'd accused or questioned him—before the heart attack began, I would have believed I had caused it. Maybe Howard would have believed it, too. Katherine, who was always looking for a connection between random events, might think I was responsible, anyway. Or that Howard had brought it on himself.

"La Rae," I said. "Don't tell anyone about this, all right?"

"You mean Katherine?"

"Well, yes," I said. "Or anybody. Not even Frank. It wouldn't be fair to Howard if I blab about it before he and I have a chance to discuss it. You're the only one I've told."

"The reward for being closemouthed is getting to hear all the juicy stuff."

"You think this is juicy?" I didn't know why that notion pleased me.

"No, not really," she said, after a pause. "Except in the context of our pathetic little lives. I mean Flaubert made literature out of provincial intrigue, didn't he? I'll probably just get a lousy column out of it."

I was appalled. La Rae did invent letters for her column when the real ones were dull. Once in a while she even let me write one. "You can't use this," I said now. "It's my *life!*"

"Relax, Paulie," she said. "The names will be changed to protect the innocent—and the guilty. I'll make it cancer of the you-know-what the husband gets, just when the wife is planning to cut it off to teach him a lesson."

"You're terrible," I said. "You're crazy," and then I started laughing.

4

*W*HO WOULD HAVE THOUGHT I'D EVER BE HUNGRY
again, drooling over anemic-looking chicken, and peas the
color of Astroturf? But it was all part of the big recovery.
The guy in the other bed eyed my supper tray the way people
in Chinese restaurants ogle the food on the next table, as if
it looks better than what they have. In this case, he was right.
I mean, I was still on no sodium and low fat, but everything
on his tray had been pureed into an anonymous gray mush.
He was my second roommate in a week, a bleeding ulcer.
The first one—Gil Danzer, another heart attack—had gone
home two days before. It's amazing how quickly you can get
to know someone in a situation like this. Gil and his wife,
Sharon, and Paulie and I became old friends in only a few
days. Like us, they'd been married forever and had a couple
of grown kids. Gil and I compared the details of how we'd
gotten sick, as if we were describing the riveting plots of
movies we'd seen. We'd both had anginal pain on and off for
months, and we'd both blamed it on something we ate, or
muscle strain, or our imagination. When his heart attack
started, Gil was sure it was only indigestion, too; he and
Sharon were in a restaurant, and he'd just polished off a plate
of mussels marinara. "Ham!" I said, and we laughed like

34

maniacs. Our heart attacks had made us war buddies; the common bond was survival. But we had other things in common: Gil was a sound man at CBS, and he'd been a professional trombonist when he was younger. He still played with a group—at one another's houses—and he said I could sit in with them sometime. Gil wore his thinning, reddish hair a little long in back, the way we all used to wear it, and he had that patch of beard right under his lip some horn men think protects it. He reminded me of people I used to hang around with, and hadn't seen in years. While we chewed the rag, Sharon and Paulie made plans to go out for dinner after we were both home. "But it has to be strictly kosher," Sharon said. "No mussels, no ham."

Those days in the CCU had really gotten me down. At first I was sure I was going to die, and then when I didn't, living didn't really seem like such a hot alternative. I spent most of the time feeling my pulse and craving a smoke. Ordinary things—using the bathroom and cutting my own food—were like privileges I'd lost forever. So it was great watching Gil get better. He'd had his heart attack a week before mine, and he became a kind of role model for me—walking around, gradually getting his appetite and energy back. Because of him, I started believing I wasn't going to spend the rest of my life in bed, pissing through a tube. When Sharon came to take him home, we were all struck by how big his clothes were on him. I'd lost a lot of weight, too. It was the hard way to take it off, but we made a pact to keep it off. Sharon tied Gil's get-well balloons to my bed and he came over and said, "So long, kiddo. Be good, and I'll send you a cake with a file in it." He hugged me hard and then he was gone.

The new guy, Gary Seiffert, was something else. He hadn't stopped grouching from the minute they'd brought him in. The bed was too short, there was too much noise in the halls, his TV didn't work right. He left it on all day, anyway, even when he was sleeping. I kept dozing off to canned laughter and waking up to Crazy Eddie screaming about his insane prices. I figured I'd get an ulcer, too, before I got out of there. Seiffert was recently divorced—for the second time—and I thought he looked at Paulie with a sort of snide and hungry look, as if to say: She's great, but how long do you think it will last?

Despite Seiffert, and my own restlessness, I was feeling much better about everything. My body didn't seem like such a double-crossing traitor anymore. I worked my fork and knife out of the plastic wrap, and was lifting the lid off the mystery dessert, praying it wasn't Jell-O again, when Janine walked in. I thought I'd have another heart attack. Paulie had just gone home—I could still see the depression she'd left on the seat of the bedside chair. I pushed the tray table away and said, "Jesus, Janine, what are *you* doing here?" and Seiffert lowered the volume on his TV and looked at us with interest.

"That's quite a greeting, Howard," Janine said. "What do you think I'm doing? I came to see you."

"You know what I mean," I said through my teeth.

Janine sat down on the side of my bed, crossed her beautiful legs, and smiled over at Seiffert. I motioned for her to close the curtain, but she either didn't notice or decided to ignore me. "I went to the studio," she said, "and your partner told me about you. I almost died. I called the hospital and you know them, they said you were *critical*."

Jesus. "When did they say that?"

"I don't know. Yesterday, a couple of days ago. Honey, I was so worried."

"Paulie was just here." I whispered. "A few *minutes* ago." Seiffert lay on his side, completely absorbed by us now, as if we were a spin-off of the sitcom he'd been watching.

"I know, silly." Janine said. "I've been waiting down the hall in the lounge for her to leave. That place is so smoky—"

"Janine," I said, with barely controlled rage, "that was a really stupid thing to do."

"Well, thanks a lot," she said, and her freckled eyelids and the tip of her nose grew pink with emotion, the way they always did when we made love.

"Listen," I said, in a kindlier tone, "this isn't the place for us to talk."

"I didn't want to *talk*," she said. "I just wanted to *see* you."

She seemed much younger than thirty-three then, and irritatingly naïve. And although she was as pretty as I'd remembered—with her strawberry-blond hair, that flecked, creamy skin—she wasn't that attractive, somehow. I thought of the day she'd first shown up at the studio, looking incredibly sexy and innocent in washed-out jeans and one of her son's T-shirts. "Hi!" she'd said. "I found you in the Yellow Pages." It sounded like the lyrics to a country-and-western number. *I found you in the Yellow Pages, and lost you when your fingers walked away* . . . But Janine was into more sophisticated music, mostly slow, pensive ballads. She told me she wanted to make a demo, that she had always dreamed of becoming a singer, and now that she was divorced it seemed like a good time for a career change. At the moment she worked at Bloomingdale's, in Garden City, as a rep for a cosmetics company. She was one of those women who stand on the main floor of the store and spray other women with perfume as they walk by, as if they're blitzing roaches with Raid. Mike wasn't in the studio that first afternoon, and I'd been taking a nap when she came in. It started out as something professional between us. I let her sing for me and I accompanied her on the keyboard. She'd picked a Suzanne Vega number: "Undertow." Her voice was pretty much what I'd expected—pleasant and thin, and definitely untrained. She could carry a tune, but she switched keys in the middle of the second verse without seeming to realize it. The wonderful thing was the way she stood there, as if she was on the stage of a concert hall, gesturing like crazy with her hands, gazing out toward the back rows of an adoring crowd. I found myself praising her a little, and then coaching her. I didn't have an ulterior motive, I was only trying to help her out. When I told her how much a demo would cost, she looked so stricken I immediately said we had a sliding scale, which wasn't true. If Mike had been there, it might not have happened, but I agreed to a price slightly below the cost of operation, and decided I'd pay the difference myself and keep the whole thing off the books. It was an act of charity, like giving to Cancer Care and the Salvation Army. She lived in Hicksville with her sixteen-year-old son. She told me she'd been a child bride, that her ex-husband was an alcoholic who'd abused her and the kid. I really didn't have a fix on her that day, only a feeling of sympathy, a kind of tenderness. Except for a few one-night stands when I was on the road, I had been faithful to Paulie since Marie. Most of the yearnings I'd had during those years were safe ones: movie stars, centerfolds, girls in bikinis I'd glimpse at the beach before they disappeared into the surf or I closed my eyes. Janine said later that she'd fallen for me the minute she'd walked into the studio, but I think she was just trying to be romantic, and her lousy life had given her a pathetic notion of romance. Anyway, the idea that I'd help launch her singing career had probably turned her on first.

The second time I saw her, at a prearranged time on Mike's next day off, she was wearing something wildly inappropriate for a rehearsal at a storefront studio in Hempstead. It was a gold jumpsuit, and so loaded with spangles it hurt my eyes. I was glad we had curtains on the windows, that nobody else was in the place. I locked the front door and took her into the control room. She was very jittery; she kept clearing her throat and wiggling her fingers, as if they'd gone to sleep. "Just relax," I told her. "You're going to be great."

But she wasn't great at all. When I played the tape back, her eyelids and nose got pink and the rest of her went dead-white, the first time I'd seen her like that. I pictured her being shoved around by her husband—a big, mindless goon like Bluto in *Popeye*—and eating lonely suppers in her kitchen with her surly, teenaged son. I would have done anything to make her happy at that moment. What I did was tell her that everybody's tape sounded like hell until it was sweetened. I fooled around with the equalizers until the mix was a little better. It was like cheering Annie up when she was a kid and got into a sulk. Janine was sitting on one of the stools, listening to herself through a headset, and I watched her face slowly change until it burst into a sunny smile. Then she jumped up and threw her arms around me. There was nothing sexual in it, at least not right away. I wasn't braced for her attack and she almost knocked me over. The spangles scratched my neck. "Hey!" I said. "Take it easy!" I'm not sure exactly what happened next, but suddenly we were locked together, kissing in a hard, serious way. Her outfit had a zipper, one of those long, greased-lightning jobs. Maybe I started opening it just to get that scratchy stuff out of the way, and then I couldn't stop. She wasn't wearing anything underneath. The gold fabric was silky smooth on the inside, like her skin. She made me think of Marie, who

was actually much darker and taller. It was the surprise of
her, I guess—that she was new, totally unknown—but I didn't
understand that then. I didn't understand anything. When she
touched me, *I* became a mindless goon, grinding against her,
lifting her into me. She wrapped her legs around me, trailing
the jumpsuit she hadn't quite stepped out of, digging her
spike heels like spurs into my ass. She was still wearing the
headset, too, but it was knocked askew. I could hear her
distant, canned voice like a backup for our gasping breath.

That was almost three months before my heart attack. We
saw each other as often as we could during those months.
She came to the studio whenever I was sure Mike wasn't
going to be there, and I went to her house when we knew
her son was in school. Once, he came home early, and Janine
sent him to the basement on a phony errand, while I got
dressed and sneaked out the door like a thief. It gave me a
sick, heavy feeling listening to the kid's voice coming up
through the floorboards as I left, saying he didn't smell any
gas leak. We should have stopped it then, as if his coming in
unexpectedly was a sort of warning or omen. But we didn't—
we started meeting in motel rooms. Quit while you're ahead,
my father used to say, before he threw all his winnings back
into the pot.

Paulie and I had been together almost a quarter of a century—our silver wedding anniversary was coming up next
June. Neither of us had ever made a big deal out of those
things, but this year was different, we really had something
to celebrate. Anyway, I *liked* being married—you didn't have
to be in a turmoil of excitement all the time. Married sex
was friendly and familiar, even if it wasn't that thrilling or
frequent. I could sleep afterward. I could sleep *instead* if I
felt like it. And Paulie and I were able to communicate in
shorthand because so much had gone down between us: the

early passion, the children, the fights, the reconciliations. I believed that we should be together when one of us kicked off, and I could see why my mismated parents had stuck it out. I'd always thought I would go first, because of my family history. And you only had to look around—about half the population are widows. More than half of Florida's. When Paulie had that lump on her breast years ago, I though I might lose her, and it seemed impossible, unnatural, for me to survive her.

I imagined her friend Katherine analyzing this whole business, giving it a neat Freudian twist. She'd say something asinine about Janine and Jason's girl both being vocalists, that I was competing with my own son, and going through a mid-life crisis. Or that I was unconsciously in love with my daughter, or my sister. She'd said plenty of that crap already about Frank Peters. Of course he screwed around all the time, and when I wasn't with Janine, I had sensible thoughts about ending the affair and getting my life out of jeopardy. But whenever I was with her again, I'd lose sight of the danger, or I'd put things off. I knew it was going to be difficult. She was ambitious far beyond her dreams of becoming a singer. Maybe being battered had something to do with it. Maybe it contributed to that feisty, stubborn quality that drew me to her and scared me off at the same time.

Now I faced her without feeling any physical attraction, only a desire to get it over with without having to go through the tortured motions. I wished I could close my eyes the way I did at the beach to end a fantasy. It was a chickenhearted wish, but I reminded myself that I was a sick man—*critical* maybe—that I'd already made a resolution to break it off with her the night I'd come here. I got out of bed and pulled the curtain around us, holding the short, ridiculous hospital gown closed behind me. "Janine," I said, once I was back in bed, with my heart knocking from the effort, from the dread. "Thanks for coming, but I'd like you to go home now. I'll call you as soon as I can." I spoke softly, because of Seiffert, whom I sensed still listening on the other side of the curtain, but I also heard condescension and coldness in my voice that had nothing to do with him.

Janine had obviously heard it, too. "I see," she said bitterly, and dramatically loud. "So this is the kiss-off. Without any kisses."

"Please," I said. "Come on, Janine."

"No, *you* come on," Janine said. "I don't want to get you upset, Howard, because of your condition. But you can't get rid of me like this. I'm a human being, too, remember, with feelings and rights. And don't forget that we have a business arrangement between us, too."

How could I forget? I'd cut three demos for her already, all of them heavily edited, and so enhanced with echo she sounded like the Supremes in the Howe Caverns, but she still wasn't satisfied.

I closed my eyes and kept them closed for a very long time. I might even have dozed off. When I opened them again, Janine was gone, someone had taken my uneaten supper, and the curtain between the beds was open. Seiffert must have been lying in wait, watching me, because soon as I looked at him he grinned and gave me a broad, conspiratorial wink.

5

*T*HE MOMENT I STEPPED OUT OF PENN STATION AND onto Seventh Avenue, I felt that old rush of excitement. So many people, and in such marvelous variety! I hadn't been to Manhattan since Howard's heart attack and I'd almost forgotten what it was like to be part of that restless throng. In the suburbs, only a nuclear accident could bring out crowds like these.

It was the day before Howard's release from the hospital and I'd told him I wouldn't visit him again until that evening. He was going to have other company in the afternoon: the kids would be there, and so would his partner, Mike. I had said I was going to Macy's to buy a new shower curtain, that the Herald Square store had the biggest selection. I walked to Thirty-fourth Street, but I only glanced across the way at Macy's, whose windows were dressed in shades of russet and gold for the fall. It was strange that the changing seasons thrilled me more here than they did on Long Island. All those years, and I was still lonesome for the soaring skyline, that artificial barrier to wind and light.

Street vendors cried, "Check it out, lady, check it out!" offering belts, umbrellas, falafel, sunglasses, watches, orange juice, batteries. It was a veritable bazaar of one-dollar

43

bargains. If I walked a little further in any direction, I might find everything necessary for human survival spread out right there on the sidewalks.

But I boarded an eastbound bus instead. There weren't any empty seats—two young toughs sat in the ones up front designated for the elderly and the handicapped—and I imagined Howard saying, "See, this is what *you* call civilization." He would look through the bus windows and indicate the added irony of the homeless shuffling along right next to the well-heeled. And he'd point out that most of the merchandise sold on the street was defective. Once he got going, he'd tackle littering, and municipal corruption, and ordinary one-on-one muggings. He'd be right, of course, and he'd be wrong. I mean if I really checked out those bargain batteries, I'd probably find they'd lost their zip. And crime in the city was as common as dirt. I knew that none of this was civilized, but maybe it wasn't civilization I was after, only a more intense reality.

The bus lurched through traffic to Second Avenue, where I got off and walked a few blocks south. I read the address in the *Times* again and found the building. It was narrow and old, just as I'd suspected, and sandwiched between two glaringly new high-rises. It was rigged with ugly fire escapes and its brick façade hadn't been cleaned in at least forty years. But the front door had a lovely art deco brass trim that I was sure could be nicely polished with one of those non-abrasive tile cleaners. "See Super," the ad said, so I rang his bell and waited. A voice burst like gunfire through the intercom. I wasn't sure what it said, but I answered, "I'd like to see the apartment, please, the one in the paper," and waited until I was buzzed in. The super was in apartment 1A. I heard the tumblers in the locks turn, one after another, and then the door opened. An East Indian man in work clothes was standing there, and a few feet behind him, a woman wearing a sari was sitting with two children at the kitchen table. In one swift glance, I got an impression of yellow curtains and flowered wallpaper, dark linoleum splashed with bright toys. There was the spicy smell of cooking, foreign and inviting. Oh, other people's lives!

The super said something to his wife in their language, and then he took a big ring of keys from the corkboard on the wall. One of the children waved gaily to me with her spoon before the door closed behind us. The available apartment was on the fifth floor. As the super and I climbed the stairs, I had another mental argument with Howard—as if I were considering this place for both of us and would have to convince him of its appeal. "A walk-up!" Howard exclaimed, inside my head. "Do you want to kill me, Paulie? This setup is for kids. Wait and see, the bathtub will be in the kitchen." "Look how clean the hallway is, though," I insisted. "Hardly any graffiti. And the rent is really reasonable." Actually, it was more than the monthly mortgage payments on our house, but it was cheaper than any of the other one-bedrooms I'd seen advertised.

It was a rear apartment. As soon as I walked in, I reluctantly took up Howard's side of the argument. It was dark and dreary in there, and the rooms were tiny, with only an archway separating the bedroom from the living room. There were bars on the windows that cast prison-stripe shadows on the walls and floors. The bathtub wasn't in the kitchen, but that might have been an improvement. The bathroom was so narrow I envisioned bruised knees and elbows from midnight trips to the toilet. The ad had said "No fee," and I thought, They'll have to *pay* somebody to take it. I knew that wasn't true, it was a sellers' market. But how did people live like this? How had *we* ever lived like this? I remembered the tumult of those early years, when all of us always seemed to be in the same room at the same time. It was noisy and nerve-racking and claustrophobic. I learned to long for solitude and space, but I'd never meant the isolation I'd felt lately in our roomy house.

I looked around and tried to picture what a couple of coats of white paint could do to reduce the gloom and make the apartment look larger. And mirrors—why, I'd just done a column on "mirror magic" that week. The bars would have to stay on the windows, of course. This was the top floor of the building, and burglars probably hung by their heels from the roof, like trapeze artists, trying to break in. But curtains would help, and an interesting old thrift-shop screen might serve as a kind of bedroom door. If I were twenty years old, I'd have been overjoyed at my great good luck in finding this place. Once, long ago, Howard and I had felt privileged to pay key money for a similar dump in Queens. But now I couldn't work myself up into a sincere state of enthusiasm.

"You like it?" the super asked.

"Hmmm," I said, noncommittally, and gave him a cowardly nod.

"Then you take it," he concluded.

"Well, not yet," I said. "Not right away. I need to think about it for a while." What I thought about was his wife in her sari in Kip's Bay, far, far from India, and that I was dislocated, too, although I couldn't say exactly from where. I thanked the super and told him I'd be back. He politely pretended to believe me.

I went next door to one of the high-rises and bribed the doorman into letting me borrow the keys to a vacant studio on the twelfth floor. At least there'll be a view, I thought. But the windows looked across the roof of the brick walk-up to the other high-rise. The square footage was about the same as the first apartment's, only here it was all crammed into one room. The walls must have been made of rice paper, because I could hear every word of a conversation in the adjoining apartment. Two people, a man and a woman, were discussing where they would have dinner that night.

"Let's eat Thai," the man said.

"What, again?" the woman said. "If I even think of lemon grass, I'll puke. Can't we ever have any variety?"

"Ho, ho, ho," the man said. "Look who's talking about variety."

"Fuck you, Mitchell," the woman said.

I tried to imagine listening to them every day for the rest of my life. And then I had a true moment of clairvoyance. I saw myself actually *living* in that apartment, or the first one, with paintings on the walls and dishes in the cupboards. My friends would come with housewarming gifts: knickknacks and potholders, plants that would die in a week from lack of sunlight. I saw Katherine climbing the five flights of stairs of the walk-up, looking behind her all the way, and hyperventilating from exertion and fear. I pictured myself living alone, making supper with the television on for company, or getting dressed for a date. The word "date" seemed like such an anachronism, something to do with corsages and soda shops. Who was supposed to pay for things these days, anyway? And how did you ask, without offending, about herpes or AIDS? Oh, God, had Howard asked?

When someone stayed over, did you hide the less glamorous artifacts of your life, like the dental floss, or the tube of ointment that says: *Apply to affected areas twice daily?* Maybe you both flossed, companionably, in bed, the way Howard and I did, and applied the ointment to those hard-to-reach places on each other's back. Years ago, when we were separated, I did go out with other men, but I was pretty young then, and more recently in the social swirl. Things were different in those days, anyway, and I only took one lover—out of loneliness, curiosity, revenge. Douglas was even younger than I was, and we had nothing in common but our hyperactive coupling. Howard was the only other man I'd ever slept with, and I suffered over my infidelity, and blamed that on him, too. It all seemed oddly innocent now, like an episode from childhood. I hadn't even thought about Douglas in years.

I knew some divorced women who complained about the "rat race," but I'd only paid distracted attention to their stories. My oldest friend, Sherry, had never married. Her disappointed, bewildered mother wasn't ever sure what to tell her cronies, as Sherry passed through the decades from old maid to Cosmopolitan Girl to liberated woman. I'd granted my own mother her two dearest wishes: to be the mother of the bride and a grandmother—although I'd almost gotten the order reversed. Sherry had always maintained that she adored her single life, that it had terrific suspense. That sounded like the last thing I needed, but I was going to move out, anyway, as soon as Howard was fully recovered. I wouldn't wait for proof, like the anonymous note a neighbor once sent about Howard and Marie, or the appearance on our doorstep of a dark-eyed, curly-haired baby. Or Howard's disappearance.

On the way down in the elevator, an elderly woman confided that the service in the building was terrible and that the landlord was a famous criminal. She whispered, as if the elevator might be bugged. When I returned the keys to the doorman, he appeared to take sadistic pleasure in telling me that the rent on the studio was twelve hundred a month. The amazing thing was that my yearning for the city wasn't diminished by any of this, and it seemed separate from my anger at Howard—more like an old, suppressed desire I was just beginning to acknowledge. I had to admit that he hadn't abducted me and dragged me off to the suburbs; in the end, I went willingly.

When we were young and poor, and drove out to Long Island on Sundays to look at model houses, I believed it was only a cheap and harmless form of recreation, a way of playing house. And it did seem like effective if unconventional therapy for Howard's depression. How amused we were by those impeccable, roped-off rooms, how smug about our own relative squalor. We kept telling ourselves we didn't really want to live out there, where they named shopping malls after poets or Presidents, even if we could afford to. After Howard's affair, though, the city began to seem dangerous in ways I'd never considered. I believed that crimes against the heart were being committed in every dark alley, on every street corner. No matter what excuses we finally invented for moving—safety, cleaner air, better schools, more space—we really did it to preserve our family.

That evening, I went to visit Howard at the hospital. I'd taken a long, hot bath first, as if to soak away the sins of an illicit rendezvous, as if I had lain with the super of the walk-up or the doorman of the high-rise. Looking at the apartments without telling Howard *was* a kind of deception, and so was fantasizing about a future without him. But it was nothing compared to the way he'd deceived me.

He was freshly shaved and showered—the perfect date— and he looked handsome, and pretty healthy, too. I wondered how much of a shock his heart could stand. What would happen if I accused him then and there and, when he admitted everything, told him what I intended to do? He might keel right over at my feet. But I couldn't kill him yet; I had to let him get well first. He was like those prisoners on Death

Row they keep in terrific shape until they give them the chair. I didn't say anything, except for some aimless small talk. We chatted about the marvelous weather, the new low-calorie wines, the lesbian nuns on Donahue. I felt wildly impatient with Howard's expansiveness, which was like a game-show host's, his manic anticipation of going home. He announced again that he was going to change his habits, and I thought of all the times he'd quit smoking and of the abandoned Exercycle in our bedroom, its handlebars hung with his ties and belts. He kept calling me "babe," a long-forsaken endearment. Liar, liar! Pants on fire! He told me Gil Danzer had called to say he'd gone back to work, that he was driving his car again, and felt like a million bucks. Howard expected to make the same splendid progress himself. Now he wanted to know all about the new shower curtain—the sort of thing he'd never been interested in before—and I had to confess that I hadn't bought one. "They didn't have the right color," I said sullenly, and he said, "That's too bad, babe. Maybe we can look for one together soon."

So that's what he planned for our future: homely excursions for shower curtains, a clever domestic cover-up for what he'd done. Soon he'd want to get into team cooking, too. I guessed his sweetie had dropped him as soon as she'd heard about his heart, that she didn't want to risk his dying on her—literally. God knows, there's nothing romantic about a sick lover. *Apply to affected areas twice daily.*

Then I noticed that Howard's roommate was acting strangely—staring intently at me, and looking quickly away whenever I returned his gaze. He had his television set on, as usual, a cops-and-robbers show, with strident music punctuated by gunshots. It was an effort for me to stay until visiting hours were over. As I went through the door, at last, Howard called after me: "Don't forget, babe, be here bright and early. I can't wait to get home!"

6

*O*NE MINUTE I WAS FLYING, AND THE NEXT THING I knew I was down and out. To begin with, Paulie and the nurses made a major production out of my leaving the hospital. Paulie opened the closet and the night-table drawer a hundred times to make sure we weren't forgetting anything. She kept asking if I wanted to take home the dying flowers and deflating balloons, all the get-well cards she'd taped to the wall. Seiffert had picked this time to shut off his TV and wander around the room, getting in the way. "Whoops, pardonnez-moi," he said whenever he bumped into Paulie. Then one of the nurses came in with a wheelchair.

"I don't need that," I said.

"Rules," she insisted.

"It's a long walk, Howie," Paulie said.

Even Seiffert chimed in, urging me to go along for the free ride.

I argued with all of them, getting hot and anxious. By the time the head nurse got into it, I felt overpowered and a little light-headed, so I just gave in and sat down. "See ya!" Seiffert called as we started down the hall.

It was a long ride and it would have been an even longer walk, but I was tired of being bossed around, and I hated to be made conscious of a simple thing like walking. I'd been especially jumpy since Janine's surprise visit, but despite her threats, she never came back. I was relieved and let down at the same time. When Mike came to see me, he said, "Who was that ditzy dame at the studio, Flax?" Luckily, Paulie wasn't there then. "Don't ask me," I said. "We're in the Yellow Pages."

Paulie brought the car around to the main entrance of the hospital and I got into the front passenger seat, holding on to the nurse and a curb-side tree for support. "Welcome back to the world," Paulie said, charging into traffic. It was a beautiful autumn day, breezy and bright. The world hadn't stood still in my absence. In only a couple of weeks, while my back was turned, the seasons had changed. It was like coming out of a movie in the afternoon, into sudden, blinding daylight and three-dimensional life. Paulie still drove like a madman. We whizzed past everything, my foot stomping the brake that wasn't there. "Hey, take it easy," I said. "Do you want to give me a heart attack?" I said it lightly, to hide the real apprehension that was building in my chest and stomach, that I was returning to things without being ready for them. I was much weaker than I'd expected to be, and we were moving farther and farther away from the protection of the hospital. I had gangs of pills to take, but we weren't really equipped for emergencies—Paulie didn't even know CPR— and what if something happened? That morning, before she showed up, I couldn't wait to get out of there, and now I almost wished I was back inside.

"Look at the trees, Howard," Paulie instructed. "Aren't they gorgeous?"

"Which ones are the trees?" I said.

Our house couldn't have changed, but it looked smaller and flatter, somehow, as we approached it, more like a *pho-*

tograph of a house. The dog went nuts even before he saw me. He whined and scrambled against the other side of the door while Paulie unlocked it, and when I walked into the kitchen he barked hoarsely, as if he was choked with emotion. I couldn't speak either. There were three fat, dusty tomatoes from my garden on the table and Paulie had chalked *Welcome Home* on the bulletin board. She stayed in the kitchen to make lunch, keeping Shadow with her, while I went down the hallway to our bedroom. The bed was made up with fresh, flower-printed sheets, and the covers were turned back on my side. I took off my shoes and lay down. The blinds had been tilted so that just the right amount of light filtered into the room, and the pulsing digital clock glowed greenly. I had a sudden desire for sleep and the drowsy, hopeful idea that when I woke up, my old life, my sense of well-being, would be completely restored. I turned the radio on, and the MJQ was playing "Trianon," those cool, restful sounds made almost to order. I was a child again, getting into bed in the daytime, listening to music and the faint, comforting noises of a meal being prepared. Paulie had said that the kids would be over soon to see me, and I was going to call Gil later to tell him I was home. It was familiar and peaceful here, and safe.

When I came to, the room was dimmer, the radio was sputtering pure static, and my mouth was sour with sleep. Paulie was standing next to the bed, staring down at me. I shut the radio off, trying to remember my dream. Paulie had been in it, I was sure of that, and she was dressed in white, like a nurse, or a bride. "How do you feel?" she asked now, and before I could answer, she said, "Are you hungry?"

I had to think about both questions. I'd slept for almost four hours, but I still felt groggy. My stomach was rumbling, but I didn't have much of an appetite. The kids had come and gone while I'd slept, and Gil and Sharon had called to say hello and good luck. I'd never even heard the phone ring. Paulie continued to stand there, like a waiter impatient to take my order. I was on eye level with the curve of her hip. She was wearing her blue skirt and she smelled of something spicy. "What's that?" I asked.

"What's what?" she said.

"Your perfume. You smell good."

She sniffed her arm and then pulled the neck of her blouse away. "I'm not wearing any perfume," she said. "Maybe it's the cardamom, or the curry. I'm making an Indian dinner. You slept right through lunch."

"It must be because I'm in my own bed," I said. "Our bed."

"You have to take your medicine," Paulie reminded me, and she handed me the vial of pills and a glass of water from the night table.

I swallowed a pill, swishing some extra water around to sweeten my breath. "Sit down for a minute," I said, shoving over to make room for her.

"I can't, really," she said. "Everything will burn."

"No, it won't. Come on, babe, just sit down for a minute."

She hesitated, twisting her fingers together the way she does when she's nervous, and then she perched on the very edge of the bed. I moved closer and put my hand on her back. It arched instantly, as if I'd touched a spring. "Relax," I said, massaging her through the soft cloth of her blouse. "Everything's going to be all right now." I said it for my own benefit as much as for hers. But how could anything ever be all right again? I was damaged; Dr. Croyden had used that word himself in his diagnosis. He said that I'd suffered moderate damage. I remembered that "damaged goods'' was what we used to call girls who weren't virgins anymore, happy to be the ones who'd damaged them.

It's hard to describe the way I felt then—I was definitely interested, but not exactly horny. And I was a little worried that maybe I couldn't, although the only part of me that had been damaged was my heart. But what about that? I didn't know how much work it could stand before it blew out. Jesus, I'd never thought of sex as *work* before. We'd met with Croyden a few days ago, to discuss my reentry to real life. "You should be able to resume all normal activities," he'd said, "as long as you take it easy. Walk at first, don't run. I think you can start working a few hours a day in a week or two. Just try to avoid stressful situations." How the hell did you avoid stressful situations?

Paulie asked him a lot of questions about diet and exercise, and I waited for her to say something about sex. When she didn't, I hesitated for a couple of minutes, and then I did. Croyden smiled. "If that's one of your normal activities," he said. "Like everything else, in moderation at first."

I expected Paulie to make a nervous joke, something about cutting down to twice a day, but she only looked troubled and sad, and she didn't say anything at all.

Now, lying there, with Paulie sitting rigidly beside me, I wasn't sure how to begin. Again, I wished she'd say or do something. She used to take the initiative pretty often, especially when I was feeling low. Her hand or her mouth would search under the covers and coax me out of hiding.

Paulie sighed. "Well, I'd better get dinner on the road," she said.

I remembered that scene in *Love and Death*, when Woody Allen and Diane Keaton are in bed on their wedding night and she says, "Not here." It occurred to me that Paulie was probably terrified about putting any strain on my heart.

"Nobody ever died of love, babe," I said, to reassure her, and immediately thought of Romeo, and Cyrano, and Nelson Rockefeller.

"Who said anything about dying?" Paulie said.

"You don't have to say it," I said. "Look how tense you are." I moved my hand to her breast and she jumped to her feet.

I stood up, too, and put my arms around her. "Paulie, sweetheart," I said. "We *need* to do this."

"Not yet," she whispered into my shirt collar.

"I want to start my life again," I said. "I'll be careful."

"It's too soon, Howard. You're not ready."

"I'm ready," I said, and as if to prove it, I grew hard against her blue-skirted belly. I thought of how my readiness had once delighted her. But now she seemed upset and unwilling, as if I was some pervert pressing against her in the subway. "Sweetheart," I said, and I began touching her the way she liked to be touched, slowly and rhythmically. I opened her blouse while I kissed her hair and her neck, and my mouth found its way home to her mouth, but it was closed against me. Her resistance seemed brave and foolish; she was one lousy border guard against a whole invading army. Oh, it was work, all right—how could I have forgotten? Soon I was breathing fast with the mean, sweet labor of it, and so was she. First her lips opened a little for my tongue, and for air, and she made a sound, more of a growl than a moan. Her nipples darkened and puckered from kissing. Then her back yielded to my hands—I could feel her vertebrae disappear, one after the other—and her trembling legs opened at the slightest prod of my knee. When I pulled her down with me onto the bed, her entire body dissolved under mine.

After that growling sound, she grew quiet, except for the frantic hiss of her breath. She usually made a racket in bed—

crying out and almost singing in some garbled love language of her own. When Annie was little, she was a light sleeper, with a sixth sense for when we were making love. She'd make her dazed, determined way down the hall from her bedroom to ours. "Tunafishy here," she would comment, wrinkling her nose, and get in between us like a bundling board. Sometimes I'd ward Annie off by holding my hand over Paulie's mouth. She would whimper and chew on my fingers, and later I would stand in the bathroom, examining the teeth marks with prideful pleasure.

This time she moved differently, too, opening and closing in a slower, more deliberate tempo, like the automatic gate on a toll bridge. It was strangely exciting, and new. I rocked over her, in her, propped on my quivering arms, so I could look at her face, at her lovely, sprawling breasts. She grimaced and ground her teeth in concentration. I could hear my own heart booming, as if the volume was up too high. Maybe it always sounded like this and I just never heard it over Paulie's cries. Jesus, was this moderation? It had to be more like running than walking. Boom! Boom! Boom! Oh, God. Oh, God, I was afraid, maybe I'd die! I didn't care! Paulie shuddered once, furiously, and I collapsed onto her, letting her take all my weight, still thrusting. I couldn't have stopped then for anything, for my life. "Oh, my sweet love, I love you!" I said, and pumped myself empty inside her.

We lay there for what seemed like a very long time. I tried to regulate my heartbeat with the blinking seconds of the clock, but my heart raced ahead. Boom! Boom! When was it supposed to slow down? It was only later, after the throbbing had gone out of my ears and back into my chest, that I realized Paulie had remained silent throughout, and was still lying under me, as motionless now as a trapped animal playing dead. I eased myself off her and she moved onto her side, with her back to me. I leaned over and kissed each of her wing bones. "See," I said. "I survived. We both survived. I told you it would be all right, didn't I?" There was no answer. I thought that she had fallen asleep. It must have been as much of a workout for her as it was for me. And the weeks I was in the hospital had to be rough on Paulie, too, running back and forth the way she did, keeping up everybody's spirits. I wasn't the best patient in the world, either—scared shitless at the beginning, and then going stir-crazy once I started feeling better. A rush of love for her went through me, and I knew it wasn't ordinary, post-coital gratitude. I understood that Paulie was *good*, in some essential and final sense of the word. And I knew that what I'd always like least about her—her excessiveness, her insistence on happiness—had probably saved me, against my will. I was racked by regret then for everything and anything I'd ever done to hurt her, sorry for the reckless anger of words, for that time with Marie. And for Janine.

"Paulie," I said, curving against her in that perfect, lifelong fit. I touched her face and discovered that it was wet with tears. No wonder she hadn't spoken. I felt like crying myself.

7

WHEN I GOT TO THE LIBRARY, A FEW DAYS AFTER
Howard's homecoming, I saw that Bernie Rusten was there,
reading at one of the study tables in the back. He looked up
from his book and waved at me. I waved back and decided
I'd try to speak to him about Howard's condition before he
left. Bernie was a family doctor, recently transplanted here
from Boston, who liked to read American history in his spare
time. He said that he wanted to figure out how we'd gotten
into this mess in the first place. I'd spoken to him often at
the library, mostly about books, and La Rae and I had seen
him at Friends of the Earth meetings. Someone there told
me he'd been married for a long time, and that his wife had
been killed in an automobile accident a couple of years ago,
but he had never mentioned her to me. Whenever any of the
other library patrons began coughing in the study section, he
would glare at them with a mixture of annoyance and clinical
concern. Bernie wasn't our doctor, but I imagined he had a
wry and sympathetic bedside manner. He reminded me a
little of pictures I'd seen of William Carlos Williams when
he was in his forties or fifties. Bernie wore similar wire-
framed glasses, and he was starting to go bald in that same
attractive, scholarly way. Maybe I was influenced by the fact

that he was a doctor, too. And because I sensed that he took an intense pleasure in the company of women, the way Williams was supposed to.

I'd told him about Howard's heart attack soon after it happened, saying that he had never seemed like an A-type personality to me. I'd already taken out a stack of popular books on heart disease—*Beating the Skipped Beat, Pumping Blood, You and Your Arteries*—and was beginning to feel like an expert. Bernie had only one question: "What did Howard's father die of?" When I told him, he simply said, "Aha!"

Now I waited a reasonable amount of time before I set out purposefully toward him, using a cart of paperback romances as a blind. He was browsing in the stacks by then, in the Civil War section. I cleared my throat and said, "Good afternoon," in my modulated library voice.

"Well, look who's here," he said, closing the book in his hand. "You caught me at Antietam."

"Antietam," I said. "I've forgotten what happened there."

"Yeah, we all have," he said. "That's the problem. How's your husband feeling?"

"He's better, he's home," I said, and to my dismay, I burst into tears.

Bernie pulled a large handkerchief from his pocket and handed it to me. It smelled as if it had been freshly ironed. "That doesn't sound like such tragic news," he said.

"It isn't," I sobbed.

"Then are these tears of happiness?"

"No," I admitted, "not really." I picked up one of the books on my cart so I wouldn't start twisting my fingers. Years ago, Howard used to grab my hands and put them in his pockets to stop me from doing that. I wasn't sure what I wanted to say, and I looked down at the book I was holding, as if for inspiration. It was called *Love in a Nutshell*.

Bernie followed my glance. "That would be a little crowded, wouldn't it?" he said, and I had a sudden longing to throw my arms around him. Crying in the library, wanting to embrace virtual strangers—I was as bad as the wanton paperback heroines, all of them made lovesick and unstable by the rise and plunge of their hormones. Of course I laughed and said it was very complicated, and Bernie said, agreeably, "What isn't?" But that was another reason to read history, he told me, because it helps put things in perspective. "Well, so does poetry," I said. He smiled and reopened his book, and I walked away toward Fiction, pushing the squealing cart ahead of me.

Howard was at home, taking a nap. That morning he'd puttered in the garden, pinching off the dead marigold and zinnia heads, but mostly just surveying things on our quarter acre of property, like the lord of a country estate. I'd watched him through the bedroom window while I was getting dressed for work. He'd whistled as he sauntered around, and I couldn't stand his happiness any more than I used to be able to stand his depression. I kept thinking of the other day, of our love-making. When Howard had brought up the subject with Dr. Croyden, I'd had the wild hope that Croyden would order indefinite abstinence. And when he didn't, I made vague plans for evasion. Nothing worked, though. I'd allowed myself to be coerced, bullied, seduced, humiliated. My hypocrisy was far worse than Howard's. I hadn't even felt lustful when he began touching me, only coldly righteous. And he'd thought I was afraid for him. "I'll be careful," he said. Exactly what he'd promised twenty-five years ago in the backseat of his car. I would have believed the most extravagant lies then. "No, yes, please!" I'd cried, in adolescent delirium. But the other day I was sensible and middle-aged, and determined not to fall for any cheap argument or ploy. The body has its own memory, though, its own mind. I shelved the paperbacks with distracted haste. The heroines on their covers smoldered, like me, while their men (some of them on horseback) commanded their passion.

Ann and Jason and Sara had come to visit Howard a few hours after I'd brought him home from the hospital. I'd been sitting in the kitchen, writing a column on mildew—"Dear Dank in Deer Park, Get those smelly sweaters out in the sun"—when the doorbell rang. Howard was still asleep, so the four of us sat at the table, drinking coffee and waiting for him to wake up. I noticed right away that things were strained between Jason and Sara, but it took several minutes before I realized they weren't speaking to each other, except in elaborate messages they conveyed through Ann and me. "Have some cake, Sara," I said. "It's coconut, your favorite." And she answered sorrowfully, "I'm not hungry, thanks. But I'm sure *Jason* will have some." Jason had already helped himself to a mammoth slice of cake. "She's trying to starve to death," he said with his mouth full.

I searched my head for a suitable, peacemaking subject. "What's happening with Blood Pudding?" I asked.

"Nothing," Jason said, and at the same moment Sara said, "We have a couple of gigs." She didn't get flustered about contradicting him, as I expected her to, and say that he was right, a couple of gigs *are* nothing. Instead, she glared at him in defiance, reddened, and turned away. As for Jason, he shrugged and drank his coffee. "Same difference," he told me. I tried to guess what he might have done to earn her wrath—she'd put up with so much until then, and with such angelic patience. I hoped he hadn't found somebody else, that he wasn't letting her go—for his sake, and mine. Plenty of groupies hung around even minor rock bands like theirs, girls who appeared to have no other purpose in life but to swoon with sensation and make themselves available. When Howard had played the clubs years ago, it was the same way. The jazz groupies wore a lot of black, too, but they'd dressed much more discreetly—I remembered berets and turtlenecks—and they tended to be older. But they were just as intensely charged by the music, and they were always, always there. I looked carefully at Sara. More than ever, in daylight, in my kitchen, her gelled pink hair and funky clothes seemed like a child's getup. And her defiance was childlike, transient as a temper tantrum. Pain was more evident in her face now than anger.

"Mom," Ann said, "I've been thinking. You and Dad have a very significant anniversary coming up."

"Ann, darling," I said, "you know that we both despise those things, so please don't plan anything, okay?"

"*You* may despise them," she said, "but Daddy doesn't. I spoke to him about it in the hospital, and he agreed that this time it's different. I mean, now we really have something to celebrate."

"Yeah," Jason said, "twenty-five years of bondage."

Sara looked shocked.

"He means imprisonment," I explained. "Marriage." God, what was happening to the language?

"Dad wants to go all-out," Ann continued. "He said we'll have to paint the town silver."

I had a flash of the Kip's Bay walk-up, of covering the grimy walls with coats of glistening silver paint. And I imagined another scene, here in this kitchen, when I told my children the truth. "Anyway, this is all very premature," I said. "It's a long way off."

"Only nine months," Ann said, and for the first time

since they'd arrived, Jason's and Sara's eyes met—locked really, with electric tension. Jason glanced away first. "Is Dad getting up soon?" he asked.

Ann looked at her watch. "I'm meeting Spence at Il Mulino at seven," she said, "and I have to go home and get dressed first."

"That should take about two weeks," Jason said.

"Oh, screw you, Jason," Ann said.

"Let me take a fast peek at Dad," I said. "Maybe he's getting up now."

I tiptoed into the bedroom. The news was fading in and out on the radio, and Howard was flung across the bed in sleep. He looked pale and beautiful. His hair was a laurel wreath of curls, like Housman's dying young athlete's. But Howard wasn't that young, and he wasn't dying; he only needed a little sunlight and some convalescent care, which I would provide. I had a sense of tremendous power over him as I watched him sleep, as if his will had been magically transferred to me.

When I reported back to the kitchen, Ann was on the telephone. Jason was staring out the window, and Sara was absently picking up crumbs of cake with a dampened finger and licking them off. "He's out like a light," I announced, wishing them all away.

Once they were gone, though, the house was eerily silent, except for the erratic signal of Howard's radio. When the phone rang, I was startled. It was my mother, calling from Brooklyn. She asked how Howard was feeling, and I said he was okay. "Okay?" she said. "Okay? I sincerely doubt that."

"What do you mean?" I asked.

"That after a heart attack you're not okay, you're not well."

"I didn't say he was *well*, Ma. It's just that he's feeling much better. He's sleeping now. I hope the phone didn't disturb him," I added meanly. There'd been a definite shift in my mother's loyalties since Howard's heart attack. One day, while he was in the hospital, she arrived at the house, unannounced, carrying shopping bags loaded with plastic containers of prepared food. She'd taken the subway and the Long Island Railroad and a taxi, and she'd brought all his favorites: blood-clogging lamb stew, sweetbreads in mushroom gravy, herring fillets in cream sauce. She advised me to stow everything in the freezer for him, so he could put some meat back on his poor bones when he got home. I explained that Howard was supposed to *lose* weight, and anyway, that stuff was more likely to put plaque on his arteries. She was disbelieving and terribly hurt. As she stood near our freezer, perspiring, and holding a tower of perspiring Tupperware, it became clear to me that she had really learned to love Howard over the years. She loved his playful, teasing manner with her, his exaggerated flattery. In fact, he'd truly become her son. Once, he was the dark villain of our lives. When I'd told her I was marrying him, her screams must have carried to every apartment in the building. A musician! A gypsy with bedroom eyes! She recruited my mild father into her camp and they berated me in stereo. At Howard's parent's home, a similar melodrama was taking place. I think his mother even fainted as part of her argument. But the winning argument belonged to Jason, my enduring, silent swimmer, and for all their carrying on, his grandparents were given the gift of generations.

"Take good care of Howard," my mother advised on the telephone. "You only get one husband." It was a confused variation of her usual, more logical theme, that you only get one mother.

The phone hadn't disturbed Howard at all. He continued to sleep while the sun moved westward and I prepared chicken tandoori and basmati rice. He even slept through two other phone calls. The first was another one of those nuisance calls, with nobody there. I knew it wasn't *her*, but still it made me feel paranoid and helpless. Everything did lately. That morning, when I was packing Howard's things up at the hospital, his creepy roommate kept getting in my way. I began to think he was trying to tell me something, or that he was going to throw his bathrobe open and flash. I had to get myself under control.

The second phone call was from Sharon Danzer, to welcome Howard home. Gil got on, too, and told me he was feeling terrific, ready to take on Leon Spinks. After he hung up, Sharon whispered that he'd actually been having a lot of anginal pain. "Don't say anything to Howard," she said. "Gil would kill me." I promised, finding myself whispering back, hushed by our collusion and the abundance of deceits. We made a dinner date for the four of us for a month from then.

When the tandoori was almost ready, I went inside to wake Howard. He needed to take his medicine, anyway. I watched his eyes open and focus, a wary Lilliputian watching Gulliver come to, and I asked how he felt and if he was hungry. I was all business, but I quickly saw what was on *his* mind, as if a cartoon balloon of lascivious thoughts hovered over the bed. Come in, sit down, said the spider to the fly. The fly buzzed in protest—Oh, no I can't! Our dinner! Your heart! Then his hands and mouth were on me, moving in blind certainty, but not in any married, follow-the-dots routine. This was desperate intention, life and death. I never lost sight of my outrage, but that didn't matter—it only served my own reviving passion. Howard aroused all those old places that long for

touch, here and here and *here*, and I opened to him, clench-
ing and unclenching like an angry fist. I did worry fleetingly
about his heart, as I'd worried once in his car—too late and
too little—about contraception. At least I didn't say anything
this time, or yell out. I managed to keep some dignity, and
the mystery of my emotions to myself. I'd often cried afterward—Howard could make anything he liked of that.

I saw Bernie Rusten leave the library. He'd put the Civil
War book back on the shelf. I picked it up and opened it to
the section on Antietam, and there it was, the bloodiest battle
of the war.

8

*P*AULIE DROPPED ME AT THE STUDIO AFTER LUNCH, AND zoomed away. We had taken our time getting there, thank God, going through local streets and stopping for gas and a newspaper. As I walked in the door, Mike collared me and hissed, "She was just here!"

I was confused for a minute and thought he'd meant Paulie. "I know," I said. "So what?"

"Oh, man, are you ever cool," Mike said. "What if Paulie saw her?" And then I understood that he was talking about Janine, and that he knew about us.

I didn't have the energy to lie or play dumb. "When?" I asked, as the day, my first one back at work, began to fall apart. I had been looking forward all week to putting in a few hours, to start easing back into the routine of things.

Mike was sympathetic, but he was also enjoying himself. "Maybe ten, no, *five* minutes ago. Man, I almost shit-freaked!" At that moment I regretted not hooking up with somebody older, somebody married and more reserved. Mike was in his early thirties, an electronics whiz kid who didn't play an instrument himself but who worshipped jazz. I'd met him on one of my last club dates, in Chelsea, when he was about twenty. He'd handled the sound and lights that week, and he impressed me so much with his enthusiasm and skill that I hired him on a part-time basis right after I opened the studio. Five years later, he borrowed from every musician he'd ever amplified, and I took him in. He was a lot more reliable than he looked, with that pasty, night-owl complexion, and the shades he affected in homage to all his blind heroes. He showed up when he was supposed to, driving in from the East Village in his battered Chevy, and he carried his own weight. Since I'd gotten sick, he'd been carrying most of mine, too. I'd always trusted him completely, but how dependable could he be if the business with Janine turned him on like this? I couldn't see his eyes behind the glasses, but the rest of his face was alive with animation.

"Look, Mike," I said, "whatever it was, it's over."

"That's what you think," he said. What the hell had Janine told him?

"What do you mean?"

"She said to give you a message."

I waited, but he paused, dragging out the suspense, glancing around as if spies were lurking in the corners of the studio. "Well, what did she say, damn it?" I said.

"She said, 'Tell Howard I'm still in his life.' "

Jesus. "What else did she say?"

He hesitated again, uneasily this time. "She said she'd be back later this afternoon."

"Mike, I don't believe it. You told her I was coming in?"

Mike put up his hands. "I didn't know who she was then, Flax," he said. "I thought she was . . . maybe just a friend. The last time she didn't say, and she didn't really say anything this time, either, at first."

The place had smelled like a giant ashtray from the minute I'd walked in, and now, as we were talking, Mike started lighting up. He was a Marlboro man, like me. He flashed the familiar red-and-white box, and then there was the sulfurous flare of the match, the sweet stream of smoke in my face. "Christ, put that thing out!" I yelled, and he jammed the cigarette against the wall so hard that sparks flew, almost igniting his shirt.

"Hey," he said. "Take it easy, will you?"

Easy! He'd put me right back in the CCU. My heart was banging in my head the way it had after Paulie and I made love. I had to sit down, take some deep breaths. I didn't have any pain, but I put a nitroglycerin tablet under my tongue, just in case.

Mike started doing a worried little dance around me. "I'm sorry, man, okay?" he said. "Just take it easy and everything will be cool."

Maybe for him it would be. I thought of his carefree, uncomplicated life, the various "foxes" I'd seen waiting for him on the sheepskin-covered front seat of the Chevy. Paulie used to say he'd installed the sheepskin so his girlfriends wouldn't get bedsores. "You have to drive me home," I said.

"I can't. I have an appointment in a couple of minutes—the gospel singers from Huntington Station."

"Leave them a note. I have to get out of here."

"She won't be back right away."

"How do you know?"

"She said something . . . wait a minute. Yeah, she said she had to go back to work. I think she was on her lunch hour."

Bloomingdale's. It was Saturday, and I was safe until five. My first feeling was one of relief—Paulie was going to pick me up around four. Then I saw the thing for what it was, a game of hide-and-seek I had to lose. Janine had shown up at the hospital, and now she'd revealed herself, *us*, to Mike. She was getting closer and closer to home. I had to face up to it, to make her understand that it was over between us, that I loved Paulie above everything, and my life depended on being with her. As for the demo, Mike could finish that for me; he'd probably make her sound better than I ever could, anyway. I would continue to cover the expenses, of course. It all seemed simple at that moment, a clear and reasonable scenario. If it was cowardly to pick a crowded public place for playing it out, so be it. The whole point was to end it, and nobody could mistake the main floor of Bloomingdale's for a motel room. And I wouldn't run into Paulie there—she was spending the afternoon at La Rae's. Besides, she'd once said that she hated Bloomingdale's. It was soon after Janine and I had begun, and I remember the way my flesh crawled when she said it. But she'd only meant that the glitter of so many worldly goods in one place was too much for here. "I get intensely greedy," she said. "And at the same time I want to take a vow of poverty."

I waited for the cab to come and take me to Bloomingdale's. Mike thought I was going home, which was almost true, since I intended to go there next. I would call Paulie then and say I'd gotten tired faster than I'd expected to. The gospel singers had arrived in the meantime, and were rehearsing. They were five middle-aged black women who sang a cappella with a thrilling vocal range. They sang "How I Got Over," building in volume and passion with every chorus. Listening to them made the term "inspirational music" seem just right. You had to be inspired to get a sound as rich as theirs. Mike was in harmony heaven in the control room, moving the levers on the console, jerking his shoulders and arms around as if he was possessed. Gospel music was much older than his beloved jazz, and was probably its ancestor, it was so jazzy in its beat and phrasing. And it was inspiring as well as inspired. As the women belted out "The

Battle Hymn of the Republic,'' I started feeling uplifted and hopeful myself, if not exactly religious. When the cab's horn tooted, breaking into the final hallelujah, it jarred me from a peaceful trance.

I heard Janine's voice even before I saw her standing next to the up escalator. She was doing her act a cappella, too, but her voice was shallow and piping in the humming crowd. She sounded like an impatient child trying to get attention at a grown-up party. "Ladies! Princess Marcella Borghese has a lovely gift for you today! Ladies! Won't you try Princess Marcella Borghese's lovely new fragrance! Ladies . . .''

She was aiming a perfume atomizer at the upturned wrist of a gray-haired woman, and she froze when she saw me. Then she smiled, that same surprising break of sunshine through the clouds. "Howard!'' she cried, as if she was still addressing the entire floor. People turned to look at us, and the gray-haired woman withdrew her wrist, smiling, too, at what she obviously assumed was a romantic reunion.

Janine had a tray of cosmetics slung from her neck, like a cigarette girl's in a nightclub. It got between us when she tried to hug me.

"Ouch!'' I said, a lousy opening, and then, "Hey, hello.''

"Hello, yourself,'' Janine answered, and she beamed at me with blinding intensity.

"I have to talk to you, Janine,'' I said.

She looked at her watch. "Just give me fifteen minutes, honey, until my break,'' she said. "But don't you dare go away.''

I wanted to go away, as far away as I could get. I remembered shutting my eyes in the hospital and keeping them shut until she'd disappeared. This time I kept them open. Janine was wearing a ruffled white dress and a load of makeup. She looked vulnerable and dangerous at once.

It was the longest fifteen minutes. Janine held me with her gaze, like a short leash that let me go in circles around the handbag counter, the gloves. I watched women try gloves on, turning their hands this way and that in admiration and doubt. I picked up a handbag or two, opened zippers, sniffed the animal smell of leather linings. Husbands and wives went by arm-in-arm, carrying crackling shopping bags, having ordinary domestic conversations. They appeared contented, pleasantly bored. Jesus, how I envied them. "Ladies! Ladies!" Janine called. I pictured Paulie and La Rae and Katherine drinking coffee in La Rae's kitchen, plotting a pro-choice counterdemonstration at an abortion clinic. I remembered their voices drifting down the hall when they met at our house, flutey and urgent, full of important female secrets. I could have written anonymously to La Rae, asking for advice. Bewildered at Bloomie's. Or asked her straight out. I saw her standing with her arms folded, a rubbery little blonde, chewing on her lip before saying, "You know what you have to do, Howie." Katherine, who gave guidance to teenagers all week, would peer at me through her glasses and say, "I think you should see somebody." But I was already seeing somebody, that was the problem. Katherine would sternly reject the joke.

A man came to relieve Janine, and she hung the tray from his neck. "Go get 'em, tiger," she said.

He seemed to be wearing makeup, too, and he carried his own atomizer. Janine pretended to spritz me with hers as we walked away. "Hey, cut it out," I said, and when I put up my hand, she grabbed it with her free one and held on. I quickly turned down her suggestion that we go to her house to talk. "Why not?" she said. "Tommy's at a game. And Rod will cover for me as long as we need."

"We won't need that long," I said.

"What is *that* supposed to mean?" she asked, dropping my hand. We had wandered into the men's department, and she stopped dead near a display of jogging suits. Two athletic-looking mannequins were also poised in arrested motion.

"Janine, we have to break it off," I said. "I don't want to hurt you, but I don't know how else to do this."

"I don't understand you, Howard. Everything was fine until you got sick. You'd think that almost dying like that would make you want to grab what you can out of life."

"It does. I mean, it makes me want to hold on to what I had, what I *have*. My family. We had a wonderful time together, you and I. I won't ever forget it, and I really want to thank you."

"Oh, I get it. Wham, bam, thank you, ma'am." I could see her color mottling under the makeup, the tears gathering.

"It wasn't like that. It's not like that."

"Then what *is* it like, Howard?"

"It's over," I said.

Just then, a woman approached us with an inquiring smile. "Excuse me," she said. "Would you wear this tie with a pin-striped blue suit?" She held the tie in question up to her own tweed-covered chest for my inspection.

"Yes," I said. "It's very nice. Perfect."

"He has your coloring," she said, thoughtfully.

"Ah," I said. "Well, good."

Janine had strutted off and I followed her, moving quickly, snaking through the busy aisles toward the exit to the parking lot. "Thank you!" the woman with the tie called after me.

"Janine, wait a minute," I said, grabbing her arm just before she could go through the door. We were caught in a two-way stream of shoppers—everyone had to walk around us. One of Janine's colleagues was a few feet away, intoning,

"Estée Lauder! Estée Lauder has a lovely free gift for you today!"

"I want to wish you luck, and happiness," I said. "And I know how much the demo means to you, so Mike, my partner, will finish the job. It's a gift." It sounded terrible to my own ears, like an echo of Estée Lauder's promotional offer. I began to feel dizzy while I was saying it. I was reaching into my shirt pocket for the nitro when Janine's hand came up. "You bastard!" she said, snarled really. I thought she was going to hit me, so I flinched, which probably saved my eyes from real damage. The perfume burst from the atomizer. I think I tasted it first, sickeningly sweet and acid-bitter, before I felt its icy sting. "Wait, no!" I said, gagging, and took another blast, and then another and another, mostly on my upraised arms. Somebody yelled, "Hey! Watch it!" as I backed blindly out the door to the parking lot. My eyes were killing me and I was retching. People bumped into me. "You all right?" a voice asked, and I reeled away without answering. I made my way to the street and walked about a block, in the direction of Old Country Road, everything around me in a brilliant, burning blur. I stopped and shoved a pill under my tongue. Shit, my heart was going a mile a minute. Slow down, slow down. When I could see a little better, I crossed the street and went into Lord & Taylor's. I stank like a thousand harems. In the men's room, I rinsed my eyes over and over again with cold water. I washed my face and arms, but the smell was still powerful. How could I take a cab? I went to the phones and called Mike at the studio. The gospel singers were gone and he had some time until his next appointment. He picked me up, and I have to give him credit, he didn't ask a single question, not even about the perfume. He opened all the windows, though, and we rode home with our hair flying and our shirtsleeves flapping like flags.

I had an hour before Paulie was due to pick me up at the studio. I showered and then I called her at La Rae's. "What's wrong?" she asked immediately, just like my mother.

"Nothing," I said. "I got a little pooped, that's all. Mike gave me a ride home, so you can take your time." After I hung up, I took the plastic leaf bag with my clothes in it and carried it to the next block, where I stashed it in somebody's trash pail that was sitting out near the curb. I was like a murderer getting rid of the bloodstained evidence.

Back home again, I showered once more and gargled with full-strength Listerine. I used eye drops and invented reasons for the residual redness: cinders, shampoo, allergies. I tried to remember some of the hints from Paulie's column about cleaning cooking odors out of the house. There was something with lemon, something with vinegar. I went to the cabinet under the sink and sprayed a couple of things around. It was no use. The first thing Paulie said when she came in was, "My God, what stinks like that?"

"Me," I said. Mea culpa. "I spilled a bottle of after-shave all over myself, the fancy stuff Annie brought me at the hospital."

"Phew!" Paulie said, turning on the exhaust fan.

It was that easy. Hallelujah!

9

WE WERE DRINKING COFFEE AND FINISHING OUR COM-
mittee work, the strategy for a counterprotest the following
week at an abortion clinic in Northport. This time La Rae
would do the telephoning, Katherine would prepare the signs
and sandwich boards, and I would draw up the formal request
to the police for permission to march. The Right-to-Lifers
had chosen a Saturday, thank goodness—I guess they had
jobs, too.

"I hope they don't wave those butcher's aprons at us, like
the last time," Katherine said.

"What I can't stand are the blown-up pictures," I said.

"Get pictures made for us, too," La Rae instructed Katherine.

"Of what?" Katherine asked. "I'm not exploiting abused
kids."

"She's right, La Rae," I said. "Our argument isn't made
with shock tactics."

"I still feel funny about abortions," Katherine said, closing her notebook. "I can't help thinking of little Ethan."

"Oh, please, Katherine," La Rae said, "spare us the viol-
ins, okay? This has nothing to do with your grandchild."

"Well, it has to do with *somebody's* grandchild."

"No, it doesn't," La Rae insisted, "and you know it. It has to do with choice, remember? With women's bodies."

Katherine sighed. "I suppose so," she said. She took off her glasses and polished them with a paper napkin.

"Don't suppose," La Rae advised her. "*Know*. Knowledge is truth, truth is beauty, et cetera, et cetera."

I didn't say anything. I remembered briefly considering an abortion when I was pregnant with Jason. It was just before I'd given Howard the news, and everything seemed to depend on his response. He loves us, he loves us not.

"Listen, Katherine," La Rae said. "Why don't you bring Ethan with you next week? We could hang a sign on his stroller: *Here by choice*."

Katherine was shocked. "I couldn't!" she said.

"They bring their babies, don't they?" La Rae said. "To show the difference between their little cherubs and our bloody fetuses."

"I wouldn't ever use him that way," Katherine said.

"Why not?" La Rae asked. "You'd be teaching him about responsibility."

"He's only four months old, La Rae," Katherine said. "I think he has time for that."

The three of us were sitting in La Rae's kitchen, where we'd been gathering for years. Long ago, our own babies crawled around our feet under the table, banging spoons against pot covers, while we tried to figure out ways to keep them from ever being drafted. This time, now that our work was done, I drifted off into a troubled reverie. I was living a double life, encouraging Howard to get well while I was planning to leave him. What if he died suddenly, without ever knowing my intentions? But I was being morbid and silly. He was making great progress—he'd started working again that day—which both pleased and disheartened me. It was similar to the conflict I'd felt when the children started kindergarten. I had to let go; it was for everyone's good. La Rae thought I was overreacting to the whole situation, but I thought that she underreacted, in the extreme, to hers. And I still didn't want to confide in Katherine, to come up against the judgment I'd see in her face: How had I allowed it to happen *again*? Mostly, I dreaded that she'd be even more outraged than I was, that she might make me want to come to Howard's defense. She'd once expressed her angry opinion of La Rae's permissive arrangement with Frank, and La Rae told her to shut up and mind her own business, that she wasn't a high-school student in need of guidance. They didn't speak to one another for two weeks. But they were in the same car pool—music lessons and soccer practice—and one afternoon they were forced to talk about the driving schedule. Katherine threw her arms around La Rae and apologized. She'd only meant to be a good and honest friend. La Rae reminded her that honesty wasn't always friendly, and that there are places friendship can't go. Marriage was one of them.

Katherine often pointed out the exceptional strength of her own marriage. She said that she and Tony discussed *everything*. When their children were still at home, there were family conferences every week in which complaints and confessions were aired. They actually voted on meals and vacations and the distribution of household chores. Years ago, La Rae and I both admitted that although we loved Katherine and Tony, we hated their perfect relationship. We made sly fun of them—"Can this marriage be saved?" La Rae asked when we saw them smooching. And we discovered that we both had secret, mean fantasies about a sudden scandal: Tony was fooling around, was gay, had embezzled money from one of his law clients. But nothing ever happened, except for the drug bust at the high school in which all of our sons were caught with pot in their lockers. And Tony was the one who got them off.

La Rae was reheating the coffee when her father wandered into the kitchen from his room in the garage. He was wraith-like, with that startled crest of white hair, and eerily quiet in his bedroom slippers. "Coffee, Dad?" La Rae asked.

"Hello, Mr. Munson," Katherine and I chimed, in cheerful chorus.

But he couldn't stay. He poured himself a glass of water, made a circuit of the kitchen, and wandered out again. He'd been living with La Rae and Frank for ten years, ever since her mother died, and had become more and more withdrawn during that time. After the children moved out, La Rae urged him to take one of their bedrooms, but he refused. He stayed on in the garage, a deposed king on his island of exile. When the door closed behind him, La Rae confessed that she dreamed sometimes of driving her car into the garage again, right over the green shag carpeting, and parking it between her father's bureau and his easy chair.

We were all silent in contemplation of that scene. I thought of my mother's solitary confinement, her regular rendezvous with soap-opera stars. She had dizzy spells that might be little strokes. Would she really be able to summon help, if she needed it, with her beeper? I listened, and imagined I heard scratching noises from La Rae's garage, like mice in the walls.

"I'd kill myself before I'd live with any of my kids," La Rae said.

"No, you wouldn't," Katherine said.

"Howard says that we're never going to put Shadow down, so the children will be merciful to us in our old age," I said. Howard says. Husband, children, dog. I saw them all in simple lines and primary colors, the stick figures in a child's drawing of a family. When Howard left us, Jason was four, and he crayoned pictures of himself, Ann, and me inside the house, with Howard floating over the roof, like a Chagall lover, like God.

Katherine went home, and La Rae and I put some of the letters for our columns out on the table. We'd worked together before, reading passages aloud, and offering one another suggestions. Once, at my house, I couldn't find the antidote for battery-acid stains on car upholstery, even in my *Encyclopedia of Spots and Stains*. La Rae took a battery out of Jason's toy robot and smashed it with a hammer. She smeared the acid on some rags, and we spent the afternoon experimenting with possible solutions, like a couple of mad scientists.

My first job at the newspaper had been as La Rae's secretary, when their offices were still in Mineola. My baby-sitter hadn't shown up the morning of my interview, and I had to bring the children with me. The baby cried nonstop, I remember, and Jason overturned La Rae's wastebasket. "Couldn't you leave them somewhere?" she asked, and I said, angrily, that I'd tried to sell them to some gypsies on Jericho Turnpike but it hadn't worked out. She laughed and told me that the job was mine.

I'd read La Rae's lovelorn column before I met her that day, and I expressed surprise that she was so young. "Why does everyone think wisdom comes with age?" she said. We agreed that our mothers had probably started the rumor. La Rae had begun at the paper as a file clerk. She'd invented her own column, out of boredom, writing all the letters to herself for a while, until the thing caught on. After I'd worked as her secretary for six months, she thought up "Paulie's Kitchen Korner" for me. When I protested that I was no expert on household matters, she picked up my purse and dumped it out onto her desk. A world of domestic litter fell out: keys, a collapsed and dusty pacifier, expired supermarket coupons, a small screwdriver, a rubber dinosaur, a can of V-8 juice. "I rest my case," La Rae said.

Now I read a letter aloud to her. "Dear Paulie, My stainless-steel sink is anything but stainless! Rust and water spots all over it! Hope you can help. My ninety-year-old Mom and I really enjoy your helpful hints! Sincerely, Betty Jean Rickover."

La Rae handed me one of her letters. It said, "Dear La Rae Peters, It's difficult for me to write this letter. Maybe everybody says the same thing, but I really mean it. It's about my husband. We never had what you would call a thrilling love life. I know Burt works hard and he really is tired, but *not all the time*, La Rae. I just can't get him in the mood, as the old song says. Any suggestions? Sign me Frustrated (Real name Mrs. Janet Workman). P.S. Please don't print that I'm from Chicago—he would *know*."

"Oh, poor thing," I said.

"Yeah, those rust stains can really get you down," La Rae said.

"Don't be funny," I said. "At least I had a wonderful sex life, once. Howard didn't ever used to be tired."

"Frank still isn't."

I looked up in quick sympathy, but La Rae wasn't being bitter or ironical, only dreamily proud.

"She can use lighter fluid," I said, thinking of Betty Jean Rickover's sink, and trying to change the subject. "Or some white vinegar."

"Yeah, that really turns them on."

I laughed. "Dear Frustrated, Get into something flimsy

and dim the lights. Then rub a little lighter fluid on those special places.''

''Behind the ears and the knees,'' La Rae said. ''And don't forget the pillows.''

''Come on, baby, light my fire!'' I sang.

''Do you think Tony is any good in bed?'' La Rae asked.

I was used to her habit of veering abruptly around the corners of a conversation. ''Probably,'' I said, plunging into gloom and jealousy. ''But let's not start picking on Katherine, okay?''

''I just can't stand her holier-than-thou attitude.''

''What we really can't stand is her happiness, that she makes marriage seem easy.''

''I'll admit that's a neat trick,'' La Rae said.

''My favorite little poem goes: 'So different, this man / And this woman: / A stream flowing / In a field.' William Carlos Williams.''

''Who else?'' she said. ''But I know an even shorter one, on the same subject. 'Madam, I'm Adam.' ''

''Well, who else?'' I said, and we both laughed.

''Anyway,'' La Rae said, ''Katherine could have brought Ethan to the clinic.''

''He's her grandson,'' I said. ''It's her choice.''

''Can you imagine being a grandmother, Paulie?''

''No. Yes.'' It was probably the only opportunity in life to bestow unconditional love. Howard's mother doted on our kids long-distance, with adoring letters and phone calls. And she was especially gaga about Jason. Against everyone's advice, she often tucked crisp ten-dollar bills in with her letters to him. And when he was a baby, my super-critical parents refused to acknowledge his flaws: his wandering eye and the way his feet toed out, like Chaplin's. ''What? Where? I don't see anything,'' my father would say. ''He'll outgrow it,'' my mother insisted, as we rushed Jason from the ophthalmologist to the orthopedist. "I wish I could have my own baby," I told La Rae.

"You still could, couldn't you? But it would probably have two heads or something. And you'd have to be class mother when you're sixty. Anyway, who would you have it with?"

"Well," I said. "I don't really want a *baby*, La Rae. I guess I just wish I were young again. You know, all damp . . . and ready."

"Like garden soil."

"Like I used to be." I meant more than physical youth, though. I meant the constant fever of excitement, the boundlessness of possibility. "I hate getting old."

"You're not getting old," La Rae said, "you're getting better. You're only maturing, like Arlene Francis and Hugh Downs."

"Soon I'll get into the movies for half price again. And get discounts on dentures and hearing aids." Live in Ann and Spence's garage.

"Meals on Wheels!" La Rae shouted.

"Cataracts!" I shouted back.

"Pacemakers!"

"Osteoporosis!"

"Wait until we start the changes," La Rae said. "My sister Carol goes hot and cold all day, as if her thermostat is shot. And you get all dried out inside, like an old shoe."

We giggled nervously. I imagined my future single life as a confusion of interior climates, with a tube of lubricating jelly always on hand. "God, I can't wait. Thanks a lot for cheering me up," I said.

"Why do they call it menopause?" La Rae wondered. " 'Pause' makes it sound as if it's going to start again."

"Do you know that novel by Thomas Mann?" I asked.

"*The Black Swan*? A middle-aged woman falls in love with her son's friend, and she starts to feel miraculously young again."

"Damp and—"

"Yes, and her periods *do* come back! But it turns out that she really has this terrible cancer."

"Well, thank *you*, Miss Merry Sunshine," La Rae said. And then she said, "Don't do it, Paulie."

"What, grow old?"

"No, don't leave Howard."

"La Rae, I have to. Before he leaves me again."

"Maybe he won't."

"I'll never feel safe about that."

"Well, then don't leave me."

"We'll see each other."

"Yeah, for *lunch*, probably. We'll go *shopping*. When are you going?"

"Soon," I said, wondering if it was true.

"Nothing will be the same around here."

"Everything changes," I said. "We may even have to grow old gracefully."

"Not yet," La Rae said.

"Not yet," I agreed.

Then the phone rang and it was Howard. "What's wrong?" I said, forgetting my vow to be calm.

He didn't sound that calm himself. "Nothing!" he snapped. "Why do you always think something's wrong?"

"I don't," I said.

"I'm only a little tired," Howard said in a gentler voice.

"Then I'll come and get you now," I told him.

"No, no, I'm home already. Mike gave me a ride."

"Oh," I said. "Well, I'll be home soon, too."

"Take your time," he said. "I'm going to take a nap, anyway. Take your time," he repeated.

So I did. La Rae and I drank some more coffee, and the caffeine rushed through my bloodstream, giving me a fast, false surge of energy. We made a pact to live together when we're both ancient and decrepit. We made another pact to never get that way. And we answered a few of our letters, giving serious attention to the universal problems of love and rust.

When I got home, Howard was awake. The house was heavily, funereally fragrant. "What stinks like that?" I asked, and Howard said that he'd spilled some after-shave. I turned on the exhaust fan and then I started supper.

10

*S*HARON DANZER HAD PICKED RISTORANTE SCALA, ABOUT halfway between our two houses, for our recovery celebration. She'd told Paulie it was expensive but festive—just right for the occasion. It turned out to be one of those pretentious new places, with menus too big to handle, and prices to match. On Saturday night, at seven-thirty, we followed the maître d' to a corner table for four in the nonsmoking section. All of the tables were spotlit little stages, and Muzak was being piped in steadily and softly, like odorless gas. I looked over at the other side of the room, where cigarette smoke swirled in the beams of the spotlights.

The captain recited a long list of the evening's specials, but I kept tuning him out. I wished we were at Sweet Basil or the West End, ordering cheeseburgers and fries, and listening to live music—somebody old and mellow, like Doc Cheatham. That was the way to celebrate survival. Sharon and Paulie paid careful attention to the captain's spiel, while Gil studied the wine list as if they were going to quiz him on it later. I began to crave all the forbidden foods I could think of—bloody, marbled steak; silky oysters; salty, saturated onion rings—anything deep-fried and greasy. I think I could have guzzled a quart of crankcase oil right then without any trouble. I'd been good for weeks, letting Paulie supervise my diet, and hardly ever complaining. "Listen, everybody," I said, keeping my voice casual and trying not to salivate. "This is a special occasion, am I right? So let's have something special this once, the exception to the rule. A steak isn't going to kill anybody, is it?"

Gil gave me a pitying smile, and the women looked shocked, as if I'd suggested eating live mice. In the end, they ordered for everybody: green salads first, and broiled lemon sole with wild rice. I slathered butter on my roll, tore off a chunk, and practically swallowed it whole. Paulie didn't say anything, but a few seconds later she moved the rest of the buttered roll onto her own plate.

The waiter brought the wine, and after the tasting ritual, we raised our glasses in a toast. "To us," Gil said, "long may we wave," and the glasses clinked together. I had the crazy notion I could hear his heart beating across the table, that I could hear everybody's heart in the restaurant, like a chorus of metronomes. Of course it was only the boring beat of the Muzak.

Another waiter went by, with platters of dark, glistening meat on his tray. When our main course arrived, looking almost as pale as hospital food, Gil said, "Ahh, good!" I had never liked fish very much, except for shellfish. Mercury poisoning probably killed more people than cholesterol, anyway. And then there was smog, and fallout, and radon, and terrorists—hell, you had to die of *something*. "Gil, they've got you brainwashed," I said. "You've become a Moonie of the health nuts. Soon you'll be bugging us in airports." Even as I said it I remembered that he was my role model, that we were both alive because we were lucky and had been given a second chance to be sensible.

We ate, and the fish wasn't so bad. Maybe it was just that

I was hungry, or that the wine had helped loosen me up. I noticed that Gil didn't really look that hot, despite his tan and his flat gut. And his happy mood seemed forced after a while, and kind of desperate. When Paulie and Sharon went off to the ladies' room together, I sang, "Gimme a pig foot and a bottle of beer," Bessie Smith style, and he didn't even crack a smile.

"You think this is all a big joke, Howie, don't you?" he said.

"Hey," I said. "What did I say?"

"It's your whole attitude," he said. "You're acting like a spoiled little kid, like a deprived person."

"Listen, Gil," I said. "I'm grateful to be alive, but I don't really enjoy living this way. If I had any choice in the matter, I'd be over there, smoking my lungs out and eating all the poison on the menu."

"Go ahead, then," he said. "Nobody's stopping you, are they? It's your funeral."

I tried to remember why I'd liked him so much in the hospital. I thought of how we used to horse around with the nurses, like a couple of sex-crazed teenagers. And late at night, before our sedatives took effect, we usually rapped for a long time, about our families, about music. We were the same age, and we'd grown up in adjacent neighborhoods. When we were kids we'd both hung around the clubs, hoping to sit in with the greats, and at the union halls, looking for work. We'd also both been drafted during Korea, and then sat out two years of the war in the States, waiting to be shipped out any minute, to be killed on foreign soil. The army itself was a foreign experience for two laid-back musicians from New York who were used to going to bed about the same time we had to get up as soldiers.

Some nights we talked about personal things we wouldn't

ever have mentioned in other circumstances, like death, of course, which we planned to beat. He told me how he and Sharon had met in high school, that neither of them had ever dated anyone else. And I told him more about Paulie and me than I'd ever told anybody, as if I'd just fallen in love and had to brag about it or die. The dark room must have opened us up, and that feeling of being shipwrecked together. He had a great sense of humor then, and what seemed like real courage and wisdom. In the morning he'd invariably greet me by saying, "You still alive there, kiddo?" When I would grunt sleepily, he'd say, "Good, then I must be, too." It was a dumb routine, but it seemed funny then, and cheering. Later, while I was trying to get my soft-boiled, salt-free breakfast egg down, I'd think *I'm alive, I'm alive*, the way I'd kept thinking *This is it* the night Paulie brought me in. Now Gil was uptight and sanctimonious—the brainy nerd in school who won't show you the answers. I was ready to tell him to fuck off when I saw him stick a nitroglycerin tablet under his tongue. He did it fast, as if he was sneaking a breath mint, but I saw him anyway. "What's the matter?" I asked.

"Nothing. Just can it, okay?" he said, glancing behind me.

I looked around and saw that the women were on their way back to the table.

Dessert wasn't much more fun. We all settled for the fresh fruit—without the crème fraîche, naturally—but by then I wouldn't have enjoyed the richest chocolate cake in the world. In fact, I felt a little queasy and there was a tightness in my own chest. I was sure it was indigestion this time, but I took a nitro, too, with the same sleight of hand Gil had used. I think he was the only one who noticed.

We livened up a little in the parking lot, joking around and making promises to get together again soon. Gil must have been sorry for acting like such an asshole, but he didn't want to apologize. Instead, he punched my shoulder a few times, and said, "So, kiddo, are you still alive?" And as his car pulled away, he tooted a farewell riff on the horn.

Paulie and I were both quiet on the way home, but it wasn't the cozy silence I used to long for whenever she talked too much. "That was sort of fun," I said, as we walked into the house. She didn't say anything, and I said, "I think I liked him better in pajamas, though." We made our way down the hallway to the bedroom. I hung my jacket on one of the doorknobs we passed, my tie on another, and started unbuttoning my shirt. I was hoping Paulie would agree, or even say something catty or spiteful of her own. One of the best things about marriage was that you could do that, expose your worst side without being judged. I dumped my change and keys on top of the bureau. When I turned around, I saw that Paulie was sitting in the window seat, with all her clothes still on, and she was looking intently up at me. I sensed that something important and bad was about to happen, and I tried to forestall it. "Boy, I'm really dead," I said, "aren't you?" I sat on the edge of the bed and let one shoe drop to the floor with a thud.

"Howard," Paulie said. "I have to say something to you." I took a deep breath, but before I could let it out, she went on. "This has been on my mind for weeks, but I waited for you to get well before I brought it up," she said. "It's something that won't go away by itself."

"This sounds serious," I said, and smiled at her to undo the seriousness.

"It is," she said. "Do you remember that after . . . Marie, after you came back to us, I said that things were changed forever?"

"That was a long time ago," I said. Why couldn't she try and let it go away by itself?

"What I meant was that the balance of power between us had changed. Before you left, the thing that scared me the most was the idea of you ever leaving."

"What scares you the most now?" I said, jumping in right over my head.

"That I want to leave you," she said.

If I hadn't asked her, she might not have said it exactly that way. Maybe she wouldn't have said it at all. "Paulie," I said. "You don't mean that." The irony of the whole thing occurred to me in a battery of wild heartbeats. I'd given up Janine, and Paulie had found someone else. Who was it? I thought of philandering Frank, of cocksure Mike, and, crazily, of Gil acting hostile in the restaurant and then popping nitro. Mine were down the hall somewhere now, in my jacket pocket.

"Yes, I do," Paulie said. "Listen, Howard, there's something I've sensed for a very long time and didn't say anything about. I guess I didn't want it to be true, so I pretended it wasn't."

"Maybe it's not," I said.

"Maybe," she said. "But I think it is. I think you've had a lover for a while, Howard, the thing I'd decided I wasn't ever going to tolerate or forgive again."

"Why do you think that?" I said.

"Oh, clues . . . this and that. Things weren't that great between us, anyway."

Her incredible calm struck me, as if she'd rehearsed this conversation for ages, and had resolved herself to its outcome. Had I said what she'd expected me to? I hadn't said anything that mattered yet, not a denial, not a confession. If I was going to deny it, I should have done that right away. It wouldn't have seemed like much of a lie anymore. I hadn't been with Janine for weeks, and I'd ended it on my own initiative. It was as if I were two separate people, the one before the heart attack and the one after. How could she hold me responsible for what the other one had done? "Paulie," I said softly, "it isn't true."

"That's hard for me to believe."

"Is it because I've been a little grouchy? Is it because we don't make love enough?" I had turned this into a game of twenty questions without meaning to. For the first time I understood Paulie's compulsion to talk and talk into the silences between us, that it came out of uneasiness, and out of a desire to change what was probably out of your hands.

"It's not any one thing," Paulie said. "It's many things. Our life together is all habit now, and it could go on like that until we die. *You* almost died, and I thought I'd be cheated of saying this to you, and it made me furious."

"Is that all you thought?" I asked, fishing for something better, but hardly feeling hopeful.

"You know it isn't," she said.

"Then you still love me," I concluded for her.

"Yes, in a way. But I'm also very angry with you, and terribly disappointed. I want to move out, Howard, and take a place by myself in the city."

"This is crazy," I said. "When did you decide all this?"

"A while ago."

"Did you rent something yet?"

"Not yet. I'll look again tomorrow, more seriously."

"You've *looked* already?"

"Only once, when I was just trying out the idea."

"Jesus, I don't believe this," I said. "Paulie, I *love* you. What do you want me to do?"

"I want you to just let me do this, peacefully."

"Peacefully! We'll get enough peace after we're dead!" As I said it, I remembered this was what she used to say about sleep when I wouldn't get up on Sunday mornings. "Our silver anniversary is coming up," I said, and my eyes filled with tears, as if that was the central and tragic fact.

"I know," Paulie said. "Exactly! Can you imagine feeling this way and going through that whole farce? With Ann hiring Madison Square Garden or someplace for a party?"

"The kids will be thrilled to hear about this," I said. Everybody would hear about it.

"They'll live," Paulie said. "And so will we."

"I don't know about that," I said. I limped around the room until I flung off the other shoe. "You sure took a long time to get even with me."

"Is that what you think I'm doing?" she asked.

"I don't know what you're doing," I said. "I don't think you know, either."

"I'm mixed up about some things," she said, "but I want to try a separation. I *have* to."

"You only have to die," I said coldly, and when she didn't answer, I said, "Go ahead then, go!" I picked up the newspaper that was lying open on the floor next to my side of the bed. "Here!" I said. "Look through the real-estate section!" I threw the paper in her direction. It fell short by a few feet and the pages scattered all over the carpet.

Paulie walked noisily across them and picked up her pillow. "I'm going to sleep in Ann's room," she said. "Maybe we can talk again in the morning."

I waited until I heard the door to Ann's old bedroom close before I went back up the hallway to look for the nitroglycerin. I put one under my tongue, but what I really needed then was a cigarette. In the bedroom again, I rummaged through the pockets of my jackets in the closet, hoping to come across a forgotten pack of Marlboros. I only found a few shreds of loose tobacco that I chewed and spit out. I thought of the silvery smoke disappearing on the other side of the restaurant that night, and of everything lost through bad choices and lousy luck. "Shit," I said, and went to the door of Ann's room and knocked.

"Yes?" Paulie said.

I opened the door. She was sitting up under the covers in the white canopied bed. The room was still pretty much the way it was when Ann lived there—posters, photographs, high-school trophies—even though she'd been married for more than a year. Her child-sized Raggedy Ann doll still sat slumped in the wicker rocking chair. Paulie had talked about turning the room into a study for herself, but it remained a kind of shrine to Ann's childhood. Being in there with Paulie now made me feel the positive vibes of the past, of the good times, at least.

"Paulie, there isn't anybody anymore," I said.

"But there was someone, wasn't there?"

"Yes," I said, and watched her whole body take that in. "But it didn't mean anything. It was just something I got into, by mistake, and then got right out of again. It's been over for a long time—I swear it—and it was never worth what this is doing to us, to you."

"Was *Marie* worth it?" she said.

"Oh, Paulie . . ."

"I don't think I can ever trust you again, Howard," she said. "I don't even really want to try."

"I know that. I know that, Paulie, and I don't blame you."

"Then there's nothing else to say, is there?" she said.

"Can't you just try and forgive me?" I asked, and her mouth curved into a bitter smile. "Listen, babe," I said.

"Do you know what I used to talk about to Gil all night in the hospital? About you—about how much I love you."

"That was probably out of guilt," she said, "and fear."

"I was scared, sure I was, but it was more than that. I felt *lovestruck*, as if we had just met for the first time. I drove poor Gil nuts talking about you. Do you remember I used to say that you were the words and I was the music? Oh, God, how can I say this?"

Paulie's face was wide open, and miserable with confusion. I wanted to move in then, climb in next to her on the narrow bed and take her in my arms. Instead, I lifted the doll from the rocker and sat down with it on my lap. "I don't think I *could* live without you," I said.

"You're the one who said that nobody dies of love."

"I guess I was lying," I said.

"That wouldn't be the first time, would it?"

"But it would be the last. I know it's corny to say this, but that first night in the hospital my life actually passed in front of me. The important parts, anyway. I remembered when we met at the dance, how gorgeous you were . . . that tremendous feeling I had when I first saw you. I remembered making love in my car. That time in Marine Park when the horn went off and I had to pull the wires to stop it. And waiting for Jason to be born. It was as if *I* was just being born then myself. I was sorry for ever hurting you. Paulie, I still am."

I waited in the awful, punishing silence until I couldn't stand it anymore. Then I put the doll on the floor and stood up. "I want you to stay with me more than I've ever wanted anything," I said. "Please, my love." She didn't answer and I went to the side of the bed and took her hand. "Please," I said again.

Paulie closed her eyes for a few moments, and when she opened them, they were darker, changed. "Oh, damn you to hell," she said, and then she moved over for me.

11

WHEN I WAS A LITTLE GIRL, MY FATHER USED TO pretend to pull pennies from my ringlets, and I fell for it again and again. Even after the magic act was over, I always shook my head a few times, waiting for some spare change to fall out. This was more or less the same thing—Howard had pulled off his major trick once more, making me believe my instincts were wrong, and that love always triumphs over everything. As soon as I let him into Ann's bed, I felt something leave me. Maybe it was courage. God knows I was relieved not to have to go through the agony of separating, but I was still sad. I wasn't exactly convinced by Howard's story, but I wanted to be, and that's what mattered, finally. *Tell all the Truth but tell it slant* . . . I didn't say any of that to him, though: I didn't say anything at all. We made love in the space that was almost as small as the backseat of his old Pontiac. We were passionate and raucous; the canopy trembled above us, the way the car had once trembled and rocked on its beat-up springs. Later that night, we woke and went hand-in-hand down the hallway to our own bed. We fell asleep again in one corner of that broad expanse, staying as close as we could without merging again. But I was still sad.

For days, Howard did everything he could think of to cheer

me up. It was a kind of courtship—that constant, anxious awareness, his earnest desire to please and be pleased. Why did I remember being much happier during our first, hurried courtship, even though I was doubled over most of the time then, in a cramp of longing?

Soon there were other things on my mind. One afternoon, about a week after my reconciliation with Howard, Sara came to see me, unexpectedly. I opened the front door, on my way out to the library, and she was standing there, about to ring the bell. "Sara!" I said. "You scared the life out of me." When I looked back later, it seemed like a blackly humorous remark, since the life was really in *her*.

She'd come out on the train, she said, and walked the two miles from the station. My poor half-extinguished Flame. She was wan and exhausted, as if she'd trudged across the Sahara. My first thought was that Jason had left her. I remembered the tension between them that day in my kitchen, right after Howard came home from the hospital. "It's a wonderful surprise, though," I said, belatedly, and her bony little body collapsed against me. She began sobbing; the sound was throaty and desperate, strangely like the way she sang.

I took her into the living room and made her sit down. I brought her a glass of water, which she held for a while without drinking. It sloshed as the sobs subsided into hiccups. "What's wrong, Sara?" I asked. "Tell me, and maybe I can help you."

When she was composed enough, she said, "I'm pregnant."

History, I thought. But it was my own mother I'd gone to. And I knew she hadn't felt the queer thrill of joy that went through me when Sara spoke. "You are?" I said. "Oh, honey, are you sure?"

It was a foolish question. Of course she was sure. Her usually modest breasts were straining her glittery T-shirt, and her face was changed in mysterious ways beyond the pallor and despair. No doubt a handy home-pregnancy test had confirmed what she already knew from missed periods and other symptoms. She nodded, anyway, sipped a little of the water.

I took her icy hand and said, "Are you that unhappy about it, Sara?"

"I was happy at first," she said, "until I told Jason."

It *was* history. I could still conjure up Howard's surprised face, the way his eyes shifted away from mine into the darkness of the future. He'd said, "What do you want to do about it?" and I said, "You know." And that was how we became engaged. "What did Jason say?" I asked Sara.

"Oh, *he* wants me to have an abortion."

My friends and I had marched at the clinic in Northport not long ago. Katherine didn't bring her grandson along, but other women on both sides wheeled strollers back and forth in front of the building. And Katherine had put her commitment into the signs she'd made: CHOOSE FREEDOM; MEN MAKE LAWS, WOMEN MAKE BABIES; WHAT ABOUT OUR RIGHTS? Across the street, there were the other signs, including the ones I'd dreaded, with blown-up photos of fetuses on them.

"How far gone are you?" I asked, thinking what an awful expression that was. Right then, it evoked an image of a pregnant woman disappearing down a dusty road.

"About ten weeks," Sara said. She put the glass of water on the coffee table and brushed her cotton-candy hair back with her hands.

"Have you seen a doctor?" I said. "Have you told your mother and father?"

"Yes," she said. "No. I know what *they'll* say."

I'd only met them once, when the kids invited both sets of parents for supper after they'd moved in together. The Bartletts had declined, and then they showed up as we were finishing our dessert. They'd come all the way in from Westport for that brief, unhappy visit. It was clear to everyone that they strongly disapproved of Jason, of what had become of their daughter, and of that tiny, barricaded firetrap in the Bronx. Sara's father was a pin-striped corporate lawyer, obviously not her model for the ideal lover. I imagined that Sara's mother, a pretty, matronly blonde, had a head filled with snapshots of Sara's childhood she wished she could reveal to us. "She had lovely hair," Mrs. Bartlett wanted to say, "like mine, only lighter. I used to brush it a hundred strokes every night when she was little. Look, here we all are at the lake. That's her sister, Peggy. I bought their clothes at Bonwit's. They had French lessons when they were three."

I had my own hidden pictures, but I didn't think she'd be interested in them, and she wouldn't have approved of my sympathy for our children's union. The leavings of dinner added further disorder to the scene. There were red-wine stains on the pale yellow tablecloth. I had to remember to tell Sara that a handful of salt or a few spills of white wine would get rid of them. The candles she'd cleverly set into balls of Play-Doh had melted down to waxy puddles, and the dessert plates were smeared with dirty-looking chocolate. Her parents stayed only long enough to register their distress, without saying anything directly about it. They merely asked polite, deadly questions: "Does your . . . uh . . . group have many engagements? Have you met your neighbors?"—even as a woman screamed close by, probably because she was being murdered, and the bass of someone's stereo thumped mercilessly overhead. I bet they'd have plenty to say about *this* news.

"I want to have the baby," Sara said.

It was what high-school girls, some of them as newly pubescent as pregnant, sometimes told Katherine. She didn't argue with them, only patiently explained their options. Of course, Sara wasn't a high-school girl. She was almost twenty-one, and had finished two years at Fairleigh Dickinson before she met Jason.

"I know it isn't practical or anything," she said. "And we didn't plan for this to happen. But it did, and now I'm . . . I'm like in *love*."

"How do you feel?" I asked. "Physically, I mean. What did the doctor say?"

"Oh, that I'm healthy," she said, with a dismissive gesture. "You know, I feel *fine*."

I'd thrown up all the time in the early days of my own pregnancies, but I knew exactly what she meant—that extraordinary sense of well-being, of containing a splendid secret.

"I know," I said.

"Except," she said, her eyes clouding up again. "Except about Jason."

"Maybe it's only the shock," I said, with my first grudging loyalty to my son in all this. Poor Jason—with everything he'd learned about it in school and at home, the connection between all that glorious sex and this unhappy consequence must have still been a blow to him. And they were too poor, and probably too immature, to raise a child.

"He's gotten over *that*," Sara said. "He just doesn't want it."

Howard hadn't wanted him, either, in the beginning. Was this the sins of the fathers, etc.? "He might change his mind," I said. "Or you might."

"I won't," Sara said resolutely, and I suddenly under-

stood that this was my grandchild we'd been discussing with
such practical detachment. It might have pink hair or play
the drums. It could look something like me! And it was
already a contender for every human pleasure and sorrow.
Sara blew her nose. "I don't even know why I came here,
Mrs. Flax," she said.

"I do," I told her. "You knew I'd be on your side."

"I don't want there to be sides," she said.

"We'll talk to Jason," I promised. "Wait and see, he'll
end up being delighted." Liar, liar! Pants on fire!

I paid thirty dollars for a cab to take her back to the Bronx.
The minute Howard walked in the door, I broke the news to
him. He stared at me so long I thought he hadn't understood
a word I'd said. Then he said, "Jesus. That poor kid."

Who did he mean? Jason? Sara? The baby? "Who's a poor
kid?" I said.

"What is she going to do?" he asked. Almost an echo of
what he'd asked me twenty-five years ago.

"You know," I whispered.

"What?"

"Sara wants to have the baby, and we have to help her.
We have to do something about Jason."

"I guess it's too late to ground him," Howard said.

"I'm glad you find this so amusing, Howard. But it happens to be our own grandchild we're talking about."

"I just can't get used to it, that's all," he said. "Jesus,
they're not even married."

"What difference does that make?" I asked.

"No difference, I guess."

"Jason has to act responsibly," I said. "I want you to talk
to him, Howard."

"All right, I will," he said. A few moments later he said,
almost to himself, "What will I say?"

"God, Howard, what do you think you should say?"

"He'll have to get a regular job," Howard said, gloomily. "They'll have to live someplace normal and safe."

"Yes," I agreed. "You can tell him we'll help them get settled. He's probably terrified right now. You know Jason."

"I thought I did. What the hell were they thinking of?"

"They weren't *thinking*. Anyway, look who's talking," I said.

"Things were different then," Howard said. "We didn't major in sex education. And contraceptives weren't out there on the drugstore shelf right next to the toothpaste. Are you sure she won't have an abortion?"

"Yes, I'm *sure*," I said. I was becoming angry, and I felt heavyhearted, as if it were me who was pregnant again, and Howard who was denying his duty.

"Why are you getting so upset?"

"Because you're acting like a fascist."

"A fascist! What's that supposed to mean? And make up your mind, Paulie, will you—didn't you march against the Right-to-Lifers a couple of weeks ago?"

"Of course I did," I said. "I'm pro-*choice*, remember? And Sara chooses to have the baby."

"What about Jason's choice?" Howard said.

I hated him then, even as I conceded his point. Woman's body, but man's seed—they did have a say in it. There'd been almost as many men as women, on both sides of the issue, the day we paraded in Northport. "We're in this together!" Howard had insisted when I was alone in my labor. And in Ann's room the other night, when I decided to stay with him, he'd spoken about Jason's birth with what seemed like reverence. "Just talk to him," I said, my old refrain.

* * *

That was Friday. I remember because I was very late for work at the library and agreed to make it up the following week. Bernie Rusten was going through microfilms of the *Times* when I got there, and although I'd promised myself to be discreet after my last outburst, I sat down next to him and said, "Guess what? I'm going to be a grandmother!"

"Hey, good for you," he said. "Congratulations. Is it your daughter?"

"No," I said. "My son. Against his better judgment, I'm afraid."

"How long have they been married?" he asked.

"They're not," I said. "Howard's going to knock some sense into him, though."

"Your husband must be much better, then."

"Oh. Yes, of course."

"And you're happy?"

What a question. "It's complicated," I said, my old standby for evasion.

"I've been reading some poetry," he said, "on your recommendation."

"Who?"

"Let's see . . . Wilfred Owen and Siegfried Sassoon. And Rupert Brooke."

"The war poets. Well, do they help explain history?"

"I don't know, they seem as bewildered as I am. But they give it immediacy. And they break your heart."

"What more can you ask?" I said. "But you ought to broaden your horizons." I recommended Williams to him, and Dickinson, and Elizabeth Bishop. He wished me luck and I went back to work.

The following Friday, I had another unexpected visitor. I was vacuuming the bedroom rug when I realized the doorbell was ringing persistently. That doesn't happen very often in the suburbs. When we lived in Queens, people sometimes rang the bells in the outer lobby at random, just to gain entry to the building, and kids pressed all of them for fun when they had nothing else to do. Out here, an occasional salesman or a couple of Jehovah's Witnesses would stop by, and that was about it.

I turned the vacuum off and looked through the window. I couldn't see who was on the front step from there, but a red Mazda was parked at the curb. Probably not Jehovah's Witnesses. "Who is it?" I yelled. A woman's voice answered, but I couldn't make out what she was saying. I opened the door. She was a stranger, a freckled redhead in a flashy jumpsuit and spike-heeled pumps. I'd never worn a jumpsuit myself. My figure was too full, and they seemed like so much trouble—you'd practically have to get undressed every time you went to the bathroom. I wondered what she was selling.

"Hello?" I said.

She looked me over, cocking her head and squinting, as if I were trying to sell *her* something. "you're Paulie," she said, "aren't you. My name is Janine."

12

*I*DIDN'T GET AROUND TO TALKING TO JASON RIGHT away, in spite of Paulie's nagging. This routine began sometime in his teens, when he turned into a stranger she couldn't reach, a puzzle she couldn't solve. When Jason was little, Paulie had never urged me to straighten him out, no matter how obnoxious he got. In fact, she'd come to his defense when I got angry about something—his disgusting table manners, or because he was acting fresh, or goofing off in school. She never threatened him with that old saw of my mother's, "Wait until your father comes home." Whenever I did come home, and Ann reported Jason's latest crime, Paulie would stop me before I could say anything to him. She always reminded me that he'd had a "bad start" in life. It was an umbrella expression that covered everything from his long-corrected strabismus, to his reading disability, to my initial reluctance to marry her.

She let him get away with a lot in those days, although she was often critical of Ann, whose worst sin was making her brother look bad. We were divided early on into two odd couples, two clearly defined teams. Paulie tried to offset things by forcing Jason and me into all sorts of father-and-son activities. We ended up on camping trips that neither of us enjoyed. I'd find myself lying awake in a stifling pup tent, next to Jason, who scratched at his hundreds of mosquito bites and ground his teeth in fitful sleep. I would wonder how the hell I'd gotten there, and I didn't mean the campgrounds at Wildwood or Hither Hills, but there in my very life.

Later, when Jason discovered music, things changed for the better between us. At last I had something to offer him that he actually wanted. We'd jam together, driving Paulie and Ann out of the house and closer to one another, too. He was very talented, a natural, and for the first time in his life he was interested in something, and willing to work hard at it. For the first time I didn't lose my temper trying to teach him something; I didn't even really mind that he was the better musician.

Music was still the strongest bond we had, maybe the only one, and now Paulie was setting me against him. "Talk to him," she'd said, but she meant for me to talk *at* him, to tell him what to do, what his moral and legal obligations were to Sara. And I was supposed to say that we'd assist them, financially and otherwise, until they could stand on their own feet.

We'd never lied to the children about the dates of our marriage and Jason's birth, and I guessed Paulie expected me to remind him that he'd come into being himself because I'd accepted responsibility for him. But I didn't think that was much of an argument. Jason tended to be a moody kid— maybe he wished he'd never been born, especially now. And, anyway, some maverick part of me wanted to tell him to run for it.

I finally got around to calling him about a week after Paulie began working on me to do it. I told him I was coming into town to buy some outboard gear, and that I'd meet him for lunch afterward at a Chinese restaurant on upper Broadway. Jason must have been suspicious, although he didn't seem to know about Sara's visit to Paulie. He showed up fifteen or twenty minutes late, looking rumpled and handsome. When he sat down, there was a rustle of attention among the women at the next table that he acknowledged with a flicker of his hooded eyes. "What's up, Dad?" he said, by way of greeting.

I wouldn't let him take the lead. "What took you so long?" I said. "Do you want a bottle of Kirin?"

We drank the beer, and ordered too much food. When the moo shu pork and the fried noodles arrived, he said, "Are you sure you're allowed to eat this stuff?"

There was more concern in his voice than curiosity. I remembered wanting to slug him for deliberately burping at the dinner table, for the mocking bark of a laugh that used to be his response to everything I said. "Yeah, I'm sure," I said. "Let's get some chopsticks. Do you want another beer?"

An hour or so later we were still sitting there, bloated and sleepy. Jason was tapping out a polyrhythm on the table with his chopsticks—four against three, no less. We'd talked mostly about music during lunch, about the new sounds that were developing, and the new techniques for recording it. He had some cockeyed, impractical ideas, but I liked the way they excited him, the way they pulled him out of himself. I almost forgot my mission or any animosity I'd ever felt toward him. "Let's take a walk, Jase," I said.

I stopped and bought a couple of cigars, and then we went to one of those benches on the center island of Broadway and sat down among the old ladies, the bums, and the pigeons. He declined a cigar, and when I lit up, he said, "I thought you're not supposed to smoke."

"That's cigarettes," I said. "I'm not inhaling this." Right after I said it, I sucked in a lungful. I almost choked to death, but it felt great, anyway—the rush of nicotine, the pleasure of the cigar in my hand. It was a gorgeous day, sunny and very warm for late September. Cars whizzed by, the pigeons pecked near our shoes—Paulie's crazy, filthy city. Jason leaned back and closed his eyes, turning his face up to catch the sun. I hated to spoil the lazy peace between us, but there was no sense in putting it off any longer. I took another puff, and as the smoke curled out, I said, "I hear Sara's pregnant."

The bench shook a little as he sat forward. "Did she tell you?" he demanded.

"Hey," I said. "That's her privilege, you know. This isn't Annie, snitching on you for some misdemeanor."

"It's between us," he said. "It's between me and Sara."

"Sure," I said. "I understand that. Your mother and I only want to help out if we can. We want to help you do the right thing." Pat O'Brien encouraging Jimmy Cagney to go straight. But didn't he always end up in the chair?

Jason rubbed his eyes, hard, as if he wanted to wipe out some terrible vision. "Maybe we could use some cash," he said. "You know, like a loan."

"How much?"

"Two, three hundred," he said.

"For an abortion?" I asked.

He hesitated for a beat before he said, "Yes."

"When did Sara change her mind?" I said.

"What is this, the Spanish Inquisition?"

"Relax," I said. "She told Mom she wanted to have the baby."

"Then let her have it," he said.

"Wait a minute, wait a minute. She's not in this alone."

"Maybe she will be if she goes through with it."

"That's really great, Jason. Your mother is going to be very proud of you."

"Dad, listen," he said. "It was a mistake—neither of us planned on this happening. Why do I have to pay for it the rest of my life?"

"Jase, you were a mistake, too, once upon a time, remember?"

"Yeah," he said. "And I ruined your life."

"What are you talking about? Does my life look ruined to you? As soon as your mother and I got married, I was crazy about the idea of a baby. I was even crazy about the baby . . . that was *you*."

"Then how come you split when we lived in Queens?"

Jesus. "It's complicated . . . I lost my head for a while. But I came back, didn't I?"

He didn't answer for a moment. Then he said, "I don't want to be tied down like you, and end up with a heart attack. I don't want to give up my music."

So that was how he saw me—somebody hog-tied and helpless, ready to be kayoed by a heart attack. It was hard keeping my voice level and reasonable. "Who said anything about giving up your music? I told you we're going to help you. But a little responsibility will be good for your soul."

"I feel as if I haven't even lived yet," Jason said.

"You'll probably always feel that way," I told him. "It's the curse of mankind."

"Oh, shit," he said under his breath.

I pretended not to hear him. "So, is it a deal, my man?" I said.

He mumbled something, or made a grunting sound, so I slapped him five on his limp hand, and then I hugged him, awkwardly.

Mission impossible—accomplished! Then why did I feel let down instead of triumphant? Because of the way Jason had described me, maybe, or because I might have just betrayed him. Driving over the Triborough Bridge later, I kept thinking that Paulie would make me feel better. Her relief about Jason and Sara would rub off on me, and she would be sweetly grateful for a long time. I'd gone off my diet at lunch, but she'd get me back on the right track again—one lousy meal never hurt anybody.

It was only four o'clock, but the traffic was building up. Construction, accidents, breakdowns. And it was Friday, when all the lemmings headed for the sea. I thought of the poor suckers who crawled back and forth in the rush hour every day of their lives. At least I'd never had to do that. I had my little garden, the shade of maple trees I'd planted myself. And my work was still music, even if I didn't play much anymore. I'd be able to show Jason that there were loopholes in the life sentence. As I drove, I remembered being stuck in heavy traffic another time, years ago, on my way to a club date in Jersey. It was summer and there were a few cars on the shoulder of the parkway, their hoods up and their radiators smoking. And then I saw this tall, thin black guy standing alone next to his car, playing the trumpet. I don't even think his car was in trouble. He'd probably just pulled out of that mess onto the grassy shoulder and started to play. He was in rolled-up shirt-sleeves, I remember, his eyes closed and his foot tapping in time to the music. The traffic slowed even more, because of the rubbernecking, like at an accident. My windows were rolled down, and as I went by him I heard the honeyed wail of his horn over all the noisy engines and exhausts. I decided to tell Jason about that next time, too, although I wasn't exactly sure why.

When I turned down our street, almost an hour later, I

realized how tired I was, and how glad I was to be home. Two little kids across the street were chasing each other around the lawn the way Jason and Annie used to. Gordon Brooks, the guy next door, was working on his rosebushes. I tapped the horn as I turned into our driveway and he waved his spade at me. When we'd first moved in, we had some disagreements over the border shrubs, and about Jason cutting across his property on the way to school. We both thumped our chests a few times, and then, over the years, we'd reached a state of détente. The houses in our development were all identical, but we'd each made some mark of distinction, with paint or lawn ornaments or landscaping. Gordon had his fabulous rosebushes. The Castellis had their ceramic frogs. And Paulie and I had a red door, with a fist-shaped brass knocker she'd found in a flea market. I banged it three times—our old signal—and then I put my key in the lock.

"I'm home," I yelled into the cool afternoon shade of the house. It was eerily quiet in there, or did I just think that later? The only sound was the clicking of Shadow's toenails as he came slowly across the kitchen floor to greet me. "Hello, you good boy," I said, rubbing his head. "Where's Mommy?" I went through the rooms, calling Paulie's name, until I came around full circle to the kitchen. It was much too neat, like those kitchens in the model homes we used to look at on Sundays. There were no signs of dinner. Paulie should have been home from the library—she was usually slicing or chopping something on the cutting board by now. I let Shadow out into the back yard, hoping I'd find her in the hammock, sleeping maybe, or reading. She wasn't there and I had a sudden moment of real loneliness, the way I felt some evenings when the grass and trees went black, and the cars became dark silhouettes in the driveways. I automatically went to the refrigerator and opened the door. I was still a little full from lunch and yet I ate a slice of cheese and poked at the last few green olives from a jar. The salty brine on my fingers was stinging and delicious.

The phone rang, and it startled me in that stillness. It was Ann, wanting to ask Paulie about the ingredients for a cake. "She's not here, sweetie," I said. "She must be taking a walk or something."

"With Shadow?"

"No," I said, and a nervous spasm grabbed my gut. "He's out back, killing off the hydrangea."

"Mom told me about Sara, Daddy. What's going to happen with them?"

"I went to see Jason today, and we had a man-to-man talk. I think I convinced him to accept fatherhood." I knew I was grandstanding, but it was Paulie's fault—she should have been home to hear what had happened.

"Jason? I can't believe it. He's still such a baby himself."

"Not for long," I said.

"And you'll be a grandpa!" She said it gently, teasingly, and it certainly wasn't news, but it felt like it anyway.

After we hung up, I let Shadow back in and I wandered through the house again, as if I might have overlooked Paulie in one of the rooms. Where the hell was she? I wouldn't call any of her friends; I hated it when she tried to track me down that way when I was late. I hated even having to account for where I'd been. I didn't have any pain, but I touched my breast pocket, where I kept the vial of nitroglycerin. The other cigar was still in there, too. I almost dumped it, but I changed my mind and tossed it into a carton of odds and ends on a shelf in the hall closet. As I was shutting the door, I noticed my saxophone case, way in the back on the floor. I took it out and carried it to the bedroom. I sat on the bed

and opened the case; the sax glimmered on the dark blue
velvet lining like buried gold. Without really thinking about
it, I put my neck strap on. I wet the reed and pressed it
against the flat of the mouthpiece, and twisted the pieces
together. The first sounds I blew were rampant bleats, like
the cries of an animal in pain. I was really out of shape—
even my breathing was harsh and uneven. I ran up and down
the scales and blew arpeggios and chords until I had more
control. Then I played a few Getz numbers: "Over the Rain-
bow," "Desifinado," and "Early Autumn." The room was
noticeably darker when I finished. The telephone rang.

13

I THINK I KNEW WHO SHE WAS EVEN BEFORE SHE SPOKE, although she might have been selling cosmetics door-to-door—she had that glamorous, glossy finish. But she was also coolly pale, small-boned and delicate, my opposite and Howard's perverse passion. It wasn't just her appearance that gave her away, though. It was also the way she eyed me, a private comparative study in which she clearly came out ahead. I saw her and I saw myself—queen-size and florid—at the same time, as if we were side by side, facing a mirror.

"You're Paulie, aren't you," she said. "My name is Janine."

Janine. I stepped backward, as if I'd been pushed, and she swished past me into the house.

Marie had never presented herself this way. But I'd stalked her for days, riding up and down in the elevator of her apartment building until I saw her at last, with a whomp of recognition. How could I blame Howard for wanting her? She had the kind of body I'd always wished I had myself, and that no amount of dieting or exercise would ever give me. And her long hair was gloriously straight and lustrous. In those days, I set mine on juice cans to get rid of its stubborn frizz, but the moisture in the air would curl it right back up again. I'd tried not to even imagine this one—*Janine*—until it became bearable. When I told Howard my suspicions that night, I said I thought he had a lover. Now that seemed to be only a modern catchword, a false nod to equality between the sexes. Janine looked more like what we used to call a *girlfriend*, or a mistress. I followed her into my own living room, so invaded by sensation that the final effect was total numbness, except for the frantic bird of my heart. She sat down and I sat opposite her, wishing she had a sample case of lipsticks and blushers to display, that she wasn't here merely to tell me the truth.

"I met your husband . . . I met Howard six months ago," she began. "I went to his studio to cut a demo. I'm a singer—not rock, though—slow, romantic ballads."

The nerve of her! What supreme vanity to think I'd care what kind of songs she sang! But I *did* care, the way my mother obstinately cared about the lives of her favorite soap-opera villains.

"And then we just fell for each other. I mean nobody meant for it to happen, but it did."

She may have been wondering why Howard had never told her I was mute. I put one hand to my throat and felt all the unspoken words crowded together there.

Janine sighed deeply. "He's been in terrible conflict," she said. "That's what probably led to his heart attack. I saw him in the hospital, you know," she added slyly. It was, oddly enough, the most intimate and terrible detail she could have revealed.

"When?" I managed to say.

"Right after it happened," she said. "He sent a message for me to come, and I did."

"And when did you see him last?"

"The other day. He came to Bloomingdale's, in Garden

City, where I work—I mean, just until I get my break as a singer.''

"Why did you come here?" I asked her.

"Because I don't like living like this," she said, "and I believe in being honest. I believe you should know what's going on."

"Thanks," I said. "That's very considerate of you."

For the first time, her confidence wavered. She wasn't certain if I was being sarcastic or just stupidly sincere. To be safe, I guess, she offered a tentative, crooked smile.

"So I'm going to be honest with you, too," I said, erasing that smile. "I've known about you all along." Wasn't that really true? "And I've decided to end Howard's conflict about us. He's all yours."

She opened her mouth and shut it again, confused, as if she'd forgotten the words to a song.

"There are a few things you ought to know about him, though. He needs a low-fat, low-sodium diet. And he's not supposed to smoke," I said, "or strain himself. You'd better keep an extra supply of his heart medicine in your purse." Her nose and eyelids flushed pink and she'd turned even paler. Before she could speak, I continued: "He gets depressed on Sundays. You'll have to ease him awake—I suppose you're good at *that*. Oh, and watch out for his mother. She lives in Florida, but she's a shark, she's a long-distance swimmer."

"I don't—" Janine began.

"The children will hate you at first, maybe forever, but that's Howard's problem, isn't it?"

Janine stood up. I was going too fast for her. I was going too fast for myself; it was making me dizzy. "You'll get to put the dog to sleep, I guess. What else is there? What else?"

Janine headed for the front door, and I walked briskly

behind her. "Don't crowd him," I advised. "He hates that. Remember, less is more, more or less."

She was on the front steps, and then she was tripping toward the curb. "I'm sorry you didn't have time to sing for me!" I called after her. I shouted other things, but they were lost in the roar of the Mazda's engine.

I went back inside and sat in the kitchen, trying to catch my breath. Twenty-five years, I thought. Twenty-five years ago we weren't missing two cups, one soup spoon, and three knives. Twenty-five years ago I carried Howard's lagging spirit over love's threshold, while my mother and father watched grimly from their own wedding bed.

I dragged a suitcase from the garage—the weekender—and stuffed it with clothes and things from the bathroom cabinets. I hadn't spoken to Sherry for a long time and I had to look up her number in the phone book. If she wasn't there, or if she couldn't put me up, I'd have to stay in a hotel. That would be expensive and lonelier than I thought I could stand. Sherry was a schoolteacher and would be home from work by now, if she'd gone directly home. The phone rang several times before she answered it. "Paulie, I was just thinking about you!" she exclaimed. "I dreamed about you last night, or was it the night before?"

"I've been thinking about you, too," I said, realizing that I hardly ever thought about Sherry anymore. She was part of some previous incarnation, that slow, glazed summer of our youth. Years ago, she squeezed her eyes shut and threw the I Ching coin to find the direction of her future. It rolled across her kitchen and disappeared under the stove. I wondered if she was still seeking practical answers from mystical sources.

"Actually, I dreamed that you'd died," she said. "But don't worry, that only means I've added years to your life."

"Thanks," I said, "but right now I sort of wish I was dead."

I was able to tell Sherry everything in a fast synopsis—she knew so much about Howard and me already. Sherry had been my closest friend when I first met him, the willing audience for all my ecstatic confidences: Howard says, Howard says, Howard says . . . Despite her sympathy for our grand passion, she worried about the incompatibility of our astrological signs, and she was always surprised and amused by my monogamy. "You're going to miss *everything*," she'd say, and of course I believed that was true of her, with her many short-lived romances.

For several years after she'd graduated from NYU, with a degree in elementary education, Sherry refused to apply for a teaching job. She worked as a temporary typist or receptionist, and as a part-time salesclerk at Macy's during the Christmas rush—anything that allowed her lots of time to play. She even used to answer those ads in the *Voice*, for people to participate in psychological experiments for two dollars an hour and a free lunch. I remembered her mother's anguish because she wouldn't settle down. And I remembered Sherry's small, smoky apartment, where people lounged among all the cats on her bare mattress, trying out marijuana and sex. Now Sherry's mother was dead, and Sherry was a tenured teacher in the New York City school system.

"Come and stay with me," she said, as I knew she would. Even before she spoke, I was fumbling in one of the kitchen drawers for a timetable.

I took a cab to the station, and waited among the home-bound day workers for the 4:36. I hadn't told anyone I was going, not even the children or La Rae. For one thing, I was afraid of being defused by argument, and for another, I had to leave quickly, before Howard came home. I didn't want to see his guilty face, or listen to his feeble denials or declarations of remorse. I tried to write him a note, but every attempt was either inadequate to the occasion or hysterically illegible. Let him worry, I decided as the cabbie honked in the driveway, and soon I was on my way, the sun flashing at the train windows like the lost knives.

The decor of Sherry's West Village walk-up had changed over the years. The beaded curtains were long gone and the mattress on the floor had been replaced by a sedate-looking fold-out sofa. There were only two cats now, elderly and arthritic females who hardly showed any interest in my presence. The place still stank of cats, though, as if the menagerie of a quarter of a century ago had left a permanent stench.

Sherry herself appeared to be straddling her former life and the present one. There was something of the bohemian in her long, dark hair and something of the schoolmarm in her sensible shoes. Once I'd tried to persuade her of my domestic bliss, and she had pretended to be persuaded. "God, I *love* it in here" was her first comment about the infant Jason's nursery, but she hit the road the minute he filled his diaper.

None of Sherry's many lovers ever won her mother's heart or approval. There were married men who promised through their teeth to divorce, and homosexual men Sherry hoped to convert. In her late thirties, she was involved briefly with another woman—"A district supervisor," she'd told me on the phone. "Even my mother would have been impressed."

After Howard left me for Marie, I used to sprawl among the freeloading, unpublished poets on her mattress, trying in vain to get high, to rise up out of my sorrow. Now we sat at her tiny dinette table, eating a Greek dinner right from those little foil take-out trays. "We'll probably get Alzheimer's from the aluminum," Sherry commented, digging in, and I was flung back in time to our "dangerous" girlhood, when almost everything seemed like a worthwhile risk. "You only live once" used to be Sherry's motto, and who could argue with that?

"I'm going to find a place tomorrow," I promised. "I'll go to the real-estate agencies."

"What? And pay a fortune *plus* a commission for some rat-hole?"

Sherry's place, where she'd lived for almost thirty years, was rent-controlled, and she loved to upset everybody by mentioning how little she paid for it. Her landlord had tried desperately to get rid of her over the years, so he could acquire a new tenant and a substantial increase. He'd sent her phony eviction notices, refused to make repairs, and he'd cut off the heat and hot water for weeks at a time. Sherry said he once even sent someone posing as an exterminator, who let a whole new generation of roaches loose in her bathroom. She fought back on every front, and by now I supposed he'd resigned himself to trying to outlive her. "Well, I can't stay here forever," I said.

"I wish it were bigger," Sherry said. "But maybe you could get a larger share. We'll look in the *Voice*."

"Sherry," I said, "this isn't a June Allyson movie. I'm forty-five years old, and I've been married for over twenty-four years—I couldn't live with a complete stranger."

"Then we'll find you a sublet. That way, you'll get furniture and linens and dishes, and maybe a low rent, too."

"All right," I said. And then I was suddenly exhausted, my moussaka-laden fork too heavy to lift. *Janine*. "Oh, God," I said, slumping in my seat.

Sherry reached across the table and squeezed my hand.

"Poor Paulie," she said. A few minutes later she said, "What are you going to tell your kids?"

"The truth—sort of. That we have irreconcilable differences, that we're emotionally incompatible."

"That sounds right out of *Divorce Court*."

"Well, the sordid details are none of their business. They've witnessed enough in the past, anyway." I thought of the day Howard left to live with Marie, how the children and I came home early from my mother's and caught him packing. It was like an opera without any accompaniment. We screamed at each other in soprano and baritone, and then I collapsed against his chest, begging him to stay. He groaned in misery and commiseration, and kissed me good-bye. The baby cried throughout the whole thing, and Jason kept yelling at us not to yell.

After we'd cleared the table, Sherry brought in some school papers to correct. She taught the fourth grade, and this pile of papers was the result of an assignment to write a report on a favorite book. Were they still doing that? The sight of those lined sheets, the earnest, chubby, penciled letters made me nostalgic, not for my children's school years, but for my own. I remembered the renewable pleasure of blank paper, the endless possibilities of inspiration. This was before rejection or writer's block had ever occurred to me, before I'd learned that rhyme and meter weren't enough, were sometimes too much. "Begin!" the teacher would say, as if we were runners at the starting line, and the pencils would scratch in chorus, sending up their dark, woody perfume. Words like "pandemonium" and "delphinium" were like rich cakes—only one to a page, I knew without being told, but, oh, how delicious! Of course I was praised for the puffed-up little poems I wrote on demand. And I was criticized for my creative errors in spelling and syntax.

I picked up one of Sherry's papers. A girl named Grace Lombardy had chosen a Judy Blume novel, the same one Ann had loved so much at the same age. "This is a god bok," Grace had written. "It esplains abot life." Well, what more could you ask of a bok? I grabbed Sherry's red marker and scrawled a giant A+ across the top of the paper. Then I asked Sherry if I could use her telephone. "Of course," she said. "Do you want me to take a walk?" There wouldn't be any privacy if she stayed, but it seemed terribly rude to ask her to leave her own apartment. "That's all right," I said. "I'll only be on for a few minutes."

Howard picked up the extension in the bedroom; I don't know how I knew that—I just did. Sherry went into her bathroom and closed the door. "Hello," Howard said. He sounded expectant, and as if he'd been running.

It was easier than I'd thought. It was like leaving a message on someone's answering machine, because I didn't really wait for his response. "This is me, Paulie," I said. "I'm at Sherry's and I'm not coming home. Janine paid me a visit today." Then I hung up, quickly, and just as quickly took the receiver off the hook again.

Sherry came out of the bathroom. I indicated the phone. "I'd like to leave it that way for a little while if it's all right with you."

She nodded and said, "Ah, Paulie, didn't I tell you Aquarius and Scorpio wouldn't work?"

14

THE MAGAZINE I'D GRABBED AT THE CHECKOUT IN Foodtown had a piece on "the new breed of bachelors." After I'd emptied the bags on the kitchen table and punched them flat, I sat down and opened the magazine to the cover story. It was a big, full-color layout about six men ranging in age from twenty-five to sixty. One of them was black, one was Asian, and they all looked as if they'd been fitted with expensive rugs. The gist of the article was that bachelorhood was a dynamite way of life, not just a state of limbo before marriage. Some of the photos showed the men at home in their bachelor condos. None of them seemed to live in a suburban development, like me, and none of them was shown eating supper on one corner of a crazily cluttered table. I'd gotten into the habit of doing the dishes after meals, for fear I'd run out of them, but other things piled up: the mail, cans of dog food it didn't pay to put away, clothes to go to the cleaners, the newspapers I hadn't gotten around to reading, the books I meant to return to the library for Paulie.

Every day it got light out before I was ready to wake up and turned dark again way before I was able to sleep. The bachelors had been photographed on the job (a doctor, a clothes designer, a construction foreman, etc.). They were pictured holding important-looking papers or chatting democratically with their underlings. I thought about shlepping to the studio every day, and having to listen to the music of hopeful amateurs and Mike bragging about his latest conquests. I also kept waiting nervously for Janine to show up. Whenever the light flashed in the control room to indicate someone had come in the front door, I'd start palpitating and get a little short of breath. I wasn't sure what I'd say to her, except that she'd ruined my life and I wanted to murder her. It was strange that she hadn't come by yet, almost two weeks after her visit to Paulie, and that she hadn't returned my telephone calls.

After Paulie called that day, to say she was gone for good, I listened to the dial tone in a sick daze for a few seconds before I hung up. The phone rang again almost immediately, and I grabbed it, saying, "God, Paulie, please listen, you have to listen to me!" My mother's voice whined through the wires: "What? Hello, hello? Howard, is that you?"

Her perfect timing. Sometimes she caught me in the bathtub, or on the can, or like Annie used to—the moment Paulie and I began to make love. The pitter-patter of little feet, the jarring ring of the telephone. "Did I wake you?" she invariably asked. "You sound funny." When we remembered, we'd knock the receiver off first, lock the bedroom door, keep the noise level down. It was a wonder we ever got together, a wonder we ever enjoyed ourselves.

"Did I wake you?" my mother asked that fatal day. "You sound funny."

"No, Ma," I said. "I just have a little headache."

"What did you say before, when you answered?"

"Nothing. I was talking to Paulie."

"She's there?"

Jesus, did she have *radar*? "Of course," I said, "Of course she's here. So, how are you?'' I asked, switching tracks, hoping to derail her.

"How can I be?" she answered. Our usual opening volley. There were at least a hundred more lines we'd have to exchange before we got around to the purpose of her call, if we ever did. And Paulie was at Sherry's, probably expecting me to call her right back.

"Ma," I said, "I can't stay on now. I'll call you soon, okay?" and I hung up the way Paulie had hung up on me, before she could rally to protest.

I had to get Sherry's number from Information. She was listed as S. Fabrikant, that pathetic ruse of women living alone, to fool the crazies. Nothing that simple would ever stop those guys. One of them used to call my father regularly at the funeral home and describe what he'd like to do to the stiffs. I dialed Sherry's number, my head jammed with opening lines, but her phone was busy. I dialed again and again, the number now memorized for life, repeating "Come on, come on, hang up." Then I called the operator and said this was an emergency, could she please break into the conversation. She got back on after a few seconds to say there was no conversation to break into, and I understood at last that Paulie didn't want to hear from me. I sat there for a while digesting that news, and then I called Janine's number. Her kid answered and said she wasn't there, he didn't know when she was coming back. I left my name and number and said it was important.

I tried to imagine Janine coming here, what she might have said to Paulie and how Paulie must have felt. It occurred to me that I always picked women who loved in an ambitious, do-or-die way. Marie drove me crazy until I went away with her, and now Janine was trying to do the same thing. Even Paulie was once that demanding and intense. And I'd had a moronic, macho pride in being wanted like that. Maybe I still did.

It was hard falling asleep that night, and most of the nights that followed. I kept the lights on in the bedroom while I watched old Westerns and reruns of *Ben Casey* and *Sergeant Bilko*. One night, some guy on *Ben Casey* had a massive heart attack, and I looked on in fascinated horror while they pounded him on the chest and then shocked him back to life with electrodes. I had to get up and walk around a little, and I ended up in the kitchen eating a bowl of cold leftover pasta, washing it down with wine, until I was groggy and glutted. Sometimes I'd fall asleep sitting up, and then wake in the middle of the night with a Japanese monster on the screen and Paulie still missing from our bed. I kept trying to call her those first days, and I kept getting Sherry's tape: "Hello. Don't hang up. This is a recording, but the real me is only a message away . . ." A couple of times Sherry herself answered, and she only confirmed what I already knew—that Paulie still didn't want to speak to me. I called Janine again, too, and again I got her kid. He said that he'd already given her my message.

The bachelors in the magazine piece had a heavy social life—they were all shown dining or dancing somewhere with great-looking women. I probed myself for feelings of envy, but I didn't have any. I could have been reading *National Geographic* and looking at the quaint customs of some foreign culture. All I wanted was what I'd recently had and lost.

My own social life was almost nonexistent. Paulie's friends seemed to go out of their way to ostracize me. La Rae would drive by without even slowing down, and Katherine turned her back on me at the 7-Eleven one night, where I'd gone to buy cigarettes. Frank Peters came to the house a couple of times, and I made room on the table for another plate so we could have supper together. He advised me to wait it out, as if it was a summer storm, something that would quickly pass. Mike asked me to hit some bars with him, to listen to a little piano and drown my sorrows, but he seemed relieved when I turned him down.

I'd broken the bad news to Annie and Spence the morning after Paulie left. Now, when they visited, it was like one of their hospital visits, or a condolence call. They talked in hushed voices and she kept patting my arm. "What can we do for you, Daddy?" she asked. "Just tell us what we can do." When I moved back home after Marie, Annie, who was still a baby, greeted me at the door like a Trojan maiden welcoming a hero back from the wars. Now I didn't give her and Spence any of the details, only that Paulie and I had had some major differences and decided to separate for a while. I had no idea what Paulie had told them. Jason called once or twice, but I think Annie made him do it, because he didn't say very much about anything. It was as if I'd called *him* and woken him up. When I tried pumping him about Sara and himself, he said he had to go now, and he got off fast.

I wasn't really smoking again, only a few cigarettes a day. I rationed them out to myself in the morning, and I wouldn't touch one before noon unless things were especially bad. Paulie had hidden all the ashtrays, so I was using a mayonnaise-jar cover. I always emptied it before the butts could pile up and depress me more. I kept waiting to feel better, for that tight feeling in my gut and chest to ease up, but it didn't. The worst thing was knowing there was nothing I could do. Even if Paulie did agree to speak to me, what could I say to undo what was done, to make her forgive me and come back? I could only die, maybe, and I spent a night or two imagining the big heart attack, my body found when the neighbors began smelling something funny.

I wrote letters to Paulie that I tore up and threw away. The language itself seemed inadequate for what I wanted to tell her. One night, while I was eating supper at the crowded table, I opened one of Paulie's library books at random and came across a slew of love poems. I read them one after the other—it was amazing the way they were about us: "Oh, think not I am faithful to a vow!" . . . "Have I spoken too much or not enough of love?" . . . "I can no more hear Love's / voice" . . . "There is a momentary pause in love / When all the birth-pangs of desire are lulled." I thought of scribbling one of them out and mailing it to her, but I knew she'd see it for the cheap, easy ploy it was. For years she'd tried reading poems to me at night in bed. "Howie, just listen to this," she'd say, and then begin reciting before I could stop her. I'd only really hear a few lines before my concentration shorted out. Sometimes phrases of music came into my head and washed away the sound of her voice. Sometimes I went off into my own reverie or I just fell asleep. There'd be no way to convey to her how moved I was, reading poetry in our kitchen, with the book propped against a pyramid of dog-food cans. And maybe it was only self-pity, anyway, something Paulie would recognize in a minute.

When I thought I could stand it, I called my mother back and lied to her about everything. "Fine," I kept saying, "fine." I hadn't told her about my heart attack until I was almost recovered from it, and then I'd played it down. Now I said that I was completely well, that everybody was just fine and dandy. I said that Paulie and I were thinking of going to Paris next spring, as an anniversary present to ourselves. My mother never asked to speak to her, so that was no problem. At first, it felt sort of good pretending that nothing terrible had happened—I almost believed it myself—but once I hung up and began making supper, I felt worse than ever.

I wasn't sleepy, but I went to bed early that night, like an invalid, the way I did those first weeks home from the hospital. The bed was getting as messy as the kitchen table. It was easier to just leave things scattered there—magazines, snacks, my Walkman and tapes. I looked at the telephone, willing it to ring, and when it didn't, I put my earphones on, blasting Miles and Coltrane inside my head until I fell asleep.

The next day, when I came home from work, I noticed right away that something about the house was different. I realized it was the smell, or smells—of cooking, of furniture polish. I rushed into the kitchen, with Shadow wagging around my legs, almost tripping me. "Paulie?" I yelled, and the name rose and died in the room. There was a cake in the very center of the table—everything else had been cleared away. The cake was angel food, the only kind I was allowed on my diet. The appliances all had a hard gleam; I could clearly see my own reflection in the glass oven door. After a while, I saw the note stuck to the refrigerator with one of the magnets. "Dearest Daddy," it said. "No little elves, just Lily and me. Speak to you soon. Love you, A." Annie and her housekeeper, putting things in order, making me feel even lousier than I had. I imagined La Rae remarking on what a sexist pig I was, expecting Paulie to not only crawl back to me but to clean up my mess besides. But that wasn't what I wanted.

The whole house had been cleaned, and there was something final about its tidiness, as if all evidence of our previous life here had been wiped and waxed away. I was reminded of the day Paulie left, when the kitchen had looked like the kitchens in model homes. Today, the bedroom seemed . . . *virginal*, with its fresh linens, everything tucked tightly in place. I lay across the bed, thinking that I would never fit in with the new breed of bachelors, that no matter what happened I would always be married in some deep, binding sense of the word. Then, when I wasn't even looking at it, the phone rang, and it was Paulie. I was so surprised my throat closed up. "Paulie," I croaked.

She was all business. "I just want you to know," she said, "that I'm coming by for some of my things tomorrow, around noon. And I don't want you to be there, Howard."

"I wouldn't get in your way," I said. "And I could help you pack."

"No, thank you. La Rae and Katherine are coming over to help me. We'll manage."

I knew they'd be there as much to keep me away as to help her. "Paulie," I said, "I'm trying to understand what happened, what Janine could have said to you."

"It doesn't really matter, Howard, and I don't want to discuss it. In fact—"

"How have you been?" I asked quickly.

"I'm okay," she said. Then, after a pause, "And you?"

"Could be worse," I said, "could be better. Oh, shit, Paulie, won't you even *talk* to me?"

"Why should I?"

"I don't know. Maybe it would lead to something. Look at Reagan and Gorbachev."

"Ha!" she said. "*You* look at them."

It began to seem a little more like a conversation, so I said, "I saw Jason, you know, and I spoke to him about Sara."

"What did he say?"

"I think I straightened him out."

"That's not what *I* heard," she said. "Maybe there's a genetic flaw."

I was going to ignore that and build my case about Jason, but instead I blurted, "Paulie, I never meant to screw us up like this!'' She didn't answer, and the silence was so heavy I thought she'd hung up. "Hello?" I shouted. "Paulie?"

"I'm here," she said, with that creepy new composure.

"Yeah, and I'm *here*," I said.

I would have been home the next day, despite Paulie's orders, if her friends weren't going to be there, too. I stayed away as long as I could, and when I finally did go home I was sick with suspense, as if I was just about to discover that Paulie was gone. And it actually was like that. I sensed the further emptiness even before I could bring myself to look in her closet. Her clothes were gone, but her smell— something like raisins—still lingered among the bare hangers, and I stood there breathing it in as if I needed it to live.

15

IT WAS DIFFICULT LIVING WITH SHERRY. SHE THRASHED around in her sleep and the sofa bed's foam mattress bounced like a trampoline. I ended up folded in half on her love seat most nights. I'd be stiff and cranky in the morning, and Sherry quickly matched her mood to mine. One small room was terribly confining for our disparate tastes and habits. She kept the blinds drawn, making the room seem even smaller and more confining, and if I opened them she squinted and threw her arm across her face, like Dracula surprised by sunrise. We got on each other's nerves, and were viciously polite in our efforts to deny it. "Excuse me . . . No, excuse *me*," we'd say as we bumped hips going in and out of the narrow bathroom.

Sherry watched an inordinate amount of television, and like Howard's last hospital roommate, she kept it on even when she wasn't actually watching it. Sometimes she read while the television was playing. "Could I please shut that off?" I'd ask, because I was trying to read, too, and couldn't concentrate, especially during the supercharged commercials. Sherry would say, "Why, of course, be my guest," and throw me a murderous glance. I had to remind myself that I *was* her guest, that it was truly generous of her to have taken me in in the first place. It was up to me to make concessions to her peculiar habits, to be grateful for every favor.

But we didn't even like the same foods. Howard and I had always eaten sensibly, or at least I had. When she was younger, Sherry had gone dangerously gaunt on a macrobiotic diet, and now she seemed to eat only overly rich ethnic dishes. One morning, I went to the market while she was at school, and brought home salad greens and fresh fruit. "Don't give me any of *that*," she said, with a little shudder of revulsion, as I tossed the salad that evening.

She left her answering machine on until she came home, and when I was in the apartment I heard the messages as they were being recorded. Almost all of her callers were men. "Sherry? Ralph here. I'm really glad you liked my picture. Why don't we get together this weekend?" . . . "Hi there, babycakes, this is the Lone Ranger—501-3420. The vibes are good for a meaningful relationship, so give me a call." One of them just sang a few bars of "I'm on Fire" at the sound of the tone and then hung up. Howard called several times, too, and when I heard his voice I stopped whatever I was doing and listened in miserable silence.

Sherry played back her tape every afternoon, scribbling numbers and names on a note pad. Finally she told me that most of her calls were the result of an ad she'd placed a few weeks before in the personals section of *The New York Review*, and she showed me a copy. "SWJF looking for a soul mate. Are you ready for a literate, luscious, liberal, lovable, lunatic Libra? I'm 38 years young in heart and body—who are you? Photo, please. NYR Box 365812." She's received over two hundred responses so far. Some of them were clearly unacceptable-raving anti-Semites and plain old garden-variety psychopaths. Three men sent nude photos of themselves; five requested the same from her. Another, whose letter was full of misspellings and food stains, claimed to be a noted surgeon who would give medical discounts to her family and friends. Sherry had answered several of the more reasonable letters and these telephone messages were in response to her replies.

"I think you're crazy, Sherry," I said. "How do you know who any of them really are?" Some of the photos she'd been sent looked like mug shots to me. I read a few of the other ads on the same page as hers. "Listen to this," I said. " 'Into good times, Dutch treat only.' That sounds like a euphemism for something sexual and weird. Maybe he wears wooden shoes to bed."

"Mmm, I *hope* so," Sherry said, and giggled.

"And this one. 'Tall, dynamic poet laureate.' Poet laureate of what—the Bronx?"

"Maybe just of his building," Sherry said. "Oh, Paulie, you haven't changed a bit. You're still so cautious, still such a little mouse."

I was shocked and offended. Was that the way Sherry saw me? Did other people? I'd always thought of myself as adventurous, even somewhat reckless. Hadn't I taken a tremendous chance on life twenty-five years before? But maybe I hadn't ventured much out of the safety zone since then. Safely married, safely suburban. Once it had seemed like a death-defying act, Howard and me dangling over the center ring without a net. But who was Sherry to be so condescending? A middle-aged woman sending out love notes in a bottle, like a starry-eyed adolescent. "Literate, luscious, liberal"—all that alliteration had a desperate ring to it. And she'd lied about her age; that struck me as both foolish and pitiful.

I simply had to get out of there—I had to find my own place. It wasn't that I hadn't tried. I'd taken Sherry's advice and looked for a sublet, but none of the ads I answered worked out. Either the rental period was too brief, or the rent was exorbitant, or the tenant wanted sleep-over privileges. One woman expected me to care for ten uncaged parrots, who shrieked their reciprocal alarm as soon as I walked into the room, and shook out a blizzard of feathers.

I began to worry about money, too. Of course I'd resigned from the Port Washington library, and there didn't appear to be any openings in the city system. The personnel people I managed to see all complained about government cutbacks. "We sure could use you," the woman in Sherry's neighborhood branch said, wistfully, "but we can't afford you." And she was talking about the minimum wage! An older man shelving books nearby looked at me with fear in his eyes, as if I were about to steal his daily bread. There was a big glass jar chained to the checkout desk, for contributions to the library, and I threw some change in on my way out.

I still had the income from my column, but I definitely needed to augment that with something else. I began to scan the want ads as well as the real-estate pages. By lying about my previous experience, I was able to get some freelance work, proofreading engineering abstracts for a professional journal.

During the day, I continued to look for an apartment and a more suitable, permanent job. At night, Sherry and I sat opposite one another at her table. She graded papers and I tried to make sense of unfamiliar technical terms, while the television competed shrilly for our attention. Whenever the phone rang, I'd listen carefully while Sherry answered it, my blue pencil poised over words like "gravimeters" or "electroplastic." I could tell instantly if Howard was on the line, by the belligerent and didactic way she spoke to him. "Yes, she is," she'd say. "But I believe I've already told you that

she doesn't want to talk to you." Didn't we learn that yesterday, class? When one of her mail-order men called, her
voice changed; it became syrupy and seductive, like a telephone solicitor's. She would wander into the bathroom with
the long-corded telephone, and ripples of affected laughter
filtered through the noise of the television.

I'd called my children from a pay phone the day after I
moved in with Sherry. Jason hardly seemed to react to my
news, as if he'd been expecting it all along. But then Sara
took the phone from him and murmured her surprise and
sympathy. I asked her how things were going between them,
and she whispered that everything was pretty much the same.
"Try and be patient. He'll come around," I said, although
I had no reason to believe that. When I asked her if she'd
told her parents yet about her pregnancy, there was a long,
troubled pause before she said that she had, and that they'd
decided to disown her. I was appalled, and bewildered—how
did you disown your own child? The instant I saw my new-
borns, even before the cord between us was severed, I knew
we were joined forever. I changed the subject, asking her
what hospital she intended to use, and she said she'd decided
to have the baby at home, and be attended by a midwife.

"Are you sure that's a good idea?" I asked.

"It's cheaper," she explained, "and a lot more natural."
I remembered my own months of training in a natural-
childbirth class, and then, during labor, yelling like a mad-
woman for gas, for anything to ease the astonishing pain. My
mother had warned me I'd do exactly that, and I was tempted
to pass the warning on to Sara, but I didn't.

"We have to take a course. Jason is supposed to be my
labor coach," she said disconsolately.

"When he was born," I said, "Howard was right there,
too, cheering us on. He said it was the most thrilling expe-

rience of his life.'' I didn't mention that he'd grown faint when I crowned, and had to put his head down between his knees.

Ann answered her phone in a grief-stricken voice. ''Mommy, you don't live at *home* anymore,'' she wailed, and I knew that Howard had gotten to her first.

''Well, neither do you,'' I said, but she didn't think that was a fair comparison.

Sara and Ann both invited me to stay with them, offers that touched and pleased me, even if they were totally unsuitable. Young people are resilient, I told myself; they would all weather this. The one I'd really dreaded dealing with, though, was my mother, and my worry was justified. She carried on as if I'd killed Howard, not just left him. ''How could you do it?'' she demanded. ''Such a sick man! Such a *wonderful* man.''

I couldn't help reminding her that she'd once passionately disapproved of him, and of us together. ''You and Dad didn't even want me to marry him, Mother, remember? You said he was bad news, you said he had bedroom eyes.''

''Spilled milk!'' my mother cried. ''Water over the bridge!''

''Well, there it is,'' I said, impervious to every mixed-up maxim.

''You'll be alone,'' my mother said.

''No, I won't. I have my friends, I have my family.''

''You'll be alone,'' she insisted, ''and it's no fun.''

Fun! It was a word outside her usual vocabulary. For the first time in a while, I thought about my mother's life, the daily rituals of housekeeping and television watching. Lately there'd been a rash of deaths among the elderly widows in her building. For all the fuss she made over less significant events, she remarked on those deaths with gentle and dignified acceptance. "We had a little excitement here today," she'd say, and that's how I learned of Mrs. Wasser's fatal stroke during a game of Rummy-O, and Mrs. Stein's quieter passing in her sleep. Maybe my mother feared that my separation from Howard was going to leave *her* more alone, her circle of family members diminished by one.

"Paulie darling," she said. "Listen to your mother. Have I ever lied to you?"

What an opportunity! But I let it pass. After all, I was using a pay phone on the corner of Second Avenue and Twenty-third Street. Cars and trucks were roaring past and the pedestrian traffic milled around me. My quarter was going to run out soon, anyway.

"If you love each other in your hearts," my mother said, "you can work the rest out. You have your whole lives to do it in. And life is short," she added, confounding her own argument.

The quarter dropped, and a bus that had stopped for a light began wheezing loudly. "My time is up!" I shouted. "I'm out of change, Ma, I'll call you!" And I hung up.

Two weeks later, I found a sublet. The building, a few blocks from the pay phone I'd used, had an elevator, a locked lobby door, and an intercom system. The three-room apartment was on the fifth floor, facing the front. It was noisy, but light, and seemed safer than the apartments in the back. The current tenants were a young engaged couple named Mary and Jim. Jim, who let me in, said that Mary had left a month before to start teaching in the English department of a small Midwestern college. They were sharing the position, and they had a one-year contract. "Maybe we'll even be renewed," Jim said, "but the year is definite." He was going to join her there as soon as the sublet was settled. I was lucky, he said, because their friend who'd agreed to take the place had changed his mind at the last minute.

The living room was modestly furnished. There was a cheap brown velvet sofa and matching love seat—the kind that are always advertised on buses—and a couple of shaky tables. But there were hundreds of books on built-in, floor-to-ceiling shelves. Jim was going to take some of them along, but he said I'd be free to read anything he left behind.

I wandered into the bedroom alone and immediately felt that I'd be able to sleep there. There was a peaceful aura that went beyond the modest decor, the slanting sunlight on the worn patchwork quilt. Although I didn't believe in ghosts, either malevolent or benign, I thought it had something to do with the happiness that had been experienced in that room. The first apartment Howard and I lived in had been vacated by a married couple who were splitting up. I used to sense a leftover sadness there that had to be dispelled by the prosperity of our own marriage.

"I'll take it," I said to Jim, back in the living room, imagining him gone and myself falling onto the bed among the pleasant disorder of pillows.

The last week with Sherry was easier; with the end in sight, we became more generous and more tolerant of one another. On my final night at her place, I saw her off on a date with someone who'd answered her ad—a guy with white socks and a Cro-Magnon forehead. He could have been a serial killer, for all I knew, but I blessed their evening like a fairy godmother. "Have fun!" I called gaily after them. As soon as their footsteps stopped echoing in the stairwell, I phoned Howard. It was something I knew I'd have to do eventually. A divorced woman I'd worked with at the library had told me that she and her ex-husband were great friends now, which wasn't ever possible during their marriage. They met for dinner regularly and talked on the phone all the time. I couldn't envision any such social ease between Howard and me. While I was dialing our number, my heart bumped and lurched, but I managed, somehow, to sound cool and efficient. Howard's voice was rusty, as if he hadn't used it in years. At first he played the game—he let me state my business, and we even exchanged a few superficial, civil remarks. Then, suddenly, he began begging me to talk to him. I knew that if we did really try to talk, I'd wail and scream and cry, and I couldn't afford to lose control like that. I couldn't stray the tiniest bit from my plan. I made Howard promise to stay away the next day, so I could pack my belongings in peace and privacy.

La Rae picked me up at the Port Washington station at noon. Katherine was going to meet us at the house later on. As we drove into the development, I had an unexpected and confusing flood of feeling. "Oh, I can't look," I said, covering my eyes. "I don't blame you," La Rae said. "It's pretty ugly, isn't it?"

Howard had kept his promise—his car wasn't parked on the street or in the garage. I noticed that the pin oak had started turning red while I was away, and the sugar maple near the front door almost seemed to be on fire.

I was surprised at how neat things were inside the house. It wasn't at all like Howard to be orderly on his own. Could *she* have been there? Or was this some new tactic of Howard's, his way of saying, *See, I can change if you'll only give me a chance*? Shadow was so delighted to see me he danced around in clumsy circles and squirted my ankles and shoes. I patted him, and then I hurried past the artifacts of my old life and began taking clothing from the closets and the drawers. Katherine showed up after a while, and the three of us worked steadily and with hardly any conversation. We filled three suitcases and then began stuffing things into the cartons La Rae had brought from the supermarket. We didn't bother with the tissue paper and plastic cleaners' bags I advised my readers to use when packing their clothes, to prevent creases.

I took my notebooks, my box of rejection slips, and some of the framed photographs from the dresser top. I hesitated and then threw in a few of our record albums—who was to say who they belonged to? I even took my favorite painting off the living-room wall, an impressionistic seascape we'd bought right from the artist on the beach in Montauk one summer. But it left a conspicuous square of lighter paint, so I put it back. Finally, we were finished, at least for now. I'd have to return sometime in the future, maybe after we'd sold the house, and go through the junk in the garage and the basement. I hugged the dog, crying a little.

We loaded both cars. I rode with Katherine because there was more room in her station wagon, and because she asked me to. When our little caravan started out, I looked behind me, forgetting what happened to Lot's wife, and I saw the house and the lawn and the trees rush away.

16

I DIDN'T TELL GIL ABOUT PAULIE AND ME UNTIL WE were in his basement den, warming up. He'd called the night before to say that his combo was meeting at his place and did I want to sit in. It was the first time we'd spoken to each other since that fiasco of a celebration dinner, although the women had been in touch. Sharon yelled in the background that she wanted to speak to Paulie when we were through. Neither Gil nor Sharon seemed to know what had happened, and that would have been the right moment to tell him. But it was too important to mention casually over the phone, and I was suddenly afraid I'd lose them both later, when everybody started choosing up sides. So I said that Paulie had gone to bed early (it was about eight o'clock), and that she'd call Sharon back the next day.

In the morning, I left a message about it for Paulie—it was only one more excuse to call her. She'd moved to her own place the week before and she had her own answering machine now. Her outgoing message was briefer than Sherry's. It simply said, "Please leave your name and number at the sound of the tone. Thanks." But it was clearly her voice, and I was haunted by the idea that I could hear it whenever I wanted to, merely by dialing her number. Sometimes I didn't say anything; I just listened and then hung up before the tone sounded. The machine probably registered the call, anyway, and I imagined she knew it was me calling and hanging up all the time. I worried that she'd think I was harassing her and that she'd get an unlisted number, so I began leaving messages, inventing reasons for calling her as I went along. *The New Yorker* was still coming to the house— was she going to give them an address change? Did she want me to send it on to her, or drop it off, in the meantime? And what about the running shoes she'd left in the hall closet? I seemed to have an adolescent fix on the telephone, but it was my only contact with Paulie, or at least with her voice. After a couple of days, I'd memorized the way she spoke those two sentences on the tape—precisely where the accents fell, and the little pause before she said "Thanks." I could lip-synch it with ease. I was like Gene Hackman in that movie, *The Conversation*, where he plays and replays the taped conversation of two lovers in order to uncover a murder plot. The fact that Paulie didn't identify herself seemed either impersonal or very intimate to me, according to my mood. And that last-minute, breathless "Thanks" could have come from her old need to be good and please everyone, or because she'd realized the lead-in on the tape was too long. I wondered why she was out so much, or if she was actually there and using the machine to avoid speaking to people, particularly me.

Gil had asked me to come over a little earlier than the others, and the moment Sharon left us alone down in the den, I spilled everything.

He said he couldn't believe it—he'd thought we were the only other happily married couple in America. "I don't know what to say, Howie," he said.

"That makes two of us," I said, opening my fake book on one of the stands.

"Do you think it would help if Sharon spoke to her?"

"No," I said. "Thanks a lot, Gil, but no thanks."

"I suppose she'd side with Paulie, anyway," Gil said. "Sharon is pretty hard-nosed about screwing around."

"I know it's none of my business, Gil, but didn't you ever . . ."

"You're right, it *is* none of your business," he said. "But no, I didn't. Not once in over thirty years, although I sure lusted in mah heart a lot, like President Jimmy. Do you think Ripley would want to write me up?"

"Well, that kills my theory about heart attacks being a kind of divine punishment."

"Unless they zap you for just thinking about it."

"Maybe you should have been hung for a lion instead of a lamb, then."

"Nah, I'm too chicken, I'm too lazy. I guess I'm actually monogamous," Gil said.

"In a crazy way, I am, too."

"Yeah, you sure picked a crazy way to be monogamous," Gil said.

We could hear the other men arriving upstairs. I blew a couple of scales, and then the melody of "No One Else but You."

"That's a cool sound you've got there, pal," Gil said, and he pumped his slide and came in a few bars later.

I *was* sounding good—maybe misery agreed with me. But I'd also been practicing every day since Paulie left. It was something to do, and it was another voice in the house. When I wasn't blowing my sax, I played tapes nonstop: mostly Miles and Ella and Billie. And I talked to the dog a lot, like some screwy old hermit. I began letting him into bed with me at night, the habit Paulie had broken him of when he was a puppy. He smelled pretty gamy and the bed was always covered with dog hairs, but his company was worth it. I'd begun to hate television, although it was a kind of drug. I still fell asleep with it on, and I still needed the lights on, too.

My social life hadn't picked up much, except for the invitation from Gil and one from Ann to come for dinner the following week. I went to work early in the morning—Mike was always surprised to see me there when he came in—and I stayed late. For a while he thought I was sleeping at the studio. We had a cot in the back, but I only catnapped on it now. It was where Janine and I had finally ended up that first time. I remember that it started rolling across the floor, and I had to put one foot down as a brake before we hit the wall.

Mike was sympathetic about Paulie's leaving, but he was confused by the whole thing. Marriage itself was a marvel and a mystery to him—something like the existence of God— and the breakup of a marriage was even more mysterious. I told him to tell me right away if Janine ever came looking for me. I had to know exactly what she'd said to Paulie, before I could adequately defend myself, and I wanted to settle things between Janine and me once and for all. She'd never returned my phone calls. I'd considered going to her house to speak to her, but I was afraid she'd take it as an overture of love, and I couldn't deal with another episode like the one at Bloomingdale's.

We'd been unusually busy at the studio, which gave me less time to think about everything else. There was a run on cassette duplications and voice-overs, and everybody on the Island seemed to want to make a demo. I was even able to get some back-up work for Jason's group. They came out to Hempstead in his guitarist's van, which had *Blood Pudding* painted on its side in dripping red letters. Sara was starting to show, and in case anyone missed it, she wore one of those oversized T-shirts that say *Baby* across the chest and have an arrow pointing downward. I couldn't imagine how they got any gigs—her pregnancy was such a bizarre note in their bizarre punk look. While they were tuning up, I noticed she had the same habit Paulie had when she was pregnant, of holding on to her belly with outspread hands, as if she was protecting it, or measuring it. I wondered if her scalp absorbed the pink stuff she used on her hair, and if it eventually got to the baby. Paulie used to worry about things like that in an almost obsessive way. It wasn't common knowledge then that drinking was bad for the fetus, but she didn't touch a drop for the nine months of either pregnancy. And she tried to get me to stop smoking the first time by insisting she heard a tiny, muffled cough whenever I lit up.

I got the fuzzy idea that Sara's pregnancy was the key to my reconciliation with Paulie. I wasn't sure how it would come about—she hadn't seemed very impressed by the pep talk I'd given Jason. Yet here he was, still by Sara's side. They weren't married yet, though. I suppose the example of people like Mick Jagger made him think he could take his own sweet time. His kid would be an usher at his wedding if he waited long enough. In the middle of one of their hard-driving numbers—something about guts or butts—it hit me that I had to get Jason and Sara married, that somehow that would bring Paulie back. Since she'd been gone, I'd felt like the youngest son in a fairy tale, the one who has to perform some heroic task to win the hand of the beautiful princess. Nothing I could come up with seemed heroic enough until I thought about getting Jason married. And I wasn't being totally selfish; it would be for his own good in the long run, and for the good of the family he'd started.

Paulie and I had both been very moved by Ann's wedding, despite the wild extravagance of the thing. That night we lay awake for a long time in each other's arms, recalling happy moments of her childhood. The circumstances would be different for Jason, but maybe they would work in our favor. Maybe his wedding would recall ours—the mad, makeshift rush of it—Paulie's borrowed, let-out wedding dress, my symbolic nosebleed just before the ceremony. But did Jason love Sara enough for a whole lifetime? It was hard to know, probably even for him.

My days had a new meaning and purpose, once I'd made the connection between his troubles and mine. I'd started my campaign that afternoon at the studio, when the three of us had a few minutes alone. I didn't beat around the bush; I came right out and asked them when they intended to get married. Jason blanched—there isn't a better word for the way his face lost its color. I might have just dipped him in a vat of bleach. On the other hand, Sara flamed up under her white makeup, reminding me again of her stage name. Marriage was obviously a touchy subject, and I tried to back off from my direct approach. "Well, it's something to think about," I said, and I put a paternal arm around each of them. Jason flinched away from me, and Sara leaned her surprising weight against my side in a return of affection. I kissed her temple. It was still damp from the exertion of their last number, and she exuded a nice perfume of sweaty girl and strawberry shampoo.

After they left, I began to map out a strategy that would bring Jason around and win Paulie back. The first thing I did was take a thousand dollars out of our money-market fund. It was an either/or joint account, so I didn't need Paulie's consent, but I was sure she would have given it if I'd asked. I mailed a check to Jason and Sara with a note saying that it was a gift, sent with our love to them both. It was too late for an abortion by then, so neither of them could mistake my intentions. I got one of Sara's cute little thank-you notes, and Jason called a couple of days later, sounding grateful and cautious. "Thanks a lot for the money, Dad," he said. "But what's the catch?" I told him there wasn't any, that I was just feeling generous. "And there's more where that came from," I added, dangling the green bait.

He didn't bite, though. I waited a week or so and then I called him. We talked about neutral things for a while, mostly work. Jason said he'd written a couple of new songs, that the money I'd sent had bought him the free time. That was my opening. I told him that he made me feel like a patron of the arts. Then I said I'd like to offer him some more financial aid, and that I had something really substantial in mind as a wedding gift. There was a silence, but I could hear him breathing. "What's going on, Dad?" he said at last. "Is this a bribe or something?"

"No, of course not," I said. "It's just that I want to make an investment, instead of throwing my money away. And I've decided to invest in your future."

"I can have a future without getting married," he said.

"True, true," I said, "but that doesn't look like such a hot investment to me."

"How about *your* marriage?" he said, going straight for the jugular, as usual.

"It's rocky right now," I admitted, getting a pained little snort from Jason. "But it's not over yet." When he didn't respond to that last statement, I said, "You love her, Jase, don't you?" A pretty belated consideration.

"Yes. Sure I do," Jason said. "I'm just not ready for any big moves."

"Jason," I said, "when your house is burning down around you, you can't say you're not ready to jump."

"My house isn't burning," he said. "Look, Dad, I guess I didn't understand the game plan. If you want the grand back, I'll try to get it somewhere."

"Forget it, that was a no-strings gift," I said. "Jasie, I know you feel pressured right now, and I don't want to add to that pressure. But you can't pretend Sara's not pregnant, or that you're not responsible. And you've got to do something about it. You've got to grow up sometime."

"I'm working things out," he said, the way he used to say that he was studying, with his stereo blasting and his eyes shut.

I decided to back off then, to give him room and time to think it over.

Now Gil's bass man and pianist were coming down the stairs. We shook hands and they set up. In a little while, after some false starts, we were jamming. I took a solo on "Sweet Lorraine," playing it legato and low at first, working up to double time on a middle register. The others stayed with me all the way, and then, without breaking, we moved right into "Satin Doll." The bass and piano player—a dentist and a computer salesman in real life—worked very well together. And Gil had a nice lyrical style that was reminiscent of Dorsey's; he did some fancy flourishes that heated us all up. I kept thinking that there was nothing else in the world like this, like making music—the consuming concentration it took, and the rich, instant reward it gave back. If only marriage worked like that.

17

I SHOULD HAVE KNOWN WHAT ANN WAS UP TO, BUT I
didn't. On the train to Larchmont, I only thought how nice
it would be to visit her and Spence, and to have someone
else cook dinner for a change. I'd forgotten Ann's stubborn
romanticism (''Now kiss Mommy'') and her inclination to
take charge.

There were no immediate clues. Spence met me at the
station, a good-looking, gangly boy leaning against his BMW
and waving. On the ride to the house, he was as he'd always
been—affectionate and polite. He managed to allude to my
new living arrangements without seeming to pry or pass
judgment. I thought how all that privilege hadn't destroyed
Spence's essential sweetness.

The imposing grandeur of their house always struck me
anew. It was a kind of miniature Tara, with a sweeping driveway and classical white columns. Inside, Ann glided down
the circular staircase to greet us. She was so fair and pretty,
a throwback to blond ancestors, probably, unless they'd given
us the wrong baby. We had cocktails in the living room, in
front of the fireplace, and I settled into the deep leather cush-
ions of the sofa. The last weeks hadn't been easy. My notion
that I could sleep well in Mary and Jim's bedroom was mis-

taken. I would doze off most nights and then wake startled, as if someone had touched me. Once I was fully awake, I'd realize how much I *needed* to be touched. And then I'd become aware of the unfamiliar room and all the strange noises from the other apartments and the street. I told myself I'd get used to them, as I'd get used to the roaches that sprang into a frenzied discotheque whenever I turned on the bathroom light. I was a city person, after all, although I'd been out of the city for almost half my life.

Howard had been driving me crazy, calling a few times every day. I thought about getting an unlisted number and decided that would be too isolating. What if I forgot to give it to someone I hoped to hear from? My friends were especially important to me now, and I had what seemed like a hotline connection to La Rae and Katherine. The day they helped me move, La Rae had snooped around, opening drawers and closets. "This is like baby-sitting," she said. "Do you remember looking in people's bedroom drawers when you were a kid?"

"Oh, yes," I said, "although I never really knew what I was looking for."

"The secret of life," La Rae said solemnly.

"Once I found a deck of pornographic cards in somebody's night table," I said. "I think I blushed for a month."

"*I* never did anything like that," Katherine said.

"Then how did you ever learn anything?" La Rae asked her.

Sherry dropped by on her way home from work sometimes, and we'd have dinner together or go to a movie. She tried to get me to go out with some of her surplus *NYR* men. Her own experiences with them had been varied, but mostly she'd just been bored. I wasn't interested in going out, especially with anyone like "Dutch Treat" or "Poet Laureate.'' I kept busy enough, proofreading the engineering abstracts and writing my column. Sometimes I played with some of the engineering terms, like ''avalanche oscillations,'' ''spin wave stiffness,'' and ''amorphous alloys,'' trying, without success, to make poems out of their imagined meanings.

Many of the letters to ''Paulie's Kitchen Korner'' seemed to be encoded cries for help with more serious matters. Women who wrote about carpet ants, and men asking what to do about wood rot in their beams, might have really been suffering deeper, human problems. Or maybe I was only projecting my own situation and feelings onto them.

The first hint I had of Ann's subterfuge was when I peeped into the dining room on my way to the powder room and saw that the table was set for four. ''Who else is coming?'' I asked with apprehension when I was back in the living room. Their immediate exchange of worried glances gave them away.

''Oh, God, I can't believe you did this to me, Ann,'' I said. ''When is the next train back to Manhattan, Spence?''

''I knew this would happen,'' Ann said, and at that moment the door chimes rang.

I could see right away that Howard hadn't been in on the plan. He was genuinely surprised to see me, and he seemed just as embarrassed as I was. When he'd recovered, he said, ''Hello, Paulie,'' and for some stupid reason we shook hands.

I was as civilized as anyone. ''Hello, Howard,'' I said. ''How are you?'' The Duchess of Windsor wouldn't have done better, greeting the Queen Mother. ''I didn't know about this,'' I told him, ''and I guess you didn't, either.''

''No,'' he said. ''I didn't. But I'm really glad to see you.''

''I don't think I'm going to stay,'' I said. ''Spence, did

you get a schedule?'' I asked, although he hadn't moved an inch since I'd come back into the room.

"Dinner is cooked already," Ann said. "Just stay for dinner." Now kiss Mommy.

Spence looked at his watch. "Well, you've missed the 7:25, anyway," he said.

We all stood there before the blazing fire, like characters in a drawing-room comedy, until Lily came to announce that dinner was being served. I gave in, even though I couldn't stand the flash of satisfaction in Ann's eyes. I would have to speak to her later, in private. I'd *murder* her. In the meantime, I went into the dining room with the others and let Spence seat me in the chair to the right of his. Howard was sitting opposite me, and every time I looked across the table, he was looking back, forcing me to drop my eyes. He appeared healthy in the brief glimpses I had of him, although he needed a haircut badly. I wondered if Lily knew what was going on, and who she sided with. But why should she even care about us—she probably had her own problems. Yet she had always seemed to prefer Howard. At least she smiled more often at him than she did at me. If she knew the whole story, I thought, she might find him less charming. I realized with dismay that *I* wanted Lily's sympathy, that I wanted everyone's. But Lily was impartial as she served our dinner. How long had Ann been planning this reunion? Except for the uncomfortable guests, everything was perfect, from the pale Belgian table linen to the artistically arranged baby vegetables. I'd once lamented to La Rae that my daughter was becoming a yuppie. "Maybe we'd be yuppies, too," La Rae said, consolingly, "if we were young and rich enough." But we both knew that wasn't true.

All that lovely food, and I wasn't very hungry. I noticed that Howard's appetite wasn't so terrific, either; he kept picking his fork up and putting it down again. And the conversation was stilted and strained. Everyone admired the poached salmon, which we hardly ate, until there was absolutely nothing left to say about it. Spence kept the wine flowing—a Château something or other—and he and Howard talked that to death, too. In one of the clumsier pauses, Howard said, ''Well, I guess I'll commit infanticide!'' and popped a whole tiny eggplant into his mouth. I was the only one who got it, and the others' bewildered laughter quickly died.

Ann was clearly miserable—her plan had backfired, and she had to bear witness to the disaster. If I hadn't been so angry, I might have felt sorry for her. Maybe I actually did feel a little sorry for her, for her innocent belief that ruined lives could be repaired by the grace of candlelight and good intentions. Poor little rich girl. Poor little everybody. I knew that I was drinking too much wine by how sleepy I was getting and the way my attention was flagging. God, they were talking about the *dessert* now. There's something so desperate about eating and talking about eating at the same time, as if there are hungers that can never be appeased.

I stood up, too abruptly, I guess, because the wine and water glasses wobbled and chimed. ''Excuse me,'' I said, and fled to the powder room. There was a Greek chorus of murmurs in my wake. I washed my hands and face with the almond-scented guest soap and then I sat down on the closed toilet seat to think. The awful thing was that I wished with all my heart that I could go home with Howard right then. Not in our present circumstances, of course. What I wished was that nothing bad had ever happened between us, not Marie, or Janine, or any of the various quarrels that lead to the failure of love. I knew it was a silly, regressive longing. But I remembered what it was like to ride away together after a party, into the privacy of the night.

When I went back inside, Ann was snuffing out the candles, and Lily and Spence were clearing away the last of the dishes. Howard leaned in the doorway, watching me walk toward him. "I'd like to drive you home, Paulie," he said. For a moment it seemed like an extension of my reverie in the powder room, but then I understood that he meant he would drive me to Manhattan, to my apartment.

"No thanks," I said. "It's a little out of your way."

"I don't mind, I'm wide awake," he said.

I wasn't—the wine had made me groggy, and it had softened my defenses, too. Otherwise, I would never had given him such an easy opening. I noticed that we were alone— Ann and Spence and Lily had disappeared. "Ann set us up, Howard," I said, "but we don't have to carry it any further."

"I want to carry it further," he said. "I'd carry it all the way to China if I had to."

"Well, you don't have to. I'm going to take the train back to the city."

"Do you want a divorce?" he said.

The word was astonishing, spoken aloud like that when I wasn't prepared for it. "Right now I just want some peace," I said. "I want you to leave me alone. No phone calls, no ruses."

"We'll have to talk sometime . . . about money, for instance, and about the children."

"Yes, all right, but not about magazines or running shoes, please."

"Do you need any money?"

I did need money. Living in the city was more expensive than I'd realized, even though my rent was pretty reasonable. I'd taken on more proofreading work than I could really handle; when I shut my eyes, rows of black print continued to move behind them. But I didn't want Howard's patronage. I didn't want him to think he could control me this way. "Yes, I do," I said. "Half of the money-market interest will do for now. We'll discuss the house and car, dividing everything up, some other time, when we're ready to talk about it."

"Okay, that's fine with me. Have you spoken to Jason and Sara lately?"

"To Sara, mostly. She's forging ahead, like I did. And Jason is being a lot like you."

"That's not fair," Howard said. "I wanted to marry you, I *did* marry you, once I got used to the idea."

"I don't think you ever got used to it."

"Paulie, what did Janine say to you? Please just tell me that."

"Oh, the usual. How *conflicted* you are about us, how she comforted you in the hospital." I clasped my hands tightly together at my waist, to keep from wringing them.

"Jesus! She just showed up there, I swear it. And I told her it was over. It *was* over."

"Were you afraid of dying in the act, Howard? Or were you just afraid of dying for your sins?"

"I can't talk to you when you're like this," he said.

"It wasn't my idea to talk in the first place," I said, and I turned and walked away from him. "Ann!" I called. "I'm ready to go!" She and Spence came into the room at once, as if they'd been waiting together in the wings for their cue. "Would you check the trains for me now, please, Spence," I said.

They exchanged further stricken glances. "It's late, Mom," Spence said. "I'll drive you back."

"No, no," I said. "The train will be fine. And I'll get a cab from Grand Central. Ann, why don't you drive me to the station?"

"I can do that much," Howard said. "It's not even out of my way."

"Oh, all right," I said, surprising everyone, especially myself.

Ann looked relieved—her hope rekindled and her own execution stayed. Spence came up with a timetable at last. "You have about fifteen minutes till the 10:25," he said.

It was chilly out; the wind shivered through the trees and I hugged myself. Howard opened the car door for me. Before he came around to the driver's side, I had leaned across the seat, out of habit, and unlocked his door. When he pulled the door shut behind him, the automatic roof light slowly dimmed, until I could barely make out his face.

"Well, here we are," he said. "Sort of back where we started."

"Have you been smoking?" I asked. The whole car stank of it.

"Once in a while," he said.

I opened the ashtray and it was filled with butts.

"Less than a pack a day," he said.

"Oh, Howard."

"I can't give up everything at once, can I?" he said.

"A dish of vinegar left overnight on the dashboard will absorb the odor," I said.

"Thanks for the hot tip," Howard said, "but that's not my main problem."

I tried to read my watch. "We'd better get going," I said. "I don't want to miss my train."

There were only a few other cars at the station, their motors humming. I hoped the train would be on time, that we wouldn't have to extend this awkwardness.

Howard kept his motor on, too, and he slipped a tape into

the deck: Bobby Hackett playing "Moonlight Becomes You."

"Wanna dance?" he said.

I opened my window and leaned out to look for the train. The couple in the next car were fused together in an embrace. I pulled my head in and rolled up the window. "I'm going to kill that Ann," I said. I looked at Howard and his eyes were dark with resolution. Then he leaned over and kissed me on the mouth, tenderly, without force, without even using his hands, and I kissed him back. It was a brief and potent kiss. Neither of us heard the train over the Hackett tape until it was in the station, and I had to run for it.

18

*A*FTER HIS NURSE TOOK SOME BLOOD FROM MY ARM, Dr. Croyden listened to my chest for a long time. "Sounds pretty good in there," he said. "How have you been feeling?"

"Not bad," I said. "Fine, really," I knew that the occasional heaviness around my heart was emotional, not physical. It came and went with my optimism, with how I assessed my chances of getting back together with Paulie. Seeing her at Ann's the other night had made me feel lousier in a way, and yet more hopeful, too. I must have replayed that kiss at the station a million times. She'd kissed me back—I was certain of that—but I'd been the aggressor, the needier one. I supposed there was a kind of poetic justice in my wanting her as desperately as she had once wanted me. But God knows none of this was any of Croyden's business. "Fine," I said again.

His nurse set me up for an EKG, and Croyden read the long sheets with satisfied grunts. He told me to get dressed and meet him in his consultation room. I had to wait there about five minutes before he showed up, and I spent the time reading his diplomas and looking at the framed photos of his wife and kids on the desk.

"Watching your diet, Mr. Flax?" Croyden asked as he walked in. It was like being given a pop quiz as a punishment for goofing off.

I turned my gaze back to the diplomas. "Sure," I said, although that wasn't exactly true. It was a lot easier to pan-broil a steak than to prepare salads and pasta. I trimmed off most of the fat, as a compromise, and used margarine to fry the onions, instead of butter.

Croyden sat down behind the desk and began reading my chart. "Not smoking, are you?" he said, without looking up.

"Uh-uh," I said, to the top of his head. Actually, I'd worked it out to odd-and-even smoking days, and I was using brands I didn't really enjoy, to help me cut down.

"Getting enough mild exercise?"

"Uh-huh."

"Good," he said, and his wife seemed to smile her approval at me, too. He wrote something on the chart and then he looked up and held me with his eyes. "I want to give you a stress test about a month from now."

"Like the one at the hospital?" I asked. That had taken place right before I was released. It wasn't too bad, as I remembered it—just climbing up and down a couple of steps a few times. And I'd passed with flying colors.

"Oh, no, this one's much more strenuous," Croyden said. "It separates the men from the boys."

"Maybe I'm not ready." I said. "Maybe I'm still one of the boys."

"I thought you said you were feeling fine."

"I did. I am," I said. "But, hell, I don't think I need any more stress right now. I've had plenty of it lately, and look, I've come through it all right."

"That's fine, but not very scientific," Croyden said. "Miss

Green will set up the appointment, and I'll see you in a month. Try to keep any other stress to a minimum until then.''

Easy for him to say, with his family in their proper places on his desk and in his life. I left his office and walked briskly around the parking lot, partly for the exercise, and so I wouldn't be tempted to have a cigarette. The Virginia Slims were on the dash of my car, where I'd deliberately left them. I hadn't expected Croyden to frisk me and find them, but I was worried that they'd fall out of my jacket, and I didn't need the lecture that would have followed. Although he might have merely shrugged and said, ''It's your funeral,'' the way Gil did that night at the restaurant.

After our jam session at his house, I'd told him that my father had been a funeral director, and that I figured I might as well live, since I couldn't get a break on the rates anymore. He didn't laugh. ''That's no joke, Howie,'' he said. ''Do you know what those things cost these days?''

''What, funerals? No, I haven't been pricing them lately.''

''Well, I have,'' he said. ''And you can't get away with less than three or four thousand.''

''You mean you can't get away *for* less,'' I said.

''And that's with a pine box you wouldn't use for kindling.''

''Hey, you're really serious about this, aren't you?'' I said.

''I sure am. I've told Sharon that I want mine short and sweet. And simple.''

''You mean cremation?''

''No, I don't like the idea of that—I'll burn enough in hell, probably. I don't like the idea of burial, either, to tell you the truth. But I'm mainly concerned with keeping the costs down, and leaving more for the living.''

I saw the lid slam shut on the light, heard the thunder of

dirt overhead. "Boy, this conversation is really making my day," I said.

"You think not talking about it makes it go away?"

I knew better than that, yet I'd always tried to avoid the subject. Visiting my father at work when I was a kid hadn't helped me get used to death. If anything, it created an earlier than usual anxiety that never went away. There was an old man named Pete who worked as a handyman at the funeral home. He looked half dead himself, but he was full of sick, morbid jokes, and I think he got off on scaring the shit out of little kids. Once, when my father wasn't around, Pete took me into the back room, which was off-limits to me, and he lifted the lid on a corpse. He shut it again right away, but that wasted, waxen image was indelibly printed on the back of my eye. I could call it up anytime I wanted to, and it simply appeared, unwanted, plenty of other times. I couldn't say whether there'd been a man or a woman in the coffin, and maybe that was the worst part—that you became an "it" after you died, a nameless, genderless nobody.

Years later, soon after Jason was born, I decided to buy some extra life insurance. I'd only had the ten grand from the V.A. until then, and I wanted to make sure Jason could go to college someday, and even on to medical or law school. But talking about it with the insurance salesman, who was a musician buddy of mine in his other life, made me feel rotten. It wasn't only the contemplation of the worst, of the inevitable—I even hated the language. Term. Straight life. Beneficiary. Manny kept saying, "If anything should happen to you . . ." and his eyes never met mine. After he left, I paced around the apartment like a caged animal. Paulie kept begging me to come to bed and forget about it. Of course, lying in the dark, with the clock ticking away near my ear and Pete's nameless corpse between us in the bed, didn't help. I loved my family and I wanted to protect them—it was just that thinking about it in such concrete terms really got me down. In the middle of the night, Paulie put her arms around me and whispered that she wouldn't ever let me die. Now maybe I'd have to do it all alone.

Gil told me he'd included instructions for his funeral in his new will. Sharon had revised hers, too, and the lawyer was coming over one evening soon for their signatures. Paulie and I had never gotten around to making out wills. I knew this was my fault—I'd invented a different excuse every time she brought it up. "What's the hurry?" I used to say. "Have you got a contract out on me or something?" Then, later, I'd remind her that everything was in both our names, anyway, and the kids were our automatic heirs, so what difference did it make? After a while, she simply gave up.

Gil asked if I'd witness the signing of their wills. "I'd ask Paulie, too," he said, "but I don't think she'd come."

"It would be like the ultimate bad blind date," I told him. "But I'll do the honors, if you want me to." One more evening spoken for, I thought. I had to be hitting rock bottom, accepting an invitation I would have fled from a few months ago, and then thinking about it as a kind of social engagement.

The will signing took place a few days after my physical. That entire day at the studio I was obsessed with thoughts of death and dying, and I felt uneasy about having lied to Croyden about everything. I'd been relieved to get away with it, at first, but now I worried that the tests couldn't be valid if they hadn't caught me out. To calm down and to keep myself from smoking, I took a couple of Mike's Valium before I left the studio.

Gil and Sharon's place seemed different to me this time. It wasn't particularly cloudy or foggy out, but I'd swear the house was shrouded in gloom as I drove up. The lawyer was there already. His car was in their driveway, behind Gil's Toyota, as if to block their escape. Sharon let me in. Gil was sitting in the living room with the lawyer and a gray-haired woman in a bathrobe, and he jumped up when he saw me. "Howard, glad you could make it," he said. "This is Don Berger, our attorney, and this is our neighbor, Mrs. Haskell. Rita, Don, this is Howard Flax." We shook hands all around and Mrs. Haskell sat down again, holding her robe closed over her knees. "You'll have to forgive my appearance," she said. "The truth is that Harry, my husband, was supposed to do this and he's not home from work yet. You know the traffic. You know the Expressway at this hour. Sharon caught me in the bathtub, and I came right over, dressed like this. I guess there's no *law* against it," she said, darting a glance at Berger, who didn't give anything away.

I was feeling pretty mellow from the Valium, and I had the giddy thought that if anyone wanted to contest the will, they could argue that it had been witnessed by a man on drugs and a woman in a bathrobe. I smiled to myself, and Sharon, who hadn't been acting very friendly toward me, said, "Is something funny, Howard?"

Her cold appraisal sobered me up fast. It reminded me of all the other things wrong with my life besides mortality. "No, not really," I said, and I dropped into one of the chairs.

The lawyer cleared his throat as soon as everyone was seated. "Thank you all for being here," he said. "This won't take very long. Gil? Mr. Danzer? Have you read this will?"

"I have," Gil said.

"And do you find that it's fully in accordance with your wishes?"

"I do," Gil said.

"Then please sign here," the lawyer instructed.

Mrs. Haskell and I each signed the will after Gil did, and then we went through the same rigamarole with Sharon. It was like a wedding, in a way—the "I do's," and the solemnity of the occasion. There was even a small reception afterward; Sharon brought in a pot of coffee and a platter of cake. Berger became less formal and more expansive once the legalities were over. He told us about a "floozie" clause that some of his married female clients were insisting on in their wills. He said it protected the children's inheritance, in case the grieving husband was grabbed up by some little gold digger before his wife was cold in the ground. Sharon cast me a meaningful look and clattered her cup against its saucer. Mrs. Haskell, who was beginning to look casually elegant, told the old joke about the woman who has her portrait painted wearing nonexistent furs and jewels so that her husband's second wife will go crazy looking for them. We all laughed politely. When the chatter died down, I found myself searching for something to say to extend the evening. It wasn't that I was having such a good time, but that I wasn't ready to go home by myself yet. The Valium was probably wearing off, and I was being overtaken by a clear and terrible consciousness. "How about some music?" I asked Gil, indicating the stereo, but Berger looked at his watch and said he had to be going. As soon as he left, Sharon began gathering up the coffee things and Mrs. Haskell yawned, as if Berger had been the life of the party and it was fizzling out fast without him. "I guess I'll be on my way, too," I said, and nobody argued with me. "May I walk you home, Mrs. Haskell?" I asked.

We cut across the lawn toward her house, which was lit by a blaze of lights. "Oh, Harry's home!" she cried, her voice so rich with pleasure it hurt my chest.

19

*O*NE MORNING, WHILE I WAS EXAMINING MY BREASTS
in the shower, I burst into tears. I hadn't found anything to
worry about, but touching my own soapy flesh that way reminded me of the time I did. It had happened ten years before, on the Friday afternoon before Labor Day. Howard was
outside, working in the garden, and I was taking a shower
then, too. The kids were both somewhere else. I wasn't even
looking for anything that day, just soaping myself and singing, when I felt a pea-sized thickening in my left breast. I
realized at once that I'd been happy for a long time, without
really thinking about it, and I stopped singing in mid-song,
regretting such careless, unguarded happiness. The water
drummed down on my head while my fingers went back
again and again to explore the same place. The thing was
there every time, and I started shivering in the hot, steamy
bathroom. I shut off the water and dried myself hastily. Still
damp, and still wrapped in the towel, I went to the kitchen
window and called Howard to come inside for a minute.

"Do you feel something here?" I asked him, lowering the
towel and putting his grimy hand on the suspect breast. I
watched his look of pleased expectation fade to a worried
frown. He couldn't find the lump right away, but I knew

when he did by the way his fingers suddenly stopped their search, and by the awful stillness in the kitchen. "Jesus," he said, "I don't know, babe. It's so tiny—maybe it's supposed to be there. Maybe it's always been there and we just didn't notice it." I told him that I examined myself every couple of months and I'd never felt anything like it before. Then we both saw that he'd left muddy fingerprints on my breast and shoulder, and he wet some paper towels and wiped them away.

We tried calling our family doctor, my gynecologist, and even the dermatologist husband of one of Howard's cousins. Everyone had left town for the long weekend. Howard asked if I wanted to go to the emergency room at the hospital, and I had to smile at that. "It's not exactly an emergency," I said. "I guess we'll just have to wait."

He was wonderful during the waiting, staying close by in an attentive, almost maternal way. We'd decided not to say anything to the children until there was something definite to tell them. They sensed the tension in the household, though. Jason cornered me in the back yard after supper and said, "Are you and him fighting?" Ever since Howard's flight with Marie, when Jason was four, he was on the alert for serious trouble between us. Our voices raised in anger could always bring him from the hideout of his room. I assured him that Howard and I weren't fighting, and he regarded me with dark, doubting eyes before he slunk off.

Ann had been a baby when Howard left us, but she had a built-in detector for domestic conflict, just as she had for our sexual activity. She was twelve years old when I discovered the lump in my breast. Her own breasts were still dormant then, but ready to bloom, and she was horribly pre-adolescent. She moped around Howard a lot, desperately in love with the idea of love. Everything she said was punctuated by a whinnying laugh I prayed she'd outgrow. That weekend she seemed particularly unstable, and her high-pitched laughter resounded in every room of the house. I felt a deep, aching pity for both of my children, as if they were already motherless, way before anyone else could possibly find them lovable.

Howard was a nervous wreck, but he rallied to give me sympathy and encouragement. He gathered evidence in my favor: that I'd nursed the children, that there was no family history of breast cancer, that he loved me madly.

"But what if it's the worst," I said, "and I have to lose my breast?"

"I'll love you just as much, babe," Howard said. "I'll love you even more."

I became furious. "That's a stupid, sexist remark!" I hissed.

Howard looked bewildered.

"We're not talking about how *you'll* feel," I said. "We're talking about *me*, about *my* body. I'll be lopsided!" I wailed.

"Then we'll put a matchbook under your foot," Howard said, making me laugh and cry at the same time.

When I couldn't fall asleep, he rubbed my back until his hands must have become numb. He kissed my breasts—for luck, he said—and it was more of a blessing than a sexual gesture. We did make love, though, several times, and with life-affirming urgency.

The suspense continued way past the weekend. On Tuesday my gynecologist examined me and ordered a mammogram. He and the radiologist disagreed on their reading of it, and by Friday I had an appointment for Monday with a breast specialist. We went through the second weekend even more terrified than we'd been during the first one. And the following week there was the biopsy and the anxiety of wait-

ing for that report. Howard and I were in the kitchen together
when the doctor called and said that the lump had been completely benign. Oh, what a benign and lovely word! I stood
there, stunned by the charge of restored happiness. "See?"
Howard shouted. "Didn't I tell you?" He was crying and
wiping his eyes with a dish towel. I remember that Jason
came out of his room again to see if we were fighting.

Since then I've only examined my breasts on Mondays,
and it was a Monday in early November when I began weeping in Mary and Jim's shower, and couldn't stop for a long
time. I wept for my lost marriage, the way my mother had
for hers at my father's funeral, with earnest, noisy grief that
bounced and echoed around the tile walls. I felt better when
I was done, relieved of some of memory's burden. While I
was getting dressed, I started humming tunelessly, and when
I went downstairs to do my marketing, I walked with a pur-
poseful stride. For the first time since I'd been living in the
city, I bought enough groceries for more than one day's
meals. And I bought freezer paper and Tabasco sauce and a
thrifty, jumbo-size box of laundry detergent. Later that day,
after a few hours of proofreading, I put one of my notebooks
into my purse and went to the Forty-second Street library.
I'd taken to writing there, at one of the individual study desks.
It was quiet, but not isolated. Other people wrote and studied
at the other desks, and the scratching pens and rustling pages
comforted and inspired me.

I wasn't writing whole poems yet, only jotting down words
and phrases—mostly impressions of the city. It had been a
long time since I'd written anything but my column, and I
felt a little timid, but hopeful. I'd been sitting there thinking
and scribbling for about fifteen minutes when someone came
up behind me and said, "I've been wondering what happened to you."

It was Bernie Rusten. I hadn't seen him since my last day at the Port Washington library, and I blushed now, as if he'd caught me in some illicit act. "Well, I've moved," I said, closing my notebook. "I live in Manhattan now."

"How is your husband doing?" he asked.

"He's better," I said. "But we're separated." I didn't know why I'd felt the need to blurt this fact. Maybe it was habit—I used to see Bernie nearly every week in Port Washington, and I'd given him news briefs of our lives before.

"Then he can't really be better," Bernie said. "Not better off, anyway."

"But *I* am," I said boldly.

"Yes, you look very well," he said, but it wasn't a medical appraisal. His gaze was acute and full of implication, and I had to glance away, as if to resist a spell. The woman at the neighboring desk was glaring at us for talking.

"What are *you* doing here?" I whispered, changing the subject.

"The usual," he whispered back. "Looking things up. They sure have a better selection than Port Washington. But am I interrupting you?"

"No, no," I said, and as if to prove it, I shoved my notebook and pen back into my purse.

"Then let's go someplace for coffee."

"Yes, let's!" I said, with so much enthusiasm he laughed, and the woman at the other desk said, "Shhh!"

We ended up in a booth at a Sixth Avenue bar, drinking beer, and I told him pretty nearly everything. He had that quality some doctors have, no matter what their specialty, that invites confession and intimacy. But at least it was reciprocal. He told me things about himself I hadn't known. I found out that his wife, Ellen, had been his college sweetheart, at Cornell, and had been forty-four when she died.

She was driving home alone from work when the accident happened; the other driver had been drinking and ran a stop sign. Ellen was a marine biologist, he said, and they'd never had any children. He told me that, right after they got married and he opened his first office, she'd sit in his waiting room sometimes, reading, to make his practice look more prosperous. He took off his glasses as he said that, and the focus of his blue eyes softened. It allowed me to look directly at him for the first time that day. I had a sudden, jarring vision of him in a white lab coat, of myself behind a screen, undressing. "Do you have a busy practice now?" I asked.

"Yes, but I'm part of a group," he said. "There are four of us, and we rotate duty. How about you? What were you writing before, in the library?"

"Nothing," I said. "I used to write poems when I was younger. I'm fooling around with that again, but I'm not getting very far."

"It's funny, but I've always thought of you as a writer," he said.

That gave me an odd sensation, as if he'd said something amorous. "Probably because we met in a library," I said. "You remind me of a writer, too, you know. Of William Carlos Williams."

He looked pleased. "The Paterson doctor," he said. "I read him, on your advice. I liked the stories a lot, and the poems, too, especially the later ones."

"I can never eat a plum without thinking of him," I said, and that, too, seemed like a confession, and to have a double meaning.

He put his glasses back on and said, "Paulie . . . Is that short for Pauline? Or Paulette?"

"Paulette."

"It's a pretty name," he said. "Your father must have had a crush on Paulette Goddard."

"No, actually, I think my mother did. But nobody ever calls me that. Everybody says Paulie," I said, remembering Howard saying it.

"Paulette suits you better."

I pretended that wasn't such a personal remark. "My mother claims I almost killed her, being born," I said, "and she never had any other children. I think that's why she really picked that name—you know, the female version of a masculine one?—to cover all bases. Most people hate their own names, don't they?" God, I was jabbering like an idiot.

"Yeah, I guess so. I never liked mine much. It's Bernhard, with an 'h.' "

"I know," I said, "from your library card."

"A few of my friends call me Rusty."

"But Bernie suits you better," I said, amazed that I'd done it, that I'd completed the overture to courtship he'd begun. We sat there without speaking for a while, and then I said, "Well, this is nice, isn't it," just to say something, to break the hush of sexual tension.

"It is," he agreed. "It just proves that it pays to hang around libraries."

"Do you ever do anything with all your research?" I asked. "I mean, are you writing something?"

"No," he said. "Should I be?"

"Maybe," I said.

"Would you help me if I did?"

"Oh, I'm not a writer," I said. "Not that kind, anyway." And we fell into another loaded silence in the crowded, noisy bar. "I'd better go," I said. "There are things I have to do," although I couldn't think of a single one at that moment.

He took my hand and the little current of pleasure I'd

dreaded and longed for quivered through me. Did he feel it, too? And could he feel my rampant pulse? We both stood, still connected by our hands. "Good-bye," I said helplessly. "This was really lovely."

"I'm going to call you," he said. "Is your number listed?"

"Yes, with Information. It's not in the book yet, though." And I took my hand back and walked away.

20

IT WAS MY DAY OFF FROM THE STUDIO, AND I'D PLANNED
to hang around the house and do some yard work, blow my
sax a little, and just relax. But I couldn't stay with anything
very long, even lying in bed and listening to music. I realized
that I was talking to the dog more than usual, which wasn't
very different from talking to myself. "Want to hear a little
Bix?" I asked him in the middle of the morning. "Or are
you more in the mood for Coltrane?" Later, I said, "What
should we have for lunch, boy? Something healthy or something good?" Shadow didn't answer, of course. But he made
three heroic attempts to get onto the bed with me—I guess
arthritis was slowing him down—and I hoisted him up and
continued our one-sided conversation "It sure is boring
around here," I said. "It's a dog's life, isn't it?" I knew it
wasn't exactly boredom I was feeling, but the kind of restless
anxiety I'd had years ago right after I'd bought the extra life
insurance. This time it probably had something to do with
witnessing Gil's and Sharon's wills, with the fact that death
didn't get more attractive just because you weren't particularly enjoying life.

I ended up back in bed with a two-sandwich lunch: peanut
butter on whole wheat and pastrami on a roll, as a compro-

mise between healthy and good. And I compromised further by eating only half of each and feeding the rest to Shadow. I wasn't that hungry, anyway. "What do you say we go for a ride?" I said.

Shadow's ears pricked up, and he struggled to get his footing on the rumpled quilt. This was language he understood: the words "ride" or "walk," the jingling of his chain lead or the sound of the garage door lifting.

In the car he sat erectly beside me, like a navigator, although he didn't give a damn where we went as long as we were rolling. At that moment, neither did I. I drove through the development and down to Northern Boulevard, where I headed west for a few miles, and then made a U-turn and went east. The last time I drove around aimlessly like this, I was young and single, and cruising for action. Now it seemed pointless, as if I was only going in circles, and fifteen or twenty minutes later I was actually back in Port Washington, not very far from home. I pulled off onto a side road, in another development, and tried to decide what to do next. A woman in the house across the street peered through her curtains at me and then disappeared. A couple of minutes later a big, beefy-looking guy came out and walked over to the car. "You looking for somebody, buddy?" he said. He put his hand on the roof and I felt the car rock.

"No," I said. "I'm just a little lost. I'm trying to get my bearings." To back myself up, I took a map from the glove compartment and started opening it. I saw that it was a map of Jersey, and I crumpled it and jammed it back inside. "I guess I'll get going," I said. "I think I missed my turnoff at the last light."

"What street were you looking for?" he said, his hand like a sandbag on the roof, and without thinking I said "Sherwood Lane," my own street. Shit! If this guy got really worked up, the cops would be prowling my neighborhood later, and they'd probably have my plate number, too, from his wife. The curtains across the street had rippled a few times since he'd come out. Maybe he was a cop himself—and how the hell would I talk my way out of this? But he seemed to know Sherwood Lane, and he got much friendlier after I mentioned it. He began giving me complicated directions back to my own house, and I pretended to listen and memorize them—"Let's see, that was a right at the Exxon station, and then I go straight for two lights . . ." I thanked him, a little too heartily, and took off.

Jesus, being alone was dangerous. "That was a close call, Kemo Sabe," I said. "Maybe we should go to work and stay out of trouble." I was already heading toward Hempstead and the studio. I could give Mike a hand there, and if things slacked off, we could play a couple of hands of gin. Having plans, any plans at all, cheered me up somewhat, and the rest of the way there I whistled, and I didn't talk to Shadow or myself anymore.

I saw the Mazda as soon as I hit the street. It was parked directly in front of the studio, right behind Mike's Chevy. My first impulse was to floor the gas pedal and keep going. I was mad as hell about Janine's lies to Paulie, and I wanted an explanation, but she'd never returned my calls, and as time went by I got lulled into thinking it was just as well, that I didn't need the hassle of dealing with her on top of everything else. And I was too depressed by then to stay that angry. But there was unpleasant, unfinished business between Janine and me, and when I saw her car, I knew my life would never get straightened out until I took care of it.

I drove around for several minutes before I found a spot three blocks away. I parked, cracked one of the windows open for Shadow, and started running toward the studio, worried that I might have missed her. But the Mazda was still there. I popped a nitro and leaned against the wall, waiting to catch my breath. When I tried to open the studio door, I realized it was locked. My fist came up to knock, and then I lowered it and took out my keys. It was quiet inside, and the lights in the reception area and the control room were off. I was pretty quiet myself, but they must have heard me, because a few seconds later Mike came out from the back room, barefoot and tousled, and with his shirt unbuttoned. "What are you doing here, man?" he asked.

"I'm with the vice squad," I said dryly. "It's a raid."

"Listen, Flax—" he began.

"No, you listen to me. I thought we were running a business here. Is this all you have to do?"

"This is my coffee break, man," he said, running his hands through his mussed-up hair. "Hey, you know how it is." He laughed uneasily and glanced behind him.

"Sure, I like something sweet with my coffee, too."

"So maybe you could come back a little later . . ." he said.

"Mike, I know who you've got in there."

"Oh, shit," he said. "Look, we finished the demo this morning. You're the one who told me to finish the fucking demo for her, remember?"

Then Janine appeared in the doorway, fully dressed, which in her case was a kind of nakedness. "Hello, Howie," she said. "Fancy meeting you here."

I turned to Mike. "Take a walk for a while, okay?" I said. "I want to talk to Janine."

Mike gave her a rueful look, went into the back for his shoes, and left without saying anything. I locked the front door behind him. "Come here," I said to Janine, and she came slowly into the reception area. "Sit down," I said.

She hesitated and then she perched on the edge of one of the plastic chairs. I sat on another one, facing her, wondering how to begin.

"Well, we're even now, aren't we?" she said, with a kind of nervous defiance.

I stared at her, not comprehending. Then slowly it dawned on me. I'd gone back to my wife and she'd screwed my partner, and now we were supposed to be even. Those were pretty weird sexual politics, even for these days. And when it came down to it, we weren't even at all, because I'd lost my marriage in the deal. I shook my head, as if to clear it. "I don't give a damn about you and Mike," I said, which was or wasn't true, but it made her wince. "But why did you have to go to Paulie? You knew things were finished between you and me. Why the hell did you have to lie to her and kill my marriage, too?"

"Is that all it took to do that?" she said, holding her hands up in mock surprise.

"You know what I'm talking about. You know what you did," I said, but a sick, hot feeling was spreading through me. It wasn't her, it wasn't only her. Still, I said, "I'd like to kill you."

"Well, go ahead, if it will make you feel better," she said, and she bared her teeth in a terrible grin.

For some reason, I thought of her thin singing voice, the flamboyant, ambitious gestures she made when she sang. Then I had a sudden flash of her Hicksville kitchen, of her husband bouncing her off the counters, the refrigerator, the walls. I stood up, shakily, and walked out of the studio. Mike was on the corner, his shoes untied, pacing like an expectant father.

"We're not running a day-rate motel," I said. "Take her somewhere else the next time."

"Listen, man—" he began, but I walked quickly away from him, and he didn't follow me.

21

*T*HE DOWNSTAIRS BELL RANG, AND I PRESSED THE TALK button on the intercom. "Yes?" I said. There was the usual static, and then a man's voice I didn't recognize said, "Paulie?"

"Who is it, please?" I said, and the answer was garbled in more static—you could never get the super to fix anything around here. I wasn't expecting anybody. It was ten o'clock in the morning and I was in my bathrobe, typing up my column, sharing wisdom with a Wisconsin reader about childproofing electrical outlets.

There had been two robberies in our building the week before, and a tenants' movement against admitting strangers had been organized. "Who is it?" I said again, and again I couldn't understand the answer. My mailbox and doorbell both listed me as P. Flax. I decided that Paulie couldn't possibly be some stranger's lucky guess at my first name, so I pushed the buzzer that released the lock on the lobby door. After several minutes, I heard the sluggish elevator whine to my floor. I looked through the peephole, which gave me a convex view of the hallway, and I saw a distorted, diminished Frank Peters approaching rapidly. What was he doing here? Had something happened to Howard? To La Rae? My hands shook as I unbolted the door and then he was there, restored to life-size, and grinning.

I'd forgotten, in that moment of fear, that Frank had called me a week or two before. Just to say hello, he'd said at first, to find out how I was doing. He told me he'd seen Howard a few times, and that he seemed to be all right, too, although I hadn't asked. There was an awkward pause in the conversation then, the sort of pause I usually feel obliged to fill with nervous chatter. That time I kept quiet, and finally Frank said, "Paulie, I was wondering if you'd like to have lunch with me today."

"Why?" I blurted.

He laughed, a mirthless heh-heh. "Oh, for the usual reasons people have lunch," he said. "Because they're hungry. Because they want to get to know each other better."

"I know you about as well as I want to," I said, feeling sick-hearted and furious. "And I've just lost my appetite."

"Hey, Paulie, relax," he said. "It was only a friendly gesture."

"*La Rae* is my friend, Frank, remember?"

"All right," he said. "I'm sorry you took this the wrong way, Paulie. Take care of yourself now." And he hung up.

He had only come on to me once before, and that was in the long-ago past. It happened at a New Year's Eve party given by a couple named Shirley and Ed Benson, who lived near us in Port Washington and have since divorced and moved away. It was nearly midnight, and we'd all been drinking a heavily laced rum punch for about three hours. I remember that most of us were pretty high, and there was a great deal of hilarity and noise. The television set was on in the den and the hosts' two young children were stationed in front of it in their pajamas, blowing noisemakers in each other's faces. They were supposed to let us know the moment

the ball began falling on Times Square to mark the stroke of
midnight. I had to use the bathroom, and the one downstairs
was occupied. I raced upstairs to the other one, so I'd be
back in time to see the New Year in with Howard. No one
answered when I knocked on the closed door. I turned the
knob, just as Frank pulled the door open from the inside,
and I literally fell into his arms. I tried to back away from
him, but he held on to me and shoved me against one side
of the tile walls. "Hey!" I said, and Frank laughed and began kissing me in a wet, sloppy way and squeezing my
breasts. He smelled strongly of liquor and a sweetish after-
shave. "Hey!" I said again. "Stop it!" I beat on his chest
and tried to knee his groin, and he fell backward, rattling
against one of the glass shower doors.

That was all that happened. I got out of there while he was
still off-balance and I went back downstairs just as the ball
on Times Square hit bottom. Everybody was kissing and
calling "Happy New Year!" I could hear Guy Lombardo's
band playing "Auld Lang Syne," and the discordant bleating
of the children's horns. I felt forlorn and frightened, not because I thought Frank was chasing me, but because I'd drunk
too much and was suddenly alone in the midst of all that
revelry. Howard came out of the kitchen then and put his
arms around me.

I'd never told him or anyone else about what happened
upstairs. Neither Frank nor I acknowledged it when we saw
each other again, a week later, at another party. Maybe he'd
been too drunk to remember, and I pretended that I'd been,
too. Every New Year's Eve since then, no matter where I
was, the sensation of loneliness I'd had at the foot of the
Bensons' stairs came back to me on the stroke of midnight.
And whenever I saw Frank after that night, I felt uncomfort-

able, as if something more serious had happened between us.

Now here he was at my door, smiling broadly and saying, "Well, aren't you going to invite me in?" He was clearly sober this time, and not a messenger of bad news. Frank sold restaurant supplies, and he had that brash expression I'd seen on the faces of other salesmen, when they're certain you need their product. He looked handsome, in a slick, overgroomed way—the words "dapper" and "suave" came to mind. And he rocked on the balls of his feet as if he were trying to make himself taller. As we stood there, the woman who lived across the hall came out of her apartment. She pressed the elevator button and leaned against the wall, gazing at us with leisurely, open curiosity.

I beckoned Frank in and closed the door. "What do you want?" I said.

"Uh-oh," he said. "This can't be the hospitality suite."

"Frank, I'm working."

He went right past me into the living room, and sat down on the love seat. I had a whiff of that same after-shave as he went by. "In that getup?" he said.

I tightened the belt of my plaid bathrobe and folded my arms across my chest, thinking that I probably looked like Sherlock Holmes's landlady. But why should I care what I looked like? "I wasn't expecting company," I said coldly.

"I tried calling you earlier," Frank said, "but your line was busy. I knew I'd be in your neighborhood today—on business—and I wondered if you'd like to have that lunch with me."

"I'm busy," I said.

"That's too bad," he said. "Maybe another time. So, how have you been doing here, all by your lonesome?"

"I'm doing fine," I said.

"Howard seems to be making it on his own, too."

"So I hear. *And how is La Rae?*" I asked pointedly.

He looked amused. "La Rae's fine, thank you," he said. "Haven't you spoken to her lately?"

I had—that very morning, in fact—probably when Frank was trying to call me. I felt myself blushing, as if I'd betrayed her in some unaccountable way. "Yes, of course I have. Frank, you'd better go now. I really want to get back to work."

"All work and no play . . ." he said, wagging his finger, making no move to leave.

"Don't make me call the super," I said, thinking how impossible it was to ever find him.

"Ah, just as I remembered—you're even more attractive when you're angry."

It was a line right out of a stupid B movie, but I knew he was referring, for the first time, to what had happened in the Bensons' bathroom. He was given to confessing his past transgressions to La Rae; those confessions, and her forgiveness, were part of their peculiar arrangement. Had he ever said anything to her about that incident, altering the details to implicate me? "I'd hoped you were simply drunk that night, Frank," I said. "It was the only excuse I could find for your behavior, and I've never mentioned it to La Rae, or to Howard."

"Oh, I was smashed, all right, and you were just the wrong girl in the right place."

"What do you mean by that?"

"I mean you were supposed to be Shirley Benson. We had a date in that bathroom. It was all arranged."

Arranged by whom? Did he mean Ed was in on it, too? That was about the time that key swapping began in the suburbs, and I was shocked and even a little thrilled then by the rumors—a spectator on the sidelines of the sexual revolution. Now I tried to remember how Shirley Benson looked that particular night, what she wore, and if she had an aura I might have recognized. But all I could think of were those pajamaed kids tooting in the New Year, and myself standing alone at the foot of the stairs. "I don't want to hear any more about it, Frank," I said, in a voice I'd never used before. "And I want you out of here this minute." He sat there staring up at me, as if he was trying to gauge my true intentions. And I stared back with icy concentration until he had to glance away.

"Going, going, gone," he said, lifting himself from the love seat.

I marched to the door and opened it wide. My nosy neighbor stepped out of the elevator at the same moment and waved.

Frank reached into his pocket and took out a business card. "Call me sometime, if you change your mind," he said, trying to hand it to me. "If you need something for your kitchen . . . or your bathroom . . ."

I let the card flutter down between us to the floor, and I shut the door in his face. I opened a window and lit a few matches to get rid of his cloying smell. Then I went back to my typewriter and angrily banged out advice.

22

I REMEMBERED BASIC TRAINING AS BEING EASIER IN
some ways than the stress test; at least you didn't think you'd
die during it. I joked with Croyden's nurse while she shaved
patches of my chest and attached the electrodes. It was what
I always did when I was scared out of my wits. "I hope you're
keeping the line to the governor open," I said. I guessed
she'd heard it all before, because she shook her head and
gave me a long-suffering smile. Croyden came in with one
of his partners, and assured me they'd done this hundreds of
times and had never lost a patient. "Well, don't let me spoil
your record," I said. I told myself that they wouldn't put me
through anything I couldn't handle, or that they'd stop it as
soon as it looked as if I couldn't handle it. And if worse came
to worse, I had two board-certified cardiologists right there
to beat on my chest, the way they did to that guy on *Ben
Casey*. Still, I believed I was going into the valley of the
shadow.

The entire test was going to take place on a treadmill.
Croyden instructed me to walk naturally, as if I was actually
heading somewhere. He said that when they increased the
speed of the belt, I'd have to increase my speed, too, or I'd
be pitched backward into the wall. "Eventually," he said,

"you'll be going very fast, almost running. We want to see if the blood supply to your heart is adequate when you're really accelerating. Hold on to the bar for balance, if you have to."

"Miss Green will say 'Now!' when we're about to shut the machine off," his partner said. "As soon as it stops, get off and go to the cot and lie still."

This was the time to confess all my sins of diet and smoking, so that they'd postpone the test until I had another chance to get in shape for it. I could have told them I'd lost weight from grief and erratic eating, not from sensible living. That I'd chewed gum on the way there to kill my cigarette breath, that there was a whole carton of Merit Menthols in the glove compartment of my car right now. But I didn't say anything. I didn't even wisecrack about hanging a marathon number on my chest, or about having to run for my life. Nothing struck me very funny at that last, scary moment. Gil had gone through this the week before, and he'd had difficulties— they had to take him off it in the middle. He'd called me up afterward. "It was like blowing up a balloon," he said, "knowing it was going to burst if you didn't stop." His doctors wanted to put him back in the hospital and do a catheterization—Jesus, that wire from your groin to your heart! They'd even discussed the possibility of surgery. For once, Gil stopped being the trusting, obedient patient. He told them, "Hell, no, I won't go."

I climbed onto the treadmill and looked down. My belly had gotten trimmer, but not hard. I patted it and watched it ripple. I was wearing my old, worn-out Adidas and a pair of running shorts. Except for the electrodes, I could have been any middle-aged Sunday jogger.

"We're going to begin now, Mr. Flax," Dr. Croyden said, and the belt started moving under my feet. I moved with it.

I'd psyched myself up for this for days, and now I tried to remember what I'd planned to do to help me through it. For one thing, I let some music into my head—a nice slow version of "Walking My Baby Back Home." And I pictured myself heading toward something, as Croyden had suggested. I saw a long stretch of country road with a tiny figure in the distance. As the speed of the belt gradually increased, I strode more quickly toward the figure, making it seem closer and closer. I switched to livelier music—an old show tune called "I Know That You Know" that builds in energy and temp. The figure was Paulie, of course, and now I was walking faster and faster to get to her. *I know that you know that I know that you know* . . . The crazy thing was that she started walking faster, too, away from me. I wanted to yell, Hey, wait! My heart was the drumbeat of the music, loud and pounding in my chest and ears. I started running then and I had to grab the bar for balance. I was sweating bullets and panting—were they paying attention? You could drop dead on this thing, no matter what they said, and Paulie was nowhere in sight.

"Now!" the nurse said, and the belt slowed and then came to a stop. My feet moved a few more paces on their own, the soles tingling as if I'd just taken off a pair of roller skates.

"Get off!" Croyden commanded. "Hurry up and lie down!" I just stood there clutching the bar, my breath having, until the nurse grabbed my arm and pulled me toward the cot. I staggered like a drunk, the first bars of "I Know That You Know" still repeating in my brain.

"You can rest now," Croyden said. "Miss Green will check your pulse, and I'll speak to you when she's finished." He and his partner went out of the room.

Miss Green sat next to me for five or ten minutes, holding my wrist and looking at her watch. When I could speak again,

I said, "Maybe your watch stopped," earning another sour little smile.

Back in Croyden's consultation room, I braced myself for the worst, but he shuffled some papers and said, "The test results are average for a man your age who's had a coronary. You seem able to handle exertion pretty well, but I'd like to get your resting heart rate lowered. Maybe some additional moderate exercise will do it. Do you walk much?" I admitted that I didn't. "I'd recommend brisk walking," he said. "Start with half a mile each day and work your way up to two miles."

At first, I felt exhilarated. I'd passed, I was going to live! I started driving home—it was about four-thirty—and the traffic on the Expressway was murder. It took me fifteen minutes to get to the next exit. I decided to get off and go somewhere local for a drink until it eased up. There was a place on Roslyn Road I remembered passing, an Italian restaurant and bar.

It was much darker inside, as if night had suddenly fallen. There were a few other people at the bar, mostly men, watching a rerun of an old fight on television. I sat down and ordered an Amstel Light. I was still feeling pretty good about the test, and the atmosphere in the place was nice and relaxed. There was a low buzz of conversation around me, broken by ripples of laughter, and the TV flickered and hummed overhead. Maybe I'd stay here for supper, have some pasta or a hero. I could call Frank or Gil or somebody to meet me. Later we could go to Sonny's in Seaford, where some good sidemen were playing. I took my beer and went to the pay phone in the back. Nobody answered at Frank's, and Gil's line was busy. I went back to the bar and ordered a Scotch and soda. I noticed it had gotten a little noisier—more people had come in and someone had turned up the volume on the TV. One word from my consultation with Croyden that afternoon came into my head: "average." I couldn't remember the exact context, but he'd said something about my heart being average. Who the hell wanted to be average? Or to have to think about your heart at all? I was only fooling myself, anyway, with the cigarettes, with everything. My good mood was fading fast, the old doom and gloom descending. I was getting ready to split when the woman on the next bar stool leaned over and asked me for a light. I got a hit of a musky fragrance while I fumbled for matches, and when I managed to light one, her face was illuminated in the brief flare. She was young—in her late twenties, maybe—and she was dark-haired and very pretty. The smoke from her cigarette drifted toward me like a friendly signal.

"God, that smells good," I said, before she could turn away. She offered the pack, and I said, "No, thanks, I've given them up. Cold turkey, in fact."

"Oh? How long has it been?" she asked.

I looked at my watch. "About fifteen minutes," I said, and she laughed.

"Don't laugh," I told her. "It's been hell." She started to slide off her stool and I touched her wrist lightly and said, "Please don't go away. I need some moral support, and I can always inhale what you exhale."

We had supper together in the back room. She had a great appetite, almost purring as she chewed, and taking bits of food from my plate with her fingers. I thought of *Tom Jones*, of that orgy of eating, and I was pretty sure how this would end. Her name was Amy Kline and she worked as a computer programmer for an electronics firm. She said that she and a couple of her co-workers usually came here to celebrate the onset of the weekend. She'd whispered something to another woman at the bar after agreeing to have supper with me.

I told her I was divorced, when she asked, and that I was a jazz musician. These were only partial lies: one truth lay in the future, the other in the past. What difference did it make, anyway? This was going to be a casual encounter, and we only needed some social foreplay before we could begin.

"Are you a good musician?" Amy asked.

"About average," I said, and she laughed again, as if I'd said something witty. Maybe I had.

We went to her garden apartment in Little Neck. Her roommate—the woman she'd whispered to at the bar?—wasn't around. I'd had several moments of doubt before we'd gotten this far. Driving behind her toward Little Neck, I'd thought about her age and mine, that I might make a fool of myself, and even if I didn't, it was still sort of incestuous. Then I worried that it might be too much exertion for me in one day. What would Dr. Croyden say about it? As we were parking outside her place, I wondered if she could possibly be a pro, if this was something I was supposed to understand without actually being told.

I didn't find any incriminating evidence inside her apartment. It was tidy and modestly furnished. She had lots of plants and family photos, and there was a computer terminal in one corner of the bedroom. There were no pimps lurking, no mirrored ceiling, no heart-shaped bed. I was ashamed of myself for even thinking those thoughts.

When we got into her ordinary platform bed, she handed me a condom. "The awful eighties," she said, sounding suddenly, girlishly shy.

"How old are you, Amy?" I asked.

"Thirty-one," she said. "How about you?"

"About average," I said, and we both laughed. Jesus,

Croyden had given me a password, and a theme for the whole evening.

I was less than average in the sack, though. It had been a very long time, and Amy was such a knockout. I was over-eager, I guess, and faster than the speed of light. "Sorry, sorry," I mumbled, ready to crawl away in shame.

But Amy wouldn't let me go. She murmured consolation, and after we'd rested, she encouraged me to try again. It took a while, but then I was ready. And this time I was able to hold off, to move slowly and to give her pleasure, too. I slept for a long time afterward. When I woke up, she was sitting in the eerie green glow of the computer, wearing a bathrobe and pecking at the keyboard. "Hello," I said.

She swiveled around to face me. "My, you sure can sleep," she said.

I hoped I hadn't been snoring. "It's been a hard day," I told her.

She came to the side of the bed and sat down. "Howard," she said, "what's wrong with your chest?"

I looked down, saw the shaved patches, the fading impressions of the electrodes. "I was about to get the chair," I said, "when the governor called up with a reprieve."

"Don't," she said. "I really want to know."

"Okay. I had a stress test this afternoon, for my heart."

"Is there something wrong with it?" she asked.

"Sort of. I had a heart attack in August."

"Oh," she said.

"Well, I'm fifty-two," I said. I waited for her to express surprise at that, and when she didn't, I said, "Things start breaking down a little after fifty. But don't worry, you have a long way to go."

"Longer than you think," she said. "I'm really only twenty-four."

"Jesus," I said. "You're two years older than my daughter." I pulled the covers further up, feeling chilled suddenly, and exposed.

"How old is your wife?" she asked. I noticed that she didn't say "ex-wife."

"Forty-five. And we *are* separated. Listen, I feel really weird about this, Amy. I mean, you're lovely, you're *wonderful*, but there's a tremendous gap here. I expect your father to come out of the closet any minute and shoot me."

She leaned over and kissed me. "My father's in Seattle," she said, "and he doesn't even own a gun."

I was somewhat relieved; at least he wasn't dead, at least it wasn't a classic case study. "Older men aren't your . . . thing, are they?" I said.

"Nope. My regular boyfriend is my own age."

"Then why did you do this?" I asked her, genuinely puzzled.

She shrugged. "I wanted to," she said. "You were so sweet and funny. And handsome, too. Why did you do it?"

"Oh, God," I said. "For the obvious reasons. And maybe as a kind of supreme stress test. Now I guess I'm going to live forever." It made me sad, saying it.

"I hope so," she said. "Will I see you again?"

I hesitated. "I don't think that would be such a good idea," I said at last, with an instant pang of regret.

It was after midnight when I got home, but I was wide awake. I took Shadow for a walk around the block and then we got into bed together, like an old married couple. He snuffled, sighed, and finally settled down for the night with his snout on Paulie's pillow. I couldn't fall asleep right away. I played the whole day back, and it was strangely unreal, as if I'd only dreamed it.

23

I VISITED MY MOTHER IN BROOKLYN ONE SATURDAY
morning and, as always, I was stirred by emotion when she
undid the locks and let me in. Her apartment was a museum
of family history, a warehouse for my childhood. Anything
I might have forgotten was recalled and commemorated in
photographs, even the pre-history of my grim-looking, im-
migrant grandparents. My mother kept the blinds lowered
and shut, so that the place was cast in somber shadow, no
matter what the weather or the time of day. In winter she'd
say it was to keep the heat in, in summer to keep it out. And
you had to protect the furniture and wallpaper from sunlight
or it would fade. This same instinct for preservation ac-
counted for the pervading stink of camphor in any season.
When it mingled with those rich, familiar cooking odors,
everything I'd enjoyed and suffered as a child came back in
a wholesale rush. Doing my homework at the kitchen table
while my mother prepared supper—the cheerful bubbling of
soup and the voluptuous curves of my own handwriting. My
father and mother behind the bedroom wall later, myself
alone in my narrow bower of dreams. How I'd longed to be
like them, to be in on the adult mysteries of conspiracy and
power. But as I grew more and more informed, they began

to seem less so, until I pitied them for their ignorance and
was freed.

As soon as I crossed the threshold that Saturday, I was in
my mother's net again, caught in that suffocating atmosphere, and under an avalanche of unsolicited advice. She
pleaded with me to straighten my marriage out before it was
too late. When you got older, she explained, all your second
chances were behind you. She managed to evoke a death
knell Poe might have envied. Quoth my mother: "Much too
late."

I sank into the quicksand of the down sofa and murmured
sympathy. I wasn't being insincere—there wasn't a gloomier
story to my mind than my mother's life of bitter regret. If
she'd only married the accountant with the squint instead of
demanding perfection and beauty. If my father had left the
post office and gone into business with his furrier brothers.
If she'd been healthy enough to bear other children after the
gory trauma of my birth. And that brought her around full
circle to me and my present life again. Didn't I know when
I was well off? Didn't I know which side my bread was
buttered on?

"Ma," I said, breaking into her litany. "I have some good
news to tell you."

Her pinched face softened with hope. "You and Howard
made up?" she said, as if it had only been a silly lovers'
quarrel all along.

"No, nothing like that," I said. "But it's something very
nice. You're going to be a great-grandmother."

Her hand went to her bosom, where her Med-Alert beeper
hung like a showy religious charm. "No!" she cried with
delight. "My little Annie—a mother!"

"Not Ann, Ma. Sara. Sara and Jason."

"Oh," she said. I watched a series of expressions cross

her face, until modified delight was restored there. She was
a modern woman, after all, and this was a crazy world. I
gave silent thanks to Donahue and Susskind for bringing its
worst aberrations into her living room and making them
commonplace, acceptable. There was no shrieking and
breast-beating the way there'd been years ago when I'd
brought home similar news about Howard and me. Now there
was only some cautious optimism. "They're getting married
soon, aren't they?" she said.

"Oh, sure," I said. "Although Jason's being mulish about
it right now."

"Do you want me to talk to him?" she asked.

Just what Jason needed—a few of her compound chest-
nuts. *You made your bed, so shall ye reap . . . Lie down with
dogs and pay the piper . . .* "No, no, Ma," I said quickly.
"It's all going to work out."

"And in the meantime," she said, "nobody has to know
our business, right?" Then she reached across the coffee
table between us and squeezed my hand. "So, my girl, you'll
be a grandmother," she said. "If only your father . . ."

I glanced at the rogues' gallery behind her, saw my father's
solemn face, the sepia gravity of his father's. No one ever
smiled for their portraits in those days, as if they knew there
was nothing to smile about, that they'd die young and we
would all flourish in their absence.

My mother and I ate a celebration lunch of cottage cheese
and canned peaches, and then she took a pair of silver candlesticks from her sideboard, polished them on her apron,
and wrapped them in paper towels and newspaper. "Here,"
she said. "Before they get stolen."

I hated when she did that, impulsively dismantling her
household, giving away bits and pieces of her life, and mine,
to me and the children. The porcelain shepherd and shep-

herdess I'd played with as a child were crazily incongruous
in the slummy clutter of Jason and Sara's bedroom. And Ann
kept what was left of the "good" dishes somewhere in her
garage, still in their newspaper shroud. She didn't have the
nerve or heart to resist the giver, to say that she didn't need
dishes, and the ornate green-and-gold floral pattern wasn't
really her taste.

"Keep them, Ma," I said now, about the candlesticks. "I
have candlesticks. And they looked nice just where they
were." I meant, stop changing, don't disappear, but she was
already rummaging in the drawers for string to bind the package. I went back to Manhattan on the subway, with the
wrapped candlesticks weighting my purse like a concealed
weapon.

On the way to my apartment, I stopped to buy cookies and
fruit. I was expecting Katherine and La Rae to visit that
afternoon, and I was excited about seeing them. It would be
just like old times, when we were all neighbors, and a regular
threesome. But soon after they arrived, Sherry showed up,
too, escorted by her latest beau. She'd been dating this man
exclusively for a few weeks now. He was a boy, really, someone who'd answered her personals ad with his C. W. Post
yearbook photo, taken five or six years before. When she'd
first mentioned Nicholas to me, I'd told her that it would be
more difficult for the mother of a son to date anyone that
young. And not just because of the sexual implications. I
said that I'd probably start nagging him to stand up straight,
or to clean up his room. My only lover, besides Howard, had
been that age, but I was a kid then myself, and not the least
bit maternal toward him. Douglas, I remembered, had been
exuberantly sexual—the word "cocksure" must have been
invented to describe someone like him—and Nicholas struck
me the same way.

He was simply beautiful, early Warren Beatty, and La Rae rolled her eyes at me as he strutted around in his skin-tight jeans. Sherry showed him off with the blatant pride of a stage mother. While he browsed among Mary and Jim's bookshelves, she told us that his degree from Post was in Comparative Literature. We sat there, gaping, as if we were the audience at some kind of improvisational theater, of which Nicholas was the star. Then he lounged among us—the four women old enough to have been his baby-sitter, if not actually his mother—and read steamy passages from D. H. Lawrence aloud. By the time Sherry carted him off, everything but his heated presence had gone out of our minds.

"Holy shit!" La Rae exclaimed before their retreating footsteps had stopped echoing in the hallway.

"Oh, come on," Katherine said. "How long do you think that's going to last?"

"All night, honey," La Rae said, and we all burst into raucous, jealous laughter.

"How about you, Paulie?" Katherine asked. "Is there a little Oedipus in your life, too?"

"Yeah, Paulie," La Rae said. "You're a swinging single again. You seeing anybody?"

I looked sharply at her, thinking of Frank's visit, hoping he hadn't told her about it, knowing that I never would. La Rae's face was open and friendly. I hesitated a moment too long before answering, and when I finally said, "No, there's nobody," and felt my own face redden, they both looked at me with skepticism. The trouble with intense friendship, I decided, is the lack of privacy. Actually, there wasn't anybody, in the most intimate sense, but I had been seeing Bernie Rusten. He'd called me, as he had promised that day in the bar, and we arranged to meet again in the study area of the library. Since then, we'd gone to dinner a couple of times, and to the movies, and back to our bar, but he hadn't ever come home with me. We took long walks in every other direction, and usually parted later in a taxi, after some strenuous necking. I knew we couldn't go on this way much longer, and I didn't really want to. My body was much lonelier than my spirit, and it longed for appeasement. But I hadn't been able to put Howard and my marriage completely away yet, and Bernie seemed hesitant, too, in spite of those galvanic kisses.

One evening, while we were sitting at a booth in the bar, disclosing more things about our past lives, I said, "This is a little like mutual therapy, Bernie, isn't it? I mean, our talking this way about ourselves and not passing judgment on each other."

He smiled and ran his long, cool fingers down the side of my neck.

"That wasn't a very Freudian gesture," I said, with a delicious shudder. "I don't think he even shook hands with his patients."

"I guess I'm more into behaviorism," Bernie said. "Or maybe faith healing." He reached under the table and touched my knee. "See, now you can walk again."

"You mean now I *can't*." There was a disquieting pause, and then I said, "Howard and I used to lie on the living-room couch together when we were first married and confess things to each other. It was a lot different then, though. We *did* pass judgment. At least I did—I hated everyone who'd ever done him wrong, and everyone who'd loved him before I did, starting with his mother."

"Ellen was like that," Bernie said. "Possessive, and unreasonable."

"It's not so unreasonable. A doctor sees all that *flesh* at work every day."

"Not just at work," he said. "At dinner parties, too. I'd go into the bedroom to put my coat down and there'd be some woman in there, opening her blouse to get my opinion of a mole."

"Ah, the old mole game," I said. "Listen, Bernie, Howard once played a wedding reception where the *bride* propositioned him between sets."

I asked Bernie why he'd left Boston, and he said it was because of Ellen, because of all the memories of her associated with the city. I told him how Howard and I had ended up living in the suburbs, and we sat there for a few moments, quietly acknowledging our respective ghosts. Then he said, "Paulette, I want to make love to you."

His words were even more disturbing than his touch had been, and I felt that old pit-of-the-stomach plunge. "Me, too," I said. "But not yet, Bernie, I'm not ready yet." I hoped he'd know it wasn't coyness on my part, or lack of response, but that my ghosts were more persistent and less benevolent than his.

"That's all right," Bernie said, fiddling with the book of matches in the ashtray. "I *want* to make love to you, but I'm not even sure I can."

"What do you mean?" I said. And then, weakly, "Oh." This was a complication I hadn't even considered. My long-ago lover, Douglas, had probably never so much as contemplated failure. His virility was almost comical, like the irrepressible spring of a child's pop-up toy. Impotence, I'd thought, only happened to husbands in the long winter of marriage.

"Don't worry, this isn't Hemingway, it's not a war wound or anything," Bernie said. "It's just that I haven't been . . . um . . . active for a while. For two years, actually."

"You mean since your wife died?"

He nodded and leaned back in his seat, seeming relieved, and grateful for my prompting. "It's not that I haven't felt lustful," he said, "especially lately, with you." He smiled. "You may have noticed. But there's something that happens, a kind of holding back, a distancing . . . Boy, this is really hard to explain."

"You don't have to," I said.

"What—explain?"

"That, or anything," I said. "It's all right."

"You mean we can just be good friends," he said bitterly, "like Jake and Lady Brett?"

"This conversation is crazy, Bernie," I said. "And it's getting embarrassing."

"That's only because people don't talk this much about sex without *having* it."

"The funny thing is," I said, "right before Howard and I separated, I tried to imagine . . . being with someone else, and I mostly worried about other things, like catching something terrible. I wondered how you asked about something like that, if you went in for blood tests together, the way people do before they get married. I know your abstinence makes you feel nervous, Bernie, but, if it's any consolation, it also makes you safe."

"Sure," he said. "You'll probably only die of boredom."

"You'll be fine," I assured him, uncertainly. "Listen, Bernie, maybe we should just—"

"No, it's okay," he said, smiling again, taking my hand and kissing it. "We'll find the right time, sweetie, don't worry about it."

I did worry about it, when I wasn't distracted by other things, especially the mess of my family's life. Despite what I'd told my mother, I didn't know if Jason would ever marry Sara. Howard seemed to think it was only a matter of time, that some small event would spark his commitment to her. I was especially disappointed that the baby's first flutters of life hadn't done it. When Howard used to lay his hand and then his ear against my restless, swollen belly, we became a perfect, imperishable unit. If Jason didn't respond in the same way to Sara, was it because we had seriously harmed him with the example of our marriage?

Howard and I were apart, but also still together in this shared problem. I began to think we needed some ceremony of separation before we could fully assume our independent lives. On Sherry's advice, I'd consulted a lawyer who advertised no-nonsense, quickie divorces in the *Voice*, but I found out that even those required time and patience.

Thanksgiving was coming up soon, the holiday I'd always liked best because there was no exchange of gifts, and its traditions seemed particularly sacred. In school we used to sing ''Abide with Me'' and ''We Gather Together,'' hymns that still moved me in a quasi-religious/patriotic way. Thanksgiving was a truly American holiday, an American *family* holiday, and one for which we'd always convened, no matter what. I loved the festive but formal table, the chaotic, fragrant kitchen—everyone safely assembled once more. Thank you, thank you, I used to think as I basted the turkey, as I stirred the bursting, jeweled cranberries. Now I wondered if Jason would be agreeably affected if we all met again this last time, and if it would also be the ritual that helped me to let go of Howard. I didn't mean for us to gather in Port Washington or at my apartment, but in some other, more neutral place. My mother wanted us to come to Brooklyn, of course, but I knew that wouldn't work. She'd be in command there, even if I brought the food, and she'd try to exercise her authority. Like Ann, she'd bang heads together, and order everybody to kiss and make up. I'd been staying away from Larchmont since my surprise reunion with Howard, and there wasn't enough room for us all to sit down at once at Jason and Sara's.

We ended up at a restaurant called Bill Tiffany's, in midtown. It was one of those oak and stained-glass places that had sprung up like weeds everywhere in the past few years. At least it was unmistakably American. Howard arrived first, with my mother, whom he'd volunteered to pick up. He'd driven for over two hours in crazy traffic, and he was sipping a martini at the crowded bar when I got there. My mother was drinking something that looked like a Shirley Temple. I ordered a martini, too, and until the children came, we talked about the traffic, and about how amazed the Pilgrims would be by self-basting, self-timed, frozen turkeys. At last Spence and Ann appeared in the doorway, and Jason and Sara weren't far behind. She walked with a swaybacked waddle to accommodate her growing belly, which we each patted in turn, greeting her. She was wearing a pleated plaid skirt that was hiked up in front, and under an army field jacket, an enormous T-shirt that said *Women and Children First*.

Once everyone was there, Howard hailed the headwaiter and claimed our table, deep in the fern jungle of the dining room. He'd brought the little crepe-paper turkey place cards from home, and he began setting them out and seating us. My mother on his right, me on his left. He'd carried the place cards in his jacket pocket and they were bent out of shape and wouldn't stand up. He rearranged their pipe-cleaner legs and propped them against the bread basket and the salt and pepper shakers, but they kept keeling over.

The rest of us attended to our menus, and everyone but Jason ordered the standard Thanksgiving dinner. He chose a dish called Sizzling Oriental Shrimp. It was brought to the table in a showy hiss of steam that made everyone at the nearby tables turn to look at us.

The food at Bill Tiffany's was well prepared and tasty, but it had an institutional quality—all those identical platters of turkey and chestnut stuffing going by. Who were the other families at the other tables, all dressed up and away from their cold, dark kitchens? We could have been inmates of a hospital or a prison, trying to put a brave front on things. *Abide with me*, I sang inside my head. *Fast falls the eventide*.

"What a good idea this was," Ann said, removing slices of dark meat from Spence's plate, and substituting slices of white meat from her own.

"No bother, no fuss, leave the cooking to us," Howard said. "We should have done this years ago." He turned to me. "Do you remember how you always used to say, 'Days of preparation for one lousy hour of eating'?"

"But I never meant it," I said. "I never really minded. I was only fishing for compliments."

"You've hardly touched your plate, Sara," my mother chided. "Remember that you're eating for two now."

"She has a T-shirt that says *that*, too," Jason said.

"That's kind of cute," Spence commented.

"She's a walking billboard," Jason said.

"Somebody has to be glad about it," Sara announced in a tremulous voice, and the whole table fell silent.

Howard raised his wineglass to her. "I'm glad," he said.

"We're *all* glad," Spence said, and everyone clinked glasses around the table, even Jason. Then my mother said, "Well, if everybody's so glad, when's the wedding?"

I was too far away to reach her, and I kicked Jason instead, who said, "Hey! Ouch! Who kicked me?"

"How's the course coming along?" I asked Sara.

"Well, I've got the breathing down pat," she said. "Jason's a good coach," she added, glancing shyly at him.

"She needs to work on the panting," he said.

"That's for the last stages," Sara explained. "I have lots of time."

"Next year we'll need a high chair for the baby," Ann said dreamily.

"He can chew on the drumstick," Howard said. "We used to give it to you, Jase, before you even had any teeth."

"Is that when you decided to play the drums?" Spence asked.

"I'll bet your mother will come up from Florida next year, Howard," my mother said.

Their extravagant plans were for an expanding family, not a disintegrating one. Next year there would have to be two parties for every occasion—the poor baby would probably be spoiled rotten and completely confused.

By the time the waiter brought the pumpkin pie and the coffee, I had moved away, at least in spirit, from the magic circle of our round table, where the paper turkeys lay on their sides, as if they'd been felled by Pilgrim gunpowder.

24

"*HEY, DAD, DO YOU WANT TO GO TO A WEDding?*"

"Who is this—Jason?" I said, struggling to come awake. It was Sunday and way too early for both of us, although the room was very bright.

"Yeah, the prodigal son," he said. "Sara and I are getting married. Do you want to come?"

"That's great!" I said. "Of course I do. When's it going to be?" I staggered to the window with the phone and saw that it had snowed again during the night.

"Soon, I guess," he said. "We haven't picked the exact date."

"Have you told your mother yet?"

"No, I called you first, since you were the one pushing for it."

"Well, let me tell Mom about it, okay?"

"Sure," he said, and I could picture him shrugging.

"She'll want to do something nice, probably. You know women, you know your mother."

"Well, don't let her make a federal case out of it. We just want to get it over with," he said, as if we were talking about an operation one of them was facing.

I asked to speak to Sara, and when she got on, I said, "This news make me very happy, Sara. I've always wanted more daughters."

"Thank you, Mr. Flax," she said. "We hope you'll be there. And Mrs. Flax, too."

"Oh, we'll be there, all right. How about your folks? Have you told them about this?"

There was a long, charged silence, and then she said, in a wavering voice, "They won't talk to me. Maybe my sister will come, though."

"Good, good!" I said heartily. "The more the merrier." I was thinking about Paulie, and how she'd react to this news. Would she give me some credit for it, even if I hadn't really carried it off? Jason might repeat to her that I'd been the one "pushing for it." I'd have to come across with the substantial wedding gift I'd hinted at, but I knew Paulie wouldn't object to that. I wondered what had happened to make Jason change his mind. Thanksgiving hadn't done it, certainly, but maybe Christmas had. All those street-corner Santas, and the store windows filled with toys. In any case, I wasn't going to rock the boat by asking too many questions.

As soon as I hung up on them, I called Paulie and got her damn tape. She'd changed the recorded message; now it said: "This is Paulette Flax. If you'll leave your name and number at the sound of the tone, I'll get back to you." Paulette! Since when did she call herself that? And she'd dropped that un- certain little "Thanks" at the end. She sounded more con- fident now—*single*, somehow, and ready for anything. When the tone beeped, *I* wasn't ready, and I sputtered and said, "Uh . . . listen, it's me. I have to talk to you—it's impor- tant—so call me whenever you get in." Shit, I'd forgotten to give my name! And those machines could distort your voice so that your own mother wouldn't recognize it. Some of the cheaper models made you sound as if you were talking in a tunnel, or underwater. Everybody and his kid sister had one now, even Jason, who could hardly pay his phone bills. His outgoing message started with eight bars of Black Flag's "Scream."

It wasn't even nine o'clock. I hated being awake at that hour—there was that Sunday stillness, like the world had stopped, and the snow only made it worse. But I couldn't go back to sleep, so I took Shadow for a walk. It was a real winter wonderland out there—no wind at all, and the sun was dazzling. Where was Paulie this early in the morning? The *Times* was still waiting in plastic bags in everyone's driveway, and the new snow was broken by only a few footprints. I let Shadow off his lead to plow through drifts for the buried scent of other dogs. As soon as he was free, he ran around barking, as if he'd suddenly remembered the bliss of a puppy winter.

When we came home, the phone was ringing. "What's the matter, Howard?" Paulie asked before I had a chance to say hello.

"Nothing," I said, "nothing's the matter. It's something good—Jason and Sara are getting married."

"They are?" she said. "Oh, that *is* good. When did he tell you?"

"At the crack of dawn," I said. "He woke me up. Where were you that early?"

"I wonder why he gave in," she said.

"Yeah, I wondered, too. Maybe Christmas softened him up, or it could have been his New Year's resolution. I know that I sure worked hard to convince him."

"Will they let us give them a little reception?" she asked.

"I guess so," I said. "If he's going this far. We could probably do it right here."

"That wouldn't be a good idea," she said. "But maybe Ann would let us use her house, or we could get a private room in a restaurant."

"They won't want anything big," I warned her. "Remember, they're not Andrew and Fergie."

After we hung up, I remembered that she'd never told me where she had been when I'd called her. But she'd said "we" and "us" each time she mentioned the wedding plans, and I took some comfort from that. Small comfort, though. My notion of us getting together when Jason and Sara married had lost most of its shine. A few weeks before, I'd received a letter from some prick of a divorce lawyer she'd hired, advising me to get one of my own. I'd finally called what's-his-name, the lawyer who'd drawn up Gil's and Sharon's wills, and told him just to make things move as slowly as he could.

I had breakfast and then I called Ann and Spence, waking them up. They spoke in tandem from the twin telephone extensions in their bedroom, and they were thrilled by the news. Ann immediately volunteered their house for the wedding. "I wish it was springtime, though," she said wistfully, "so the ceremony could be in the garden."

"I don't think we ought to wait," I said.

"Unless the caterers boil lots of water," Spence threw in.

"I'll have to take Sara shopping for a wedding dress," Ann said. "God, will they have anything decent in the maternity shops?"

"See if you can get one that doesn't say anything across the chest," I suggested.

"Oh, I don't know," Spence said. "Why not 'Just Married' or 'I'd Rather Be Hang-gliding.' "

"Very funny, you moron," Ann said, and then I heard

shrieks and muffled laughter that probably meant the onset of a pillow fight.

I was so high I called Paulie's mother, who said, "Oh, Howard darling, you should see me—I'm crying from happiness. Just remember that good news always bring more good news. You wait and see—a little child shall lead them." My own mother was less cryptic and less ecstatic. Maybe long distance encouraged economy and clarity. "Jason's still a baby himself," she remarked, Ann's words of a few weeks ago, but with a more sympathetic inflection. I asked if she'd come up for the wedding, and she said, "We'll see."

Later, as I was reheating the coffee, I remembered that that was what she'd said all through my childhood whenever I'd wanted something: a new toy or money for the movies or candy, that it was her way of withholding pleasure, of exercising power and control. In the long run, I always got what I'd wanted—everyone said she spoiled me silly—but the game left me feeling weak and angry. Well, I wasn't going to let anybody or anything get me down today. I whistled while I was cleaning up, and I even made the bed for a change, without reasoning that I'd just be messing it up again in a few hours. Only the business of Paulie's early-morning whereabouts stayed in the back of my mind.

When the doorbell rang after lunch, I was sprawled in the living room with sections of the paper all around me, and Ruby Braff blasting on the stereo. A couple of kids had been by before, and I'd hired them to shovel the snow from the driveway. I thought it was probably them again, coming to collect their money, although I could still hear the scrape of snow shovels over the music. I opened the door and Paulie was standing there in the blinding light. "I thought you were Robbie Castelli," I said stupidly, blinking at her. She was wearing a red knitted hat, and her cheeks were as pink as a girl's. "But what a nice surprise this is," I said, recovering. "Come on in."

I began getting scared as soon as she stepped inside. The vestibule seemed ominously dark after the glare of the snow. Shadow had rushed in to welcome Paulie with rapturous yelps, and she'd greeted him absentmindedly. "Let's sit down," I said. "Can I get you some coffee? Would you like something to eat?"

She sat on the sofa, with the sports section crushed under her, still wearing her hat and coat. "I don't want anything. You sit down, too," she said, patting the cushion beside her.

I shut off the music and sat down next to her on the sofa. Her face was grave. I knew she hadn't come on some minor errand, or even to discuss plans for Jason's wedding. "Tell me," I said, thinking: Don't tell me.

"Howie," she said, taking my hand between her mittened ones. I smelled the cold air on her clothes and skin, her own scent of raisins. "It's bad news," she said. But her mother had told me good news brings more good news.

"Who?" I asked.

"Gil," she said. "He died this morning, clearing a path to his house."

"Oh, Jesus," I said, starting to shake.

Paulie gripped my hand harder. "Sharon called me. She said it happened very quickly. A massive coronary."

"Oh, sh-shit," I said, my teeth rattling.

"Howie," Paulie said. "Please, honey." She pulled off her mittens and put her burning hands on either side of my face. I wouldn't look at her; I couldn't stop shaking. "I know," she said, "I know. Can you cry, Howie? Crying helps a little."

I looked up at last and saw that tears were streaking her own face. I wasn't sure why, but that calmed me somewhat.

"I just don't b-believe it, you know?" I said. "We were supposed to play again this Tuesday. I witnessed his w-will a few weeks ago. It was like a wedding, somehow. This woman was there in a bathrobe . . ." I started to cry then and Paulie put her arms around me. I don't know how long we stayed like that, embracing on our sofa, until the doorbell rang again.

"I'll go," Paulie said. "You rest."

I heard her talking to the Castelli kid. "There's money on the kitchen table," I called, and listened to her footsteps in the house. She came back inside and I said, "Paulie, thanks for coming here to tell me."

"Well, I didn't want you to be alone when you heard about it," she said.

"I appreciate that," I said. "It started off like such a good day, didn't it? Jesus, poor Gil." I reached into my pocket for the nitroglycerin.

"His condition was worse than yours right from the beginning," Paulie said. "He suffered a lot more damage. You have to keep that in mind."

"He didn't even pass the fucking stress test," I said.

"I know, Sharon told me."

"Then why the hell was he out shoveling snow?"

"To test himself, maybe. Who knows?"

"When is the funeral?" A plain pine box, I remembered. More for the living.

"Tuesday or Wednesday. Gil's sister is in Europe. They're trying to get in touch with her."

"Paulie, can you stay here with me for a while?"

"For a little while," she said. "Not too long." At least she didn't say, "We'll see."

There were a few beats of silence, and then I said, "Did

I tell you that I stopped smoking?'' It was true, as of that moment, anyway.

"You did? That's great," Paulie said. "It's about time."

"I called everybody about the wedding."

"I know, you rat, you beat me to it. It's an awfully mixed-up day, isn't it? Such happy news, such terrible news."

How long was a little while? I didn't want her to leave, and I scrounged around for something else to say that would delay her. "Where were you this morning when I called?" I said. That just popped out; it wasn't what I'd meant to say at all.

"Why do you want to know?" Paulie said.

"I was just curious. And I couldn't wait to tell you about Jason and Sara."

"Please don't be curious about me anymore, Howard," she said. "We have separate lives now."

"Yeah," I said. "I've noticed that. And in case I hadn't noticed, I got a letter from Perry Mason."

"I'd better be going," she said, looking at her watch.

"How did you get here?" It was the first time I'd thought about that; it was as if she'd simply materialized because I'd been thinking about her.

"The train. And I took a cab from the station."

"Give me a minute, and I'll drive you back there," I said, remembering the kiss in the car at the Larchmont station.

Paulie must have been having the same thought, because her face closed and she said firmly, "No, I'll call Port Taxi."

When she was gone, it was as if she *had* materialized because I'd willed her to, except for the news about Gil she'd brought, and the sorrow that lay around the house afterward, like drifts of snow.

25

*B*ERNIE AND I WERE BOTH NERVOUS OUR FIRST TIME TO-
gether. It was a Friday evening soon after Thanksgiving, and
we'd left in the middle of a movie, by mutual, unspoken
consent, and gone to my apartment. I'm still not sure what
that movie was about. Bernie stubbed his toe on the night-
stand getting into bed, where I lay huddled under the blan-
kets, naked and shivering. He whispered a curse into the
darkness, and I had to control a wild urge to laugh. Not that
I was merry, and not that it was dark enough in there for me
to relax. I'd been able to put aside my fears about social
diseases and the protocol of conducting an affair. And I
wasn't that concerned right then about Bernie's problem, either. I was more worried about revealing my weathered body
to someone who hadn't witnessed its weathering. How did
Sherry manage that with Nicholas—by using veils? Bernie
was a few years older than I was, but he was slender and
solid. I could see that much in the shadows as he approached
the bed. He smelled good—wintry and a little medicinal—
and when he reached for me, I forgot almost everything but
the instant, urgent pleasure of his touch. "Don't be afraid,"
I whispered to both of us. "It's probably like riding a bicycle."

But it wasn't simply a matter of physical memory. We didn't know each other's bodies, and there was that awkward groping toward discovery. But what is sweeter or more absurd than first sex? Something hurts a little, but you can't complain, not even if your arm falls into numbness under his weight. The springs are noisy, your bellies slap, and then get sucked together with sweat. Sweat, spittle, scum! A minute ago you were vertical and dressed and deodorant-dry. It's worse for the woman, I thought, who has to coax the man to rising and guide him in. More like trying to open a door while you're carrying a tray than like riding a bicycle. And it's worse for the man, who has to direct the flow of his own blood, and whose watch glows and ticks like a bomb at your ear, and catches the hair on the back of your neck. "Sorry, hold still a minute," Bernie murmured, trying to engage and disengage himself at once. He was fine, though, finally, just as I'd falsely promised he'd be that evening in the bar. "Oh, sweetie," he sighed, drowning, like a man saved from drowning.

Later he said that he thought my body was lovely, a veritable garden of delights. Of course he was being gallant, and manic in his relief about his own performance. And he'd taken his glasses off on the way to bed—that's probably why he'd stumbled, although I liked to think it was the distraction of desire. Perhaps, I thought, doctors have a special fondness for the human form in any shape or condition. I told him that he'd made me very happy, which was true. My happiness was complicated, though. When we lay beside each other, in what Howard and I used to call "the aftermess," I remembered being married, and imagined that Bernie did the same. It wasn't that I made anatomical comparisons, not consciously, anyway. It was more a question of habit and mood. Howard had always smoked a last cigarette after making love, while I stayed close to him and plunged into a deep, safe sleep. The cigarette's flare was a kind of night-light I saw behind my heavy, closing lids. I didn't dare fall asleep now, for fear of being rude. Bernie and I were still polite strangers, no matter how intimate we'd just been. I felt awkward again, and he seemed to be trying to think of something to say, as if we'd only just met and he wanted to make the right impression. Finally he said, "Oh, come here, you," hugging me to him roughly, and soon we both slept.

After a few exhausting, passionate weeks, we stopped falling on each other the minute we were alone indoors. We became cozy together, almost married, sharing confidences and the Sunday paper in bed, keeping our ghosts at a safe distance. I told Bernie that he mumbled in his sleep. He said that I was a noisy mouth breather, and he was probably just telling me to be quiet. "Didn't they take those adenoids out when you were a kid?" he asked, and I opened wide and said "Ahhh," so he could see. I couldn't help thinking it was Howard who really needed a doctor in his life.

Bernie didn't move in with me, although we discussed that possibility, and decided against it, at least for the time being. He did stay overnight whenever he could. One Saturday, his service woke us at 2 a.m. with an emergency call, and he had to leave. I gave him a sleepy, wifely kiss good-bye and rolled right over. When he came back, sometime after dawn, I turned to him the way I used to turn to Howard coming home from a late gig.

But I discovered that even when I was alone I was less lonely than I'd been before. I'd gotten into a regular work routine—the proofreading became easier as I became more familiar with the language of engineers and editors, and my column seemed to be inspired by city living. I'd learned ingenious new ways to combat roaches and mice, and how to

make the most out of limited closet space. After much hes-
itation, I had joined a health club, during one of those dis-
count membership drives they hold every week. I told myself
I needed to get in shape for my new life, and that it wouldn't
be anything like phys ed in high school. But it was. It took
nerve just to undress in the communal locker room, where
some ravishing young creature was always wriggling in or
out of a shimmery, flesh-colored leotard. I tried to remember
Bernie's pleasure in my body, and my own. And I tried not
to listen to my desperate breathing during Slimnastics.

The most important and daring thing I'd done, though,
was to register for a poetry workshop at the New School. We
met on Tuesdays at 8 p.m. around a big conference table:
twelve men and women and the instructor, a woman about
my age named Ruth Trueheart, who'd published seven books
of poetry, none of which any of us had ever read. She wrote
their titles on the blackboard the first evening, but admitted
that they were very hard to find. In fact, they were impossible
to find, in any library or bookstore, so I'd placed an order
for one of them with a book-search service that advertised in
The New Yorker.

Ruth was a good teacher, charitable but honest, and she
became a model for me of courage in the face of lost causes.
What was a boxful of linty rejection slips compared to *seven*
out-of-print, out-of-mind books? Every Tuesday evening, we
read and discussed the poems of two or three of the workshop
members. We would dissect each poem, see how it was
made, and then try to put it together again in a better way. I
hadn't had a turn at bat yet, but even the thought of it made
me sick with anxiety. I would have to bring in something
old—I still hadn't completed a poem out of the fragments I'd
written at the library—and the old ones had all been rejected
everywhere, without a single personal comment. If I put any

of them up for class criticism, maybe the comments would be unbearably personal. I'd never even shown my work to Bernie; I was shyer about that than I'd been about my body.

One afternoon in January we made love, and after we'd slept we got dressed and went out to get something to eat. We walked from restaurant to restaurant on Irving Place, and then Twenty-third Street, reading the menus hung in the steamy windows, unable to make up our minds. I remember that we were holding hands, swinging our arms and laughing about something, when I saw Ann and Spence coming toward us down the street. It's true that lifelong roles can be instantly reversed; in that moment I became the child, caught at some forbidden activity, and Ann became the omniscient parent. I dropped Bernie's hand and moved away from him a little, without thinking about doing it, but I'd already seen the shock and disapproval on my daughter's face. Spence was only on the edge of my vision, a neutral figure in a puffy down jacket and a jaunty scarf, part of the blur of other figures and awnings and neon signs. He said something, and I said, "My, what a happy coincidence," in what Ann used to refer to as my phony telephone voice. Her face was white and unforgiving. "What are you two doing around here?" I chirped, and then I tucked my arm through Bernie's in a belated gesture of loyalty and bravado. Spence said they'd been visiting friends on Gramercy Park. He was like an interpreter between two ill-humored, opposing heads of state. "I wish you'd called," I scolded, "to let me know you were going to be in the neighborhood." That sounded as if I would have made plans to see them, when I really meant I'd have hidden out with Bernie until they were gone.

They knew about him, at least vaguely. I'd made a point of telling Ann and Jason that I had a new, close male friend. They could make of that whatever they liked, I'd decided, and in those first excited weeks I hardly thought of my children at all. Now I introduced Bernie. "This is Dr. Rusten," I said. "Bernie, this is my daughter, Ann, and her husband, Spence." I realized why I'd used his title and only their first names—I was trying to throw a smoke screen around Bernie and me, and to right the reversal of family roles. But who did I think I was fooling? Surely Ann knew that we'd just come from bed, if not from her old instinct for sexual action, then from that hasty separation of our hands.

We all stood there a while longer, suffering the cold and chattering mindlessly. Bernie asked them to join us for supper, but Spence said it was late, they weren't hungry, and they wanted to get home before it snowed again. Bernie and I went into the next restaurant we came to, a crowded Greek taverna with live bouzouki music. He ordered a bottle of retsina with our meal. It was strongly bitter, like the cough medicines of my childhood, but we drank every drop of it. On the way back to my apartment, I felt tipsy and terribly blue. Bernie put his arm around me. He said, "You have your own, separate life now, you know." It was almost an echo of what I'd said to Howard the day Gil died.

"I know," I told Bernie. I didn't remind him of how sad and withdrawn he'd become at the end of December, right before his wife's birthday, or that my ghosts, at least, were still alive.

I called Ann the next morning, after Bernie was gone, and we made a date for lunch at a quiet place in the mid-thirties. After our food was served, I spoke directly and swiftly to her, the way I'd removed Band-Aids from her knees and elbows when she was a child. I told her why I'd left Howard, how much I had loved him, and how deeply betrayed I felt by what he'd done.

She was very quiet while I spoke, turning her fork over and over in her hand, ignoring the salad on her plate.

"I know this all makes you very unhappy, Ann," I said, "and I'm sorry."

"I was thinking about how I used to get into bed between you when I was little, in what I always thought of as 'the warm place,' " she said.

"I have some happy memories, too," I said.

"Well, don't they count for anything?" she asked.

"You're an old married woman yourself now," I said. "How would you feel if you discovered Spence was unfaithful?"

Her eyes glittered with tears, either for Howard and me, or for the awful possibilities of her own future. "Well," she said after a long pause, "maybe I wouldn't mind so much if it was someone I didn't know." It was practically a question.

I smiled. "That would give him a pretty wide field, wouldn't it?" I said.

She smiled back, weakly, bravely. "Can't you ever forgive Daddy?" she asked.

"Oh, Ann, it's not as simple as that, it's not just that single issue," I said. "It's the whole sense I had of our marriage, of my life. I felt limited. Oh, dear, I'm making this sound all wrong, like a delayed adolescence or seventies narcissism. I mean I'm not 'looking for myself' or anything like that—but I do want to be on my own right now."

"Are you in love with him . . . with Dr. Rusten?" she asked.

"I don't know," I said. "It's pretty early. I certainly *like* him a lot."

"I'm too old to care this much," Ann said. "But I can't help it, it's like a death in the family." She sighed. "Mom, do you remember my friend Jane Somkin, in fifth grade?"

"I remember you carried your Barbie dolls back and forth to each other's houses in those hideous cases. Her parents were divorced, weren't they?"

"Yes. I think they used to beat each other up or something. Anyway, it was horrible. We'd sit on the twin ruffled beds in Janie's room, dressing our dolls in their cruisewear or their wedding gowns. Then Janie would hold her still little dressed-up Barbie against her chest and rock back and forth, back and forth. I used to ask her what she was doing and she never answered me. Her eyes were sort of glazed over and far away. At first I thought she was just rocking her Barbie to sleep, the way we did our baby dolls. When I was older, I wondered if she'd been masturbating. Now I think she must have been mourning."

"You're probably right," I said. "Darling, it takes time, but everyone recovers."

She sighed again and put the fork down alongside her plate. "Not Jason," she said. "He needs about forty years on the couch."

"He's making an effort, Ann. And next week he'll have his own marriage to worry about. It's wonderful of you and Spence to have the wedding at your house."

"You know I love parties," she said. "And I get to be one of Sara's attendants. When we bought her dress at Great Expectations, the salesclerk didn't even bat an eyelash. They had a whole *selection* of wedding dresses with expandable waists."

So the subject was changed, if not resolved, and we were able to turn our attention to lunch.

That night I dreamt of being lost in a maze of streets. Before I was fully awake, I reached across the bed for some-body. I wasn't sure who I wanted to find there. I had a moment's panic in which I didn't recognize the room, either. Then, slowly, the tide in my chest subsided, and the dark shapes around me were furniture once more.

26

I T WAS CRAZY, BUT I FELT AS IF I WAS ON THE WAY TO MY own wedding again, instead of Jason's. Except for the pregnant brides, the circumstances were completely different. Paulie and I were married in a small private room in a neighborhood restaurant in Brooklyn, during the lunch rush; I can still hear the not-so-distant banter of the kitchen workers and the crash of china as we said our vows. Jason and Sara's morning wedding, in Ann's elegant living room, would certainly have a lot more class. She and Paulie had hired some fancy local caterers to do the breakfast—crepes and Irish salmon and good champagne. This time I was driving there by myself. Twenty-four years ago I was in a cab, wedged between my father and mother, who tried to talk me out of going through with it all the way there. "What's your hurry?" my mother kept saying, as if Paulie wasn't three months gone, as if twenty-eight wasn't considered overripe for bachelors in those days. She even hinted that the baby might not be mine, a claim no one could ever make once he was born. The taxi got stuck in traffic, and we arrived at the restaurant almost a half hour late. There was no private entrance to the private room, and I remember rushing through the main dining room with my parents right behind me, past all the gaping diners, the waiters with their loaded trays. In the little side room, our friends and relatives were standing around impatiently, as if they were waiting for an overdue train to pull into the station. An accordionist was strolling among them, playing a desperate medley of love songs. I didn't see Paulie right away, and I felt a rush of relief, tinged with disappointment. She was in the ladies' room, and when she came out, I was right near the door. We looked at each other in an intense way that almost married us right then and there, without the benefit of a ceremony. Still, we went through with the ceremony, although I was a jittery mess just before it was supposed to begin. The end of freedom! My bass man, Roy, who considered himself a card, mimed putting a noose around his neck and stringing himself up. Paulie's parents flanked her like bookends, and glared at me, and my own mother pinched my arm hard as I broke away from her. The accordionist began to wheeze "Because," a number I've always hated, and I felt something warm trickle, and then run, down my face as I went toward Paulie. It was a nose-bleed, a gusher, the first and only one of my life. Years later, during a quarrel, Paulie would accuse me of bringing it on deliberately, as a symbol of the period I wanted her to get. But that day she was all concern and tenderness, running to the bar herself for ice cubes to put on the back of my neck. A few minutes later the nosebleed was stanched, and pale and splattered, my collar soaked and my neck numb with cold, I was joined to Paulie in holy matrimony. The accordionist broke into the finale of "The Wedding March," and there was scattered applause, the way there is for a third-rate act in a noisy club.

Sara's sister had agreed to stand up for her today, but her parents had stuck to their boycott. We'd invited several friends, but only a few members of our families, so Sara wouldn't feel even worse about the poor representation of hers. My mother had declined the invitation, saying that her feet were bad, as if we'd asked her to *walk* up from Miami. Paulie's mother was there, though, and her corsage was crushed between us when she hugged me. "This is the day, Howie darling," she said. "Our chickens are going to come in. Wait and see."

I was early this time—only a handful of guests were there before me. Jason hadn't even arrived yet; he was coming directly from Atlantic City, where his group had played a gig the night before, without Sara. She'd stayed overnight at Ann's, and I imagined the serious, sisterly talk they must have had—Ann bestowing love secrets and expensive lotions and perfumes on Sara. They seemed to be in cahoots now, along with Sara's sister, Peggy, whispering and giggling together, looking gorgeous in their wedding clothes. I talked to them for a while, and to Spence, who pinned a red carnation to my lapel. There was an earthy, springlike smell from all the flowers heaped in baskets around the living room. Ann and Spence had rented little gilt chairs with red velvet seats, and a guitarist in a long dress was sitting on one of them, plucking out strains of Albéniz. Paulie was nowhere in sight, and I walked casually around, looking for her. I hadn't seen her since Gil's funeral, when she'd stood beside me as they lowered him into the ground. Now I found her in the kitchen, giving last-minute instructions to the caterers. She was wearing a blue silk dress and she had a flower in her hair. Blue is my favorite color, which Paulie once remarked was predictable and not very interesting. But she'd always worn a lot of it to please me, and she even favored songs with the word "blue" in the title: "Blue Moon" . . . "Am I Blue?" . . . "My Blue Heaven."

"You look nice," I said. "Not at all like your typical mother of the groom."

"That groom," she said, ignoring the compliment and elbowing me out into the hallway, "should have been here by now."

"Traffic," I said. "You know how it is."

"You were late on our wedding day, too," she reminded me.

"Our taxi got stuck in a tie-up. Those things happen."

"Your mother probably set up a roadblock," Paulie said.

"Jason's not really late," I said, determined to be pleasant. "There's plenty of time. Do I look nice, too?"

"You'll do," she said. I'd hoped she'd make some fussy, wifely gesture—straighten my tie or the boutonniere, or find some lint to pick off my sleeve—but she didn't.

Guests kept arriving. The door chimes rang and voices rose in greeting. La Rae and Frank were in the living room when we got there, and Katherine and Tony were just coming in. Mike had a stunning strawberry blonde on his arm. I never expected he'd bring Janine, and he swore he was finished with her, anyway, but I was spooked when I first saw the blonde. The room was humming with conversation, the guitarist was into Vivaldi, and there was an air of excitement and celebration. Through the open drapes, I could see the row of sugar-coated junipers at the edge of the snowy garden. It was cold, but very sunny, and everything glittered and shone. "Look at that," I said to Paulie. How could she fail to be moved by the occasion, by the beauty of the day?

Spence introduced us to the judge who would perform the ceremony. He was a big, hearty man, someone I wouldn't mind coming up before if I'd committed a murder. "So you're the groom's parents!" he said in resounding tones, clamping one hand on each of our shoulders. "Well, well!

Congratulations to you both!" After he'd wandered off, I said to Paulie, "I feel as if he just married *us*." She laughed and I said, "Can we leave on our honeymoon now?" She stopped laughing and sidled away from me into a group of guests.

I talked to a few people myself, but I wasn't having a very good time. Jason actually was a little late, and I was getting edgy and worried. "So where's my handsome nephew?" Paulie's deaf aunt Mildred shouted, and I saw the judge frown and look at his watch. I went down the hallway again and found Sara by herself, leaning against the wall outside the kitchen. "How are you doing, kid?" I said. "Any last requests?" To my horror, her eyes filled with tears. "Hey, Sara," I said. "Did I say something wrong?"

"No, no," she said, just before she really started bawling. I took her arm and herded her into the powder room. After I'd locked the door behind us, I grabbed a few Kleenex from the dispenser and handed them to her. She wiped her eyes and blew her nose. Then she sat on the closed toilet seat and said, "I'm sorry, I couldn't help it."

"That's all right, it's your big day," I said. "You're entitled to a little nervous hysteria."

"It's not that. It's that Jason isn't going to sh-show up," she said.

"Sure he's going to show up," I said, hovering over her, wanting to touch her veiled head but afraid of mussing it. I wished there was a bathtub ledge I could perch on, so we could be at eye level. Instead, I crouched before her, and when that proved uncomfortable, I got down on one knee, as if I was about to propose. "Of course he's going to show up."

"He's not," she said, with stubborn confidence. "I knew it the minute I woke up this morning. I knew that his heart was never in it, and that he wouldn't go through with it. Now he's not here, and I'm g-glad my parents aren't, either." And Niagara Falls began gushing again.

"That's crazy, Sara," I said. "Why would he have agreed to get married in the first place? It was hardly an impulsive decision."

"It was, in a way," she said, dabbing at her eyes. "He decided to do it after one of our birth-training sessions. We were lying on the floor with all the other couples that day, everybody breathing together in one long, whooshing sound—like the ocean? It was so beautiful. I closed my eyes and pretended I was at the beach—that's one of our relaxation techniques—and when I opened them, Jason was staring at me. I knew right away that something was different about him. My heart started pounding, and I was afraid to say anything."

"Did Jason say anything?" This seemed like the beginning of a very long story, and my knee was starting to ache from the cold, hard tile.

"Not then. We walked home, and it began to snow again. The whole world was quiet, and we were sort of in tune with it. But much later, when we were in bed, he said something about the cool way the group breathing had sounded, and that maybe we could make some music like that. I said that was a good idea, and I was reaching to turn off the light when he grabbed my wrist, real hard, and he said, 'Sara, I love you.'"

"Hadn't he ever said it before?" I asked.

"Oh, sure, lots of times. But never like that. He looked . . . angry, almost, or like he was going to cry."

"Yeah, I know that look," I said. "And what did you say?"

"You know—that I loved him, too, and all that."

"Then what happened?" I said, shifting to my other knee.

"Then he said, 'Let's get married,' and I said, 'Let's,' and 'How wonderful,' or something, and he said, 'Let's call my father up and tell him he's won.' ''

Jesus. "And?" I said, already knowing the rest.

"Well, it was after midnight, so I told him we'd have to wait until the next day, and that's when we called you.''

"It practically sounds like a religious conversion,'' I said. "Why do you think he'd back out now?''

"The last few days he's been very moody.''

"That's only natural before your wedding,'' I said. "And Jason's a moody guy to begin with, Sara. You know that.''

"No, I mean *dark* and moody. I couldn't say boo to him. He sat at the drum pads all the time, working the same rhythms over and over again.''

Someone knocked on the door then, and rattled the knob. "We'll be right out!'' I called. "See, he's probably here already,'' I told Sara. "They probably want to get started, and they can't do that without the bride.''

I stood up and tried to rub the circulation back into my knees. Sara stood, too, and we walked out together. All the way to the living room, I silently prayed he'd be there, but I knew that he wouldn't be. The worst thing was the stupid relief I felt when I saw the other members of Blood Pudding. "What took you guys so long?'' I asked Iggy, their keyboard man, who had a string of paper clips hanging from one ear. When he didn't answer me, and they all looked at one another like guilty kids, I said, "Where's Jason?''

"He didn't come with us,'' Iggy said, and I heard a little cry from Sara as she disappeared behind me, like a ghost.

"What do you mean, he didn't come with you?'' I demanded. "Where the hell is he?''

"We dropped him off in the Bronx,'' Iggy said. "He said

he had to take care of some business, that he'd catch a train or a bus in a little while."

"Did he take his drums out of the van? And his drum box?"

"Well, yeah. Sure," Iggy said.

"Oh, shit," I said. Paulie was standing next to me by then, and I could see by her face that she'd taken everything in. "What are we going to do?" I said.

"I guess we've done all the wrong things already," she said.

"He's a grown man," I told her. "There comes a time when he has to be accountable for his own life, for his own actions."

"You say that now," she said.

"Paulie, what do you want from me? I talked to him, remember? And he came around."

"*You* thought he did, anyway."

Iggy was listening to us, his head swiveling from side to side, as if he was watching a tennis match.

"Oh, shit," I said again.

"I'm going in to Sara," Paulie said.

"And I'll try calling Jason."

"Hah!" she scoffed, walking away.

I told the guitarist to keep playing until I got back, and she immediately began something jazzy and upbeat. As I climbed the stairs toward Ann and Spence's bedroom, I thought of the band playing as the *Titanic* went down. Of course Jason didn't answer the phone, and when I heard the Black Flag screaming on his answer tape, I yelled, "You rotten little bastard, why don't you get your ass down here!" and I threw the phone across the bed.

I conferred with Spence in his study downstairs. After a while we went into the living room, and he announced that the wedding was being postponed because Jason had been unavoidably detained. There was a stunned silence, followed by an excited buzz of conversation. The guitarist started packing up her guitar, and the bewildered caterer stood at the entrance to the living room, holding a dripping ladle. Paulie's mother was crying. "Maybe something happened to him," she said. "Maybe he got sick. Or maybe he was mugged. Let's give him the benefit of the doubt."

It was like an untimely, senseless death, a funeral without a body to mourn. People left quietly, shaking their heads sadly and pressing the hands of the bereaved. I drove Paulie and Sara to the Bronx. As we'd expected, Jason wasn't in the apartment, and his equipment and most of his clothes were gone, too. Paulie pleaded with Sara to come home with her, and finally she gave in. I took them to Manhattan, and then I drove back to the Island by myself. At first, I walked around the house, kicking things and cursing, madder than hell at Jason for jilting Sara, for screwing everything up like that. As the day wore on, my anger wore off, and by nighttime I was left with only a feeling of flatness and terrible fatigue. When I got into bed, I decided to start looking for Jason the next day, but in the meantime I couldn't keep my eyes open another minute.

27

We are all living these lives,
four-generation novels
that are plotless
except for birth and death.
Halfway through we're bored,
we skip pages.
Truth plus fiction
make the best story,
so we lie and invent passion.
Dozing, we dream
a new dream
with tough symbols,
without heroes.
We wake, our breath
drugged with ink,
our heads mobbed
with characters
found in subways
and offices.
The dustcover promised more.

Now I was going to school twice a week. There was the poetry workshop on Tuesdays, and every Saturday afternoon

I accompanied Sara to her program at the Natural Birth Center in SoHo. I'd become Jason's stand-in, her new labor coach and potential birth partner. The other women in Sara's group all had their husbands or lovers with them, but at least she wasn't alone. I knelt beside her as she lay on her floor mat, and we breathed slowly and deeply in unison. Right after my first class, the instructor gave me a private crash course in everything I'd missed. Howard and I had taken a similar course when I was pregnant with Jason, and maybe that's why I was such a fast study. Some of the relaxation exercises, and the business of soft lights and soothing music during delivery, were new, but other details came back to me: the various stages of labor, the lower-back massage to ease tension and pain, the panting and pushing near the end. And the language, with words like "show" and "presentation," still had a wonderfully theatrical quality.

One afternoon I went with Sara to visit the nurse-midwife who would deliver her baby, a stocky, middle-aged woman named Carmen Gomez. She'd been recommended by the doctor who'd confirmed Sara's pregnancy. Sara clearly had a crush on Carmen, like the one I'd once had on my obstetrician, Dr. Kramer. I remembered sitting in his waiting room among other pregnant women, all of us extolling his virtues, like a bunch of fat harem wives in thrall of our sheik. We were strangely unjealous of one another. Each of us harbored her own obvious, marvelous secret, and each of us lived for her final rendezvous alone with him.

Mine turned out to be a lot less romantic than I'd dreamed. When my contractions were ten minutes apart, but not really strong, Howard stood in our bathroom doorway, timing them with his stopwatch, and watching me comb my hair and put on makeup. "Come on, babe, let's go," he urged. "It's snowing hard out there—we'll have to crawl. And the kid'll know you without lipstick.'' But I was lovestruck and giddy, and I wanted to be perfect for my child and our deliverer. Never mind that Dr. Kramer was at least fifty years old, and pretty fat himself. Never mind that I had to call him Dr. Kramer and he called me Paulie. When is love ever fair or reasonable?

Twelve hours later, I was in the delivery room with my hair in a matted, sweaty tangle. The lipstick had all been gnawed off, along with little bits of my lips. I was calling Dr. Kramer ''Marvin'' between screams, but the honeymoon was definitely over. I hated him and I hated Howard— I despised the treachery of all men who brought women to this destiny. Yet now I felt sorry for Sara because she had no men in her life, except for Howard.

On what would have been her wedding night, she and I got into bed together at my apartment. She'd stopped crying in the car, and before I could even say good night, she'd fallen into a deep, exhausted sleep. I lay awake for a long time beside her, and then I escaped into sleep, too. The next morning, Howard showed up while we were having break-fast, and we talked about calling the police to help us look for Jason. Sara became very upset. ''What are they going to do—arrest him for not loving me?'' she said. ''I don't want him back, especially if he has to be dragged back.''

''He's our son, Sara,'' I said gently. ''We're furious with him, too, but we're also worried.''

''It's not as if he was kidnapped or anything,'' she said, and we had to concede that. ''He's just hiding out in the Bronx or in Queens somewhere,'' she said, ''until the baby grows up and I die.''

Howard and I went into the bedroom to confer privately. Sara was probably right about Jason's whereabouts; he had musician friends all over the city who'd take him in. We decided that Howard would question a few of them and try to track him down himself. Involving the police might only complicate matters—what if Jason was staying with someone who dealt drugs? When we went back to the kitchen, Sara asked Howard if he'd drive her to the Bronx.

"You can't stay there alone," I said.

"Why not?" she said. "It's where we . . . where I live." I wondered if, despite her bitterness, she imagined Jason would show up there by and by, languishing with love and remorse.

"It isn't safe, for one thing," Howard told her.

"But I can't stay here," she said. "You don't have an awful lot of room."

I thought wistfully of the privacy I cherished, of Bernie's visits. But it would have been inappropriate for Sara to stay with Howard in Port Washington. While we were musing over all of this, Ann called to see how Sara was and to ask if there was anything she and Spence could do. Her call seemed providential in its timing, even inevitable, but I broached the subject with extreme care, anyway. "We'd love to have her," Ann said immediately. "We rattle around in this big old place. And Sara's so much *fun*."

I glanced at grim and gloomy Sara, who sat with her arms folded resolutely across the mound of her belly. Had it risen considerably since yesterday? "Sara, guess what?" I said. "Ann wants you to stay with her! Isn't that great?"

My enthusiasm wasn't exactly infectious, but at least Sara sighed deeply and nodded.

"It will only be for a little while," I whispered into the phone. "Dad's going to find Jason."

But three weeks later he was still missing. Howard had spoken to the other members of Blood Pudding, who led him to musicians and booking agents and clubs. He went through all five boroughs, and even spent a day or two in New Jersey. No one had seen Jason anywhere. Howard and I spoke on the phone more often now. He reported in, like a detective calling headquarters. We talked about selling the house; he could rent a garden apartment in Hempstead, near the studio, and we'd have enough money from the sale to provide living space somewhere for Sara and the baby. We talked about future employment for her and about the logistics of day care. Sara had already sublet the Bronx apartment to a couple of her friends. It was as if we never expected to see Jason again.

Howard and I were both anguished, but somehow our own lives proceeded, with the daily persistence of my mother's soaps. He went to work at the studio, and I continued writing my column and doing the proofreading. On Tuesday nights I went to my workshop at the New School. At last it was my turn to have something critiqued. I'd tried to get out of it by telling Ruth Trueheart that my life was a mess right now, and that I hadn't much time to write. She told me to bring in something old, if I had nothing else, although she preferred work in which our interest was still alive. I went through the yellowed pages of old poems, hating them all. I finally chose an untitled one, almost at random, and made Xerox copies for the whole class. The poem looked a little fresher on new paper, but not more accomplished. In fact, it seemed contrived to me now, and terribly simplistic. It was at least twenty years old—I was practically a child when I wrote it—but that was no excuse. What business did I have in this class if I wasn't writing?

Three of us were scheduled for that session, and I was up first. I distributed the copies of my poem around the table, filled with self-loathing and fear. There was that dreadful silence while it was being read, broken only by the occasional groan of a chair, or somebody coughing or rattling a page. I wished the fire alarm would go off—that had actually happened another night—and that we'd have to vacate the building. I wished I was at the Natural Birth Center with Sara, simply breathing, or asleep in my own bed, where I would wake soon, like Dorothy, from this bad dream.

Ruth cleared her throat for attention and then she read my poem aloud to the class. It sounded a little better than I'd expected. Her reading, in a low intense voice, gave it some authority. Still, my face burned and my cold hands clutched one another and writhed. When she was finished, no one said anything. It was like those moments of silent prayer in high school before chaos erupted again. Ruth looked around the room. "Who's ready to start?" she said. Nobody answered—nobody even made eye contact with her, which had to be a bad sign.

"All right," she said. "You seem to be in a collective coma tonight, so I'll get things going. We've had several poems in the first person this semester. What is the effect here of the plural, the 'we'?"

A young woman named Lisa said, "It makes it seem as if everyone leads boring lives, not just Paulie."

"In other words," Ruth said, "it makes it more universal, more of a philosophical argument than a personal complaint."

"Yeah," Lisa said, "I guess, but didn't you say the 'I' voice is more immediate?" All of Lisa's poems were in the first person and were explicitly sexual. I remembered one line: "He touched my vagina, the gateway to my heart," and the man next to me whispering, "Boy, she must be really short."

I had a pen poised over my copy of my poem, ready to

take notes on the criticism, and now I wrote in the margin: "We universal, I immediate." It looked like something Tarzan would say. Then I began to doodle boxes inside boxes until I'd covered what I'd just written and a few words of the poem, too.

"Maybe Paulie wants this distance from the reader," Ruth said. She looked at me with an encouraging little smile, but I knew I wasn't supposed to speak. The writer's comments were always reserved for the end of the critique, so I merely smiled back—mysteriously, I hoped—and continued to doodle.

Tim, who looked something like John Travolta, and was probably the best writer in the class, said, "I like the irony at the end, although it might be a little too neat."

"What's actually happening in this poem?" Ruth asked. "How did she reach that ending?"

"Well," Lisa said. "We go through life, dah dah dah, and have a kind of midlife crisis in the middle . . ." Everyone laughed.

An elderly woman named Rose said, "But I can't tell if the dream changes the way she feels."

"Ah," Ruth said. "That's a bit of a problem, isn't it? If she dreams a new, tough dream, why does she come back to wanting more than was promised?"

"I think you're being too rational, Ruth," Tim said. "Everyone wants more than they get," and I drew a row of tiny hearts in his direction across the top of the page.

"What do you think are the strongest parts of this poem, and what are the weakest?" Ruth asked.

"I love 'our breath drugged with ink,'" Tim said, "I could practically taste it."

Rose said, "I like 'Truth plus fiction make the best story,' but the line breaks seem predictable . . ."

"Which line breaks would you change?"

"Well, the one after line 10 is good because we pause and think of her dreaming a long time—is that enjambment?"

"Sort of," Ruth said, "What if we raised 'The dustcover' to the next-to-last line? Tim, do you think that would make the ending seem less pat, less gimmicky?"

"Yes," Tim said, and I drew a circle around "The dustcover," and attached a little upraised arrow.

A woman who always brought her supper to class in a plastic container poked at her salad with a plastic fork. "I'd like to know where the *energy* is in this poem," she said. She'd said that about every poem presented so far, and now everyone ignored her. Instead, they discussed my use of language, the absence of adjectives, and any possible influences on my work. "Have you ever read Mark Strand's *The Story of Our Lives*?" Ruth asked, and I shook my head and wrote that in the margin, too.

"What about a title?" Lisa said, when there seemed to be nothing left to say. "I hate poems without titles."

"What would you call it if it were yours?" Ruth said.

" 'Dustcovers'?"

"That sounds like a poem about upholstery," Ruth said. "We'll have to let Paulie ponder the title herself—it's her poem. What I like best about it is how well the central metaphor is controlled. It isn't strained or forced, although it easily could have been. I hope you'll think about the line breaks, Paulie, and about your diction, in certain places. I've marked my copy for you. And I'd like to see more development, especially in the middle. But the tone is quite compelling. Maybe you should all try a poem in the 'we' voice." She asked me if I had anything to say now in response, before we took a break. I only said what everyone always said, that many of the comments were useful and I was grateful for their help.

It was over, and I'd survived! I clutched my scribbled-over poem. And I looked past the bustle in the room, at Ruth, with a tremor of feeling that was close to love.

28

I WALKED MY TAIL OFF LOOKING FOR JASON. PHONE
calls wouldn't have worked, I knew, because it's so much
easier to lie on the phone than it is in person. Still, I felt like
a bill collector or a cop, the way people's faces closed against
me when I asked if they'd seen Jason Flax, or flashed his
photograph at them. It was a wallet-sized print of his high-
school yearbook portrait, and it was five years old, but it was
the only decent head shot we had of him. In all his pictures
onstage, his face is contorted with the concentration and ec-
stasy of playing. Lots of musicians grimace like that when
they play, as if they're in pain delivering the music. I do it
myself, and Paulie once said that I made some of the same
faces during sex.

Most of the kids I went to see, like Iggy and the other
members of Blood Pudding, lived the way Jason and Sara
did—close to the poverty level. Whenever they had some
extra dough, they'd blow it on a few snorts, or on equipment
or fancy duds from the thrift shops. Their parents tended to
give them food instead of money, to make sure they were
eating right. They were all waiting to "make it" with a recording, to be discovered by some entrepreneur or deejay,
and then the world. While they waited, they crashed together

in tenements that should have been condemned. I suppose I didn't live much better when I was a young musician. My band was on the road a lot, and we'd flop in crummy hotels, so strung out after a long gig that we could have slept anywhere. Jason's musician friends looked much weirder than we ever did, maybe because their appearance was such an important part of their act. Not that we didn't have a dress code of our own. We always performed in tuxedos at weddings and bar mitzvahs, although we had a more casual look at the clubs—sport shirts, pegged pants, wing-tipped shoes. Horn men wore fancy pinky rings that caught the lights, and shades were almost obligatory. At my own wedding, Paulie's mother thought that most of my friends were blind.

But these kids either had shaved heads or more hair than a Neanderthal. They wore paper clips for earrings, like Iggy, or heavy crucifixes that made me wonder how they held their heads up. And they weren't much help in my search. "Jason? Is he that curly-haired dude hangs out with a fox name of Flame? Hey, he looks like you a little? Nah, I ain't seen him."

Some people said they *had* seen him somewhere, but when I followed through, it always turned out to be a false alarm. I'd put ads in *The Village Voice* and *Rolling Stone*, carefully worded so as not to embarrass him or scare him off. *J.D.F. Call M or D. We can work it out together.* Once it was in print, it looked a little kinky, but who cared? The J.D. was for Jason David, picked from that long string of names we'd played with before he was born. Paulie would have given him six or seven of them, like the Crown Prince of England, if I hadn't stopped her. M and D, for Mom and Dad, of course, were his and Annie's early "code" names for us. Once, after one of Jason's tantrums, Paulie discovered that he'd written

I hate M and D with a crayon inside his closet. "Well, at least he spelled it right," I said, in an effort to console her.

I ran the ads for three consecutive weeks, without any luck. In the meantime I made the rounds of rock clubs in the East Village and uptown, places called Drag Race (where the performers and most of the audience were in drag), Broken Arms, and the Incest Café. *Their America*, I thought, in the dazzle of noise and strobe lights, an expression my father always used when someone of my generation confounded or frightened him. But how innocent we seemed now in comparison, with our daring, duck-assed hair, and all of those lovesick songs with women's names in the titles.

One day, when I was checking some of Jason's Brooklyn hangouts, I stopped in to see Paulie's mother. She was disappointed that I wasn't bringing good news about Jason or about Paulie and me, but she was still glad to see me. I did a few things for her—got a box down from one of the high shelves in her bedroom closet, interpreted a letter from Medicare, and changed a washer in her kitchen faucet. She made me stay for lunch, shoveling food onto my plate until I had to beg her to stop. I kept assuring her that nothing terrible had happened to Jason, that he'd gone off on his own, and I was going to find him. She sat near me, knitting while I drank my coffee, clicking her needles and counting stitches in a cozy whisper. It seemed strange that she had once been my mortal enemy, the one who'd tried to talk Paulie out of having anything to do with me.

A couple of her neighbors, elderly widows like herself, came in to visit while I was there. "You know my daughter's husband he has a music studio on Long Island," she said breathlessly, by way of introduction. I wished then for her sake that I was a dentist or a lawyer, professions that would have had more clout with her crowd. She seemed proud of me, anyway, and I could tell that she'd never told them about the separation. "Give my love to *everybody*," she called after me as I left.

The next day, when I was talking to Paulie on the phone, she had a brainstorm about Jason. "Leila!" she cried, as if we'd both been struggling to come up with her name.

Leila had been Jason's high-school girlfriend, the one we guessed he'd lost his virginity with, the one we suspected of supplying him and his friends with dope. "What about her?" I asked, trying to conjure up the sulky, pretty face that was always half hidden by a mess of dark hair. Paulie had privately dubbed her Leila the Wolf Girl, because of her wild behavior, the rare glint of teeth when she smiled. I hadn't thought of her in years. As far as I knew, Jason hadn't, either. She used to come to our house and go directly to his room and close the door behind her. The continuous blast of music in there covered everything they may have said or done. Paulie was terribly worried about it. "They're only *sixteen*," she reminded me. "And we're responsible, because he's our son and they're in our house."

I was a little worried myself—but I tried to make a joke out of it. "Well, then send them to her house, and let *her* parents worry," I said.

Paulie wasn't amused. "By not saying anything," she said, "we're giving them permission, Howard, we're in *collusion*." But she couldn't bring herself to interfere. Jason, who'd been so unhappy, was suddenly blissful, and nicer to everybody, even his sister and mother. Maybe being in love with a girl made him more generous to all females. Paulie tiptoed around him, still worried, but afraid of jinxing the peace. Finally, she talked me into knocking on his bedroom door one day just to see what was going on in there, and to let them know we were aware of them. "Be casual," Paulie hissed after she'd worked me into a frenzy, and then she retreated to the safety of our own bedroom. I knocked and knocked. Jesus, they had more than enough time to get dressed, to throw anything illegal out the window, and themselves after it. When my fist was starting to get sore, Jason opened the door a crack, and I tried to think of something casual to say—"What's new, kid? How's tricks? Would you like some milk and cookies?"—when I really wanted to push the door open wide and shout that they were in mortal danger, playing at being adults like that. It was the year of Jason's greatest growth spurt, and we were on eye level with one another, the first time I'd noticed that. His eyes slitted and cold, his mouth was curled with contempt. The stink of incense seeped out into the hallway, and I thought I glimpsed Leila lounging brazenly on Jason's bed. The main horror was my sense of their freedom. They probably *could* go to Leila's house—her parents didn't seem to know or care much what she did—or they could just pool their fat allowances and drive to a motel. "Can you keep the music down a little?" I said at last, chickening out. "Mom has a headache."

On another occasion, Paulie conned me into talking with Jason about his behavior, and about contraception. "They study it in *school*, for God's sake," I protested at first, and then I went upstairs and knocked again. He was alone this time, and the incense was as thick and sickening as ever. I remembered with wonder that my father once beat the hell out of me for lighting matches in the bathroom. I felt like a jerk—Ward Cleaver going upstairs to have a heart-to-heart with Beaver about the birds and the bees. When I asked if I could come in, Jason glanced behind him, as if he was checking it out with some invisible companions, before he shrugged and let me by. As soon as I began talking, his face became a mask of pity and disdain. I stumbled through the whole thing, anyway. "What I mean," I said, at the end of some tortured sentence about true sexual maturity, "is that I know how you feel."

Oh, yeah, *sure*, his face said. He kept fiddling with a ball-point pen while I spoke, clicking it open and shut.

When I couldn't stand it anymore, I shouted, "Put that damn thing down!" It was the way we'd always handled bad moments between us. Jason would do some small, repetitive thing to annoy me, and I would jump on him for it. As soon as he got me good and angry, he'd become infuriatingly calm, so I'd pick on him until he found another tic—blinking, sucking his teeth, kicking his foot against my chair—that set me off again. I saw it happening with a kind of detached amazement, amazed, too, that I couldn't or wouldn't do anything to stop it. "Listen, you don't know everything," I said, "even if you think you do. If you knock that girl up, the world's going to close down on you, mister." Cleaver never spoke to Beaver or Wally between his teeth that way, with the vengeance of age and experience. And they never smirked at their dad the way Jason did that day at me. "Swell, thanks," he muttered, and the wall was back up between us.

As usual, Paulie was waiting in our bedroom for the results of the talk she'd instigated, and as usual I lied, or varnished the truth, to please her. "I scared the shit out of him," I reported with simulated pride, and Paulie wailed, "That wasn't what you were supposed to do!" But maybe I had actually scared Jason a little. Something happened between him and Leila soon after that, and they stopped seeing one another as often. He got more into his music, opening the way for a temporary truce with me.

"Leila?" I said to Paulie on the phone. "The Wolf Girl? What made you think of her?"

"I don't know," she confessed. "Intuition, maybe. I've

been trying to trace Jason back a little, to figure him out, and I just came up with Leila. Do you remember how happy he was when he began going out with her?''

''You mean when he began staying home with her. And you were so worried she'd get pregnant.''

''Well, somebody did.''

''So you think he's with Leila? But they've been out of high school for years, and I haven't heard him mention her in ages. Where is she, anyway?''

''Connecticut or someplace. She got married, I think, although maybe that's over by now. I know her parents moved to the city a few years ago.''

''Can you find out?'' I said. ''Jesus, we're like Nick and Nora Charles, aren't we?''

''I'll try,'' Paulie said. ''Katherine might be able to help.''

''Yeah, she might. Listen, how's Sara doing?''

''Fine, considering everything. She's being introspective, concentrating on what's happening to her.''

''That's good,'' I said, ''if it takes her mind off Jason.''

''I did that, too,'' Paulie said, ''and I wasn't trying to forget anybody. It's the state of being pregnant, as if you're weaving a house for your child out of your own body, and it takes all your energy, all your attention.''

''You were beautiful, pregnant,'' I said. I didn't say it with any secret motive; it was simply the truth.

''Sara is, too,'' Paulie said, ''and Jason is missing everything.''

''Check out Leila Stark,'' I said. ''I'll call you tomorrow. And by the way, your mother sends her love.''

Paulie was right—Katherine *was* able to help us find Leila, through some school records for one of her younger brothers. He'd transferred to a prep school in Manhattan, and they gave

Katherine a current telephone number for Leila's parents. Her mother answered the phone when I called. I told her I was one of Leila's old classmates from Port Washington High, and that we were planning a fifth reunion. I thought of asking if Leila was still married, as a sort of casual, survey-type question, and then decided against it. Unsuspecting as ever, her mother gave me Leila's address in Westport. By a strange coincidence, that was where Sara's parents lived, too. I looked them up in the phone book at a gas station near Leila's, and decided to drive past their house later just to see how they lived. First I had to see Leila, though, and find out if Jason was with her, or if she knew where he was.

It was a bleak Saturday afternoon and there were only a few children and dogs on the quiet suburban streets. Leila's house—she was Leila Catalfano now—was modest for that area, a weathered-looking saltbox on a small plot of land. I rang the doorbell and waited, listening to a dog's hoarse barking inside. When the door opened at last, a young guy was standing there holding the big, barking dog back by a choke collar. I don't know why, but I wasn't prepared to see Leila's husband. I'd pictured her coming to the door herself, puzzled at first and then suddenly recognizing me. I thought I'd catch her off-guard, so that she'd spill anything she knew about Jason before she could think. Now I needed a different approach, and fast. The dog, lunging and strangling on his collar, gave me a few seconds. "Stay, Bozo, stay!" Leila's husband commanded, and he kept slapping the crazed dog across the muzzle.

"Uh . . . um," I said, and coughed to buy myself a little more time. I remembered the day in Port Washington when I was caught in my car by that couple, and made up the story about being lost. I would have done the same right then, except that someone else came up behind the guy and the dog. It was Leila, of course, although I didn't know her immediately. The hair had been cleared from her face, pulled back in a ponytail. She looked scrubbed and ordinary, not wild or mysterious at all. And she was very pregnant. Jesus, it was an epidemic. I'd have to tell her the truth now that she'd seen me, that Jason was missing and I was hoping she had a clue. But the idea of his hiding out here seemed ridiculous now—did I think they'd adopted him? I drew in my breath and was about to speak when I realized that Leila was looking at me with only mild curiosity. She didn't recognize me! All those times she'd fled past Paulie and me to Jason's room, our faces had probably never registered on her brain. Maybe she couldn't see us clearly through that tangle of hair, and we were only "them," anyway, the old folks, the parents, the enemy. I bet she never dreamed on those steamy afternoons that she'd become us someday, or a reasonable facsimile of us.

"Whatever you're selling," she said, "we've already got two of." She leaned over awkwardly to stroke the struggling dog. "Nice boy, good boy," she crooned.

"Aha," I said. "Even central air-conditioning?"

"Yeah, yeah," she said. "And a central vacuuming system. And a central burglar alarm."

"Well, you sure don't need that," I said, indicating the dog. It was incredible that she still didn't know me, especially considering the strong family resemblance.

"Isn't this a bad time to sell air-conditioners?" Leila's husband asked, not without sympathy. "I mean, it's still winter."

"But that's my product," I told him, "and I'm a man for all seasons."

"Well, good luck," he said, and began to close the door between us.

"Leila!" I said. "Wait!"

The door swung open. "You know each other?" the husband asked. Even the dog seemed surprised; his growl had changed to a pitiful whine.

"I'm Jason Flax's father," I said.

"Jason," Leila said, like someone coming awake from a dream. "God! How's he doing?"

"I don't know," I said. "We can't seem to find him."

"Who's Jason?" Leila's husband asked, and she reached out absently to pat his arm, the way she'd patted the dog before.

"Jason's missing?" she asked.

"Sort of. Yes," I said. "But you haven't seen him." It wasn't really even a question.

She laughed. "No, not recently, not since high school. God!"

"I didn't think so," I said. "I'm just following every possible lead."

"Well, when you find him," she said, "will you give him my love?"

"Sure," I said, thinking that she'd already given him more than his share. Walking back to my car at the curb, I was sorry I'd told her who I was, and for blabbing about Jason. I knew it was my pride that had made me do it, my resistance to being invisible. But I felt invisible again a few minutes later, when I drove slowly down Sara's parents' street and looked up at their swanky house. It was set way back on a sloping lawn, and it seemed even further away than it was, and unapproachable. Sara was their loss, I told myself. Jason was ours.

29

"*L*ISTEN," CARMEN SAID, PUTTING THE FETAL
stethoscope to Sara's belly, and I heard the gallop of the
baby's heart. "My God," I said, knowing by Carmen's com-
placent smile that it was probably what everyone said.

Later, while Sara was getting dressed, Carmen beckoned
me into her office, where the walls were lined with photographs of babies. "Is anything wrong?" I asked, my hand
pressed to my own beating heart.

"Oh, no, no," she said. "Everything's normal, perfect.
It's the daddy I'm thinking about. Still no sign of him?"

I shook my head. "My husband's been looking everywhere. Sara is really depressed, isn't she?" It was something
I'd known all along, but was unable to admit before, even to
myself. Instead, I'd pretended she was merely concerned with
the metamorphosis of her own body.

"Yes," Carmen said. "And she's getting a little scared,
too. A baby on the inside is one thing, you know . . ."

"I know. But at least we'll be here for her, won't we?"
And then I confessed that I wished the baby was going to be
born in a hospital. I told Carmen that I'd discussed it with
Sara more than once, arguing that it would surely be safer

there, with all that high-tech equipment, all those people. "Yeah, and all those germs," Sara had said.

To my surprise, Carmen agreed with me. "I'll be honest with you, Paulie," she said. "If something goes wrong, I'd rather have that equipment handy myself—the intensive-care nursery, the blood bank, anesthesia. I don't *advise* home births, but I'll attend them as long as my insurance covers it. If the mother is completely healthy, that is, and if there's a backup hospital nearby."

Sara had decided to be delivered at Ann's house, and there was a hospital only minutes away. And I'd already asked Bernie if I could call him to come if there was trouble. So far, Sara's troubles were all of the spirit. She was deeply distressed about Jason, and it was difficult to comfort her. What had my mother said when Howard went off with Marie? "Leave them alone, and they'll come home, wagging their tails behind them." That turned out to be true, in a way, but it was hardly encouraging when she said it. Despite Howard's daily progress reports, I wondered if he was really trying hard enough to find Jason. Maybe this was a vicarious way of regaining his own early freedom, although God knows he was free enough now.

After we left Carmen's, Sara took a cab to Grand Central, and I walked over to the St. Marks Bookshop to meet La Rae. We browsed a little and then went to have lunch at one of those Indian restaurants on Sixth Street. It was a tiny, dark place with relentless canned sitar music.

"I can't even read the menu," La Rae complained, "and that music is driving me crazy."

"Typical Western intolerance," I said, squinting at my own menu and tilting it to catch the candlelight.

"I'll probably have heartburn all the way home," La Rae muttered.

"Stop being such a pill. When it's your turn, you can choose someplace *American*, okay?" I said, remembering her bitter prediction that we'd end up meeting for lunches. But it didn't really matter where we met—I hadn't felt truly comfortable with La Rae since Frank's "visit." We argued more than we ever had, mostly about silly, petty things like this. "Listen, I'm sorry," I said, leaning forward to touch her arm. "I'm just in a lousy mood."

"You haven't heard anything from Jason yet, have you?" she asked.

"No, although Howard says he's looked everywhere . . ."

"Don't you believe him?"

"I don't know. Maybe he's compensating, maybe he's acting out his own old fantasies through Jason."

"Oh, will you stop playing Freud, Paulie," La Rae said. "It's so boring."

I became unreasonably angry. "Look who's talking," I said. "*You* could be arrested for practicing without a license. At least I don't mess around with the lives of perfect strangers."

"Well, it's better than wasting your own life on bathtub rings and plant mold, isn't it?"

How could she! Why, she was the one who'd gotten me into it in the first place! I was so angry I almost told her about Frank's pass, and I think she almost revealed worse things she thought or knew about Howard and me. But instead I mumbled, "Let's order, okay?" and we bent to the menus as if they were scripts that would tell us what to say next.

We managed to make polite, artificial conversation until dessert, when La Rae confided that she was having serious problems with her father. He was accusing her and Frank of stealing things from his room in their garage: underwear, newspapers, money. She said he was hoarding food against some imagined Armageddon, and the whole house was starting to stink.

"Your poor dad," I said. "And poor you," I added, as a kind of olive branch.

"Frank is pretty good about it," La Rae said, as if she'd read my mind before and felt obligated now to speak in his behalf. "In fact, he's a lot better than me. He tries to draw my father out, to talk him up. I just want to shake him and say straighten up and stop acting like this."

"He's *your* father, that's why. I get that way with my mother, too, when she starts singing Howard's praises, when she repeats things. God, she tells me everything about thirty times."

"I hate when my father coughs and clears his throat. I swear he does it just to annoy me."

We both laughed, guiltily, comfortably, the tension between us relieved. And later we parted with affection, but I mourned the unqualified easiness we'd once had, and I feared the eventual end of our friendship. All relationships seemed fragile to me then. People changed without fair warning, or they died or went away. If you left them first, you saved face and protected yourself from the pain of abandonment. Still, I sorely missed everyone who was missing: Howard, Jason, my long-lost father. And although he'd stopped talking about her, I knew that Bernie continued to ache for his wife.

I had been writing whole poems, in the middle of everything. At least they seemed whole until the class got at them, and then I knew they were still fragmented and badly flawed. The criticism was much harsher than it had been the first time. Somehow, it didn't discourage me, once I'd gotten over the initial shock and hurt. It actually motivated me to work harder, as if even a negative response proved my poems were viable, were worth the effort of revision.

I went to the health club after leaving La Rae, and joined an aerobics class that was already in session. "Get it up, get it up!" the instructor ordered, in time to the hard-driving rock blasting from the speakers. How did people ever exercise during the big-band era? I had trouble keeping up with everybody else, even the only other woman who looked my age. Maybe their head start had given them momentum, and maybe it wasn't such a good idea to work out right after lunch. I crawled away before the class had ended and went down to the Jacuzzi, where the same kind of music was playing. There was a woman sitting there alone, with her eyes shut, and I sat beside her in the rushing water. "Ahhh," I said. It was actually too hot for comfort, practically scalding, but I thought I'd get used to it.

"It's good, isn't it?" she said, opening her eyes. "It draws all the poisons out of your nerves."

What did she mean by that? There were so many disturbed people in the city, and although most of them were probably harmless, you couldn't ever be sure. The towel attendant was reading a magazine and listening to his own personal Walkman. You could easily drown without ever getting his attention. I looked at the other woman and she was smiling companionably. I smiled, too, and tried to relax, to release my nerve poisons to mingle with hers in the steaming foam.

Back at the apartment, I found that one of Ruth Trueheart's books had arrived in the mail. I had ordered it so long ago I'd almost forgotten about it. There was a bill tucked inside that described it as a "First Edition, d.j. slightly torn and sunned." I knew that there had only been one edition of each of Ruth's books. This was her second, a slender volume called *Wrong Turn*. I opened the back flap and there was a photo of her, taken, it seemed, during another lifetime. She looked only slightly familiar, the way my friends and I looked in our wedding pictures. The hair that was mostly gray now, and worn in a careful French knot, was dark and willfully unkempt in the picture, like Colette's, like mine. Who was this? It wasn't only that she was incredibly young but that she had the striking radiance of someone in love.

The book itself was handsome, with a simple art deco design on its jacket, which had been mended with yellowed tape. I wondered what "sunned" meant. Did it refer to the faded corners, the bleached spine? The word evoked a sun-filled room where someone sat reading poetry in a happy, golden daze. I opened the book and saw the dedication: *To A.* Oh, the holy mystery we make out of ordinary, mortal love. *Wrong Turn* had been out of print for years. This copy had to be hunted down for a modest fee, and was probably found on some dusty old shelf somewhere. There was a bookplate pasted inside; the book had once been part of Judith Lehmann Pearl's library. *Ex Libris.* Did she still exist? Did A. ? And were Ruth's later books dedicated to B., and C., and so on? I turned to the first poem. It was titled "A Winter Prothalamion" and began:

> *Come to the window now;*
> *can so much snow*
> *be simply bridal?*
> *Does love*
> *remain*
> *a sword of flowers?*

My eyes filled with tears, making the poem run off the page like rain off a window. The words had taken me by surprise, the way music does sometimes, or sudden, unbidden memories. So this was poetry! Of course, I'd always known the real thing when I read it, but now I faced the truth that my own writing was not and never would be, despite Ruth's kind encouragement and all my diligent revising. And worse, I had always known this, too. Then why did I persist, and with such sinful pride and hopefulness? It certainly wasn't for any fantasy of fame and fortune—even the real poets shared such stingy rewards. Why else did so many great ones die young, if not from the complications of disappointment? And here was Ruth with seven lost books, trying to teach her secret music to mostly tone-deaf students. I knew that I was moved to write by something like desire, although I couldn't name it exactly. Yet it had to do with naming, and with giving shape to the scary shapelessness of being.

I called La Rae later and apologized for being so cranky at lunch. She was friendly, but I detected an edge of coldness to her voice. And she insisted there was nothing to apologize for, which gave me no chance to try and repair things between us. Helplessly, I made another date to meet her for lunch. Then I got into bed with a pile of books, including Ruth's, even though it was only eight o'clock. This was what I'd dreamed of doing when the children were young and I hardly ever had time to myself. I used to read in the locked bathroom, while Jason or Annie jiggled the knob and hammered on the door with a toy. I read during their brief naps, and even while I fed them, the volume of stories or poems propped on my cookbook holder on the table. Some of my favorite books are still marked with smears of baby food and tiny fingerprints. "Mommy is reading now," I'd announce when they demanded my attention, and then I'd try to get a few more lines in before I had to stop. Did that have anything to do with the reading problems Jason developed later? Maybe I wasn't the best mother in the world, despite my passion for mothering. I had the domestic life I'd wanted so badly, and yet I'd escape into other people's imagined lives every chance I got. Katherine kept assuring me that someday my children would be adults who'd leave home, and that I'd have plenty of time to read. I told her that the way things worked out, I'd probably go blind first.

In the meantime, there were other, more serious concerns. I saw our family slowly dividing into opposing sides, and I warned Howard that something was very wrong. "We should be all for one and one for all," I said, and he said, "Jesus, Paulie, we're not the Three Musketeers." He continued to favor Ann and I championed Jason, even when he was perversely bratty. I thought I was close to him, that I understood him in some special, symbiotic way. But as he grew older the distance between us grew, too. He became so unpredictable—manly one minute and babyish the next—that I wasn't sure how to treat him anymore. The insistent high-pitched voice deepened and cracked; his body began to grow too quickly into the promise of his oversized hands and feet. He was being transformed, like some poor creature in a horror movie who can't help turning into a monster. When he was sixteen, Leila Stark, that sexy, feral-looking girl from school, started hanging around him. She would go right past me into his room and close the door behind her. "Talk to him," I'd beg Howard, and later I'd hear embattled voices from another part of the house. I was always grateful for the ultimate, peacemaking noise of their music.

Bernie was at a medical meeting in Chicago, and I wouldn't see him for a few days. He'd asked me to go with him, but I said I couldn't leave town because of Sara, and wondered later how true that was. I'd just finished proofreading a huge stack of engineering papers; they were on the dresser, neatly bundled for delivery the next morning. There were no demands on me as I lay in Mary and Jim's bed, propped on pillows like an invalid, surrounded by a landslide of books. But I was unable to read. Of course, there was nothing wrong with my eyes that my reading glasses couldn't fix—it was simply that life had completely invaded my consciousness. I gave up and reached for the telephone, which was still my main connection to the outside world. I called Ann, and she and Sara answered at the same time. Then Spence picked up a third extension somewhere and yelled hello. We all said the inane things families say to one another on the phone: "How are you? . . . I'm fine . . . Take care . . ." As if the mechanics of phoning interfered with natural discourse. I hung up, feeling restless and dissatisfied, and then I called Howard, something I rarely did.

He was surprised to hear from me. "Nothing's happened yet, has it?" he asked, and it took a few moments before I realized he was referring to Sara.

"She's not due for over three weeks," I said. "You know that. And I think she'll hold out as long as she can."

"Then is this an ordinary social call?" he said, with clear delight. "I mean, you're not selling magazines or anything, are you?"

I had to laugh. "No," I said, "but maybe that's not such a bad idea."

"Why? Do you need money?" he asked.

"Who doesn't?" I said. "But I'm okay, actually. I live pretty sparely now, like a cloistered nun."

"Are you celibate, too?" he said, and then, into the awful silence, "I'm sorry, Paulie. That was really out of line, wasn't it?" His pain was palpable, and I thought: Ah, now you know what it's like.

"Yes, it was," I said, thinking I might have led him into saying it for that small moment of revenge. But that wasn't the whole purpose of my call, was it?

Howard must have been wondering the same thing. "What's new?" he said. "That I'd want to hear about, that is."

"You're the one who's supposed to have news for me," I reminded him.

"I only wish I did."

"Maybe you're not trying hard enough," I said.

"Are you kidding, Paulie? What do you think I've been doing for the last few weeks?"

The truth was, I'd pictured him starting out to look for Jason and then staying on at some club to listen to the music and meet women. "I'm not sure, Howard," I said, suddenly wanting more revenge. "But you haven't found him, have you?"

"Why don't you try it yourself if you think it's so easy," he said.

Why, indeed? Because, I told myself, I had enough to do comforting Sara. And because I still longed for some unlikely bond to develop between Howard and Jason. But I said, "Maybe I'll just do that," and we said good-bye with the courtesy of contained rage.

I dialed Sharon's number immediately, afraid of having to think too much between calls. We talked about Gil mostly, and Sharon kept lapsing into the present tense and correcting herself. "Gil says—I mean *said* . . ." It was as if she were trying to resurrect him through memory, and then convince herself that he was really gone. She said that her days were all right once she got to work. But when she came home, the silence of the house was oppressive. "I keep thinking I hear his key in the lock," she said, and then she began to cry. If we'd been together, I would have put my arms around her. Instead, I murmured, "I know, I'm sorry," until she stopped crying. Her despair made me feel ashamed of my own, without actually diminishing it. "It could be worse," my mother always said when something trivial seemed tragic to me, but that had never cheered me up, either.

I opened Ruth's book again, with determination this time, but I didn't even get my money's worth of solace. Art was like love, in some ways—it wasn't dependable, and you had to give your whole self up to it. It was only when I remembered the baby's heartbeat that I began to feel a little better. I realized that I hadn't told anyone else about it, as if it were some great secret I couldn't share, or as if I hadn't really believed my own ears.

30

*S*O PAULIE HAD A LOVER, AND I WAS PROBABLY THE LAST
to know. Of course the possibility had occurred to me before,
but I'd given it the same fast, nervous attention I usually gave
to thoughts of my own death. I knew that she'd had somebody
while I was living with Marie. When I used to take the children out on weekends, Jason would tell me all about
Douglas—how he played horsey with them, and made good
grilled-cheese sandwiches for breakfast. So-called friends
hinted that he was a good-looking, good-natured kid, a drugstore cowboy and probably a stud. It was completely unreasonable and unfair of me, but I was jealous then, too. It didn't
matter that I was the one who'd left, the one who'd been
unfaithful first. All I kept thinking was that I wanted to kill
the guy. I controlled myself, of course. I didn't even pump
Jason about what else Douglas did, with Paulie, and he never
volunteered that information. I simply let my imagination fill
me in.

This time I found out what I didn't want to know by trick-
ing Annie into telling me. She and I were sitting in her living
room after dinner, waiting for Spence and Sara to come back
from Baskin-Robbins with our dessert. "Have you seen Mom

lately?'' I asked, and Annie blushed so violently I had to look away.

"Yes,'' she said in a small, careful voice. "We've had lunch a few times. She's doing fine.''

"Yeah, I know,'' I said, and then, without losing a beat, "Have you met what's-his-name yet?''

"Dr. Rusten? Only once, by accident. Spence and I ran into them on the street.'' My heart tripped along without interruption, and Annie cleared her throat. "He wears glasses,'' she said.

I tried to imagine that street scene, and was touched by Annie's discomfort, her obvious loyalty to me. I wondered what kind of doctor he was, but I didn't ask. Jesus, I thought bitterly, Paulie's mother will be thrilled. I made myself smile at Annie's anxious face. "He's divorced, isn't he?'' I said, pretending this was information I'd once known but had simply forgotten.

"No, he's a widower. I think his wife died a few years ago.''

And now he had my wife. "Well, it's good that Mom's not lonely,'' I said, as if we were talking about an elderly person in need of simple companionship. In the meantime, the news was slowly seeping through me, like poison.

When Sara and Spence showed up with the ice cream—ices for me, in deference to my diet—I said I wasn't too hungry, the understatement of the year. They were all solicitous, worried that I wasn't feeling well. "I just don't have enough room,'' I assured them. "Keep it in the freezer for next time.''

Sara ate her Rocky Road sundae steadily, with a preoccupied expression on her face. God, she was tremendous. Maybe there was a gang of babies in there, all of them rejected by their daddy. The last time I'd seen Sara, I asked if she had any leads for me before I went out to look for Jason again. She drew herself up with effort and said fiercely, "Don't. I don't want you to find him," and the subject was slammed shut between us. But that night Spence took me aside and told me that Sara had received some money in the mail from Jason. It had been forwarded by the friends who'd sublet their apartment. I got very excited. "Where is he, for Christ's sake?" I demanded. "And why the hell didn't you tell me this right away?"

Spence put his hands up as if to ward off a blow. "Listen, Sara would kill me if she knew I was telling you now. And it doesn't matter much, anyway. She burned the envelope in the fireplace, claimed she couldn't make out the original postmark."

"Did she burn the money, too?"

"No," he admitted. "She tried to give it to me, toward expenses. Boy, it was like Monopoly money. She had this stack of tens and twenties."

"He sent *cash* like that through the mail?" I said. I don't know why I was so surprised; it was something my mother always did, and Jason wasn't famous for his common sense, either.

"Shh, Dad. Hold it down, will you," Spence said. "Yeah, he sent cold cash."

"Was there a note?"

"She wouldn't tell me that. And she got a little crazy when I asked her, so I guess there wasn't."

I remembered Sara's defiance that afternoon, the sorrowful, furious way she'd said, "Don't. I don't want you to find him." I knew that she wouldn't tell me anything, either—if there was anything to tell—even if I grilled her for a week. So far, I had done everything I could to find Jason, except go to the police. The news about the money was reassuring;

at least I knew for sure now that he was safe somewhere. But how could a big, strapping kid with a bulky set of drums just disappear like that? I probably should have hired a private detective a long time ago, before his trail had cooled. But I'd read somewhere once that you couldn't deliberately get lost in America anymore because of the technology. They'd put your face into a computer, and it would show up on computers everywhere in the country. Someone would recognize you before too long. Jason didn't even have to be in the metropolitan area; he could be anywhere at all. He had a couple of friends in L.A., for instance, musicians who were trying to make the Hollywood scene, and he might have gotten the same idea. The Coast would certainly put a lot of mileage between him and his troubles.

Now, as I watched Sara eat her ice cream, I thought I'd ask around, then maybe head out West myself, and prove to Paulie that I was trying hard enough to find him. *Dr. Rusten*. Shit. Who the hell was he, and how had he latched on to Paulie so fast? But I really didn't want to know anything about him, didn't want to picture them together. I already saw him taking off his glasses and turning blindly to kiss her. The moment I'd asked her that stupid question about celibacy, I knew the answer. Probably before I'd asked it. Paulie was an intensely sexual woman; she'd always be with someone. The rotten joke was that I was the celibate now. It wouldn't go on forever. One day, I'd go into another bar and meet a woman who was as lonely as I was, and I'd go home with her and stay for a while. But right then that seemed even lonelier than being by myself.

That day long ago, when Paulie caught me packing to go off with Marie, she demanded to know what we did that was different, that was better, and I had a flash of sexual frenzy—of tongues and tangled limbs. But God knows I wasn't going to give Paulie any of the details. I didn't want to hurt her more than I already had. Things had been pretty rough between us for a while by then. It was one of those endless winters—snow piling up over slush over snow. I remember looking out the window of our building at the empty, ghostly playground and wishing that I'd loved my father better, that I'd learned to ski, that I'd taken more courses in music theory and had tried composing. One of the kids or the other always had croup or something that winter. We'd try to make love and listen for their breathing at the same time, which really put a crimp in desire and performance. But maybe that's too easy, only a handy excuse. The thing was, I was almost always tired in bed, more inclined to sleep, to go unconscious, than anything else. And Paulie would crawl in next to me, smelling of Shalimar and Vicks and sad desperation. "Talk to me, Howie," she'd beg, but what could I say? That we'd made a bad bargain in the backseat of a car? That good intentions become shit in the grind of years? Or maybe just that I loved her and the children more in the abstract than I did in the flesh.

And what could I say about Marie and me? I'd met her one Saturday morning in that same dreary playground, where she sat reading on one of the benches, uniquely, alluringly childless. The only one not pushing a swing or a baby carriage, or screaming orders about sharing toys and not throwing sand. Of course I loved my children—God, I was crazy about them! We could have been a family of devoted chimps as we entered the playground, with Jason swinging from one of my hands and Annie wrapped like Cheetah around my neck. When they released their hold on me and ran off to the monkey bars, where they belonged, I sat down on the other end of Marie's bench. I couldn't say what I intended, beyond settling my ass somewhere, and maybe making some grown-up small talk. It was a cold day. The kids were bundled into their snowsuits like a couple of inflatable toys. Annie's cheeks were brightly chapped, and the snot was already frozen on Jason's upper lip.

Marie and I said hello to one another and the words floated out in clouds of vaporous breath. We introduced ourselves and pointed out our respective buildings in the complex. She kept jiggling her high-heeled boots in place to keep warm. Her long hair was gypsy-black, and even in her red winter coat I could see the compact tension of her body. "Do you know who you remind me of?" I asked, and when she shook her head, I said, "Carmen. When she does a few flamenco steps before she starts singing the Habanera?"

Her feet grew still, and she laughed in a surprising, rich contralto. "Don't worry," she said. "I promise not to sing." But she knew it was her dark passion I'd perceived, not any musical impulse.

We talked a little about the book that lay face-down in her lap now, some best-selling spy thriller that I was sure Paulie would have sneered at. We both said, agreeably, that it was supposed to be good escape reading.

"What do you want to escape from?" she asked suddenly. I laughed this time and opened my arms in an all-encompassing gesture. "This," I said, and I might have meant Queens, or February, or Planet Earth. "How about you?" The kids began calling to me then, the usual "Daddy, watch me, hey, look at me, Daddy" routine they pulled whenever I had a minute to myself. I just waved to them, as if they were casual acquaintances whose friendship I didn't want to encourage.

Marie smiled at me in conspiracy and I smiled back. "The cigarette factory," she said. And then softly, seriously, "My husband.'' It took me a few moments to realize she was still answering the question about escaping.

We stayed there on the bench, even when the wind began whipping around us and Jason yelled that he was too cold, he wanted to go home. He was probably getting tired, and his mittens were soaking wet from some sandbox slush. I called him over and gave him my gloves, and he ran off again, flapping them around like useless leather wings. I put my hands in the shallow pockets of my windbreaker and then took them right out again to blow on them. They were freezing, but the rest of me was warm, was racing with blood. I felt myself begin to thaw, to rouse from my long hibernation. And I thought by her face that Marie knew I'd just bought us a few more minutes of whatever it was we were beginning.

''Tell me what she *does*, what you do together,'' Paulie cried, in the agony of my going. But it wasn't so much what we did that was mysterious or special; it was more a condition we were in, a perpetual state of heat and wildness. And even though I knew it would have to burn out eventually, or that we would, I was willing to give up everything else for it. If Paulie's current situation was anything like that, maybe I only had to wait it out. *Only*. But my instincts told me that this was different, somehow, more complicated. What really scared me was that she might be connected to this man out of bed, too, that they might have a life together. My life.

''Dad,'' Annie was saying, ''Daddy, how do you feel now?'' She was looking at me with grave concern. All three of them were.

''I'm fine,'' I told them, ''great,'' and I patted my tender, aching gut. ''Let's have those ices now,'' I said.

31

*T*HE BABY SHOWER WAS KATHERINE'S IDEA. SHE INsisted that what Sara needed, in Jason's absence, was a show of community support, a committee of friends to welcome her baby. It sounded sensible to me and even better than that to Ann, who had despaired of ever cheering Sara up again. It was pretty late in her pregnancy, and we made our plans quickly with a chain of phone calls and some hurried shopping. Katherine volunteered to have the shower at her house the following Sunday, and almost everyone else offered to bring food for the buffet brunch. We decided not to make it a surprise, because Sara had had enough surprises recently, and looking forward to the party would be a pleasure in itself.

Ann and I went shopping together in Manhattan for baby gifts. Howard and I had already agreed that we'd provide Sara with the larger items of equipment, like the crib and stroller and high chair. The gift I most wanted to bring her, of course, was Jason, not dragged in by his hair, but willing and contrite, and eager to make up for lost time. Instead, I browsed with Ann in the infant department at Saks, both of us exclaiming over the exquisite tiny garments.

''Isn't this adorable, Mom?'' Ann said, holding up a pair

of delicate pink rompers for my approval. "Oh, this is so much *fun*."

Exactly what she'd once said about Sara, I remembered, and now look at her. I pictured the rompers all soiled and smelly, and I remembered the relentless sound of colicky screaming. It was astounding to think of my first, intimate connection to this full-grown woman, to her missing brother. "Sort of," I said. "And then you have them forever."

"What?" Ann said, looking confused. "These things?"

"No," I said impatiently, "the *children*." I grabbed her arm. "Listen, Ann." I said. "Having a child is probably the most radical act of your entire life."

She wriggled free of my grasp. "You sound kind of sorry you ever did it, Mom," she said in a hurt voice.

"Oh, no, darling, never! Well, sometimes," I admitted, under her critical gaze, "but not for long."

"Don't worry about Spence and me," Ann said. "We're in no hurry to populate the world. We're still mostly each other's child."

And Sara was like a child, too, at the baby shower—a fat, sullen, reluctant child the grown-ups were trying to amuse. Why couldn't she have been this sullen and reluctant a few months ago, I thought meanly, as she was being steered into the room, and I was shocked by my own treason. But I'd begun to have a grouchy, skeptical view of our forced gaiety, of the whole celebration. All those foil-wrapped casseroles we'd lugged in, along with our gifts, as if this were a disaster area and we were the Red Cross. Most of the dishes would probably turn out to be variations of rice pilaf. And Katherine had rented a centerpiece, a huge Styrofoam stork with a baby doll slung from its beak in a diaper. Why would we want to perpetuate *that* myth, and especially now? There was a des-

peration to the shower that seemed particularly and patheti-
cally female to me.

Later, when Sara was surrounded by a mess of crumpled
wrapping paper and tangled ribbon, she seemed happier and
more relaxed, and surprisingly, so was I. Everyone had been
very generous. Practical, pedantic Katherine had given Sara
a book on breast-feeding and a little step stool that converted
to a potty chair when you lifted the top. La Rae had brought
a large, square box filled mostly with tissue paper, which
Sara pulled out with half-feigned impatience until she came
to the antique silver mug and spoon near the bottom. "Ahh!"
and "Ooh!" we cried in spontaneous chorus as each gift was
revealed. Oh, God, I thought, we'll never be liberated from
the burden of children and all their apparatus. Jason was
traveling light, in comparison, with only his drums.

Sherry gave Sara a musical mobile of fuzzy clowns that
bobbed to the tune of "Send in the Clowns." Someone kept
pulling the ring and the plaintive song played itself out over
and over again. My mother had crocheted an amazingly
beautiful afghan for the baby, in brilliant primary colors.
Sara cried out when she saw it, and then buried her face in
its folds. Just when I was starting to get worried, she came
up for air with a shimmering smile. And she actually laughed
out loud at the mother-and-baby T-shirts I'd had inscribed:
Born to Rock. Then she threw her arms around me, saying,
"Thanks, Mrs. Flax, thanks for *everything*." She still called
me that, although I'd said it was too formal under the circumstances, that she could call me Paulie, or even Mom, if she
liked.

There were duplicate gifts, of course: two sets of crib
bumpers, three teddy bears, and two identical diaper bags.
A couple of Sara's friends had bought baby clothes in the
wrong size for the intended season. It didn't matter. We made

an elaborate fuss over everything, even the greeting cards that Ann insisted on reading aloud as each gift was opened. "Welcome, little baby dear / You fill our hearts with hope and cheer."

My own heart expanded and filled as I watched Sara being coaxed out of her funk, until she was almost her old winsome self again. We were an odd assortment of cheerleaders—three generations of women with clearly divergent lives. My friends and I were studiedly casual in our jeans and sweaters, and most of Sara's friends were studiedly bizarre. One of them even had a completely shaved head. My mother clucked her tongue when she saw her, and whispered, "Oh, that poor girl." But we all got along well together. We devoured the delicious potluck food, and drank the champagne punch in a series of suggestive toasts, punctuated by laughter and applause.

We were getting boisterous, the way women sometimes do when there aren't any men around. Tony had been banished to the tennis courts for the afternoon, and husbands and lovers, like Spence and Nicholas, who'd dropped some of the women off, had been instructed not to come back until they were summoned. I thought of something I'd once read about Jane Austen, that she never had any conversations between men in her novels, unless there were women present, too, because she didn't know what they said to one another when they were alone. Could men ever imagine this locker-room rowdiness among women? Even my mother joined in, in her own artless way, when she wasn't thriftily rolling up the discarded ribbons for future use.

If Sara's cold and proper mother had been there, the rest of us would have behaved properly, too. We would have been high-pitched and silly, rather than playfully crude. I'd called to invite her, for Sara's sake, but a housekeeper had answered in an imperious voice and said that Mrs. Bartlett was unable to speak to me. I pictured a literal inability, her hand clutching her corded, constricted throat, through which no sound could pass. Sara's sister, Peggy, came to the shower, though, an unofficial family ambassador, as she'd been at the failed wedding. Like Ann, she wore expensive, tailored clothes, and she was beautifully groomed. If you looked carefully, you could see her resemblance to Sara—the good cheekbones, the small, catlike family chin. The differences between them were mostly superficial, as if they were before-and-after models of the social revolution. I had a moment alone with Peggy in the kitchen, and I asked her what I could do to bring her parents around. She laughed, a sardonic little laugh, and said, "Nothing. You'd better forget it, Mrs. Flax—they don't forgive and they don't forget. If they knew I was here, they'd probably cut me off, too."

"But Sara needs them so badly now," I said. "And it's their grandchild, too, whether they like it or not."

"They *don't* like it," Peggy said. "And they'll never acknowledge it, either." She hesitated, and then added quietly, "You have to understand . . . it's a matter of *class*. Jason wasn't ever good enough for Sara. And now, well, now Sara's not good enough for us, either."

"Are they both like that?" I asked, throbbing with the insult.

"Yes. No. Mother is really the hard one, but Dad's her slave."

"Jason sent Sara some money," I said.

Peggy nodded. "I know, she told me," she said, and I was ashamed of offering such feeble evidence in his favor.

"I'm going to call your parents again," I said stubbornly. "For Sara's sake. Or I'll write them a letter."

"It won't help," Peggy assured me, and then we went inside together, carrying platters of cake.

The party had grown even louder and merrier in our brief absence. Katherine was playing the piano for Sherry and Ann, who were singing a medley of show tunes, off-key, like a couple of drunks in a cocktail lounge. When they were finished, someone began urging Sara to sing something. She hadn't worked for a while, and Ann had told me she never sang around the house, not even in the shower. Now she was saying, "No, I can't. Come on, stop it," as a few of her friends gently shoved her closer to the piano. It reminded me of people pushing a stalled car along, hoping the engine would catch once it was in motion. Katherine played a grand flourish on the piano and Sara leaned toward her and whispered something. Katherine shook her head, repeating the flourish, and then there was further whispering and another, faltering flourish. Finally, one of Sara's friends replaced Katherine at the piano and began to plunk something out. And Sara began to sing. I'd forgotten the special rusty, husky urgency in her voice. She sang a song I'd never heard before, something weird about someone being ready to be baked. The words pulsed from her in a steady, thrilling rhythm, though, and I realized that popular songs are always about the same thing, no matter how they're disguised. As Sara sang, I looked around the room at the faces of the listening women. They seemed to be shining with accord: yes, life is difficult, with its swift peaks of pleasure, its swooping dives into despair; and yes, love is impossible, but we willingly waste our hearts, our energy, our entire glorious potential on it. Sara belted out the chorus of her song like a battle cry to action, and I felt a rush of camaraderie, of sisterhood. How terrific we were, rallying around one of our own like this, how remarkably loving and loyal. I forgot my initial annoyance with Sara for getting herself into this mess, my recent discord with La Rae, and even my lifelong disagreement with my mother on almost everything that mattered. I knew that the Styrofoam stork was only an ironic symbol, not a foolish denial, of the facts of life. I had a dreamy vision then of a society without men, of only self-sufficient females. It certainly wasn't a very original idea, but I imagined we could live without men if we really tried to, if we wanted to. We didn't have to be their adversaries, like the Amazons, only separate. I wasn't thinking of war, but of a conditional peace. The worst condition would be the denial of longing for their otherness, for the scrape of beard, the gorgeous shock of penetration. But I supposed we'd get over that sooner or later. Phil Spitalny's All-Girl Orchestra, without Phil. It wouldn't simply be an extended hen party, either. We would work together and quarrel among ourselves, the way we did now with men, but without the threat of domination or loss. "Put me in cold, I'm ready to bake today!" Sara sang, and we all moved our feet and shoulders in time to the hypnotic beat.

When the party was over, when we were gathering the gifts into a tidy pile, and cleaning up the crumbs and empty glasses, my exhilaration slowly ebbed. Some of the women used the telephone, and in a while the men began showing up. Tony, that exemplary husband among husbands, came in carrying his tennis racket in one hand and flowers for Katherine in the other. They kissed—heartily, sexily—while I watched with the awe of a movie audience watching screen lovers kiss.

Tony hugged each of us in turn, and his sweater was rough and sweet-smelling from the fresh air. It was that time of day when the natural light begins to fade and families draw together into little constellations. It reminded me of winter evenings in the Queens apartment, waiting for Howard to

come home. The windows would grow dark and steamy, and
when I rubbed a space clear to look out, all I could see were
the lighted windows of other apartments. The children and I
were often locked up together for days because of the weather
or somebody's earache, and we were all a little crazy by the
time Howard appeared at last, the romantic relief in our domestic drama. I used to inhale that same smell of the out-
doors, of freedom, that he brought in with him, as if it would
make me high. It *did* make me high, and the deep, mellow
tone of his voice, after the children's strident whining and
the strident noise of the TV, was music I couldn't get enough
of. I must have been envious of him then, and even resentful,
but now I simply remembered the joy of reunion, of welcoming him back among us. The way the other women at the
shower welcomed their returning men.

Spence came in, and later Nicholas arrived for Sherry. The
men and women were a little shy together, but also excited,
as if they'd been separated for a long time, against their will.
Their voices mingled in pleasant cacophony—flutes and bass
fiddles—like a symphony orchestra tuning up. Then they began leaving, two by two. I hadn't asked Bernie to come for
me—it was too close to home, my old home, for me to feel
comfortable there with him. And I didn't want to subject him
to the once-over he'd surely get from my friends. But I
couldn't help thinking how much they would like him, and
how they would envy me. I felt bereft as the party ended, a
wallflower at the senior prom, even though several of the
women drove happily away by themselves, and Sara and my
mother were also unclaimed, except by Spence. Some of us
could live without men—we had already proven that—but I
knew that I didn't want to. Given my freedom of choice, I
would always choose the dangers of integration and conten-
tion, the blood-curdling risk of their love.

32

*L*OOKING FOR JASON CONTINUED TO BE A DEAD END, and after hanging around the rock clubs for a while, I began to think about playing my sax again. I had hardly touched it lately and I didn't even listen to my tapes much anymore. I wasn't exactly inspired by the music Jason's friends played, but you could hear the strains of jazz history in it, if you listened hard enough, and I realized how much I missed my own music.

A few weeks after Gil died, one of the men in his group, the bass-playing dentist, called a couple of times to ask if I wanted to sit in with him and the pianist. I always had some excuse handy—I was busy, tired, under the weather—and I promised to get back to him, but I never did. Not playing was a kind of mourning, I suppose, for Gil, for my marriage, for Jason. I thought of how Orthodox Jews are forbidden to listen to music, go to the movies, or watch television for at least a month after a death in the family. Some even hold out for a whole year. I think the idea is not to interrupt the grieving with entertainment, because it only prolongs the agony. Sooner or later you have to serve the whole sentence. After Paulie's father died, her mother stopped watching her favorite soaps for such a long time she lost track of the characters.

Later, she was surprised to find out that some of them had died, too, knocked off by the networks during her period of mourning. And yet, as she would be the first to say, life goes on—and now music invaded my head, pushing out some of those troubling thoughts. As I drove to work, I found myself tapping out a lively tempo on the steering wheel and singing little riffs under my breath. Finally, I called Irv Jacoby, the dentist, and asked if he and his pianist wanted to get together at my place that Friday night. Gil must have told him about Paulie and me because he said, with obvious discomfort, that Fridays were kind of a family night for him, and would Wednesday be okay instead? The sad truth was that I was free almost any night, and I said sure, that was fine with me.

I left the studio early on Wednesday afternoon and went to the liquor store and the supermarket. When I got home, I looked around the house, the way you do when visitors are coming, to see if it's presentable. I examined the spot that was wearing down on the left sofa arm, and ran my fingers up a fine jagged crack in the wall that came from the house settling. Paulie had been after me to sell the house, so we'd have the money to provide a home for Sara and the baby. I'd told her to look for a rental for them, and that I'd pay most of the rent. She and Sara found something only a few days later. It was a small one-bedroom, with a convertible dining area, in a new building near Union Square. Now they were busy fixing it up and sending me the bills. It was going to cost an arm and a leg, but I'd manage it, even if I had to take out a second mortgage on this place.

Paulie could also have the lion's share of our savings in the divorce settlement, to make up for her share of the house. And I'd will the whole thing to her, anyway, no matter what happened between us. It wasn't that I was so sentimental about it. I was used to living there, though, and I couldn't imagine living anywhere else, with the light coming in through the windows at a different angle. And during the night, I could find my way to the bathroom and back to bed without ever opening my eyes. I sat on the sofa, my elbow covering the worn spot, and wondered, as I often did, what Paulie was doing at that moment. I had never seen her apartment and didn't really want to, didn't want to set the images I had of her and her lover in an actual, known place.

I got up and plumped the pillows, wiped some dust from the coffee table with my handkerchief. Shadow sensed that we were having company, and he perked up as I puttered around, sniffing at the dish of peanuts I set out, following me from room to room. But when I took my sax out and began to blow, about a half hour before the other men were expected, he gave me a mournful look and padded back to the kitchen. The sound always hurt his sensitive ears, and this time it hurt mine, also. In a matter of weeks, I seemed to have lost most of the polish and confidence I'd gained with all the recent practice.

Irv and the pianist, Marco, arrived together in Irv's station wagon. I hadn't seen either of them since Gil's funeral, when we'd stood around, empty-handed and solemn in our dark suits. Now, like me, they were dressed casually and eager to get started. We set up in the den, and in a few minutes we were jamming again. Nobody had said anything about Gil— what was there to say? Instead, we'd made small talk about the weather, music, the latest White House mess. I'd apologized in advance for being rusty, and they were both quick to assure me they sounded rotten themselves. They didn't, though, and to my surprise, neither did I, once we really got going. "Hey, not bad, kids," Irv said, modestly, when we took our first break.

I brought out the Scotch and ice and passed the peanuts

and some cheese around. Still, none of us mentioned Gil. I'd been having a lot of dental work lately, and I asked Irv if he could recommend a good root-canal specialist who wasn't a highway robber. He insisted on pulling me over to the desk lamp to take a look at my mouth before he wrote down a couple of names for me.

Marco was a younger guy who had recently married and moved from Queens to Northport. He kept grilling me about Port Washington, asking how high the taxes were, if the schools were any good, and if the sewers were in yet and paid for. He wanted to know if my basement was as damp as his, and we all tramped downstairs so I could show him the dehumidifier. I explained how it worked and that the humidistat was its essential feature. Once we were down there, Marco looked over the furnace, and the water heater, too, as if he were a plumber and this was a service call. Irv stood under one of the tiny, darkened windows with his hands in his pockets and remarked, almost to himself, that he needed a new set of plastic well covers at his place. The basement had never seemed so eerie before, like a cave in which our separate voices echoed and dwindled. In the dim corners I saw the shapes and shadows of things we stored there during the winter: the barbecue, the lawn chairs, the carton with the string of Japanese lanterns we'd always used for outdoor parties. ''Well, let's get back to work,'' I said. Marco lingered briefly at the water heater before he followed Irv and me upstairs to the den.

We did a whole set of Mingus next, including ''Celia'' and ''Diane''—Marco's wife's name was Diane. And then we went right into ''Sentimental You,'' in which I took the long, melodic solo with just the right blend of cool and schmaltz. We got high on how good we sounded, and we began making plans to meet again, to meet regularly at someone's house at least twice a month. In the middle of that happy rush, I could practically hear Paulie saying "Is *this* how you're looking for Jason?" just as I used to fix on dying right after making love, and it brought me down in the same fast, heart-stopping way. But I had to live, didn't I?

After that, we noodled around for a while, playing a few bars of this and that, and then we broke into some slow but joyful Dixieland. We ended with an aching version of "Jazz Me Blues," a number the marching bands in New Orleans play in funeral processions. When we finished, Irv mopped the sweat and the tears from his broad, reddened face. "Well, that's it for me, fellas," he said, dropping forward with his arms around his bass.

"Yeah, me too," Marco agreed, and he went into the bedroom to call his wife.

I wanted to say something to Irv about Gil, to formalize what wound up being a kind of musical service for him, but I didn't, and by the time Marco came back the mood was gone, the thing was over.

33

Dear Stuck-up,

You can remove that chewing gum from your hair with ordinary cold cream. Pull it through the affected strands with a dry cloth or towel. If that doesn't work, try freezing the hair with ice cubes—the gum will peel right off!

Dear Off-Your-Rocker,

Avoid scratches on your wood floors by using floor wax on the rocker arcs. And pick up that sagging cane seat by bathing it in hot water and setting it out in the sun to dry.

Dear Dog-Daze,

Try vacuuming Fido instead of the sofa. Use one of those handy little battery-operated car vacuums. Speak soothingly to the dog until he gets used to the noise, or use it around him on the furniture before you use it on him.

Dear Scout Leader,

Store all those marshmallows in the freezer and just snip them apart with scissors before the next campfire!

Sometimes I imagined people all over America, in Kansas City and Buffalo and Sarasota, vacuuming their shedding dogs, or freezing their marshmallows and their hair simply because I'd told them to. No matter what La Rae said about the triviality of my column, it gave me a queer sense of power, and of communion with strangers. The stationery some of their letters were written on, embellished with flowers or smile faces, like Sara's thank-you notes, and the handwriting that slanted forward earnestly or was modestly tiny, never failed to touch me. I "knew" these people, in a way. Some of them wrote back to say the gum was gone from their hair, the dog had run away from home. And I began to imagine other aspects of their lives. I saw a vegetable garden near a kitchen door, tomato plants neatly tied with pantyhose, on my advice, and a woman going inside, where the soup simmered with a potato in it (to absorb the excess salt), and a man waited on the repaired rocking chair to pull her down onto his lap. I began putting these images into a poem called "Advice." I told the woman in the poem to let the soup boil over and away, to let the tomatoes, nourished in babyhood by ashes mixed with the soil, grow until the house was hidden by the vines and she and the man were trapped inside forever.

When I showed the poem to Ruth, she said that I seemed to be moving more and more toward a prose style. She wanted to know if I had thought of names for the man and the woman. I admitted that I had—sometimes they were Joy and Robert, and other times they were Leslie and Paul. "What else do you know about them?" Ruth asked, and the beginnings of a story rolled out. They'd married too young, I said, and their backgrounds were too dissimilar, but their real tragedy was that they were unable to have a child. Joy,

or Leslie, kept the garden as a kind of token of fertility, and
it was also something she could nurture.

"And then what happens?" Ruth asked, the way Ann or
Jason used to during a bedtime story.

"I don't know," I said, startled and pleased by the question. "Maybe a baby grows on the tomato vine, in a caul of
pantyhose. Maybe Robert goes berserk and tramples the garden. Maybe they live happily ever after. I don't know. I guess
I'll have to write it to find out." And that was how I stopped
trying to write poetry and started trying to write fiction. Ruth
suggested I take a workshop with an old friend of hers the
following semester, a short-story writer named Alec Bres-
low. Was he the "A." she'd dedicated *Wrong Turn* to? Suddenly everything took on the remarkable mystery of an
unwritten narrative.

Early the next Saturday, Sara and I met at her new apartment to hang some pictures and line the kitchen shelves with
paper. Afterward, we went to a local luncheonette and ordered waffles and ice cream for breakfast. Sara told me that
one of the couples in our childbirth class had had a baby girl
the night before. "Debby and Ralph wanted a boy, though,"
she said.

"How about you?" I asked. "Do you have a preference?"

"Not really," Sara said. "Well, sometimes, maybe, I hope
it's a girl. Like a little friend of my own. Like Peggy." She
sighed and put her fork down beside her plate. She'd hardly
eaten anything.

"Aren't you hungry?" I asked. "Sara, honey, try not to
be so sad."

"I'm okay, Mrs. Flax," she said. "It's just that my back
is bothering me," and she squirmed in her seat.

"Since when?" I asked her.

She picked up her fork and poked at the ice cream melting in the waffle craters. "Just now. But there, it's better, it went away."

"Where did it hurt?" I asked, as casually as I could.

She was eating again, but she motioned behind her with her free hand. "All the way down," she said, "but it's gone now."

"That's good," I said, and looked surreptitiously at my watch.

"Oh, it's not *that*," Sara said quickly.

"How do you know?" I asked her.

"I just do. And it's too early, anyway."

But she put her fork down again, for good this time, and just sipped some water and pleated and unpleated her paper napkin.

Ten minutes later, there was another twinge in her back, and this one traveled to her lower abdomen and her thighs.

I went to the phone near the rest rooms and called Carmen's number. Her answering service told me she was out but would be checking in very soon for messages. I thought of Bernie, who was back from Chicago, and then I called Dr. Norman, the obstetrician who'd first confirmed Sara's pregnancy. He said he'd meet us at his office right away. Sara was in his examining room only a few minutes when he came out and told me that she was in labor. I was oddly unprepared, as if I hadn't already guessed this news, as if I hadn't really believed until that moment that she was pregnant.

"Sometimes our calculations are a little off," he said. "But don't worry, she's full-term—the baby is a good size. And the heartbeat is strong,"

"What happens next?" I asked.

He smiled. "Don't you remember?" he said. "Nature

happens next. She seems to have plenty of time. Primips—first-timers—usually do. Where did she say she's going to deliver—Larchmont? You can start out with her now and I'll get in touch with Mrs. Gomez.''

I tried to call Ann, but I got her machine. ''The baby's coming!'' I said. ''We're on our way!'' And I prayed that she, or *somebody*, would be home when we got there.

The car service Dr. Norman called sent a stretch limousine, although we'd requested a regular sedan. It had a fitted bar and a television set in the back. ''All we got,'' the Russian émigré driver explained when I inquired. He was looking critically at Sara, probably wondering if she was going to ruin the upholstery. Sara was delighted to be traveling in such high style. As soon as we swerved into traffic, she put her feet up on the facing seat and turned the television on. ''Oh, rats, it's *Saturday*,'' she said, switching from cartoon to cartoon. Finally she settled on one of those civic-minded talk shows from New Jersey. ''Thanks very much for joining us today,'' the host was saying. ''New Jersey's highway development and maintenance is certainly a subject for everyone's concern.'' I took a pencil and some paper from my purse to write down the time and duration of Sara's contractions. Whenever one began, she held onto my hand and squeezed it until the pain passed, but she never took her eyes off the tiny screen.

Our driver was skilled but reckless, and I rapped on the glass panel several times, signaling him to slow down. Mostly, he ignored me. ''Here, one pieces,'' he said with disdain as we pulled up to Ann's house. After I'd paid him, Sara asked him his name. ''Serge Polanovitch,'' he said. ''You like?''

''Not bad,'' she told him, ''but only if it's a boy.''

Lily was off for the weekend, and Spence was on the golf

course, but Ann ran out to greet us. She had just come from playing tennis and was still wearing her whites. She looked like a nurse in a blue movie as she bustled around the guest room in her tiny pleated shirt. It was the same room where Sara had been sleeping these past months; there were bottles and tubes of her makeup scattered on the dresser top, her socks and pajamas flung over the bedside chair. Ann closed the blinds, canceling out the brightness of the day. Now the baby wouldn't emerge from that familiar darkness into blinding light, which Carmen said was probably more traumatic than anyone realized. I remembered staring up into the klieg lights of the delivery room, waiting for Jason to be born, stunned by my sudden, unwelcome celebrity.

I cleared the chair so Sara could sit down, and knelt to take off her red high-tops. The Velcro rasped in the dim and quiet room. Sara said, ''Ahh! Thanks,'' and wiggled her toes contentedly. Then she undressed completely and put on the short, frilly nightgown Ann had bought her for this occasion. She asked if I'd please bring her the box of cassette tapes on the night table, and she hummed cheerily as she rummaged through them. Her euphoria, I decided, had to be related to this early stage of labor. Hadn't I been that way myself, at first, an absolute model of civility and heroism? And didn't my mother, whose favorite stories were about her tortuous delivery of me, wash and wax her kitchen floor right before she left for the hospital?

Sara's contractions were still manageable and still ten minutes apart, enough time, I knew, to make her think: *This* isn't so bad—what's all the fuss about? I'd had the same thought on my way to the hospital, certain that my mother, who had advised me to beg for gas, had blown things up out of proportion again. ''It's not bad at all,'' I told Howard, which was exactly what he wanted to hear. ''This is a cinch, so far,'' I told the obstetrical nurse a few minutes later as she bent to the fetal heartbeat. She snorted loudly and sauntered out of the labor room. Much later, Howard was with me in that same room, which had become pink with morning. By then the pains were murderous, and clearly only going to get worse. When I was way beyond reason or consolation, I was shaved, purged, and tethered to a table under those blazing lights. This was a horrible mistake, I decided, an aberration—everyone couldn't be born this way, or the human race would have died out long ago.

Carmen was on her way—she'd left a message on Ann's machine, too—and I kept going to the window to see if she'd arrived yet. Sara, queenly and calm, selected several tapes and handed them to Ann to feed into the tape deck. I glanced at the top one: the Talking Heads' *Little Creatures*. Appropriate enough, I supposed, but shouldn't Mozart, or maybe Sarah Vaughan, be welcoming my grandchild into the world?

Sara had a pile of books on childbirth that she flipped through, like a patient in a dentist's waiting room looking at magazines. "How do you feel?" I asked her, and she said, "Great! I feel perfectly great!" a little too loud, as if she were deaf or stoned.

Then Ann inserted the first tape, and the vibrant sound of the Talking Heads filled the room: "And she was lying in the grass! And she could hear the highway breathing!"

I sat cross-legged on the floor next to Sara with a pencil and pad in my hands. "Don't forget to do *your* breathing," I reminded her.

"Oh, I've been breathing all along," Sara assured me. Then she said, "Here comes another one!" leaning forward and arching her back.

I wrote down the time and announced, "Ten minutes again ."

A half hour later, we were still at ten-minute intervals, and Sara was still presiding from her chair. We heard Spence come in, and Ann went down to tell him the news. He rushed up the stairs, with Ann right behind him. "Uncle Spence coming in!" he shouted, and then he was in the room, hugging Sara, who was between pains and able to hug him back. How marvelous she was! Maybe it *would* be a cinch this time, all the way through. I'd heard stories of women who swore they'd simply "dropped" their babies, without any of the usual agony. Athletes were supposed to have an easier time of it—could the elaborate gyrations Sara went through when she sang put her into that category?

Spence and Ann arranged the bed for the delivery, spreading a shower curtain under the bottom sheet, and a layer of disposable pads over it. They propped a number of pillows against the headboard, and then Spence stretched out to see if it was comfortable. Ann carried a tray table to the side of the bed and laid out the scissors and nasal syringe she and Sara had bought, on Carmen's instructions. They were minor instruments compared to the cart of surgical steel they'd wheeled to the delivery table before Jason was born, but I suffered a pang of anxiety when I saw them. I picked up one of Sara's childbirth books, which was illustrated with photographs. The baby's father was in almost all of them, smiling and being supportive and loving.

"The camera!" Ann said, clapping her forehead. "We forgot the camera!" She and Spence raced down together, and when they came up again with the video camera, Carmen was with them. As soon as she walked into the room, I felt safer and more relaxed. Carmen lowered the volume on the tape deck, and shooed us all out of the room while she examined Sara. When we came back in, she told us that Sara was dilated two and a half centimeters, and I dutifully wrote that down, too. Then I gave Sara a back rub between contractions, another part of my coaching duties. "Mmmm," Sara said, purring happily under my hands.

Spence took video footage of the room, of Carmen taking things out of her bag, of me rubbing Sara's back. Sara waved at the camera. "Say something, dummy," Spence directed her. "These are *talkies*." "Hi, everybody," Sara said. "We're at two and a half centimeters now."

She paid no attention to the small cylinder of oxygen and the mask that Carmen had transferred from her magic bag to the dresser. I thought of the trepidation I always felt on a plane, when the use of similar equipment was demonstrated just before takeoff. "In the event of a loss of cabin pressure . . ." the stewardess would explain, matter-of-factly. And at the Natural Birth Center they'd told us that the mother might be given oxygen during delivery if the baby was in stress. I could never imagine an actual loss of cabin pressure, but what could be more stressful than being born?

The room gradually grew darker and Ann lit the bedside lamps, which had been fitted with low-wattage light bulbs, almost like candlelight. Sara fell asleep on the bed and the rest of us sat around her, trying to read in the weak light, or dozing off ourselves. We could have been part of a golden tableau in a nineteenth-century painting. Sara slept and was jarred awake by contractions. She and I did the deep breathing together. I rubbed her feet and lightly massaged her lower abdomen. I realized that the Talking Heads tape had played itself out a long time ago, and no one had replaced it.

In a couple of hours, the contractions were stronger and closer: only eight minutes apart. Carmen encouraged Sara to take sips of water and herbal tea, to walk around, to empty her bladder. She took Sara's blood pressure and listened frequently with the fetal stethoscope, saying, "Good, very good. Ah, that's lovely," After the next examination, she said "Four centimeters now."

"Ooh, it *hurts*," Sara said, coming awake again later. She turned onto her side, her legs drawn up in pain. Spence and Ann went downstairs, and I lay next to Sara on the bed, stroking her back and shoulders, talking softly to her. "There," I said. "There. Does that feel better?"

"Oh, no," Sara moaned, moving restlessly. "What's happening here? This is *awful*." She hoisted herself from the bed and paced the room, still moaning. I paced behind her, mute Harpo chasing after Groucho. Was this how Howard had felt at the ringside of Jason's birth—eager to help and helpless?

"Maybe a bath would be soothing," Carmen said.

"I thought you weren't supposed—" I began.

"She'll be fine," Carmen promised. "Some women even deliver in the bath."

So Sara took off the drooping, wrinkled nightgown, and went into the tub for a while. Lying there did seem to soothe her, even if it didn't lessen the severity of the contractions. I sat on the closed toilet seat and continued timing them. I noticed that Sara's eyes had changed. That peaceful dreaminess was gone, and in its place was a deeper look of understanding that there was no turning back from this.

In the middle of everything, the phone rang. "Mom, it's Nana," Ann yelled up the stairs.

"Oh, God, what does *she* want?" I yelled back, and then I went into the guest room and picked up the extension. "What is it, Ma?" I said impatiently.

"Annie told me about Sara," my mother said, "and I'm opening all my closets and drawers."

"What for?" I asked.

"So she'll have an easy time." I could hear Sara groaning loudly in the bathtub.

"Thanks a lot, Ma," I said, "but we're not superstitious."

"Is Howard there?" she wanted to know.

"Howard!" I said. "What would Howard be doing here?"

"I don't know," she said. "He has a right to be there, doesn't he? I thought maybe you called him."

"I'm not making any calls right now, Ma," I told her. "I'm trying to help Sara. I have to go now," I said, and hung up.

Carmen had gotten Sara out of the bathtub and back to bed, where she was sucking on frozen chips of orange juice, and eyeing the cylinder of oxygen with suspicion and fear. Now she was wearing one of Spence's plain white T-shirts and a pair of fuzzy knee socks. "Five centimeters," Carmen reported a few minutes later. "We're halfway there." Ten centimeters was the goal; then Sara would be able to start pushing.

"See, you're making great progress," I told her, but she acted as if she didn't hear me. Ann and Spence came into the room with the camera and went quickly out again.

"Mom," Sara murmured.

"What, dear?" I asked, before I realized she hadn't meant me. "You'll see," my mother had warned, when I was pregnant with Jason, "you'll curse your husband and scream for your mother." Had I really done that? Howard had stayed with me, even when I knew he wanted to flee, to be anywhere else, maybe in another life.

Sara, released from a long contraction, said, "Sometimes I think how crazy love is, you know? What is it, anyway? It makes me laugh even to think about it." But she wasn't laughing; she looked distraught and exhausted.

By eight o'clock, she was talking rapidly between pains, even though Carmen urged her to use that brief time to rest. She talked about Jason in a feverish babble. Did I know he had a patch of lighter skin on his thigh that looked just like a lion? He used to tap out songs on her back in bed and she had to guess what they were. And once, he'd made supper when she had a cold, modeling hamburger into misshapen hearts. But she'd never forgive him for this, never! She talked about her childhood, and how she and Peggy had had studio portraits taken every year on their birthdays. "What's today?" she said. "It's my baby's birthday, isn't it? Paulie, I really don't think I can deal with this."

I felt feverish myself by then, and as if I hadn't slept in years. Carmen suggested I take some time out while I could—she would stay with Sara. I went slowly downstairs to the kitchen, where Ann was making sandwiches. The fluorescent light was glaring and I had to cover my eyes. "I think I'm going to call Dad," I said.

34

*I*T WAS APRIL, BUT IT FELT MORE LIKE FOOTBALL WEATHER as I ran into the outfield. "Go, Slammers," somebody called half-heartedly from the bleachers. There were only a few people sitting huddled there—mostly the hard-core wives and kids of some of the other players. It was my first night back in the game since my heart attack. Our shortstop's cousin had filled in for me during the opening games of the season, but he'd relinquished the position as soon as I said I could play again. I'd been working out at home for a few weeks, carefully, just to get the kinks out of my muscles, but I was still pretty stiff, and the glove felt heavy and awkward on my hand. The last couple of games had been called because of rain, and even though the grass was soggy, we'd decided to play. I was especially eager to get going, to see if I'd survive the exertion. Everything I did again for the first time since my heart attack turned out to be another survival test I had to pass.

It felt weird out there under the lights, especially in that weather. As soon as we took the field, it started to rain again. It was actually more of a mist than a downpour, and it made the other players seem farther away than they really were. But I reminded myself that it was always a little lonely in the

297

outfield. I smacked my fist into the glove, to keep warm, to do something. Stu Kramer was playing first base, as usual, and it was comforting to have a doctor nearby. Nothing was going to happen, but if it did, he'd be right there. Hell, I felt ready for anything, "Play ball!" some kid called from the bleachers, and the words bounced around, sounding like several voices.

Only one pop fly came my way in the first inning, but it was Bayville's third out. It was hit almost directly over me, and I just drifted around a little, until I was in position for it, and let it fall into my glove. There was some mild cheering and booing as I loped back toward our bench. I saw that I was loosening up, moving with less effort.

Sitting on the bench, I looked over toward the bleachers, remembering sultry, starlit nights and Paulie and the kids yelling and clapping for our team. After the game, I'd let Annie and Jason run around the bases a few times and then, whether we'd won or lost, we'd drive somewhere to celebrate with hamburgers and ice cream. I'd still be all sweaty, and Paulie would open her window, saying, "Pee-*yew*! Doesn't Daddy stink?" But she'd keep one hand on my damp thigh while she drove, and we often made love on those nights as soon as the children fell asleep. I was sure that only fools saw everything in such rosy retrospect. And although I knew it wasn't true, Jason's defection seemed to be the main cause of all my problems. Yet I'd really stopped looking for him, just as Paulie had accused me of doing. Whenever I made myself think about it, a kind of lethargy came over me and I had trouble concentrating, and even staying awake. I still stopped in at the rock clubs from time to time, and I was still in touch with a few of the musicians Jason had hung out with, but there hadn't been any new leads for a while. One of these days, as soon as I could arrange another stretch of time away from the studio, I was going to head West and put in a really heavy search for him. I couldn't lay everything on Mike again right now, and Sara wasn't due to give birth for a couple of weeks, anyway—I had that much leeway.

By the time I came up to bat, it had stopped raining, but a dank chill hung in the air. Stu had reached base with an infield single, and there were two outs. So the pressure was on me, which was just the way I liked it, at least in sports. After my heart attack, Paulie told me that maybe I was an A-type after all, despite appearances, and that I'd have to change if I wanted to live. Later I understood that it had been a coded message, that she was really talking about Janine and me. And I did change, and I did want to live, but not without Paulie.

I dug my spikes in as Jim McNulty went into his windup. His first pitch sailed high and away—ball one. He put the second one almost in the same spot, but I swung at it anyway, and missed by a mile. "Hey, get glasses, blindo!" some moron yelled from the bleachers, and I enjoyed a twitch of irritability, a quickening of the blood. I let the next, near-perfect pitch go right by me for spite, and there were more catcalls from the stands and from the other team. Now I was behind, one ball and two strikes. Our first-base coach, Lenny Schultz, clapped his hands and called out his usual string of chatter, like an auctioneer. Stu, dancing on and off first, yelled, "Take your time, Howie baby! Wait for a better one! Wait for a beauty! Send me home, Howie baby!"

McNulty's control was off tonight, and his fourth pitch was low. It would have been an easy ball if I'd taken it, but I started chasing it and my whole body followed through before I could check my swing. Thwack! I'd hit a solid grounder that went right through McNulty's legs into center field. It was a single, but the center fielder bobbled it, and

Stu, who was greased lightning, started around second for third. I thought they'd try to nail him there, so I headed for second, but they decided to go for me instead. Everybody was yelling and my legs were pumping like pistons to beat the throw. I had to slide in headfirst, and it was close, but I was safe. "Way to go, Howie Baby!" Stu hollered from third as I scrambled to my feet, even though I was clearly having another heart attack. It couldn't hammer away like that without suffering damage, could it? My legs were wobbling and I was breathing like an accordion. Our handful of fans had worked up an enthusiastic chant. "Go, Slammers, go! Go, Slammers, go!" I kept my foot on the bag and continued wheezing while Shecky Snyder walked up to the plate. Shecky was a good hitter. Like me, he did better at bat under pressure, and he even seemed to relish the heckling from the other side. When somebody on the Bayville bench yelled, "Fan the air, Snyder!" he yelled back, "Fan your ass!" without taking his eyes off McNulty. I put a tentative hand to my chest. My heart was still blasting off in there, but maybe it was slowing down a little.

It went to a full count on Shecky, and I hunkered down, ready to break for third. I glanced from McNulty, who pawed the mound nervously, to the plate where Shecky was waving his bat. And then, at the edge of my vision, I saw a scrawny little woman sprinting from the parking lot toward the diamond. It looked like La Rae, but what would she be doing here? Frank didn't play softball, and she wasn't much of a fan, especially not one of mine. But it *was* La Rae. What the hell did she want, and what was her big hurry? McNulty went into his windup and delivered a perfect curveball to Shecky. He swung at it as La Rae came closer, calling "Howard! Howard!," her voice carrying over all the other noise. Shecky had connected with a line drive that flew right

over everyone's head. Stu started to go, and so did I, but in
the wrong direction, away from third and toward La Rae. In
that brief moment of chaos, I thought the worst thoughts,
that someone had died—Paulie or one of the kids. And I had
the same terrified, heartsick feeling I'd had years ago when
my mother appeared suddenly at the door of my third-grade
classroom in the middle of the day. Someone *had* died that
time. It was only my aunt in St. Louis—my mother's older
sister—someone I hardly knew. But I didn't find out immediately, and my mother's grieving face was bad enough news
itself. I saw that La Rae looked something like that when she
was only a few yards away, and in sharper focus. There were
outraged cries from the diamond and the bleachers. "Hey,
Howie! Hey, Flax! Shit, man, where you going? Lady, get
off the field!"

"What's the matter?" I shouted at La Rae, who could
hardly catch her own breath and was flapping her hands to
tell me to wait a minute. "I . . . looked . . . everywhere for
you!" she sputtered finally, indignantly. You'd think we had
a date and I'd stood her up.

"What is it?" I demanded, grabbing her arm.

"It's Sara," she said, wrestling her arm free. "Whew! It's
. . . Sara's time, and Paulie wants you to come."

"What do you mean?" I said. "It's too soon!" And I
hadn't gone to California yet, hadn't brought Jason back.
Dumbly, I remembered my mother pulling me along on the
way home from school that day, how my feet had only
skimmed the sidewalk. "And did you write to Aunt Essie
like I told you?" she'd said, weeping, hurrying as if we were
late for something. "Did you thank her for your birthday
present?" It was cruel of her, and completely unfair. I had
just begun the third grade; I hardly knew how to write. And
children didn't send letters much in those days, or receive

them. A few years later, at the funeral home, Pete would show me death in a unisex shroud, in a polished box. But first my mother demonstrated its main quality, absence. No more Aunt Essie, who I hadn't learned to love in time, or even written to. What had she sent for my birthday, anyway? I began to cry, too, flying along the street with my mother, stricken with bewildered grief and regret.

"Is there trouble?" I asked La Rae now. "What did Paulie say?"

"I don't know," La Rae said, still huffing. "She was so excited she hardly made sense. 'Find Howard,' she kept saying, that's all I know. She called your house, she called your studio. You men are never where you're supposed to be!" She was in a suffocating rage that I figured had little to do with me.

"Stop it!" I said. "You found me, didn't you? Is she . . . are they at the hospital?" I realized that I'd never really believed Sara's plans for a home delivery. The whole thing seemed so romantic and impractical. Paulie was *surrounded* by doctors and nurses when she gave birth, and it was still a bloodbath.

"No. No, Paulie said they were at Ann's, and that the baby was coming soon."

"Hey, listen, the baby's coming!" I called to the men on the diamond, who were gathering like a lynch mob, and there were more disgruntled cries. Someone even yelled, "So fucking what? Play ball!" But Stu waved me on, shouting, "Good luck, Howie baby! I hope it's a boy!"

35

*H*OWARD DIDN'T ANSWER, SO I CALLED LA RAE AND asked her to track him down for me. He was entitled to be here if he wanted to be; my mother was right about that, at least. I ate half of one of Ann's sandwiches and went back upstairs. "She's in transition," Carmen said as I came in the door. For a moment, I forgot what that meant—it sounded trendy, like an excuse people might make for not settling down. And then I understood that Sara was approaching the final stage of her labor. She began howling, as if to confirm it, and I heard a door slam downstairs—Ann or Spence trying to hide from that ferocious sound.

I went to the bed. Sara was sitting on the edge now, swaying from side to side. Her face was glossy with sweat. When I touched her hair, she shuddered and cried, "Don't! Leave me alone! Let me out of here! I want to go home!"

"What should I do?" I asked Carmen, and she said, "Just stay here with her. Come on, lovey," she told Sara, "why don't you lie down now." Her voice had a steady, lulling rhythm I tried to imitate. "Lie down, Sara," I said. "It will be over soon. We love you."

"I'm going to push!" Sara threatened when she was half

lying, half sitting against the pillows. "Oh, shit, oh, fuck, I can't stand it anymore! I'm going to push!"

"Not yet," Carmen warned her. "In a little while you can. Now, blow out through your mouth. You know how, like you're blowing out candles."

"Blow out the candles," I echoed. "For the baby's birthday," and I pursed my lips and demonstrated, until I thought I would hyperventilate.

Carmen propped Sara's legs open, planting her feet flat on the bed. Sara blew and blew before she howled again. Her belly had risen to a point, like a witch's hat. In the middle of her next contraction, her bag of waters ruptured, flooding the bed, smelling strangely like summer rain. I worked with Carmen, pulling out the wet pads, replacing them with dry ones, grateful for something practical to do.

The door opened and Ann peeked in. "Can I help?" she asked in a high, tremulous voice. I hesitated, but Carmen said, "Sure, come on in. Come tell Sara how good she's doing."

Ann tiptoed to the bed, whispering, Sara? It's me. You're so wonderful, Sara, and we're here with you."

Sara was wild-eyed, and blowing in quicker, more frantic breaths, as if this was the only language she could remember now. Carmen murmured a steady singsong of encouragement, like a lullaby.

When it was time, at last, for Sara to push, she did it in great, grunting efforts and with what looked like ecstatic concentration. "Oh, God, oh, God," she said before each animal expulsion of noise. "Why doesn't somebody help me!" she yelled. "I *hate* this shit!" I saw that Spence had come back into the room, drawn here more than he was repelled—lonely, in that large house, for this singular event. I was glad he didn't have his camera with him. I couldn't imagine sitting around watching a video of this someday, the way we used to watch our silent, innocent home movies. Who needed more than memory's record, anyway? And Jason would be missing from it, would always be missing from it, no matter how many times we played it back.

"Only a few more pushes," Carmen said. "You're doing great, Sara, you're opening up just like a flower." I thought of those accelerated nature films, where flowers bloomed with miraculous speed. I thought of the shells we'd bought in Chinatown for our little children, the ones that opened in water to release a paper bouquet.

"Look, she's crowning," Carmen said, and I saw a small, dark, glistening circle of scalp. "Don't push now! Wait!" she ordered Sara. "Let the head come slowly, let it just come." But it retreated for a moment, as if stricken with stage fright, before it reappeared. Carmen cupped it gently as it emerged, allowing the tiny, mottled face to turn to one side. It was frowning fiercely, its eyes squeezed shut against even that meager light, and its tongue was out, tasting the air. Then Sara reached down and helped catch the shoulders as they came slithering through. "Oh," she said. "Oh, I don't believe it! Does it have everything?"

It was a boy, with all his fingers and toes, with his elaborate, miniature parts intact. He was pink and blue and spangled with blood, and still connected to Sara by the thick, pulsing cord. Carmen held him in one arm and used the syringe to suction the mucus from his nose and mouth. Then she wrapped him in a receiving blanket and laid him on Sara's still-inflated belly, where he wailed in that creaking, newborn tremolo for all the world to hear. "Hello," Sara kept saying to him. "Hello. Hello."

The afterbirth was born with ease a few minutes later. When the cord stopped pulsing, Carmen clamped it, and handed me the scissors from the bedside tray. I cut the cord, which was as tough as gristle, thinking of how city officials snipped ribbons to commemorate new buildings. I felt I should say something to observe the occasion, the way they do, but I was too clogged with emotion to speak. Ann, or maybe Spence, was sobbing, and the room shimmered and melted around us.

"This is Byron," Sara said, with the baby snuffling on her breast now. "Say hi, Byron." She waved his little fist at us.

How had she recovered so quickly? And when had she chosen that name? We'd discussed names weeks ago, and she'd only mentioned Jesse and Wesley for a boy. I was relieved that she hadn't come up with something more radical—wasn't there some singer's child called God? I wondered if Sara had named the baby for Lord Byron, unlikely as that seemed, and when I found my voice again, I asked her. It turned out to be for another Byron, who'd been her seatmate in the first grade, and the first boy she'd ever liked. But maybe *he'd* been named for the poet.

"Oh, we forgot the music, didn't we?" Ann said.

"Everybody does," Carmen assured her.

Spence went downstairs for the champagne he'd kept chilled for weeks, and we all toasted the baby's health, and Sara's, and Carmen's. She looked almost as worn out and happy as Sara. "I don't know how you can take this on a regular basis," I said. "Do you just get used to it after a while?" And she smiled and said, "Oh, no, no. And I hope I never get used to it."

Howard showed up a little while later, and I went into the hallway carrying the swaddled, screaming baby. Howard was in his softball uniform, the knees mud-splattered as if he'd slid on them all the way here. It became difficult for me to speak again. I opened the blanket so he could see it was a boy. "I know," he told me. "Jesus, just listen to him, will you!" He touched the baby's hands, his feet, and let out a laugh of desperate joy. "I think he's going to be a sideman, Paulie," He said.

"Here, Howie, take him," I said, and handed him the baby.

Spence, who had retrieved his camera, began filming us in the hallway. "And now the new grandparents are making their first public appearance," he announced in a deep, mock-serious voice. He followed us like a paparazzo into the guest room, where Sara, cleansed and combed, was enthroned on fresh pillows. She held out her arms and Howard lowered the baby into them, kissing her on the top of her head. Sara put the baby to her breast and coaxed him with her fingers until he began to root and then nurse. Spence recorded everything on tape. "Smile," he kept commanding us. "This thriller will be opening next week in a theater near you."

Then Howard took my hand and led me back into the hallway, out of the range of Spence's camera. I could still hear its faint whirring and the more urgent sound of the baby's sucking. I leaned wearily against the wall. "Paulie, listen," Howard said. He hadn't let go of my hand. "This is really crazy . . . But listen," he said again, "I think I know where Jason is."

36

*T*HE MINUTE I LEFT THE ARCTIC ZONE OF THE AIRPORT,
the heavy tropical air hit me. It brought back all my earlier
visits to Miami, especially that extended one right after my
father died. Lying under the palm trees then, during those
burning days and sluggish nights, made me forget about winter back in New York. What reality did snow have in all that
summery green, that golden sunlight? And along with winter, I managed to lose sight of Paulie and the children, too,
for a while. Oh, I knew they were there, all right, waiting
for me to get over my craziness and come home. I spoke to
them daily, but their disembodied voices were changed by
distance, became thinner and less familiar. The connection
between us was stretched too far for them to reel me back
in. Paulie said much later that it must have been an enchant-
ment, and I suppose she was right.

But how long had I known where Jason was? Longer,
maybe, than I'd ever care to admit. There were clear enough
clues all along. The fact that nobody had run across him
anywhere in town. Those tens and twenties he'd sent Sara
through the mail, just the way my mother had always sent
them to him. And she hadn't called for several weeks—her
way, I realized now, of avoiding uncomfortable questions.

When I got worried and finally called her, she didn't ask about either of the children, for the first time in memory. She doted on them both, but she had always favored Jason, much the way she'd favored me when I was a kid. My sister used to complain about it. "He gets away with *everything*," she'd say, and that was a pretty fair assessment. The wonder is that I ever got away at all.

I rented a van and drove out to my mother's place without calling first. Jason might have taken off again if he knew I was coming, and I think she would have warned him. As it was, I took them both by surprise. It was late morning when I got there. She was in the kitchen making breakfast and Jason was taking a shower. I heard the boom of the plumbing as soon as she opened the door. Her jaw fell open in shock when she saw me, and then it just hung there, as if the hinges had come loose. I looked around and the setup was famil-iar—two place mats and two coffee cups on the dinette table, the pair of Barcaloungers positioned to face the TV. The only major difference was the set of drums in front of the picture window. When the shower stopped, I could hear the air-conditioner's siren song. "Jesus, Ma," I said. "How could you *do* this?"

Jason came out then, barefoot, in a kind of sarong-towel. He had a terrific tan—even the beads of water on his torso looked golden. I don't think he recognized me for an instant, but when he did he put his hands up, as if to show me he wasn't armed.

"You have a son, you son-of-a-bitch," I said. All the way here from New York, I'd wondered what I would say when I saw him, and nothing that abrupt or crude had come to mind. But everything I *had* thought to say was just as awkward and off the mark. The thing was, I'd never talked to him, really, so how could I begin now? Could I describe the way I'd felt when Paulie brought the baby out to me? It was like a wonderful dream of restored youth, and like pitching headlong into eternity at the same time. The baby, who was all lopsided, and red as a peeled tomato, was howling his head off. I saw his naked gums, his tonsils, his old age and mine in that wrinkled, toothless face. Paulie pulled back the blanket to show me it was a boy. I think I knew that right away, but I looked with amazement at that stub of a penis, the scrotum too big for the rest of him. The down on his head and shoulders was standing straight up from static or surprise, and I could actually see his heart beating, so fast it scared me. I thought he was probably going to resemble Jason, and me, too, once his face straightened out and his color came in. Poor kid, with that mashed nose and his eyes swollen shut, he looked like he'd gone down for the count, his fists still swinging. But I was thrilled, as if I'd just met someone I'd been admiring from a distance for a long time. I thought I might cry, but I didn't—I laughed instead, and I reached out and touched the baby's waving hands, his funny-looking feet. I said something stupid to Paulie that had nothing to do with what I was feeling, and she said, "Here," and put his featherweight into my arms.

Jason's hands had come down slowly until they hung helplessly at his sides. "Is Sara okay?" he asked at last.

"A hell of a lot better than you," I said, and imagined Paulie saying: Talk to him, Howard. Why can't you ever just _talk_ to him? "She's doing fine," I added grudgingly. "And so is the kid."

"Dad, listen, I'm sorry—" Jason began, but I didn't let him finish.

"Don't tell _me_ about it, mister," I said. "Save it for Sara. Just pack up your goddamn stuff now. We've got a flight out of here at three."

My mother, who had been fluttering around us in her apron, swore to me that she'd never meant any harm. She had only been giving Jason time to think, to straighten himself out. He'd come to her for refuge, what could she do? "Sit down for a minute, Howard," she said. "Let the boy have his breakfast at least. And tell me about the baby."

Jason fell asleep on the plane. He was sitting in the middle, between me and the elderly woman in the aisle seat, who was reading a Bible. He began to slump in her direction and I pulled him over toward me. His head dropped onto my shoulder. It was heavy as lead, and smelled of sunlight and perspiration. I remembered the baby's sweet, yeasty smell, Paulie's face when she handed him to me.

On the way to the airport, Jason had tried to explain what had happened, how he'd suddenly seen his life as a big black net dropping over him. And how he'd panicked and run. He swore he'd been planning to go back on his own, as soon as he got himself together again. No matter how it looked, he did love Sara, he did care about her and the baby. He sounded as if he was trying to convince himself as much as me. I let him talk this time, but I didn't say anything. I knew I was bringing him back like some sporting trophy, like a slain deer tied to the roof of my car. Except, of course, I was bringing him back alive. I was using him in one sense, but it was for his own good, too. And eventually he'd see that.

The woman looked up from her Bible and smiled at us. "He's all knocked out," I whispered, over Jason's head. "He's just become a father." Her mouth opened in surprise—he probably looked too young to her—and then she blessed him with a beatific smile. When he woke up, she'd be sure to congratulate him, to ask him a few embarrassing questions. Well, he'd just have to start getting used to it.

At La Guardia, we collected his gear from the belt and

finally found a taxi big enough to handle it all. I dozed off on the way to Larchmont, and when I woke up, it was dark out. We were on the Hutchinson and Jason was looking out the window. It was easier to say something conciliatory to him then, in the darkness, and on our own home ground. "We're going to help you, Jase," I said. "You really screwed up, but it's never too late to start over. Everything will work out, wait and see."

37

*T*HE NIGHT HOWARD AND I FIRST MET, AT A DANCE HE was playing at NYU, there was a mirrored ball suspended from the center of the ceiling. It began to slowly revolve when the music started, and bullets of light ricocheted around, striking me painlessly, pleasurably, on my face and sweater and arms. Everyone there was united by the restless pattern of light we all wore, like the spots or stripes of our species. But in that crowd, and in the mysterious order of things, Howard and I singled each other out.

Now he believed he could win me back through acts of faith and heroism, and I would let him continue believing that. And I'd let him woo me with the romantic rituals we'd skipped twenty-five years ago, in our hurry to be in love. I wouldn't tell him I was flung back that far last night, after Byron was born. When I leaned against the wall in the hallway of Ann's house, I was leaning against the wall at NYU again, pierced by the tender, insistent voice of Howard's saxophone.

38

*J*ASON HAD WANTED TO CALL SARA FROM THE AIRPORT, just to prepare her. For once he was trying to use common sense, but I wouldn't let him. I figured it was better to surprise everybody, the way I had done down in Miami. And I imagined a grand finale to the whole mess, with the lovers embracing and Paulie sobbing with happiness.

It didn't work out that way, though; Sara didn't exactly throw herself into Jason's arms. In fact, she shrieked and ran out of the room the instant she saw him, abandoning the baby, who was asleep in the cradle next to her bed. Jason paused for only a moment to look at him before he chased Sara down the hallway, shouting her name.

The baby started crying, a little mewling sound at first, and then he worked himself up into that squalling vibrato. I could hear Jason calling to Sara somewhere in the house, and their running footsteps, and a door slamming shut. Where was everybody else? Ann had let us in, and then she'd disappeared. I didn't even know if Paulie was there, and I wasn't sure anymore that I wanted her to be. I had brought Jason back, just as I'd promised, but so far his reunion with Sara was less than ideal.

There was an ominous silence now, except for the baby,

who was still going off like a siren. "Hey, you, calm down," I said, and I nudged the cradle with my foot. When it stopped swinging, I bent to pick him up, but I'd forgotten how their heads wobble, as if their necks are broken. Jesus, it took three tries before I could scoop him up in one piece. He was soaking wet and stinking, and he hadn't stopped yelling for a second. I carried him all over the house until I found Jason and Sara in the kitchen, where he had her pinned to the refrigerator.

Maybe it was just as well that Paulie wasn't around, that she came in later, from some local doughnut shop, when things had settled down a little. The baby had been changed and fed. Sara and Jason were upstairs, talking. At least that's what I told Paulie they were doing. The last time I'd looked, Jason was doing all the talking and Sara had her hands over her ears.

The doughnuts that Paulie had brought were still warm. Ann and Spence appeared from nowhere, and we all sat down to drink coffee and eat the warm doughnuts. I looked around the table and something like music kept rippling through me. We could have been any family, anywhere, doing this ordinary, marvelous thing. I began to think about the lyrics to songs I'd played, and how they asked all those unanswerable questions. How deep is the ocean? How high the moon? What is this thing called love?

SILVER

T HE SURPRISE PARTY WASN'T REALLY A SURPRISE, BE-
cause there had been so many hints, and a few dead give-
aways. The Thursday before, when I was visiting my mother,
she'd said, "What time on Sunday—" and then stared at me,
stricken, covering her mouth. But even before that, Spence
and Ann had spoken too broadly about their plans to go away
that particular weekend. And when I'd looked in their freezer
for coffee beans, I found hundreds of tiny meatballs and
stacks of cakes and pies. Still, there were considerable ele-
ments of surprise that Sunday—like the adrenaline that surged
through me as we approached our shuttered, waiting house.
And when Howard unlocked the door and we heard the whis-
pers and scurrying that preceded the shouts, he sucked in his
breath and seized my arm. "Surprise! Surprise!" they all
cried, and I turned to bury my face in Howard's neck.

The only trick Ann had actually pulled off was having the
party here instead of at her own house. That would have been
the logical choice; it was so spacious and handsome and well
equipped. I suppose she relished the challenge of fooling us
on our own territory. But it wouldn't be ours much longer—
we'd put the house up for sale at the beginning of the month.

I pretended to be surprised when we walked in, and so did

Howard. We had discussed the imminence of this event for
days. Our actual anniversary had been Friday, and except for
my mother's slip, I would have guessed Friday or Saturday
night as a more likely time. They didn't have to do anything
to get us out of the house on Sunday, though. At noon, we'd
driven to Bayside, where one of Howard's cousins' children
was playing the cello in a music-school recital. We'd agreed
to attend in a weak moment—Howard's cousin had phoned
to invite us a month ago—and whenever I regretted accepting, Ann would remind me of how sensitive Cousin Sheila
was about her kids, and how she'd sent that lovely quilt when
Byron was born. So we'd dutifully left the house at noon.
Getting us back there in time for the party was harder; Howard and I might have gone into Manhattan after the concert,
and stayed for dinner. They had to invent a ruse about the
real-estate broker bringing hot prospects who could only view
the house today at five. I'd almost fallen for that part—they
had even gotten the broker to call us himself. And they'd set
up another blind by sending us anniversary gifts in advance.

There we were now, at the party I'd vowed last August
never to have. It had started without us—some of the guests
had been there since three, drinking the wine, nibbling the
cheeses and pâtés and then smoothing them over. The rooms
were festooned with silver streamers and bells, and a flotilla
of Mylar balloons had been allowed to drift to the ceilings.
A poster-size blowup of our wedding portrait was on prom-
inent display in the living room, with the signatures of all
the guests scribbled around its borders. And there was live
music—two new friends of Howard's, a pianist and a bass
man, had played "The Anniversary Waltz" at our entrance,
and then swung right into a jazzy rendition of " 'S Wonderful."

"Were you *really* surprised?" Ann wanted to know immediately, and of course we swore that we were. "Just feel my heart," I told her, and Howard said, "Does this mean we're not showing the house?"

It was the first joke he'd made on that subject. Selling the house was an essential term of our reconciliation, but he had resisted the idea until June. All the old arguments against living in the city were dragged out once more, and it was hard to dispute them in this season of bloom and regeneration. But I was adamant—in order to heal our marriage, we had to go back where we'd begun.

We had put a deposit on a two-bedroom co-op on the Upper West Side, the final deal contingent on the sale of our house. The apartment was half the square footage of the house, but it was in one of the city's older buildings, with thick plaster walls and high ceilings. There was a sunny southern exposure, and you could just see the spire of the Chrysler Building from the master-bedroom window. Howard was going to rent studio space nearby. He would commute to Hempstead two or three days a week, until he built up his Manhattan clientele, and then he'd probably sell his share in the other studio to Mike.

Mike was at the party with a beautiful black woman named Trish. When he introduced us, she said, "Congratulations. I didn't think *anybody* stayed together that long."

"We did it in installments," Howard explained. We did it with mirrors, I thought.

The house was jammed with friends and relatives—even Howard's cousins had beat us here from their daughter's recital. La Rae came over to greet us. "You can return what I bought you," she said. "It's only a book, a walker's guide to the city. I know how you hate to polish silver, Paulie, and nothing else seemed appropriate." La Rae was at the party without an escort. She'd left Frank early in May, suddenly,

as if struck by lightning or inspiration. Her father had been
quickly moved to a nursing home in Elmont—Katherine had
gotten him in there, through political connections, past a
long waiting list. If I were more generous, I knew, I'd intro-
duce Bernie to La Rae, or to one of my other unattached
friends. In one of our private sessions, Dr. Lewin wondered
if I was, perhaps, keeping him on a back burner.

I found out that Katherine and Tony had been in cahoots
with Ann about the party. They'd served as her local liaison,
drawing up a list of neighbors to invite, ordering the balloons, and providing flowers from their own fertile garden.
The flowers had been set out everywhere in fragrant profu-
sion: white and lavender lilacs; tea roses; foxgloves; and
long-stemmed Japanese irises, my favorite. "Thank you for
everything," I said. "The flowers are simply wonderful.
Everything is."

Katherine stood in the circle of Tony's arm. "Just be
happy," she said doubtfully.

Sara carried Byron around in a canvas Snugli. He was
asleep, and so closely curled against her I might never have
cut the cord between them. We'd starting calling him "By"
right from the beginning, and a thousand other pet names as
they occurred to us. He responded to all of them, to everyone, with a crooked, naked smile. His eye hardly wandered
anymore, and his hair was a crown of golden feathers. Sara
had stopped coloring her own hair, and the emerging roots
were a surprising, ordinary brown. She was beginning to
look more and more like her sister Peggy.

Ann and Spence had hired a bartender, and two waitresses
who passed among us, serving hors d'oeuvres. The meatballs I'd seen in Ann's freezer were sizzling hot now and
skewered on silver toothpicks. There were stuffed mush-

rooms and bite-sized quiches, and triangles of black bread studded with blacker caviar.

My mother washed a meatball down with a swig of ginger ale. "Things work out for the best, knock wood," she said, rapping on the marble top of an end table. "But I almost gave it away, didn't I?"

"I never had a clue," I told her, the harmless and harmful lies continuing between us.

Later, I found her in the dining room with Sherry, advising her to "stop running around" and settle down with somebody. It certainly wouldn't be Nicholas—he'd recently found someone even older than Sherry, through another personals ad in *The New York Review*. She had brought her old friend Dave Becker to the party, and my mother said, "*He* looks very nice, Sherry, although, believe me, looks aren't everything." Sherry didn't bother to tell her that Dave was gay, and spoken for, in any case. Nor did she say how much she liked the unpredictability of her single life.

Sharon Danzer was making her first formal social appearance since Gil's death. A few weeks ago, when I told her that I was going back to Howard, she said that all separations were only dress rehearsals, anyway. Now she stood on the sidelines of the party, trying to remember how to enjoy herself. Shadow, who had grown just as wary of large gatherings, stayed close by her, and she absently fed him bits of caviar and quiche.

Jason had been in the bathroom before me, smoking grass. I opened the window to air the place out, and then went looking for him. I found him hiding out in his old room. He was lying on the bed, in a crush of silver-wrapped gifts, with his arms folded behind his head. I sat on the edge of the bed, the way I did sometimes when he still lived here, and we talked a little, mostly about his music, and about Byron. He

said that the punk sound was on the way out, and that Blood
Pudding was moving toward heavy metal, to attract a larger,
younger audience. They were thinking of changing their name
to the Cattle Prods. He tried to write new songs for their new
image when the baby wasn't sleeping or crying. Jason's
speech was slightly slurred and his eyes had a remote, ab-
stracted look. I got up at last and left him there, saying,
"Come back in when you're ready, Jason. We'll see you
later, okay?"

Our next-door neighbor, Gordon Brooks, cornered me
near the kitchen. He wanted to know who we were thinking
of selling our house to. "Whoever wants to buy it," I said,
remembering how he'd once marked off his property line
with a shoveled trench that left our azaleas on the wrong side.
So far, several people had come to inspect the house, but
nobody had made a serious offer. And one of them may have
stolen a gold bangle from my dresser top. It was missing,
anyway, after a series of prospective buyers had been through.
I'd suspected that some of them were only browsing, looking
for a little distraction on those boring Sundays, the way Howard and I used to do. "Well, don't forget that we still have
to live here," Gordon reminded me.

Sara's parents arrived at the party about an hour after we
did. "What a lovely occasion," Mrs. Bartlett said, kissing
the air near my cheek. I had followed up my unreturned
phone calls to her, during Sara's pregnancy, with a furious
and imploring letter, which she didn't answer, either. But
she had been unable to resist the actual, born, named baby,
although she'd held out a week longer than her husband. I
had called his law office the Monday after Byron was born,
and he burst into tears over the phone. They gave Sara an
allowance now, and they'd set up a trust fund for Byron,
carefully keeping the money out of Jason's reach.

I looked at the oversized wedding picture, and remembered a double sarcophagus I had seen years ago, when Howard and I were in Boston, and wandering through the Museum of Fine Arts. *Etruscan, 4th century B.C.*, the little sign said. The stone couple were facing one another in an embrace on their stone bed. I realized they bore an uncanny resemblance to Howard and me: the very curve of their features, their carved, eternal curls. The man even had a beard, the way Howard did then. "Look, Howie!" I'd cried, but he had gone ahead into the next room. Now Gordon's younger daughter came up beside me and stared at the photograph. "That's not *you*, is it?" she said.

I went into Ann's room and took By from Sara, who had just finished nursing him in the rocking chair. I inhaled his milky breath, nuzzled his talcumed neck. "Who's the most beautiful boy?" I asked. "Who does Grandma love best?"

There was a murmur of excitement when I came back into the living room, still carrying him. Someone swooped him from my arms, the lights were dimmed, and I saw Jason coming from the kitchen, balancing a three-tiered wedding cake high on one hand, like a basketball. "Watch out! Be careful!" people warned, and the bride and groom on the cake seemed to whirl near the silvery spackle of the ceiling. Howard was on the other side of the room, being pushed toward me, as if he were a shy and reluctant suitor.

I thought of Bernie again as Howard claimed me, to a burst of whistling and applause. When I'd told him that Howard and I were getting back together, he said, with a rueful smile, that he'd expected as much all along, that I had never really let go. I denied it fervently, because it shamed me, although I knew it was true.

"Oh, Paulette," Bernie said, "we could have had such a damned good time together."

"But we did, didn't we?" I said, realizing too late that he might have only been quoting Brett Ashley.

When the children were little and broke one of their toys, Howard would promise to fix it, to make it as good as new. But, oh, dear reader, I'd married him—and toys are one thing, marriage another. Dr. Lewin spoke more conservatively to us of forgiveness, of renewal. At first, Howard had resisted counseling as much as he'd resisted putting the house up for sale. He'd sit in Dr. Lewin's office, brooding, and silent, like a prisoner in the docket, as I leveled charges against him. But then he began to defend himself and bring those old countercharges, until we were interrupting each other and shouting, while Dr. Lewin beamed at us across the steeple of her hands. "Listen to yourselves," she said. "Still so much passion!"

Had it endured, despite everything, or had it merely been revived? I'm not sure. But at his little cousin's concert that afternoon, as she sawed her way through Mendelssohn's D minor Trio, we held hands like the sweethearts we'd once been. And later, after the wedding cake was ceremoniously cut, we waltzed around the perimeters of the living room, the winners in an arduous marathon dance.

That night, when the party was over, Howard went to our bedroom and lay in wait for me, wearing only his suit of tarnished flesh. I walked toward the bed through the pewter light, dressed in all the awful beauty of my years. We looked at one another.

About the Author

Hilma Wolitzer has taught at the Bread Loaf Writer's Conference and in the writing programs of the University of Iowa and Columbia University. Her short stories have appeared in *Esquire* and *New American Review* and she has written four novels for adults and four books for young readers. She is currently living on Long Island with her husband, a psychologist. They have two daughters, Nancy and Meg.